WHAT SHE DESERVES

CLARE BENTLEY

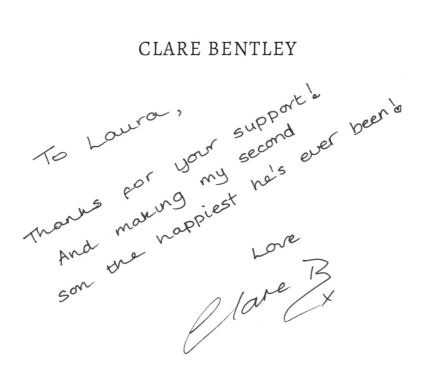

To Laura,

Thanks for your support!
And making my second
son the happiest he's ever been!

Love

Clare B x

Printed in the United Kingdom.
Published by Clare Bentley
Cover Design: © Clare Bentley
Cover Art: © Clare Bentley
License for Cover Image provided by Shutterstock.
First Printing: 2020
ISBN: 9798613881314

For those who have walked away
and those still fighting their battle.

It took me a while to get here. I had to overcome my own demons to have the confidence to put this novel out into the world. But here it is and whether I can captivate you, is something only you can decide.

For my husband, who supported the dream and patiently awaited me finishing this novel. Thank you for understanding when I needed a minute to finish my written thought before answering your question. I promise to take less time to respond in future. I love you.

For the children who inspire me every day. You're the reason I can follow my dream. Remember, you can be anything you want to be, you just have to believe. I love you both.

For my mother and mother-in-law who fought not to be another statistic. Thank you for being an example of how your past doesn't have to define your future. Your strength is inspirational.

For the friends who tried to get me to believe in myself, who contributed in some way to the words I've written, who let me bounce ideas off them, who read first drafts and gave me feedback on pretty much every aspect of this book, thank you for your support over the years.

This novel is for all of you.

STATISTICS

- According to the Office of National Statistics (ONS) about 4.2% of men and 7.9% of women suffered domestic abuse in the UK during 2018.
- This equates to about 695,000 male victims and 1,300,000 women.
- One in four women and one in six men will be affected by domestic abuse during their lives.
- On average two women are murdered every week and thirty men are murdered every year.
- 16% of violent crime is related to domestic abuse, although it is least likely to be reported to the police.

Source: Wikipedia

24-hour National Domestic Violence
Freephone Helpline
0808 2000 247

www.nationaldomesticviolencehelpline.org.uk

CHAPTER ONE

Kaidence Hadaway cowered on the floor and watched him draw his fist back before he drove it into her face. Another day and another fight meant more bruises to cover in the morning. She knew they'd ask at work how she got this one, once her face was healed enough to go back, and she knew she'd have to lie. She always did. Her cover stories for her injuries were always so pathetic; maybe that was because she secretly wanted someone to notice she was being abused. No one ever did. Maybe they didn't care. Maybe they thought she should do something about it herself. But she wasn't strong enough. That was a power he'd beaten out of her. She wished she had someone familiar enough to see through her lies; however, all her close friends had been driven away when he had made her choose. She knew now that this was designed to isolate her. He didn't want her to have anyone who would give her the strength and encourage her to leave him. He wanted her to depend on him, so he could treat her how he pleased.

She looked up at his face. He seemed so angry, as he repeatedly connected his fist to any part of her body he felt like hitting. She didn't understand why he hated her so much. She always tried so hard to please him, but sometimes she didn't know what would set him off.

'Please.' She began to beg. But that only made his punches even more determined and painful.

He grabbed her by her long curly brown hair and lifted her to her feet, without much effort. It amazed her how much strength he had when he was angry. She wished she had the courage to fight back, but she knew she would be no match for him because although his rage masked the features of the man she'd fallen in love with two years ago, she knew he was still in there. His face was a reminder of the gentle man she shared a home with the rest of the time. The man who made simple gestures to show how much he loved her, the one who would curl up on the sofa with her in his arms and would make love to her with tenderness. She didn't want to see him like this. This man was the one who brought her flowers the next day to cover his guilt and had rough sex with her every night after he'd thrown his weight around.

She wondered why it had all gone wrong. She knew the exact moment her life was turned upside down; it was a few months after he'd been made redundant and she was the only one earning. He got frustrated being at home all the time and started losing his temper little by little over the slightest things. Then he began to get angrier over less important things. His fuse shortened, and his voice seemed to be in a constant raised position. It wasn't until ten months ago that he first laid his hands on her, when she had told him she was pregnant. Something inside him snapped; she saw it in his empty brown eyes. He'd beaten her so badly that night that she'd had a miscarriage and it just hadn't stopped since.

She prayed every night for more and more good days, days when she'd do everything right, so he wouldn't hit her. But all she got lately was a run of bad days. She didn't know what it would take to stop him, although she needed to find something. He was slowly killing her, and she knew that one of these nights, he wouldn't stop until he had.

Above the noise of her whimpers, she could hear the phone ringing and she prayed he would answer it so he would stop hitting her. However, the world around him seemingly didn't exist while he was laying into her, inch by inch taking away pieces of her soul. The ringing stopped and instead she prayed for someone to knock on the door and save her. That knock never came and by the time he'd had enough she could barely speak, let alone move.

This was the worst yet. He'd punched and kicked her body so much in his rage that she was becoming numb to the blows because each one seemed to be weaker than the one before. But she didn't care any more. Her feelings were slowly being beaten out of her. She didn't cry any more because she was all cried out. She didn't smile any more because she had no reason to. She didn't care enough to scream out for him to stop because the louder she screamed, the harder he forced his hands onto her. All she could do was hope and pray she would be freed soon. Her saviour seemed to be listening to her prayers, and as he dropped her limp body back down to the floor, all she could think about was that it was over for another night.

She watched as he walked away, leaving her where she lay face down on the floor, and thanked God that he'd stopped to allow her to see another day. She could see her blood coated on his knuckles as he disappeared from the room. She could smell her fear contaminating the air, the feel of the internal bruising forming on her vital organs. She could hear her heart tissue ripping that little bit more and feel the aching of her limbs. The cuts above her eye stung, and the copper taste of her blood tainted her tongue as she licked the wound on her lips.

Her head spun with all the ways she could go from here. Did she try to get up and risk him hitting her for it, or did she just lie there and risk him hitting her for not moving? She was weak. She knew she was in no shape to survive another battle. So she lay there a while longer, bleeding on the floor.

She hated living her life like this. She was constantly fearful every day with every little act because she didn't know what set him off any more. It was different every time. She tried to only do things that pleased him, but it seemed like she couldn't even get that right these days.

She wanted to scream out, demand that he couldn't do this to her any more. She wanted to fight him every step of the way until he realised that he wasn't going to get away with hurting her. But every beating she had taken had left her weak and she couldn't fight with strength she didn't have.

She lay dormant on the cold floor of the kitchen, secretly wishing God would take her life because it wasn't worth keeping, except he couldn't have heard her. She hadn't believed in a higher power before meeting him because she didn't have much cause to. She soon found faith though, the first night she had lain on those tiles bloody and broken, praying to stay alive long enough to get as far away from him as her legs would allow. However, his desperate pleas of apology had her convinced it was the lapse of an otherwise passive man, until it happened again.

Still she lay there, listening to the dull sound of the television in the other room. She had to fight. She had to block the pain out of her mind and reach deep inside to build up enough courage to move. That's when all that was left in the room was silence. The only sound ringing in her ears was the echo of determination. She was going to lift herself from the floor, to walk up the stairs and wash his handprints off her skin. God help her, if it was the last thing she was going to do, she was going to show him he hadn't won. But in reality, he had. He always won.

It took her an hour to make it to the bathroom. Her ribs were aching, her legs were wobbly, and her head felt light because of the cut on her forehead. Her determination kept her going and now she struggled to stand upright at the sink as she washed away the evidence.

The water was tainted a deep red from the blood and as she looked into it she could see her faint reflection. She didn't have a mirror anywhere in the house. She didn't want one. Not after he'd forced the back of her head into the last one. That was the only time she'd been to the hospital with injuries, because he was careful how he hit her. She'd had to get stitches that day, and she remembered the look the doctor gave her while he tended to her wound. She could tell he wanted her to confess that her boyfriend had assaulted her and that the mirror hadn't broken her fall when she had slipped on the bathroom floor. But she didn't, because it had been her fault he'd done it. If she hadn't been putting on make-up, he wouldn't have got mad.

She didn't wear make-up any more. She didn't style her hair. She didn't wear clothes that exposed any flesh. She kept low-key. She tried not to do anything that he would punish her for. She always tried to behave. But sometimes she couldn't help it when his peas touched his mashed potato. She couldn't help it if sometimes his gravy was lumpy. She couldn't let the phone ring out without answering it if she was the only one home. Sometimes her punishment came when she hadn't realised she'd done anything wrong. Nevertheless, she knew it was still her fault. If she didn't make so many mistakes, he wouldn't have to discipline her.

Lifting down the first aid kit from the small cupboard hanging on the wall, she opened it and pulled out a plaster for her cut. Having no mirror in the bathroom, it was going to prove difficult to dress her wound; it always did.

Then she felt his eyes on her, burning into the back of her skull. Turning slightly, her eyes met with his and she could feel herself beginning to shake at the prospect of what was to come. But he was compassionate when he spoke; 'Do you want me to bandage that for you?'

She wasn't sure what her response should be and took pot luck with a nod; 'Please.'

Slowly he walked over and took the plaster from her hand. 'This looks nasty,' he said, pulling off one of the tabs. 'You know I'm sorry I had to punish you again, don't you?' She nodded, not daring to speak. 'If you hadn't made me angry, I wouldn't have had to do this.'

Again, she nodded. 'I know,' she whispered, as her bright peridot-coloured eyes instinctively made contact with the floor.

As he finished covering her cut, Mitchell stood back to admire her bruise-covered face and a slight smile appeared on his lips. 'I love you so much. You know that, don't you?'

She bravely raised her chin and forced her eyes to meet his. For a moment she was tempted to scream at him and ask why, if he loved her so much, he subjected her to such torture. She wanted to lash out and give him a taste of his own medicine, though she knew she was no match for him. So instead she reflected his small smile. 'Of course I do.'

She flinched as he raised his hand to her cheek before she realised that it was a sign of affection and not anger. She closed her eyes and concentrated on the intimacy of his touch, instantly remembering back to when it was always like this. Although that seemed like a lifetime ago.

The kindness she'd seen in his eyes the day they'd met had all but disappeared now. The gentleness of his fingers when he touched her skin had vanished and left only weapons of mass destruction. The sweetness of his lips when he kissed her was untraceable and all that was left was bitterness.

'Are you okay?' he asked softly.

Her tear-filled eyes opened and met his. 'Yes,' she replied, her voice cracked and saturated with pain. 'I'll be fine.'

'Do you need me to kiss it better?'

She knew all too well that what he was asking wasn't a question for consideration. It was more or less her warning that he wanted sex.

'Can I take a shower first?' She asked permission, hoping for a small reprieve from his abuse.

He circled his arms around her waist. 'Want me to take one with you?'

She forced a smile through the pain of the pressure he was applying to her injured midriff, knowing it was a rhetorical question and there was only one answer he was expecting. 'Sure,' she said through gritted teeth, hoping she'd put enough enthusiasm into her response for his liking, and when he didn't react negatively, she knew he'd bought her zeal.

Once they were showered, they returned to the bedroom and his mouth found hers without much effort at all. His lips were hungry, and his tongue probed deep into her mouth until she was sure she'd choke. But she knew that all he cared about was to get what he wanted, never stopping to consider her injuries or her pain from their altercation in the kitchen.

Undoing the secured bathrobe, he slipped it over her shoulders, allowing it to fall to the floor around her feet. His eyes travelled the length of her exposed body as her arms defensively came up across her chest in an uncomfortable attempt to cover herself.

He gently pushed her hands away. 'I want to see you, all of you,' he whispered in her ear as he took a small step back.

Reluctantly she allowed her arms to fall to her sides, giving him full view of her battered body. Although the bruises seemingly didn't matter to him as a satisfied smile appeared on his face. 'My God, you're beautiful,' he complimented her, somehow thinking it would make a difference to how she felt about him and the sham their relationship had become.

He opened his robe, forcing her eyes onto his naked aroused body. There was a time when that vision alone would make her wetter than running water and begging for him to take her body to do with it as he pleased. But now all it resulted in doing was turning her stomach and making her want to run for the hills.

He stepped closer to her again, his body barely touching hers but making her flesh crawl all the same, and he devoured her in a kiss as his hands came up to fondle her breasts roughly. She gasped against his mouth as his lips hardened against hers and his touch became firmer, more demanding. Her nipples swelled up in response to the pain, puckering into two peaks of pure agony.

Breaking away from her lips, he dipped his head, so he could suck first one, then the other. His mouth was hot, his teeth scraping the tender flesh of her nipples, which caused her to suck in a breath of anguish. His touch had no sexual effect on her at all. Still, she faked a pleasured moan through the wracking pain of her internal bruising.

Gently, he pushed her back, so she fell onto their bed, and he climbed on top of her, his hard male body pressing her into the mattress. He pried her clasped thighs apart with one knee and slipped his fingers between them. He found her clitoris and began playing with it, pressing it against her pubic bone and rolling it, making her call out with the sensation that shot through her. He could feel how moist she was now and moved to rub the head of his penis against the sensitive flesh of her vagina. She gritted her teeth as he sank slowly inside her, wincing at the sharp stab of pain as he burrowed deeper, twisting his hips so he could knock against the neck of her womb.

The walls of her emotions came crashing down, bringing tears to her eyes as a bitter taste formed in her mouth. She closed her eyes to try and block out the invasion of him within her. But all she could feel were her inner muscles clenched around the only evidence that he was a man.

Opening her eyes again, she saw that he was oblivious to her presence as he heaved and grunted his way towards climax, a vision she was used to seeing. The expression on his face was that of pure concentration; his eyes were fixed on a point on the wall just above her head. His breathing had become heavier as a film of sweat formed on his forehead. Then she got that familiar feeling of being outside her body, looking down on the two of them on the bed, consumed by, yet curiously detached from the scene. While at one extreme she was completely caught up by what was happening, at the other she was watching her reaction to it.

She missed the times when he was gentle, loving and caring while making love to her. She missed the sensations his touch used to arouse in her body. She missed the tenderness of his kisses. She wanted her Mitchell back. Her tears unleashed from her eyes and rolled towards the bed beneath her. Soon it would be over, and she could sleep to recover, only for him to abuse her again tomorrow. She hated this life. She wanted someone else's so badly that she was willing to go to any lengths to get it. But that was just a dream she escaped to at night while he lay snoring beside her. Many times she would think of climbing from the bed and escaping into the dark. Except the idea of him finding her always forced her to reconsider it. She was too afraid he would kill her if he caught her trying to leave.

The tendons in his neck stood out like cords as he strained to reach his climax. It didn't matter to him that she wasn't even close to orgasm; it used to, but now as long as he got his, it was enough. He let out a pent-up gasp and collapsed across her like a deflated balloon before rolling off onto his back.

Flinging one arm across his forehead, he closed his eyes, letting out a long, low whistle between his teeth. 'That was some great make-up sex, baby,' he said, when he had gathered enough breath to speak.

She lay very still beside him and said nothing, knowing that within minutes he'd be asleep. She could feel the ache of her clitoris; sore and bruised just like the rest of her body. She closed her eyes as tears escaped unheard and prayed hard that things would go back to the way they once were between them. Though she knew that even if he went back to being the Mitchell she'd fallen in love with, she'd be scarred forever by what he'd made her tolerate over the last ten months. She kept telling herself that this was a phase he was going through, that he was stressed by having started a new job, but she knew it was more than that. The man had an evil streak that no amount of financial security was going to diminish. There was something inside him that made him think this was normal behaviour, and it was bound to come out at some point regardless of the condition of their relationship.

Lying there naked, she could hear his contented snores already bouncing off the walls. But it would be a while before she slept tonight; if she did at all with the pain she was in. Her ribs ached as she breathed in and out. The muscles in her stomach burned from the tension she'd held while he kicked her repeatedly, hoping it would prevent any major damage to her internally. She could feel that this beating had done more harm to her insides than any she'd had to take in the past. It hurt in a different way.

His anger was escalating, and it wasn't going to be long before he put her life at risk. She knew he didn't have enough control to stop himself from killing her, so the question became, how long was she going to live this miserable existence before she broke away or he ended her life?

Turning away from him, she curled up in a foetal position and allowed her emotions to break free. Her tears started as a trickle and before long she was fully sobbing. She couldn't imagine what she'd done that was so bad to deserve this. But she had been forced into the position she was in, and now she just had to decide how long she was going to tolerate it. She wasn't lying there long before she fell into a light sleep.

Her eyes fluttered open as much as they could with the swelling to find Mitchell smiling down at her. His eyes were sparkling, and she found herself reflecting his expression. For a minute, what had happened the night before was forgotten and they were a 'normal' couple, happy to be waking up to each other. But everything came rushing back as he lowered his lips to hers and the bitter sting of her cut presented itself. She winced automatically and, with concern etched on his features, he pulled away.

'Sorry, did that hurt?' he asked softly.

She could tell he was in a good mood and that the Mitchell staring down at her was the man he was before he'd moved in with her. Tenderly she dabbed her injury with her hand. 'It's okay. It doesn't hurt that much.'

He smiled and leaned in for another one. But as his lips connected to hers for a second time, she winced yet again. 'You know what, maybe it does,' she said as he pulled away.

He reached up and brushed her fringe from her forehead. 'Then I'll just have to kiss you somewhere else,' he said, lowering his lips to the skin he'd exposed and placing a gentle kiss there. He rose to his original position, so he could take in the view of her face and his smile kept its place. 'What do you want for breakfast?'

Her brow furrowed softly. 'You're making breakfast?'

He kissed her forehead again before jumping off the bed. 'I am, and you're going to stay right there because I'm going to bring it to you, in bed,' he ordered as he walked from the room.

A giggle escaped into the air. That was Mitchell. That was her man. He was back; at least for now.

Standing at the top of the stairs, Kaidence watched Mitchell walk out of the front door and relaxed. His good mood had been a nice change from the rage of the night before, but she had still been on edge and now he was gone, she was free to let go of that tension.

She headed straight to the en suite to take a shower. Although she'd had one the night before, she still felt dirty because she could smell him on her skin. She wanted to wash it off, so she could go about her chores without any reminders of him. She stripped down and climbed under the shower. It wasn't until she started washing that she could see the effect her relationship was having on her body. There were bruises beneath the surface of her skin that had developed overnight, and they were blacker than any she'd had previously. Still she continued to clean herself, wincing only when she touched the places of her internal trauma. She tried to ignore the pain she was in as she climbed out of the shower cubicle and wrapped a towel around her naked form, but it was getting harder to do the more she moved.

Once she was dry and dressed, Kaidence made her way downstairs to start cleaning up the battle arena, otherwise known as the kitchen. She'd barely managed to pick up the things that had been strewn about the room when a determined knock came at the front door.

Knowing it was dangerous to answer it when Mitchell wasn't at home caused her to stand still and hold her breath. Maybe whoever it was would go if she didn't indicate she was home. But her curiosity got the better of her and as she moved towards the spy-hole to find out who was on the other side, she kicked a piece of broken plate across the hallway; the noise of it ricocheted off the surrounding walls, creating a much louder sound than she expected.

She got closer and the knock came again, causing her to jump. She managed to glance through the spy-hole, and saw a police officer stood the other side. Her instinct was to open the door, but her hand hesitated on the lock. Balanced against the fear she had of Mitchell was her fight to survive, and this could be the only chance she'd have to cry out for help. Worried that the officer might already be halfway down the path, she quickly pulled open the door blocking her from the rest of the world, only to find he was still stood the other side.

He was about six feet tall with the same chocolate-brown hair as hers and the clearest ice-blue eyes she had ever seen. But she didn't have much chance to take in any of his other features before he broke the silence with his deep English regional accent.

'Morning miss, I'm Officer Chase,' he introduced himself.

She was confused, because he didn't seem to respond to the cuts and bruises that were evident on her face. If he wasn't there because someone had reported the disturbance from the night before, she was unsure why he'd been called.

Her bright green eyes could have easily distracted Jackson Chase from the black bruises beneath them, but he saw them and instantly wanted to rescue her; his past experience with women who were being abused, however, made him refrain. He had to allow her to be the one to reach out and not push her into acting.

When she didn't speak, he continued to explain his reasons for being there. 'Last night there was a break-in across the road, and I'm just knocking on doors to find out if anyone saw anything.'

Suddenly her brain kicked into gear. He wasn't there for her. He hadn't received a phone call about the battle the night before. He was there for something else entirely. Not meaning to catch him off guard, she reached out and grabbed his hand to pull him inside. If he wasn't there to help her, she couldn't risk him being seen there in case Mitchell found out. She shoved him into the hallway and slammed the front door shut.

She turned to him with small beads of sweat on her brow. 'I didn't see anything.'

'I guess not,' he said, noticing the mess of the kitchen instantly from his position opposite her. He motioned to her swollen eye. 'Are you okay?'

She shrugged as if to appear nonchalant, when what she really wanted to do was beg him to save her. 'It's not as bad as it looks.'

'Have you had worse?'

'No, this is the worst yet. But I'll survive.'

'I wonder how long that will be true if you stay.'

'He'll kill me if I leave,' she said, dropping her eyes to the floor.

'He'd have to find you first.'

She met his gaze, hopeful for a second that he could save her. But she knew she couldn't expect him to. 'He'd find me,' she confirmed adamantly, feeling it in her gut.

He took a second to recognise the unfaltering belief she had that her abuser wouldn't rest until he'd located her, and reached inside his jacket pocket to retrieve a card with his contact details printed on. He wanted her to have somewhere to turn when she was ready to get help.

He passed it to her. 'Well, if you hear anything about the robbery or you need anything, any time day or night, feel free to call me.'

She reached out to take the business card he offered. 'Thank you.'

He gestured to the kitchen. 'Do you need help cleaning up?'

'That's okay. Clean-up duty is like therapy,' she said, forcing a smile.

He glanced down at the white tiles and noted the dried-up blood stain.

He couldn't believe how flippant she was about what was obviously going on. He'd seen women like her before who made excuses for the men who beat them; it almost always ended in tragedy and he didn't want it to happen to another woman if there was some way he could help her escape.

'You shouldn't stay.' He tried again to encourage her to act.

'I can't leave,' she countered with sadness.

'You're not safe here. This...' He waved his hand in the direction of the mess in the kitchen. 'It's not normal.'

'It's not always like this.'

'The fact that it's sometimes like this should be enough to make you want to walk out of that door with me right now.'

'I want to. But what kind of life would I have if I'm looking over my shoulder all the time?' She was honest with him.

'I would send you to the other side of the world if it meant you were safe.'

'It wouldn't matter how far away I was; I'd be living in constant fear that he'd be around the next corner and that wouldn't be living at all.'

'Many more beatings like the one you took last night, and you might not be alive to live in fear.'

She shrugged. 'I'm not ready to give up on him yet.'

He sighed in defeat. 'Then you have my number for the day you decide to stop being his punching bag.'

'Thank you, Officer...'

'Chase, Jackson Chase.'

Seeing him out, Kaidence closed and locked the door that Mitchell kept her behind long enough for her injuries to become less noticeable. She'd used up all her holiday on recovery days and had taken so many sick days that she wasn't sure how she still had a job. She ran her thumb over the edge of the business card she held between her forefinger and middle finger. She wanted to keep it, so she had a place to turn if things got really bad, but she couldn't risk her abuser finding it. She didn't think for long before deciding to bury it in the drawer of paid bills, so she would have easy access to it, knowing Mitchell wouldn't have cause to go hunting in there. She bolted towards the hiding place she had picked out and shoved it beneath the mound of paperwork inside before going back to her original task.

<hr/>

Jackson climbed into his squad car and looked back up at the house he'd left. It had been the last on his list and so far, no one had given him any leads concerning the burglary. But that was the furthest thing from his mind right now. He was concerned about the beaten-up woman he'd seen because he knew there was a chance that the next time he saw her, she'd be hospitalised or deceased.

He'd only been a police officer for six years, but he'd already had his fair share of domestic calls and a handful of those had ended in tragedy. He couldn't help the pull that drove him to not want to experience that again, but he knew that she wasn't ready to be rescued, so he would have to bide his time and gain her trust. Showing his face from time to time would lead to her eventually confiding in him, and then he could work on getting her to leave. He just hoped the opportunity to save her came before her boyfriend killed her.

Starting the engine, he headed towards the police station. He wanted to do some research about the couple to see if there had been any reports of domestic abuse and any hospital visits for injuries in the past, so he had a foundation to build on.

Taking another look at the mess in the kitchen, Kaidence decided to document her injuries before tackling the clean-up. It was something she had been doing since he had started hitting her because she knew proof of her abuse would be valuable if she wanted to prosecute. She headed to the office and removed the framed picture hanging on the wall behind the desk to reveal the small hidden safe. Punching in the six-digit code, she pulled open the door and removed the camera. She had all the photos stored on a memory card kept inside a journal, locked away securely, in which she recorded the date and full description of the things she'd had to suffer. She hadn't got around to telling Mitchell about the safe before he hit her the first time, and now it was a secret she guarded with her life.

She headed to the window for the best light to get her battle wounds on film and photographed what seemed like every inch of her body before she took the journal from the hole in the wall and sat at the desk to write the encounter as best as she could recollect it. Her pen moved across the page fast – she wanted to get every detail out of her head and down on paper before she forgot it, not that she ever could. Every incident was burned into her skull like data stored on a flash drive.

She didn't know how far into reliving the ordeal she was when she'd started crying but as her tears fell onto the last page, she wiped them from her cheek. Somehow seeing the words describing what had happened made it more real than the actual evidence she felt internally. She was heartbroken that her once great relationship had turned into this.

Putting a full stop at the end of the five pages she had written, she put down her pen, removed the memory card from the camera and slotted it into the pocket inside the back cover of her journal. She set that aside and took a fresh book from inside the desk, opened it and started an entry about the officer. When she was finished with her first impressions of him, she returned everything to the safe and made sure she heard the automatic lock snap into place before putting the framed picture back on the hook above it and going about her usual chores.

Sitting behind his desk at Kingstanding Police Station, Jackson's hands were poised over the keyboard. It suddenly dawned on him that he didn't have a name to put into the system so instead he typed in the address he'd visited last to see if there was a history of officers being called to the property. He was surprised to find that there was no such record. It stunned him. He took it to mean that either the abuse hadn't been going on for long or the woman he'd met hadn't sustained any severe injuries that warranted a police presence. However, he had found the name of a woman from the same address attached to two reports made by doctors at the local hospital. One was for a miscarriage ten months ago and the other was about a minor injury to the back of the head from eight and a half months ago. The doctor had noted that he suspected the wound was a result of domestic abuse but that the woman had maintained her story of a slip and fall. She'd had to have twelve stitches that day, but still no incident report had been filed. Of course, he knew based on the bruises he'd seen on her face less than an hour ago that both hospital visits were almost certainly a result of abuse. He just had to subtly insinuate his way into her life, so she barely noticed, and hope that one day he could get her away from the man she had attached herself to.

CHAPTER TWO

Jackson pulled up on the opposite side of the road to the residence he was there to spy on and shut off his engine. It had been a couple of days since he'd found Kaidence bloody and beaten, and he wanted to make sure his visit hadn't had any adverse effects on her because she had allowed him inside. He was fearful that if there had been another incident so close in time to her last injuries she may not have made it out alive.

He had timed his stakeout for the time most people were leaving home to travel to work in the hope he would see some activity. He had been watching the building for half an hour when he saw a man leave the premises and concluded that he was her partner. It took all his energy to resist the urge he had to jump out of the car and confront him before putting him in handcuffs despite being off duty. Instead he watched as the stocky five-foot ten-inch male drove away in his vehicle, and then waited. He didn't want to move too soon and have the boyfriend return home unexpectedly, because that would undoubtedly spell the end for Kaidence.

Having two younger sisters meant he would do worse than arrest any man who thought it was okay to lay his hands on either of them. He'd forgo the rules set in place by the badge he was beholden to and give him a taste of his own medicine. That's what he wanted to do now.

He couldn't explain why he felt instantly protective of the woman he'd encountered by accident forty-eight hours ago, but he had been obsessing about how he could get her out from under her boyfriend's control sooner rather than later. He knew the timing of an escape was essential to her survival, but it was about more than that for him. He didn't want to lose another life to abuse if he was able to do something to stop it.

It had been hard to see past the black eyes and the cuts on her face; still, her green orbs projected a certain vibrancy that he suspected had used to shine brighter. He could tell from the clothes she wore that she had probably started her relationship a dress size bigger than she was currently and that the woman who had once seen a little bit of exposed cleavage as playful was now scared to show any flesh that Mitchell deemed disrespectful to their union. Her lack of make-up was almost certainly a result of his control too, although she didn't need it. She was pretty enough without masking her face behind a more socially accepted one.

As far as he could tell, the male of the relationship had done much better for himself than she had, and it mystified him how she couldn't see this too – although he suspected that had a lot to do with the way she'd been groomed.

The story was always the same, girl meets guy and he acts like Prince Charming until she thinks she's found the one she'll spend the rest of her life with. Then the abuse starts, sly little comments to make her doubt her worth and feel degraded, sometimes in front of friends who pay no mind to it because it was said with a smile. Then he starts to shout because he can't contain the temper he's been trying to hide since the day they met. It isn't long before that escalates to a back-handed slap, which turns into a balled-up fist, and before long he's throwing her around like a rag doll.

It was an all too familiar tale to him and he wished he had more power to stop repeat behaviour, but a night in a cell was as far as he was able to go, and if the abused didn't press charges how else was he supposed to help? He had also seen his fair share of women who had got to the point of enough only for the judge to allot a diminutive sentence. The men always returned home to the women who had prosecuted them, despite the restraining order, and it would end with her in hospital or the morgue. Of course, it wasn't always male-on-female abuse; sometimes it was the other way around, but only sometimes. Eighty-five per cent of the time it was the men doing the abusing.

He continued to watch the house for a further fifteen minutes but when he saw no additional movement, he decided it was time to make his way to the front door. He had purposely shown up in his civilian clothes so as not to cause suspicion to anyone who might report back to the boyfriend, and he had parked at the distance he had so no one would recognise his car if he felt the need to drive by on occasion. But his conscience wouldn't allow him to just forget about her until he was called to a crime scene where she was the dead body.

He knocked boldly on the heavy wooden door between the two of them and waited for any signs of life the other side. It wasn't until he heard the faint sound of discontent that he realised she was fully aware of him, but it still took her a minute to pluck up the courage to open the barrier.

'Officer Chase,' she said, letting him know she recognised him. 'What are you doing here?'

'I wanted to come and check that there were no ramifications regarding my visit a couple of days ago.' He was honest with her.

'And your instinct was to risk possible exposure by visiting again?' she questioned, not meaning to sound ungrateful.

'Oh, I watched your boyfriend leave first. Then I gave it quarter of an hour just be sure he wasn't coming back.'

She opened the door fully, 'You better come in.'

He crossed the threshold and took in the grand interior. He knew from his records that the property belonged to her and that Mitchell had only moved in twelve months earlier due to unemployment. He wondered if that was how he had justified his temper at first, when it had simply been because his masculinity had been threatened by her being the breadwinner.

The staircase was positioned to the right of the entrance and the high ceiling meant the landing overlooked the front door, with a spindled banister for safety. The walls were decorated in a grey marble-effect paper with three bulky framed family photos spaced out in a triangle opposite the access to the upper level. He assumed the top photo was of her parents and the one below that wasn't of her was likely her sister.

He followed her to the kitchen on the right and almost didn't recognise it with the lack of blood and crockery on the floor. He walked under the archway that had replaced the door that had once been there, and he found himself wondering if that was a result of abuse or if she'd made that modification because she liked it that way.

The kitchen was just as grand as the previous room, with black granite worktops and mahogany cupboards in a 'c' shape around the inside wall. In the middle of the room was a stationary island that housed the sink and drainer. He noticed the greys of the large appliances blended with the wood and the small appliances were coloured red with matching accessories.

By the front window there was a large mahogany-stained dining table that seated ten people, although he assumed she'd never had that many guests for dinner.

She drew his attention back to her as she lifted the kettle from its circular base and turned to fill it with water. 'Do you want a drink?'

He nodded. 'As long as you think it's safe.'

Her five-foot-four height meant she had to go up on tiptoes as she reached into the cupboard above her head to remove two mugs. 'He's going to be gone all day. I think you've got time to have a brew.'

'But I don't want to risk possible exposure.' He smiled, using her words against her, hoping to get a smile in response.

But she remained stone-faced, 'Well you're here now. What do you want and how do you take it?'

'Coffee please, white with one sugar.'

Despite her diminished capacity to smile he could tell that at one time she had been so full of life that all she did was laugh. There was just something she emitted that suggested her life was so different now compared to the one she lived before she met Mitchell. He could still see evidence of the vigour she used to have in her step whenever she moved, even though her footsteps seemed heavy, as if she was weighed down by the man who was supposed to make her lighter. He knew he had paved a change in her the minute he thought it was acceptable to lay his hands on her and that she would never be the same again, despite wanting to be. He had put an end to the woman she'd been and replaced her with a frightened little girl who would be scared to breathe if it didn't come naturally.

He watched her move about the kitchen in silence, allowing her the chance to talk to him if she wanted to. But as she poured the boiling water into the cups, she didn't utter a word. He made his way to the island directly opposite the sink and sat on one of the bar stools there. Still the room remained quiet. He observed her as she finished off the drinks and came closer to place a mug in front of him. She put her cup of tea on the worktop in front of the seat a foot from him and lifted herself onto the stool. But it was like she didn't know how to be around people any more because instead of trying to make conversation, she sat staring into her cup, not daring to make eye contact with him.

It occurred to him then that maybe avoiding his gaze was the way she was made to react around men, in order to appease Mitchell so he felt less threatened. So instead of waiting for her to speak, he did.

'So, I take it he doesn't know I was here?' he asked rhetorically.

She shook her head. 'No. I'd probably have more bruises if he did.'

'The fact you're willing to joke about that is evidence of everything that's wrong with this relationship.'

She was immediately angered. 'Do you think I don't know that? Do you think I don't live every day scared to do anything in case it upsets him, and I get smacked around? Do you think I'm delusional and don't know how dysfunctional my life is?' she asked, knowing he couldn't understand.

'Then why do you stay?'

She shrugged as her temper dwindled in an instant. 'It's too late to leave.'

'It's never too late,' he insisted compassionately.

'He waited just long enough that I had real feelings for him before he hit me the first time, and I had every intention of kicking him out. I just fell into the trap of believing he was sorry.'

'So why didn't you get him out after the second time?'

'That happened later, and I was too invested by then. It's not like he hit me every single day.'

'Why haven't you called the police? That's what we're here for.'

'I chose to stay. It didn't seem right to expect the police to do something about it when I wasn't willing to.'

'It goes in your favour to have a record of this abuse.'

'I think that's why I opened the door to you, so at least someone knew.'

'But I can't do anything about it unless you file a report.'

She was silent for a minute before she responded, but she still didn't dare to look in his direction. 'I lost my child because of him, and I still haven't walked away. I'm just not ready to give up on him yet.'

'I know it only started ten months ago, but he's escalating quickly. You might not make it another year.'

That's when Kaidence forced her eyes to his. 'How do you know how long it's been?'

'I checked the system at work. We have his change of address on file from a year ago and the report of a hospital visit for your miscarriage. It doesn't take a detective to work it out.'

'Has he got a police record?' she asked curiously, maintaining eye contact.

He nodded slightly. 'He's been involved in a few incidents of fighting at some pubs around town and he's spent some time in the drunk tank at the station, but nothing for domestic violence if that's what you're wondering.'

She moved her gaze back to the cup in front of her. 'So I'm the first,' she muttered, somewhat shaken.

'I highly doubt that.'

'Then where's the record of the other women he's beaten?'

'They probably didn't file a complaint, or they got out at the first sign of violence.'

She nodded slowly as she pondered his sentence. 'So they were smarter than me, is that what you're implying?'

'No, because I know what kind of hold men like him have on the women they abuse, and I know how hard it is to break the cycle.'

She was silent as she considered the next words to come out of her mouth and she knew as she thought them that it sounded ridiculous, but she said them anyway. 'This is my home and I won't have him force me out of it. But I can't get him to leave. He will keep coming back until he convinces me he's changed, and I'll let him back in because he knows exactly how to manipulate me. Then, one night when I thank God I gave him a second chance because of how different he is, that night he will start hitting me and not stop until I'm dead. At least this way, I'm ready for it.'

'He's already killing you. Every punch and kick you take in his rage is causing irreparable damage to you inside.'

'I know you don't understand, and that's okay. I'm not asking you to. I'll reach my breaking point eventually.'

'I'm worried that point won't come before you're lain dying on these tiles.'

That's when it occurred to her that he was extremely invested in her well-being and it made her curious. 'Why are you here?'

'I told you, I came to make sure you hadn't incurred any rage following my visit the other day.'

She nodded slightly. 'Why are you really here?'

'During my time on the force, I've encountered too many abused women who didn't manage to get out before the men in their lives killed them, and I made a promise to myself that I would do everything in my power to prevent it happening again.'

'I appreciate your concern, but you can't save me. I have to be willing to do that myself.'

'Well, until you're ready to leave him, prepare to see more of me.'

In a panic, she twisted on her stool to address him. 'You can't come back here. If any of the neighbours see you making regular visits and let it slip to him, that'll be the end of me. He won't believe we're not sleeping together and if he was to find out you're a police officer...' She trailed off at the thought of how much pain he'd inflict on her. 'You have to trust that I'm reaching my limit for this life and just keep away until I call for your help.'

'I don't think I can go about my life not knowing if you're okay. I need to feel like I'm doing something to help.'

'You'll be helping by not giving him a reason to kill me.'

There was a hush that followed her plea as they each sipped at their hot beverage and processed the honesty of their conversation.

For her it was the first time she had spoken to anyone about the abuse, which was better than writing it down. At least this way she got a different perspective to the voices in her head that told her she somehow deserved this life.

For him it was an insight into her mental state. It was now obvious to him that she had no confidence. She was willing to take the abuse Mitchell dished out because she had picked him and didn't believe she deserved any better. Jackson aimed to change that, regardless of her resistance. He would abide by her wishes to stay away from the house if it meant their alliance remained undetected. He just had to think of another way to keep an eye on her.

'Do you remember the woman you were before he beat her out of you?'

That's when she smiled, like the memories were happy ones. 'It seems like a lifetime ago that I was that person.'

Kaidence barely remembered the carefree individual she'd been when she had met Mitchell. But she had been so different to how she was now. She loved to laugh and did it as often as possible. She was always so happy. She'd take every opportunity to dance like no one was watching, even when there was a room full of people. She was the life and soul of any gathering she held or was invited to because she enjoyed being around everyone she loved. She was a social butterfly and never shied away from meeting new people, so to be the stark contrast had been hard to adjust to. But the transition was so subtle that she didn't realise it was happening until she was already being influenced to cancel plans with the friends she'd had since school. They stopped calling her a long time before Mitchell first laid his hands on her, which gave her no outlet when it came to asking for help. It meant she had no one to influence her fight to survive. She had to endure alone, until now.

'Don't you want to get her back?' Jackson asked in a soft voice, bringing her out of her nostalgia.

She sighed. 'I don't think I'll ever be her again. I'm too damaged now.'

Jackson allowed her sentence to linger in the air for a while as he sipped at what remained in his cup. He realised now that she was willing to sacrifice herself in order for her boyfriend to work through his masculinity issues, but his past experience told him that Mitchell would always have that problem regardless of the time that passed. He also realised she wasn't ready to hear desperate pleas to leave and Jackson wasn't about to force her out, otherwise he'd be no better than the man he was trying to get her away from.

'You still remember how to be her deep down,' he offered, knowing it to be true.

'But she's hidden so deep that I just don't know where to find her.' Suddenly tears sprung to her eyes and spilled onto her cheeks. 'I'm just so scared all the time and that won't change whether I'm here or not. I wish I could leave, you don't know how much, but he's not just going to let me go. He'll come after me and then I'm dead for sure.'

'You could go so far away that he can't find you.'

'My family are here, and I'd need them to learn how to live again.' She sighed. 'It's just a no-win situation. The worst thing I did was allow him to move in.'

'He'd have shown his true colours eventually regardless of where he lived.'

'But at least then I could've hid behind my front door if I didn't want to deal with him. I hate anticipating him coming home at night and weekends are horrible because I've got no escape. My friends gave up on me a long time ago thanks to him, so I don't even have anyone to talk to.'

'You can call me any time you want to if you need to talk.'

She wiped her tears from her face. 'He checks my phone. It would be a risk to call anyone. I'm forced to write everything down in a journal so if anything happens to me at least someone will know why I died.'

'Aren't you worried he'll find your journal?'

She shook her head. 'It's in a safe that he doesn't know about.'

His eyes wandered the room. 'Where is it?'

She got to her feet and encouraged him to follow her to the office. She wasted no time lifting the framed picture from its hook and putting it on the floor at her feet.

'It may be useful for me to know the combination?' Jackson suggested, approaching the dial pad on the front of the fortified door.

'It's my date of birth backwards,' she clarified so that if he were to forget the numbers at least he'd have a clue as to what they were. 'Eight, eight, six, zero, four, two.'

'May I...' He asked reaching up to the numbered buttons but before he pressed the eight his finger hovered over, she gently grabbed his wrist to stop him from gaining access to her innermost private thoughts.

'I'm not ready to show you that yet,' she explained.

He forced the corners of his mouth up into a small smile and lowered his hand to his side. 'Then I'll wait.'

She countered with a slight smile that she didn't hold for long. 'Thank you,' she said, putting the picture back in its place.

The air between them suddenly became heavy. She was trying to decide whether he was trustworthy, and he was trying to gain her trust. The silence lingered for a while and he took the time to take in his surroundings.

Floor-to-ceiling dark wooden bookcases made up the two walls that didn't have a door or a window, like an old-fashioned library. The desk in the centre of the room was situated opposite the double doors that had led them inside and the large window to the right of it allowed enough light in that it didn't appear dim. What walls you could see were painted in a cappuccino colour, which countered the bulky walnut wood, and the few pictures that mounted the shelves were of happy times she had lived once upon a time.

Out of the blue the phone that sat on the bureau started to ring, causing them both to jump at the sudden interruption to the peace. But when she didn't move to answer it, he frowned.

'Aren't you going to get that?' he asked, motioning to the intruding object.

She shook her head and lowered her eyes to the floor. 'Mitchell doesn't like me answering the phone when he's not at home,' she clarified. 'He doesn't like me talking to anyone because of what I might tell them.'

As the ringing stopped, Kaidence took a deep breath. 'Look officer, I appreciate you dropping by, but I've got jobs to do before he gets home, otherwise he'll get mad.'

He nodded his understanding. 'You're right, I've already taken up too much of your time.' He made his way to the front door. 'Promise you'll call me if you need anything, any time day or night.'

'I will.'

Jackson immediately picked up that she hadn't used the word *promise* and would have pressed to hear more definitive assurance if he didn't think he'd already reached his limit for pushing his luck. So he gave up trying for an outcome that wasn't viable. 'You have my card?'

'Yes, I've got it.'

'Is it in a safe place?'

'As safe as it's going to be if I need it for an emergency.'

'Okay. Well I'm stationed at the local station if you need to find me,' he said, opening the front door and letting himself out.

As he walked down the drive, Jackson permitted himself to glance back over his shoulder at her, only to find her closing the door. She didn't linger to say goodbye or dare to meet his eyes with her gaze as she shut the world out. He wished he'd been able to convince her to walk out with him, but she was adamant to stay, and he had a solution.

Pulling his mobile phone out of his pocket, he held the speed dial number for his female partner and put it up to his ear. He made his way to his car as the line rang the other end. His partner wasn't on shift either, so he knew she was probably just catching up on the chores she hadn't been able to do for six days, so he waited for her to answer.

'Jackson?' Louisa Jessop quizzed, unable to contain her surprise.

'I need you to keep an eye on someone for me,' he stated, wasting no time getting to the point of his call as soon as she picked up.

'I'm fine, Jackson, how are you?' she countered sarcastically.

'Sorry Lou, but she's told me to stay away and I need her to have someone she can count on,' he said, unlocking his car and getting inside.

'Are you talking about that woman you met while you were knocking on doors the other day?'

'Yes. I've just left her, and she's scared her boyfriend will see me coming to the house, so I've got to find another way to check in with her.'

'And your solution is to make me the stalker?'

'I just want to introduce you, so she knows she can get to me through you if she needs to.'

His partner was silent for a while before she spoke again. 'What is it about this one that's got you so invested?'

'I can't lose anyone else, not if I can do something to prevent it,' he admitted, starting the engine and connecting the call through his in-car Bluetooth.

'Can't you just seduce her without getting me involved?'

'This isn't about sex, Jessop. I just think the world will be better with her in it.'

'All right partner, get me an introduction and I'll be her safe place to fall if things go wrong.'

'Thank you. I owe you one,' he said, hanging up and driving away.

Kaidence pulled back the net curtain slightly and watched as Jackson drove his car out of sight. She had no idea why he had made it his mission to save her, but she was grateful she had been able to have a conversation with him about how serious her situation was. If she were to meet her end any time soon, at least she had a witness to what she'd had to endure, Mitchell wouldn't be able to plead innocence, and someone could be her voice.

It was difficult to admit that she'd let it get this far, but she just wasn't prepared to uproot her whole life to put him in her rear-view mirror. She knew she'd have to fight for her freedom; he wouldn't just accept they were over. She had considered butchering him in his sleep and claiming self-defence, but she'd watched enough crime shows to know that the evidence would give away her deception and she wasn't prepared to serve time for him. Instead she was biding her time, hoping she could come up with another way to be free of the man that she was so petrified of.

The officer's visit had come as quite a surprise, simply because she expected him not to give her another thought once she couldn't help with his investigation. The fact that she seemed to matter to him was an experience she hadn't had before. People just expected her to do something about the abuse, because no one would be stupid enough to stay with a man who thought that behaviour was acceptable. They didn't consider that she would have real feelings for him, and it wasn't so easy to just walk away. Before long the fear he drummed into her would render her unable to leave. He convinced her he would find her, no matter where she ran to, and he would kill her simply because if he couldn't have her, no one would.

Kaidence was somewhat uplifted by having someone else in on the secret she'd had to keep to herself for so long. It gave her an optimism she hadn't felt before. It meant that if she survived, she had more than the photos and her journal to use as evidence in court; she had credibility because it wouldn't just be his word against hers. But if she died, at least she had someone who would fight for justice on her behalf.

She made her way to the kitchen and collected the cups on the breakfast bar. She didn't want to be found out because of a stupid mistake like having an extra dirty cup in the sink, so she washed them out, dried them and returned them to the cupboard where they belonged. It was just one job in a long line of chores she didn't get help with and seeing as she couldn't go to work, busying herself with housework was the next best way to prevent dwelling on a life she had once dreamed of.

But as she went about cleaning the breakfast things, Jackson was on her mind. He looked exactly like the kind of men she dated before she was pursued by Mitchell, who was the complete opposite. Jackson appeared like military, just by the way he carried himself, which she would've picked up on even if he hadn't been wearing his uniform when they met. He had an oval face, short brown hair and an athletic build with biceps that were just defined enough without looking like he spent his life in the gym when he wasn't working. His ice-blue eyes pierced into her soul, making her trust that she was safe, and that's why she had opened up to him as easily as she had. The facial hair that grew on his top lip and outlined his chin was trimmed so that it looked neat, which contributed to how handsome he was. He was the perfect image of the man she had once seen herself marrying, before Mitchell had damaged her beyond the expectations she'd had as a teenager, but all she saw him as now was her saviour.

There was already a change in her attitude. It was like sharing how awful her life had become with someone made her lighter somehow. She was almost weightless as she swept and mopped the floors. Her positive mood made the monotonous tasks around the house seem to take less time to complete and before she knew it, she was preparing vegetables for dinner.

It was lunchtime when she finally sat down with a sandwich and a cup of tea in the back garden. The British weather was still quite warm considering they were a week into September, and she wanted to take advantage of the fresh air because she'd been forced into isolation since Monday.

She could feel how crisp the air was compared to inside as soon as she pulled open the double doors at the back of the house, and it settled her. The birds were singing and there was a slight breeze that she welcomed after the sweat she'd built up doing her chores. Raising her chin towards the sky, she closed her eyes and relished the feel of the sun on her face. She barely had a chance to enjoy the sunshine these days, because when she wasn't working, cooking or cleaning, she was hiding out because of her war wounds. She seemed to have no freedom to be herself since she'd become one half of a couple, and that wasn't only down to the abuse she suffered. When they'd first started dating, she wanted to spend as much time with Mitchell as she possibly could. But since he'd moved in, she had felt like she shouldn't go out without him. His comments that made her feel guilty for leaving him at home alone had seen to that, and soon she stopped doing things if he wasn't with her. It was suffocating. She welcomed the weekdays when she had to hide just so she could be alone, not that she wanted to take the beating that made it possible, but it did afford her time to breathe.

She moved to one of the chairs on the patio and took a seat. She basked in the silence as she started to eat. The street where she lived was just outside the main town so there was rarely any traffic noise to drown out the nature that came from the small wooded area behind her property.

The privacy was one of the main benefits to her buying the house in Walley, Abybridge six years ago. She had viewed many properties, wanting to invest the large lump sum she had inherited from her parents, but when she had walked through the front door of what was now her home she had fallen in love with it. The house was far too big for her, but she intended for it to grow with her and the family she wanted to have one day, so had overbid for it straight away. Ultimately, she had paid the asking price because there was no other interest in it, and that meant she had some money left over to keep in the bank for when she needed it.

Her career as a teacher meant she lived quite comfortably on the wage she was paid, so fortunately she hadn't had to touch her savings, which had allowed them to steadily gain interest. It gave her money to fall back on when she was forced to have time off, like now.

Taking the last bite of her meal, Kaidence picked up her cup of tea and relaxed back in her chair to enjoy the peace that surrounded her. She had four hours to do nothing before she had to start cooking dinner, so it was ready for when Mitchell got home, and she was determined to enjoy the rest.

CHAPTER THREE

The house was still and quiet, almost like someone had hit pause on the day. If it wasn't for the fact Kaidence clock watched during the time she got to relive being the only occupant at the address, she would swear she'd not long got out of bed. She had enjoyed the relaxation she'd basked in since the police officer had left and had happily taken things at her own pace. Now she was cooking dinner. She had made the mistake of glancing at the clock half an hour ago, so she knew Mitchell's arrival was imminent and as much as she tried to push it out of her mind, it was stuck there looming over her like a huge weight she couldn't shake off.

She tensed immediately as she heard his key in the lock and she was overcome with fear. She didn't know which Mitchell was going to walk through the door, despite the good mood he'd left in, and she held her breath as he came into view.

'Something smells good,' he said, walking over and applying a kiss to her cheek. 'What are we having?'

'I saw a new Mediterranean chicken recipe on TV today, so I thought we could try it to see what it's like,' she replied, still feeling tense in spite of his sunny demeanour. She knew from experience to never rest on her laurels because his temper often came out of nowhere.

'Have I got time for a shower before we eat?' he asked courteously.

She nodded. 'Of course.'

Kaidence watched him leave the room and turned her attention back to the cooker; the last thing she wanted was to burn the food and have his mood turn into rage because of it. She was somewhat relieved that there was still no trace of his bad temper. It made her hopeful that the damage to her body would have a chance to heal before she had to endure any more of his anger.

The microwave pinged, and Jackson opened the door to remove the meal he'd taken out of his freezer five minutes ago. He didn't have time to cook for himself, not that he could if he had the opportunity to, because he was a terrible chef. He only had home cooking when he visited his parents and he rarely had chance to do that.

He kept in contact with his mother over the phone because he knew that, due to his chosen profession, she worried about him, and he met his father at lunchtime on a Sunday if he wasn't working to have a pint with him, but he barely saw them otherwise. The same could be said of his siblings. Although he got to see Riley, his younger brother, and Taylah, the youngest of his sisters, when he was at home since they still lived in the house they all grew up in, he saw Autumn the least because she had moved out a little over three years ago, when she'd been twenty-four, just to assert her own independence.

He took a bite of the meal, which looked about as appetizing as dog food with some mashed potato added for good measure, and he pulled a face of discontent. Usually he would drop by any of his local takeaways on his way home, but he was waiting for payday for a cash injection, so he was forced to eat whatever he had in his freezer and had opted for a cottage pie; now that he was sat looking at it, he fancied anything else.

Suddenly his mobile phone started to echo throughout the quiet two-bedroom apartment he had moved into as soon as he'd joined the police force when he was twenty-five. Picking it up from the coffee table in front of where he sat a frown etched his features as he caught sight of the caller's ID. It was rare for his partner to call him at home unless they were on a case or there was an emergency. He slid the green icon across the screen and put the phone to his ear.

'Jessop, is everything okay?' he quizzed.

'Sure. I've just put the girls to bed, so I thought we could brainstorm about how to get me close to your abuse victim,' she said, getting straight to the point.

'You didn't seem very enthusiastic before. Why so eager now?'

'I was thinking about it and I've never seen you like this. So, I figure that she must be some girl to get you so hung up on saving her. Besides, what kind of partner would I be if I didn't help you nail this guy to a wall?'

'I appreciate your loyalty, but I don't know enough about her to come up with an in yet.'

'Then we need to do some recon. Give me her address and I'll drop by to do some surveillance after I take the kids to school tomorrow.'

Kaidence was dishing up their food by the time Mitchell returned to the room. She enjoyed cooking and often lost herself in the kitchen to escape his company when she just wanted time alone. She was limited to how she could find sanctuary because he didn't like her to leave the house without him if she didn't have a valid reason. It was almost like he was jealous of her ability to function without him. It was as if he expected her to cease to exist without him when the opposite was true; she would often come to life when she was allowed to be who she had been when they met.

He had apparently fallen in love with her because she'd been the kind of woman who lived large, enjoying even the most mundane task and radiating optimism to everyone she came into contact with even if they didn't want to feel it. Yet, those were the traits he'd been trying to change since he got control of her.

She had been the right balance of kindness without being a pushover, she used to be carefree while still being responsible and whenever she made a mistake, she would correct it if she could. This time it wasn't as simple as an apology to repair something she said in anger, it was going to take much more to get her out of the situation she had convinced herself she could handle while she fixed what was broken in him, but she had underestimated how evil he was and each beating she took pushed her further from wanting to be with him. She was just in too deep to walk away now that he was living with her. It wasn't as simple as asking him to leave. It came down to survival and she wanted to live. She knew having the officer on her side was going to give her the push she needed to get out from under his rule, but the timing had to be right.

She didn't need to look to find out where he was because she knew he'd be sat at the head of the table expecting his dinner to be brought to him like he had done since the day he'd moved in. She heard the familiar sound of him opening the beer she had to make sure was on the table by the time he sat down, and she rolled her eyes. Some nights he'd stop at one with his dinner and other nights he would have enough to make him want to fight the world. His abuse wasn't always linked to alcohol, but it was 80 per cent of the time. Although she was devastated to have lost a child when all she wanted growing up was to have a family, she was glad she hadn't brought a baby into this mess. It would have been so much harder to get out if she was forced to share custody with him.

Once they were loaded, Kaidence picked up the plates and walked over to lay his dinner in front of him before turning to put her own down in her usual spot and taking her seat. She didn't speak. She knew better. She had made that mistake when he'd got comfortable in her house. The first time he jabbed her in the jaw for talking at the dinner table came as quite a shock, but she had learned a lesson and it wasn't one she intended to repeat. Now she only spoke if she was spoken to, and that was a rare occurrence.

She couldn't express how much she hated her life. She missed having the freedom to do as she pleased whenever the feeling overcame her. She missed picking up the phone to have a chat with her friends and going to bed in the early hours of the morning. She missed sleeping in on the weekend if she felt like it and deciding to spend Sundays lazing in bed watching movies. She missed so many of the things she used to do and couldn't any more. She usually had to be up before him so she could cook breakfast, and then she had washing and ironing to do while Mitchell pleased himself with what he got up to. It was getting monotonous and she was done with putting up with it.

She didn't socialise any more; she was scared to in case Mitchell found out she had acquired someone to lean on. She knew he didn't want that because of the way he'd gone about getting rid of her friends. He only tolerated her having contact with her sister because he knew she'd be suspicious if she suddenly didn't hear from Kaidence since they only had each other to rely on. He'd only met Meredith twice and he'd been on his best behaviour so that she didn't suspect him of any ill intent towards her little sister – he could sense how fiercely protective she was. Meredith was also the only person she was allowed to call, without exception, in order to avoid suspicion but Kaidence didn't see her until her bruises had healed because she knew her older sibling would detect something wrong as soon as she laid eyes on her.

She sat at that table like a robot every night just going through the motions. She was there but not really present; instead of sitting silently while he noisily consumed his meal, she disappeared inside her head, dreaming of life after she got away from him. At first, she would see herself on a beach basking beneath the hot sun while a handsome gentleman from an island far away brought her cocktails every twenty minutes and took her walking on the sand at night. But now she imagined she was anywhere but at that table with the man who didn't even have the manners to thank her for the food she'd cooked. She was free. She hated being alone in her past life; now she welcomed it. She prayed for it, except it always came at a price.

She was so lost thinking of an alternative life that she almost didn't catch the words that had left his mouth before they disappeared into the ether. She could hear the sound they made and took a minute to decipher what his question had been before she attempted to answer it, knowing that if she was wrong in her reply he'd probably punch her in her mouth. Although giving no response at all or asking him to repeat himself was certain to get that reaction.

'I mostly spent the day catching up with chores,' she replied meekly.

'I can tell. The house looks spotless,' he countered.

Kaidence internally rolled her eyes. Of course it was spotless, there was never anything out of place unless they had a fight and then he didn't care about the state of the house. The fact he could believe that she would have to catch up with chores when all she seemed to do was clean was laughable to her. But her answer seemed to satisfy his inquisition, and then the silence returned between them. She liked it when he was quiet. It meant she didn't have to force an interest in any conversation he felt the need to generate. Although lately it was getting harder to fake her happiness and she feared that the sudden appearance of the police officer was only going to make it harder.

She picked at the food on her plate while he ate contentedly. She never really had much of an appetite when he was at home due to her inability to function when he was around. He had always been able to immobilise her, except now it was for completely different reasons than it had been when they'd first met. Her palms weren't sweating because she was hoping to impress him; it was due to her fists being clenched in expectation of him picking faults. Instead of being tongue tied, she just had nothing to say even if he would allow her to. Her heart didn't beat faster because she was anticipating his touch, it was because of fear; and instead of butterflies in her stomach, it churned. She spent her life constantly on a knife edge and she wished she could rewind time to make a different decision when she had impulsively given him a key to her home.

Suddenly a phone ringing distracted her from pushing food around her plate. It was his; she could tell by how close it was because hers was still in her handbag, where it had been since she got home from shopping with her sister on Saturday. There wasn't much cause for her to keep it on her given that she wasn't authorised to use it and that way it removed any temptation.

He wasted no time removing the intruding object from his jeans pocket and answering it, even though he was at the dinner table in the middle of his meal, which was just another thing about him that annoyed her.

'Johnny!' he exclaimed gleefully, and she knew right away it was one of his brain-dead friends from high school she'd had the displeasure of meeting once. He was just as sexist as Mitchell, believing women should behave a certain way and not live as freely as men. They had laughed about keeping the fairer sex in line and only giving them enough rope to hang themselves to save them the job. That was sufficient for her to realise she didn't want to be around him, and thankfully her boyfriend had never invited him over to drink because preserving her life would be virtually impossible if she had cause to jump on her soapbox.

She continued to listen as they shot the breeze until John got to the point of his call, and although she couldn't express her feelings, she smiled inside when Mitchell agreed to meet him for a beer at the pub they frequented.

She wasn't looking forward to the state he would undoubtedly return home in, but she hoped that, like most nights when he went out drinking, he wouldn't be able to make it up to bed and instead would fall asleep on the settee. She was going to be able to do what she wanted for the rest of the night before getting into bed alone, and not be pressured into fulfilling his needs, which rarely happened.

More than once she had thought about packing what little belongings he had and leaving them on the driveway for him to discover when he got home, but the thought of the backlash had always prevented her from acting on the idea.

She pretended not to be paying any attention to the conversation he was having as she put some food in her mouth and forced herself to chew. With any luck, he would go out as soon as he was changed, which never took him long when he had a purpose, and then she could spend the evening the same way she had spent the day – hassle free.

He hung up and rushed to empty his plate, barely taking time to chew before he swallowed. Once he was finished, he leaned back in his seat, allowing the back to support his weight, and exhaled as he rested his hands on his engorged stomach.

'Thanks for that baby. It was delicious,' he complimented. It was a sign he was leaving her; he was being as nice as he could manage with his limited ability. 'I'm going out with the guys for a few drinks, so you can watch that chick flick I brought you for your birthday.'

She grinned and nodded her response as he got to his feet and left the room. Her smile disappeared with him. The birthday he had been referring to consisted of no celebration at all. She had cooked, she had cleaned up afterwards and she had gone to bed when he determined it was time for her to fulfil her womanly duty; exactly like every other night. The only small change was that he'd presented her with a badly wrapped gift, which – when she'd opened it – she discovered she already owned. He had obviously made no effort to know her at all because it was a movie she didn't even like that much.

When he had announced she could only watch it when he wasn't home, it added further insult to injury. That was eleven weeks ago, and he was giving her permission to watch it. Not that she planned to, but he didn't need to know that.

The television was playing in Jackson's living room, but he wasn't really paying any attention to it. He had been consumed with finding a way to get Kaidence out from her relationship since he'd met her and on reflection, he had an idea why.

The minute he'd seen the petite brunette with her long loose curly hair and piercing green eyes he had made an emotional association to her. She reminded him of someone he knew once who he hadn't been able to save from her abusive boyfriend in time, and he knew that was why he was holding on so tight, unwavering in his determination to not make the same mistake.

He'd been undercover at the time, trying to become indispensable to a drug dealer who his colleagues hadn't been able to pin anything on, and he'd succeeded. He'd got close, some would argue too close, and had instantly felt empathy for the girlfriend he used to knock around whenever he felt the urge. He had made promises to her, promises he ultimately couldn't keep, and before he got her away from her boyfriend, she had been killed by him. Knowing he couldn't blow his cover to stop the abuse he was witnessing, he had stayed close to her, expecting to have enough time to help her get out. He'd been wrong. It wasn't until the perpetrator had asked for his help with disposing of her body that he could finally do the job he'd been hired to do, and by then it was too late for her. It haunted him that he hadn't acted sooner and ultimately, he decided to leave the unit.

Jackson had returned to being a beat cop a month later when the trauma had proved to be too much for him to live with, and he'd only been back doing that for seven months when he came across Kaidence. It was as if he had been guided to her door that day by a higher power in order to provide him with closure of some kind on the chapter that had already been written and couldn't be changed.

As predicted, Mitchell was wearing his best clothes ready for a night boozing with his friends before Kaidence had even had a chance to clear the table. Eating after he'd left the room became so much easier; maybe it was because she was happy he was going out, or maybe it was because she didn't have to stare at him. Either way, she had emptied her plate by the time he returned to the room searching for his keys.

'They're on the counter by the fridge,' she pointed out as she swilled off the plates under the tap to remove the bubbles before drying them off and returning them to the cupboard.

She heard the jingle as he lifted them from their resting place and felt him suddenly breathing down her neck. She half spun towards him in time to catch the kiss he applied to her cheek.

'Thanks babe. Don't wait up,' he suggested, rushing for the door.

I *didn't intend to*, she thought with a wry smile as she heard the door slam shut behind him. Finally, she was alone. Nights like these were the ones she enjoyed the most because she only got to spend a short time in his company, meaning less time spent watching what she said and how she said it. Wasting no time, Kaidence headed to the door and knocked the snib button down on the door latch, deadlocking it so that if he returned home unexpectedly the lock would be inoperable by key and she would have to let him in. She could explain it away like the snib button had dropped when he'd slammed the door.

She went back to the kitchen and sifted through the bill drawer to find the card with Jackson's contact number on before retrieving her mobile phone from her handbag. Unlocking it, she touched the phone icon and punched his number into the dial pad.

The other end rang a couple of times before she heard his voice and an involuntary smile found its way to her lips.

'Hi Officer Chase.'

———

Jackson was sat in front of his police-issue laptop, punching on the keys and trying to find a common denominator to use in order to get his partner closer to the woman he was hell-bent on getting out from the threatening relationship she was in. So far, his searches had come up with nothing but the fact that she was a teacher in his district; he couldn't find out which school she taught at and he was getting frustrated.

He sighed as he reached another dead end and was immediately distracted when his phone rang, and an unknown number was displayed on the screen. Picking it up, Jackson slid the green icon from the left to the right and put it up to his ear. He didn't get a chance to speak before he heard her voice and instantly panicked.

'Kaidence, is everything okay?' he asked.

'Yes, I just wanted to call you and say thank you for this morning.'

He exhaled in relief. 'Thank God. For a minute, I thought...'

'Oh no, he was in a good mood when he got home tonight. But I saw an opportunity to call and let you know I appreciate you looking out for me.'

He frowned. 'What if he hears you on the phone?'

'Oh, he went out drinking with his Neanderthal buddies.'

'Does that mean there's a risk of you getting another beating tonight?'

'I plan to be fast asleep by the time he gets home so he won't have anyone to pick a fight with. Besides, he usually doesn't make it up the stairs. He crashes on the settee instead.'

He thought he could hear how much happier she sounded compared to earlier and he hoped it had everything to do with the promises he'd made to her. Promises he planned to keep this time. His contact with her seemed to be working. Although they'd only had two meetings, the fact that she'd used her free time to ring hopefully meant that she was beginning to trust him.

'So, what are you going to do with your night off?' he asked to break the silence.

'I figured a nice long relaxing bath was in order after I call my sister to see what I've missed out on for the last four days since I saw her.'

His brow furrowed again. 'You've got a sister?'

'An older sister, who's very protective of me since our parents died.'

'I take it she doesn't know about the abuse.'

'I'm not sure Mitchell would still be alive if she did. No, you're the only one who knows.'

'You must be an expert at hiding bruises.'

'I just avoid seeing her until they've healed so she's none the wiser.'

'Your isolation isn't healthy, Kaidence.'

'You know, and that's enough for me at the moment.'

'I'm going to find a way to keep an eye on you without drawing any attention to us. I've just got to figure out how to do it under the radar.'

'I've got your number. If I need it, I'll use it.'

'And what if you can't?'

She sighed; he had a point. 'I'll try and call you every couple of days.'

'I can't rely on that. What if you call me on the day he decides to knock you around and kills you? I wouldn't know until you didn't call me a couple of days later. That doesn't work for me. No, I need to have a daily check-in. I've just got to figure out how to get Louisa close enough to you while avoiding suspicion.'

'Who's Louisa?'

'She's my partner. I trust her with my life.'

'And mine.'

'I just thought she'd be less conspicuous than me.'

'At least Mitchell won't think I'm sleeping with her,' she commented, and he could hear the playful suggestion in her statement. It was nice to hear that side of her personality coming out, even if it was just over the phone. He knew it was easier for her to closely resemble the person she used to be when she had the protection of not being seen.

'If he does, he might leave.'

'Doubtful. But he used to be the kind of guy that would ask to watch.'

'He sounds like a real catch,' he countered sarcastically. 'My little sisters would be lucky to meet someone like him.'

She laughed, and the sound was so infectious it made him smile. He suspected she didn't have much cause to make her diaphragm dance and so he was honoured to get to hear her happy. It encouraged him to keep the sound going.

'I can only hope my little brother will be half the man he is,' he added. 'Sadly, it's too late for me to aspire to be like him.'

Her laughter died down slowly. 'So you've got sisters and a brother?'

Her question forced him to return to being serious. She was obviously trying to determine whether he was worthy of the trust she was willing to put in him.

'My sisters are Autumn and Taylah, and Riley is my brother.'

'Are they all in the police force?'

'Oh God no,' he said with a small laugh. 'Autumn is a fashionista, whatever one of those is. Taylah is working towards being a vet and Riley has just decided to join the army, following in mine and our father's footsteps.'

'I knew you were military of some kind.'

'Is it really that obvious?'

'It's the way you carry yourself, it's not just police training that gives you that kind of confidence.' Then a thought occurred to her. 'Aren't you a little young to have finished your service already?'

'I enlisted straight after school when I was seventeen and I left at twenty-two when I'd decided to go into the force. I had completed my police training by the time I was twenty-five and I've been an officer ever since.'

'I bet your father wasn't happy about you leaving the army.'

'Actually, my dad has always been supportive. He understood that the army, although it taught me a lot, just wasn't right for me. However, he is beyond happy that Riley has felt a calling to follow in his sizeable footsteps.'

'Is your dad still serving?'

'He retired last year after thirty-four years of service.'

'He sounds like a great man.'

'He's the best. Where do you think I get it from?'

Another laugh escaped down the line and filtered into his ear. He was getting to like hearing her laugh and he liked even more that he was the one causing it.

Kaidence was laughing so hard she snorted. It had been a long time since she'd had anything to bring a smile to her face, let alone a giggle, and it was surprising to her that a stranger had that effect on her. Usually she didn't let anyone in for fear of being judged but Jackson had forced his way in, and it occurred to her that maybe it was easier to open up to someone who had no preconceived ideas of her. Plus, there was something comforting about him that made her feel like she'd known him forever.

She had only intended her call to be short and sweet, but he was just so easy to talk to and it had been a while since she spent time unwinding on the phone, so she was in no hurry for it to end.

'So, I know about most of your family. But what does your mum do?' she asked, getting her breath back.

'My mum ran the family. She made sure the house was kept clean, that our clothes were always washed and ironed; she ensured we always had a meal on the table even when we were living on very little money. She had the hardest job of all but somehow she managed to keep us all together even when dad was away.'

Hearing him speak so highly of the woman who had given birth to him increased her immense respect for him; not many men recognised just how hard their mothers worked behind the scenes and so to hear him appreciate all the things she had done for the family over the years made her sure she could trust him to fulfil the promises he'd made to help her.

'You're close to her, aren't you?'

'Yes, some would say I'm a mummy's boy.'

She sniggered. 'I didn't say that.'

'No, but you were probably thinking it.'

'Actually, I like that you speak so highly of your mum. It makes me sure I wasn't wrong trusting you with my secret.'

'Now all I need to do is get you as far away from that boyfriend of yours as is possible.'

'Still haven't had a flash of inspiration while we've been talking?'

'No, I'm none the wiser as to how I'm going to get Louisa close enough to you without making Mitchell suspicious.'

'Having me prattle on won't be helping so I'm going to leave you to figure out the logistics. Just let me know what the plan is when you come up with one.'

'Okay Kaidence. Stay out of trouble.'

She smiled. 'Bye, Jackson.'

Hanging up, she immediately went into the internal phone log and deleted all trace of the call, which was almost an hour in duration, before searching her favourites list for the picture she'd assigned to her sister and hitting the green icon.

'Kiki,' her sister greeted her, using her childhood nickname.

'Hi Mimi,' she countered with her pet name for her older sibling. 'I just sat down after my dinner with a glass of wine and thought I'd call for a chat,' she lied. She hadn't had an alcoholic drink since Mitchell had moved in because he had expressed a dislike for the party girl who emerged whenever she drank. It was ironic given that he was abusive when he had a beer, but she hadn't known that at the time.

'I've forgotten what wine tastes like,' Meredith responded.

'Well that's your fault for breast feeding!' Kaidence laughed.

'I was led to believe it was what was best for my little boy. There was no mention of raw nipples and the difficulty of getting him to latch on in the middle of the night.'

'It's not like Cole can help,' she said, speaking of her brother-in-law.

'Oh, he can if I use the breast pump, but that's worse than having a three-month-old suck me dry.'

'The joys only a mother would understand.'

———

The silence in the apartment seemed louder than usual as Jackson sat with a beer in front of the television. His call with Kaidence had been a nice surprise, and one that was evidence of the bond they were beginning to forge. It was a good indication that she wanted to trust him; it had just been so long since there had been anyone for her to rely on that it was difficult for her to readily put her faith in someone. That's why she remained guarded and found it easier to talk on the phone. It allowed her to be herself while being hidden. It was safe, and he suspected she didn't get much chance to feel that.

He felt positive about his plan, even though implementing it was going to be difficult. If she was as willing as he was, he knew they could work together to be successful to reach his end game. Ideally, he wanted her to be out from Mitchell's rule as soon as possible but it was going to be tricky given that she wasn't willing to move as far away from him as she could, and he understood her not wanting to leave the only family she had left – it just limited his options.

***

Hanging up the phone from her conversation with her sister, Kaidence headed straight upstairs and hummed a tune in her head as she bounced her way to the floor above. With the deadlock on the door, it meant she could have a bath in peace without fear that Mitchell would walk in and try to join her or sit with her in the bathroom, meaning she wouldn't be able to unwind, which was the purpose of soaking in the tub. She started to shed her clothes as she made her way through the bedroom she had once considered her sanctuary but was now the backdrop to countless nights when her boyfriend would rape her after knocking her around just because he thought sex made up for hurting her somehow.

Entering the bathroom, she turned on the taps before discarding the rest of her outfit. Once she was naked, she examined as much of her body as she could lay her eyes on to see what kind of damage Mitchell had done to it, only to find there wasn't much external evidence of the internal pain she felt. The purple bruises on her sides were starting to fade a little but that's because she'd learned to place ice on them in order to reduce the blood flow to the area, and her ribs had no indication of bruising, even though it hurt when she took too deep a breath. The only real evidence of Sunday night's abuse was the marks on her face, and she only knew about those by using the camera on her mobile phone, which showed her the remains of the fading black eyes and cut lip. She was close to being able to return to work, which was useful given that the kids had started a new school year on Monday. At least they wouldn't miss much of the curriculum if she were to follow them just a week later. She just had to do her utmost to make sure she didn't need to have any more time off. That would mean being extra vigilant when it came to keeping Mitchell happy. Although she was no closer to figuring out how to do that than she was to leaving him.

Turning off the taps as the water threatened to spill over the sides of the bath, she dipped her big toe in, testing the temperature before submerging the rest of her body. She exhaled a long, satisfied breath that she'd held since her housemate had returned home as she lay back and closed her eyes. She was going to relish the warmth of the water as it gave relief to her aching muscles for as long as she could before it turned cold and she had to get out. But it was only eight o'clock, so she had plenty of time to relax before she got wrapped up in bed and basked in the comfort an empty bed provided.

CHAPTER FOUR

The house was quiet as Kaidence lay in bed. She had remembered to remove the deadlock from the entrance only after she'd got comfortable in bed. She had drifted off more easily than she had for the past twelve months and managed almost three hours' unbroken sleep before the slam of the front door jolted her awake. Mitchell was home and she could hear him rambling to himself. It wasn't unusual for him to shout the house down to get her attention, but she always pretended not to hear him because he never remembered in the morning. Although tonight he seemed content with his own company, as she heard him rummaging through the cupboards for something to snack on. He always got peckish after he'd filled his gut with beer and since there was no danger of him cooking anything, she didn't need to intervene in order to make sure he didn't burn the place down. She could picture him swaying drunkenly about downstairs until he settled in the living room on the settee. It wasn't long before she heard his snores through the floorboards and she knew she was safe for the night, which made it easier for her to drift back off to the land of nod.

The sun broke through the curtains where they didn't meet properly, and cast a light on Kaidence's face, which stirred her awake. Her eyes opened slowly, and she grimaced at the bright sunshine that blinded her. It wasn't until she rolled out of its beam that she realised she was still in bed alone. She had slept soundly for almost ten hours, which made up for the three previous nights when she had catnapped through until morning. She knew it had helped to have the evening to relax before climbing into bed alone because it was a luxury she didn't get very often. But things would return to normal later. She'd be forced to sleep on what little of the mattress he deemed to give her because he didn't care enough to share, then she'd have to listen to him snoring as she tried to limit her movement, so she didn't end up on the floor.

Turning to lie on her back, she stared up at the ceiling. She didn't hear him moving around yet so she had time to mentally prepare for the day before she was forced to get up and start slaving for the man she shared her life with. All the ways in which she was a slave were only just starting to grate on her nerves and she suspected it was the Jackson Chase effect, because it hadn't bothered her so much before.

The usual morning rush always kept Louisa Jessop on her toes as she navigated getting breakfast together while trying to motivate her eight-year-old and five-year-old daughters into getting ready for school. But this morning it seemed harder than the day before because she had promised to do a favour for her partner.

'Juliette! Alicia!' she called out as she filled two bowls with their favourite cereal. 'Breakfast is up.'

She rushed to place the crockery on the table in their usual spots where the litre-bottle of milk already awaited use before going back to the kettle and filling her mug with hot water. She steeped her fruit teabag for a minute and when her children didn't surface, she went in search of them.

She didn't hesitate to knock on her elder daughter's door before opening it like she normally would, which got a shriek of protest from her. 'Juliette, come on, I promised Uncle Jack I'd run an errand for him.'

'I'm getting ready, aren't I?' Juliette snapped at her mother.

'What have I told you about the way you talk to me?' She pulled her up on the disrespect she was showing. 'Do I have to stop you hanging out with your friends, so you learn not to talk to me like I'm one of them?'

She dropped her head and stared at the floor, 'Sorry Mum.'

'Thank you. Now hustle please,' the adult said, leaving the room to check on the progress of her younger daughter.

She headed across the landing only to find Alicia's door wide open and no sign of Alicia. As a frown appeared on her brow, Louisa shifted to the bathroom but again, didn't see any sign of her daughter. She was about to panic when she heard a clatter come from the lower floor, which did nothing to quell her nerves. She rushed down the stairs as fast as she could and entered the kitchen in time to see the five-year-old attempting to mop up spilt milk from the table with a tea towel.

Her shoulders dropped as she relaxed. 'What happened?'

'The bottle was too heavy,' Alicia replied, looking upset.

'Why didn't you call me?'

'Because you and JJ were fighting again,' she said with a roll of her eyes. 'You're always fighting.'

'I'm sorry baby, but you'll understand when you're older that families fight because they love each other,' she countered, picking up the milk and splashing some in her bowl before taking over clean-up duty.

By the time Kaidence had plucked up the energy to make it downstairs Mitchell was starting to stir. She didn't go into the living room, knowing he would emerge when he was good and ready; instead she headed to the kitchen to get a pot of coffee on and begin cooking his breakfast. His hangover remedy the morning after drinking was a bacon and egg sandwich so she knew that's what he'd want. She was concerned that if he felt worse for wear that he'd take the day off work, opting instead to lie on the settee watching daytime television, but she forced herself not to think about it until she knew for sure. By the time she cracked an egg in the small frying pan, he had shuffled into the room dressed and ready for work.

She felt lifted by the idea of having another day to herself as she kept her eye on the bacon under the grill so that it didn't burn while watching the egg to make sure the yolk didn't break. This was routine to her, although it was usually Sundays when he needed to soak up the beer from the night before, not the middle of the week.

'Did you have a good night?' she enquired to quell the silence.

'Yeah, but I tell you, I'm feeling it today,' he replied, walking over to lean his backside against the fixtures and supervise what she was doing.

'Are you sure you're okay to go in to work today?' she asked, playing the role of concerned girlfriend while secretly hoping she didn't encourage him to take the day to recover.

He sighed. 'The boss called a meeting yesterday. If I don't show up, he's going to notice, and I don't want to lose another job, so I'll go in. I might not get much work done but I'll be at my desk.'

She smiled, happy in the knowledge that she was going to have yet another day to do as she pleased, especially given that the majority of her chores had been done the day before. All she had to do was clean up the breakfast things and give the kitchen a wipe-down before she spent the day lazing around in front of daytime television. She hated sitting around, but her bruises weren't quite healed enough for Mitchell to be comfortable with her leaving the house so for now she would abide by the rules he had gradually set in place until it was time for her to walk out of the front door.

The car was usually quiet on her drive to the school, but this morning Louisa was deafened by the sound of her daughters arguing. She rolled her brown eyes as she pulled up at the red traffic light. They'd both woken up in the mood to fight the world and she was reaching the end of her tether.

Juliette was going through a stage in her childhood when she wanted to be treated more grown up than she actually was, and Alicia was an inconvenience to her so the two butted heads more frequently of late. The same could be said about Louisa's own relationship with her. Although she hadn't even reached double figures in age yet, Juliette was acting more like a teenager with every passing day and Louisa was trying desperately to allow her the space to develop while constantly battling her attitude.

'For God's sake you two, enough arguing! Please just give it a break!' She yelled to be heard over their bickering.

'She started it,' the oldest sibling stated.

'Did not!' the youngest protested.

'I don't care! Just stop it. It's hard to concentrate on driving with you both screaming in the background and I'd really like to get us to the school in one piece.'

As if a switch had been flicked, Juliette and Alicia fell quiet, causing their mother to sigh in relief. It had already been a long morning and it wasn't even nine o'clock yet. Every school day was the same, whether she was working or had the day off. She had to fight them to get washed and dressed and then she had to drag them kicking and screaming to the car. Only then would she get peace because they'd had it drilled into them how important it was to concentrate while she was behind the wheel. But today they were determined to be as disruptive as possible.

Once their journey got back under way, it wasn't long before she was pulling up outside the school gates, which were clear simply because of how early they were. The girls wasted no time climbing out from the back seat as their mother turned off the engine and joined them on the pavement. Pressing the automatic lock button on the key fob, she led her daughters inside the grounds. The teaching staff, being familiar with her flexible hours, were always accommodating when it came to allowing her children inside the doors before the bell and keeping them in the classroom a little longer if she was running late at the end of the day. Although she had a really good relationship with her ex, she couldn't rely on him to drop everything the minute she needed him, and there were only so many family members that she could call who would be there to help. Being a single mum was tough, even with her ability to lean on their father, and especially now that she was pursuing a career in law enforcement.

Proving herself in a profession that was heavily male orientated was difficult, but she liked to think that after four years on the force she was making headway regarding being seen as an equal and not as a girl playing cop. She knew that Jackson had been on her side since they'd been part-nered together, but she'd lost count of how many jokes she'd had to listen to over the years from the rest of the station about having pre-menstrual stress when she had lost her temper with one of them or having to reapply her lipstick when she made a mad dash to the toilets. She couldn't just take time off because she couldn't find a babysitter; that would be inappropriate, and she wasn't about to give them any more rope to hang her by. She had never been late for a shift, she'd never had to duck out early and she was always the last one out of the door with Jackson at the end of the day. Of all the things her colleagues could tease her about, slacking on the job wasn't one of them.

Opening the entrance door of the small building that led to the class-rooms, Louisa cut across the corridor and looked around for signs of the teacher who had introduced herself at the end of last term sat behind the desk; instead she saw a face she didn't recognise.

'Jules, where's your teacher?' she asked her daughter with a frown.

The girl shrugged. 'She's sick. She hasn't been in all week.'

'But it's the beginning of the new year.'

'So?' she countered before walking inside the class.

With a sigh, Louisa turned her attention to Alicia. 'Okay A-bug, let's get you to class.'

Kaidence filled the sink with water, adding a squirt of washing-up liquid, ready for her to clean the grill before wiping around the cooker hob, while Mitchell sat on a stool at the breakfast bar eating his sandwich. She could feel his eyes on her as she worked; it was a pastime he was fond of. It made her just unsettled enough that she made sure she did a thorough job.

She had the cleanest house she had ever had because she had more time to clean it. Instead of working all day and grabbing a quick bite to eat before she went out at night to meet friends, she spent most of her life stuck indoors, so if she wasn't prepping work for the next day or cooking, she was working out her frustrations on every surface available.

She missed the days of having to do the washing-up because there were no fresh cups for her to drink her morning tea out of; admittedly she only had six of them at the time but that wasn't the point. The point was that she had the choice to do nothing if nothing was what she wanted to do. Now she cleaned to be doing something other than sitting with Mitchell watching whatever TV programme he deemed interesting. She'd never seen him do housework, and he never offered to help, but he hadn't insisted she kept a tidy house either. It was the one thing he didn't seem to have an issue with, although maybe that was because she'd never let it get dirty. Still, she wasn't about to test whether it set him off; she didn't need to give him another reason to get mad.

Traffic was heavy from the school to the address Louisa was headed to. Although she had left early enough to drop her daughters off, she had hit rush hour on her way out. She checked the clock on her dash and huffed in frustration as she halted to a stop at another red light. She was convinced that by the time she reached her destination she'd be too late to witness the boyfriend leaving and miss her chance to see his girlfriend as she waved him out of the door, therefore missing her opportunity to get a visual in order to report the woman's well-being back to her partner.

A couple of minutes after reaching the street and finding a place to park a safe distance away, she saw a man leave the premises, but there was no sign of the girlfriend in the doorway like she expected. For a second it crossed her mind that the woman had met her end, but it occurred to her that it would be unfortunate for that to have happened the minute she joined the fight to save her. She had to use her police training to be rational and not react with her emotions just because they were the same gender. Knocking the door was out of the question given that they hadn't been formally introduced; she needed Jackson to do the honours, so they had a foundation to begin building their trust on.

Relaxing back behind the wheel, Louisa reached for the flask of coffee she had made at home just before leaving. She usually needed two cups to be able to function in a morning, especially when it was her day off, but the arguing had given her the kick that was required to motivate her. Usually she'd drop the kids off at school and then head back home to clean the house she had neglected all week. But her partner rarely asked for help with anything, so she couldn't deny him when he did.

She had been sitting observing the house for a couple of hours when her phone rang to distract her, and she answered it through the Bluetooth wired into her car. 'Hi Jackson.'

He jumped right to the point. 'Have you seen her yet?'

'No and it doesn't look like she's going to leave the house today.'

'She's probably waiting for the cuts on her face to heal,' he reasoned. 'You can go ahead and leave; I'll give her a call to make sure she's okay.'

'Are you sure?'

'Yes – why don't you go and do whatever you do on your day off? I'll see you at work tomorrow.' He paused. 'Thanks for helping me out, Lou.'

'It's what partners are for. Just let me know if you need anything else.'

The house was peaceful, just the way Kaidence liked it. She had said goodbye to Mitchell as usual and retired to the living room with a cup of tea. She was now sat on the settee watching the mind-numbing talk show of the morning. It helped her to put her life into perspective, although the problems of the people who appeared on that show seemed to pale in comparison to her own, and it would make her mad if it wasn't for the fact that she could now see a light at the end of the tunnel – thanks to the officer who had got more than he bargained for when he'd knocked on her door.

Thinking of Jackson seemed to trigger a ripple out into the world, and when her phone started to ring, she noticed the withheld stature of the caller but didn't hesitate to answer it, somehow expecting it to be him.

'Hello.' She held back on her theory until she heard his voice.

'Kaidence, thank God.' He sighed in relief.

'Officer Chase, you sound worried.'

'I'm just checking in after last night.'

'I'm okay. As predicted, he fell asleep on the settee and I had the best night's sleep I've had all week.'

He exhaled deeply. 'I hate not knowing if you're okay from one minute to the next.'

'I'm sorry, but I need to leave him in my own time.'

'I know, and I understand. I just hate feeling helpless.'

'You've still got no idea how to get your partner close without it looking suspicious?'

'Not yet. But she dropped by your place this morning and reported back to me that she hadn't seen you.'

Kaidence shot to her feet and headed to the window. Pulling back the net curtain, she looked out onto the street for a strange car, hoping to catch sight of his partner. 'Is she still there?'

'I told her to leave and decided to use the number you called me on to get proof of life.'

'Oh,' she responded, not meaning for it to slip out. She was curious about his partner. Not because she was jealous or felt like she had a claim on him somehow; she just wanted to know what kind of woman he trusted enough to enlist her help. Realising almost instantly that she had verbalised her disappointment, she attempted to cover for it. 'I was going to invite her in for a cup of tea; I bet she has a lot of stories about all kinds of shenanigans you two have got up to while you've been working together.'

'I'm an open book; you can ask me anything.'

'Okay then,' she countered, trying to think of a question to test if he really meant what he claimed. 'Have you ever committed a crime?'

'Never,' he answered instantaneously.

'You haven't even stolen a chocolate bar from the local shop?'

'I'm the oldest son of a military man; I didn't have the courage to try something like that.'

'Did you always want to follow in your father's footsteps?'

'That didn't matter, it was just expected.'

'So, are you more like your mum or your dad?'

'My dad is typical military; he doesn't have time for his feelings because they got in the way of him doing his job whereas my mum wears her heart on her sleeve, so I hope that I'm more like her.'

'Well I know I haven't known you long, but I'd say you are. I'm not sure any other officer would go to the lengths you have for me.'

'I'm just doing my job.'

'You say that, but every day you've checked on me so far you haven't been on the clock.' She let him know she had noticed. 'I bet your wife isn't impressed with how much of your time has been spent on me,' she said, fishing for information without being direct.

Jackson's smile went unseen. He knew what she was doing. But he indulged her anyway.

'I'm not married,' he replied, answering her circumlocutory curiosity.

'Dating?' she probed.

'No.'

'How is that possible? You're handsome. You must have women falling over themselves to date you.'

'I've been known to get some phone numbers in my time. But I haven't met the right woman yet.'

'When was the last time you were in love?'

He considered his response carefully before he gave it. He wasn't sure if she'd believe him and yet it was the truth. He sighed. 'In high school.'

'You haven't been in love since high school?'

'I've been too busy with my career.'

'Wow! Just, wow!'

'That wasn't what you were expecting, was it?'

'No. I expected you to be in a serious long-term relationship with a woman who was perfect for you.'

'I'm sorry to disappoint.'

'Actually, it helps that you're single; at least I don't have to feel guilty that I'm causing a rift between you and the woman you're intended to by taking up all your time.'

The corners of his mouth lifted into another smile she wouldn't see. 'So is that the end of the interrogation or do you have more questions?'

'I just have one more; why me?'

'I can't answer that because I don't know, but yours is not the first case of abuse that I've happened upon by accident. I just want a chance to change the outcome this time.'

'Oh.' she countered understanding immediately the tragedy he must have witnessed and how it must have affected him for him to be so determined to integrate into her situation. 'I'm sorry, I shouldn't have asked.'

'Well, you've confided in me, it's only right that I do the same.'

'But I can hear in your voice how painful a memory it is. I hate making you relive it.'

'I live with the pain of it every day regardless of whether I talk about it or not, so I don't want you to feel bad.'

'Still, I didn't mean to pry.'

'Kaidence, if I didn't want to tell you things about my past, I wouldn't.'

By the time the weekend came Kaidence was fully healed and ready to leave the house. Every Saturday she and her sister would go shopping; it was something they'd always done and therefore Mitchell allowed her to keep the arrangement. She always looked forward to spending time with her sister and it was rare she had to cancel the plans, because whatever injuries she had sustained the Sunday before were usually gone or easily covered.

Kaidence had dressed the way she always did: covered from the neck down with only her hands and face exposed to the conditions outside. Her long hair was scraped back into a ponytail and her face, although covered with foundation in places to hide the imperfections Mitchell had added, was otherwise untouched by make-up. She got less attention if she looked like she didn't care about her appearance. Her older sibling had commented on her lack of effort at first, but she'd played it off like she didn't need to look for a man when she had one at home. She hoped her sister had bought it because she hadn't mentioned it since. But if she knew Meredith, she was silent in her curiosity and it wouldn't be long until she had to say something because she wouldn't be able to help herself. Since becoming a mother, Meredith had been more protective than she ever had in the seven years previous.

Kaidence smiled as she spotted Meredith ahead of her on the pavement and her pace hastened. Her bruises had meant it had been a week since she'd seen her, despite living only quarter of an hour from each other, and she missed dropping by for a visit whenever she was close. It made it difficult to be the godmother to her nephew that she wanted to be, but she was hopeful that it wouldn't be long before she could be.

When their parents had died, Meredith had assumed the role of overprotective sister bordering on overbearing mother, and Kaidence couldn't give her a reason to be disappointed. Kaidence knew her sister only wanted the best for her, so it was natural that she wouldn't want her sister to settle down with a man who beat her. But she just wasn't ready to tell the woman she looked up to that she had accepted the type of behaviour that put her life in danger.

Kaidence walked into her sibling's comforting arms and held on to her for a second or two longer than she usually would. It caused her sister to frown slightly as she pulled away.

'Are you okay?'

Kaidence sucked back the tears that threatened to form in her eyes. 'Yes, I'm fine. I'm just having a bit of an emotional day, that's all. It'll pass.'

The older female studied her face. 'Are you sure it's nothing more than that?'

'I'm sure, Mimi.'

'I wasn't going to say anything, but you haven't seemed like yourself for a while, Kiki,' she said, vocalising her concern.

'Who else would I be?' she asked, forcing a smile.

There was a silence between them as they made their way to the coffee shop they visited every Saturday morning before going shopping.

'Are you happy?' Meredith asked as they walked arm in arm towards their destination.

'Of course, I am. Why would you ask that?'

'You just seem really different to the girl I knew growing up.'

'Well, a girl changes when her parents die in a car crash the day after her twenty-first birthday,' she said, bringing up a painful memory in the hope it would appease her sister and stop her looking for an answer to the difference she'd noticed in her.

'That's not what I meant,' Meredith clarified. 'You've changed since being with Mitchell and I didn't want to say anything before because I didn't want it to seem like I was judging him, but I don't think he's good for you.'

'You barely know him.'

'That's because every time I invite you two around you always have other plans.'

Kaidence shrugged. 'He works hard. The last thing he wants to do when he gets home from work is to socialise.'

'I'm your sister.'

'Maybe that's the problem. He probably feels like his every move would be evaluated.'

'That's my prerogative as the only family you have left.'

'You should trust me enough to have the ability to pick the men I want to date.'

'I do. I just want to make sure he's good enough for my baby sister.'

'I understand that. But you have to let me choose my own path in life.'

'I worry about you.'

'You don't have to, Mimi. I'm okay,' she lied, to save being lectured.

'You don't have anyone else looking out for you, I'm all you've got left.'

'Thanks for pointing that out, Sis. Your brutal honesty always makes me feel so good about myself.'

If there was one thing Kaidence could rely on her sister for, it was her candour. It was one of the qualities she loved most about her, and it was why she sometimes had to hide aspects of her personal life. It was hard for her to be deceptive, even though technically she wasn't lying; she just hadn't disclosed the details of her relationship because she knew Meredith wouldn't approve and would do everything in her power to get her as far from Mitchell as she possibly could, damn the consequences.

'How's that nephew of mine?' Kaidence asked after the three-month-old in order to change the subject.

'He's growing like a weed,' Meredith responded. 'Why don't you come home with me and spend the day with us?'

'I've got to get back; I've got things to do.'

'Surely they can wait until tomorrow? You never spend any time with us any more, we miss you.'

She sighed. 'Let me give Mitchell a call to see if he minds us pushing our plans until tomorrow,' she said, to cover for her having to ask permission.

Her sister smiled and thought of her husband. 'Cole will be so happy to see you.'

Kaidence fished her mobile phone out of her oversized coat pocket and found Mitchell in her contact list before connecting the call. She was initially worried that he wouldn't answer, and she'd be forced to find a way to get out of the invitation her sister had extended to her; otherwise he'd be angry, and she didn't fancy another week indoors when she'd finally been allowed to leave the house.

The line rang a couple of times and he picked up. 'Hello.' His voice filtered through the speaker pressed to her ear making her feel instant fear. But she had to act like a woman in love for the benefit of her sister. 'Hi baby. Mimi has asked me to spend the day at her house – would you mind if we changed our plans until tomorrow?'

'Sure, go; spend the day with your family. I'll just wait around for you,' he said abruptly before hanging up.

As the phone disconnected on his end, anger began to course through her veins. She'd only rang him so he wouldn't wonder where she'd been all day and then punish her when she finally did get home. He hadn't even been able to dignify her with enough decency to talk to her like she was a human being instead of something he'd stepped in, and she was rapidly losing the patience to put up with it.

Still, she had to continue with the show. 'Great. I'll send you a text when I'm on my way home,' she said, pretending the call was still connected. 'I'll see you later.'

He had beaten her so badly last time that she expected to have at least a week of him being sickeningly nice to her, but he was lacking sincerity in his apology this time, so she knew the worm had turned. That meant he didn't value her enough any more to try and make excuses for his bad temper.

She hung up her phone and looked at her sister. 'Looks like I'm all yours for the day.'

The supermarket was as busy as any normal weekend. A few of the people perusing the aisles were familiar to Kaidence, not because she knew them but because they were creatures of habit, like her and her sister.

She was only half paying attention as she headed to the box of beer that Mitchell couldn't live without, so she almost didn't see Jackson, but he noticed her. Instinctively he began to get closer, forcing her to warn him off with small repeated shakes of her head. She wouldn't know where to find an explanation for knowing him and she could do without the third degree from her sister until she was forced to submit the whole torrid tale.

Jackson stood in front of the selection of canned beer trying his best to pretend he didn't know the woman standing four feet from him. He could only fathom that Mitchell was nearby. But when a female, who seemed to be an older replica of Kaidence but for the curls, appeared behind her he was confused by Kaidence's determination not to interact with him. Still, she was calling the shots and he had to abide by them.

He acted as if he was studying his choices as Kaidence and her female companion walked past him. He didn't make eye contact, as hard as that was, and only looked in her direction when their voices were too faint to hear. He saw her glance back at him as she disappeared out of sight on her way to the next aisle. He couldn't help himself, he had to follow. He just hoped that due to his police training, he would be stealthy enough to go undetected by her escort, but he walked straight into Kaidence's path. They were close enough to touch, which caused him to smile apologetically.

'I'm sorry,' he said, maintaining the cover that they were strangers.

'It's okay. No harm done,' she countered as he stepped around her and allowed her to go on her way.

Meredith raised her eyebrows suggestively as they walked away. 'It's a pity that accident was avoided, it might have been nice to have been violated by that man.'

'Mimi! You're a married woman!'

'But you're not and he's handsome.' Meredith giggled like a teenager who had been caught talking dirty about her crush.

'Was he? I didn't notice,' she lied.

'You noticed; you just don't want to admit it because of Mitchell. It doesn't hurt to look – it's healthy.'

'Is it? Because usually looking means you're not happy.'

'It does not. It means you have a pulse. Touching means you're not happy.'

***

It was a couple of hours later when they arrived at the Tate residence and Kaidence had spent the morning worrying about what awaited her at home when she finally got there, which had prevented her from enjoying the time with her sister. Mitchell wasn't happy and, after spending the day in his own company, she knew that unhappiness would grow into anger, which he would undoubtedly take out on her. She was on edge. She wanted to be as far away from him as she could possibly be, but she knew her unscheduled day out was going to cost her. He couldn't stand that she had a life outside their relationship because it meant she wasn't fully dependant on him, and he relied upon her being weak due to isolation; but he wasn't able to rid her of the influence her sister had on her, as much as he wanted to. She could only imagine how crazy that made him.

'Are you sure you've got room in your freezer for my stuff?' Kaidence asked as they placed their heavy shopping bags on the floor in the kitchen.

'I've got a large chest freezer in the utility room,' Meredith responded.

'There are three of you. How do you need that much freezer space?'

'I buy meat in bulk at the butcher's in town once a month; luckily for you, I don't fetch that until next week.'

'And for you; otherwise I'd have to go home so my shopping wasn't ruined.'

'Do I hear my sister-in-law?' Cole asked rhetorically, appearing in the doorway before rushing to envelop her in a hug.

Kaidence tensed for the impact of his affection and winced as her body felt the pain of the bruises she hid underneath her clothes. He didn't know about them, but she wished he'd let her go so she could breathe. 'CJ, you're squeezing the life out of me.'

He released his hold on her. 'I haven't seen you since Justin came home, so that's three months and a week worth of hugs.'

Meredith had met Cole in college fourteen years ago, when she was seventeen and he was two years older. He had pursued her for a little over three months before she agreed to go out with him, but the two had been inseparable ever since despite him finishing the last year of education when she was only just beginning. He had proposed to her four years later and she had accepted straight away. But Meredith had wanted to do it properly, so they lived together first and only married four years after that, once they were familiar with any bad habits they had and knew they loved each other regardless of them.

Their wedding day had been six years ago, and they had been trying to conceive ever since, only to be disappointed when it didn't take. They talked about the option of in vitro fertilisation, but it was so expensive that they decided instead to mate like bunnies whenever the two lines appeared in the window of the ovulation kit their lives revolved around, and then finally a year ago they had got pregnant. Meredith hadn't wanted to get too excited, so she'd kept it secret until she was passed the danger trimester and even then, she only really had Kaidence to tell.

Kaidence smiled and nodded. 'I appreciate the affection, now where's my little nephew?'

'Oh, I just put him down for a nap,' her brother-in-law answered.

She looked at her sister. 'You lured me here under false pretences.'

Meredith laughed. 'Relax, you'll have plenty of time to see him when he wakes up.'

It was dark when Kaidence used her key to let herself into her house, struggling with the bags of shopping she hadn't had the foresight to leave in the car and make repeat trips for. She expected Mitchell to be waiting for her despite the house being in complete darkness, because he'd waited for her with the lights out before. It was only when she flicked them on and he didn't appear out of the shadows that she realised he wasn't at home. She kicked the front door closed behind her and struggled into the kitchen, illuminating that room with her elbow as she entered. It wasn't until she placed the heavy carrier bags on the floor in front of the freezer and stood up straight that she noticed the note beneath one of the magnets on the fridge. She snatched the piece of paper free and read the message he had been considerate enough to leave.

I've gone out with the lads. See you when I get back.

She screwed the piece of paper into a ball in her hand and sighed. She was glad he wasn't home, but it was only going to prolong the agony. God only knew what state he'd get back in and this time he'd make a point to wake her up just because he felt like he had unfinished business with her.

She tried to push the worry of what awaited her once he got home from her mind as she started putting the provisions away, but it set up shop right in the frontal lobe of her cerebral cortex. She could even envisage what was going to happen when he walked in and it petrified her. She knew he would make a point to climb the stairs, regardless of how intoxicated he was, and drag her out of bed by her hair before he'd even bothered to make sure she was awake. He'd then proceed to make her pay for leaving him alone all day in whatever way he wanted to because she couldn't stop him. Even in his inebriated state she was no match for him, and she'd be lucky to make it to morning alive.

Kaidence rushed her task as if her life depended on it and then fished around in her handbag for her mobile phone. She wanted to call Jackson, so he could be forewarned about what she suspected was going to happen, because she needed him to answer if she was able to ring for his help later.

It didn't take him long to pick up.

'Hey, Officer Chase.'

'Kaidence, is everything all right?'

'No, it's not. When you saw me today, I was with my sister and she asked me to spend the day with her. I rang Mitchell and he let me go but he wasn't happy. Now he's gone out drinking with his friends and I'm scared that when he gets back, he's going to hurt me.'

'Well, I'll come and get you. I can put you up in a hotel for the night.'

'No, I can't leave; that would make it worse.'

'Then what do you want me to do?'

'I'm going to store your number in my phone and take it to bed with me. If I feel like he's being threatening, I'll lock myself in the bathroom and call. I might not be able to let it ring for long, but I'll need you to come over the minute you see my number. Can you do that?'

'It'll take me twenty minutes to drive over and you could be dead by then. I need to be there.'

'If you're here it's going to be worse, believe me.'

'Not if I'm outside.'

'You can't sit in your car all night. He's not going to get back here until the early hours; it'll be about two a.m.'

'That means I can get a couple of hours sleep and set my alarm for one. Then I'll come over and sit in my car.'

'I don't want you to uproot your life.'

'It's only one night and, truth be told, I'd be willing to spend every night parked out on your street until you're away from him.'

'Thank you, but I just need you on high alert for tonight. You can go back to amber alert in the morning.'

'I think that's an American thing and I'm sure it's something to do with child abduction, not domestic abuse.'

'I heard it on TV once and blurted it out; I guess I should have done some research before I said it.'

He laughed. 'It's not important. I just wanted you to know that in this country amber alert isn't a thing in the police force.'

'That's another piece of useless information stored in my head. Thank you for that.'

'Sorry. I just thought...'

'Officer Chase, its fine. I know you weren't making fun of me,' she said so he wouldn't feel bad. 'Will you just be at the end of the line if I call?'

'Yes Kaidence. I'll answer.'

'Thank you,' she said, hanging up.

CHAPTER FIVE

Taking advantage of having the house to herself for a second night that week, Kaidence filled the bath with water but – like the rest of the day – her mind wasn't on the task. She was anxious about what was to come once Mitchell got home because she knew his anger was going to reach new heights once he'd been around Dale, John and Alan. She hadn't been lying when she told the officer that she feared for her life; tonight, more than any night before. She knew he hated her to spring plans on him, even if they didn't involve him, and his rule allowing her to have regular contact with her sister didn't extend to days when he was expecting her to be at home. Had he been invited, he would have found an excuse not to join them because he disliked being around Meredith. But the fact he hadn't been asked was only going to add to the rage he would penalise her for later.

She distracted herself thinking of ways she could appease him in order to soften the punishment, but her mind was clouded, and she couldn't clear it. There was nothing she could think of to say or do to get her out of this one. She couldn't even leave, like Jackson had suggested, because eventually she would have to face him, and he would still want to teach her a lesson.

It had been a long time since she'd been expecting a beating, but it always made her uneasy. She wasn't going to be able to relax, despite being at home alone when she'd usually be able to. She could already feel the tension in her shoulders from carrying the weight of worrying all day; that's why she'd run a bath, hoping to relieve it a little bit.

Turning off the taps, she removed the robe she had changed into and dropped it on the floor behind her as she climbed into the tub. She slowly lowered herself into the water and relaxed back so she was submerged from the neck down. In truth, the temperature was hotter than she liked it in order to be comfortable, but she was hoping the heat would soothe the pain in her body, so she had allowed the hot tap to run for longer than usual.

She had stored Jackson's number in her phone temporarily, intending to delete it again after the emergency of the night had run its course because if Mitchell were to find it while he was checking it, there would be another fight and she could only deal with one at a time.

Jackson lay in bed staring at the ceiling; his phone call with Kaidence was playing on his mind. He fully intended to get a couple of hours of shut-eye before heading over to watch the house. He was hoping to be parked on the street by the time Mitchell came home so he could better judge his level of intoxication, but sleep was evading him because all he could think about was making sure she survived until morning.

With a huff of frustration, he rolled over to try and get comfortable, but the wheels were turning in his head with all the possible outcomes of the evening and that made him apprehensive. He hated that the conclusion was out of his control, because he wanted to ensure her safety although he knew that was unrealistic. He had visions of it all going wrong and he could do without a repeat of the events that had happened while he was undercover. He planned to be vigilant this time and set up watch right by her back door if he had to, because he was not going to investigate her murder. But at least he had access to the photographic evidence she kept updated.

With a heavy sigh, he kicked the covers off his body and swung his legs out of bed. His attempt to sleep was futile. He wasn't going to be able to rest until he knew Kaidence was safe.

It was eerie for Kaidence lying in bed in the darkness anticipating Mitchell's return. She had her phone under her pillow so that if she heard him making his way up the stairs she could hit send on the text she'd drafted in preparation to alert the cavalry and pretend to be asleep by the time he got to the bedroom. Her eyes were heavy because she was tired, but she wanted to stay awake so she could be prepared for when her worst half got home. Now she was staring at whatever she could make out in the dark. Her mind was finally quiet for the first time since climbing beneath the duvet and she was able to relax, resulting in her drifting off to sleep.

Kaidence jolted awake. She had unintentionally fallen asleep. She tried to adjust her eyes in the darkened room, so she could make sure Mitchell hadn't snuck in sober and was watching her sleep, waiting for the opportune moment to strike. He wasn't.

She checked the illuminated numbers on the alarm clock and a frown set up camp on her brow. It was after three a.m. and he was usually home by now, but there were no signs of the man she cohabitated with.

Reaching down, she fished beneath the bed for the phone she had strategically placed there and – assuming Jackson was sat outside in his car – connected the call she had been expecting to make all night as she climbed out of bed. She barely waited for the call to connect before she spoke. 'Is he home yet?' she asked in a whisper, in case Mitchell was asleep somewhere in the house.

'No. He's still out.'

Standing on the landing overlooking the front door, Kaidence frowned. 'He's usually back by now.'

'Maybe he's staying out later tonight.'

'He's never done that before.'

'Have you ever unexpectedly spent the day with your sister?'

'No. Usually I know ahead of time that I'm going to be out all day.'

'That'll explain it then.'

'But what if he's not home because he's hurt?' The thought occurred to her and she actually felt concern. That was the power of the brainwashing that Mitchell had subjected her to during their time together. Her rationality told her that the abuse was wrong but the months of having it drilled into her that every punishment was her fault lingered on in her psyche and caused her to interpret his abuse as love. Thus she felt real concern when she thought he had come to harm. It made no sense and yet it was the way it worked.

Jackson knew reliance was what violent relationships depended on, but he couldn't believe the woman who was petrified of being home without a police escort was now worried about the man that jeopardised her safety.

'Do you want me to check at the station to see if there have been any accidents?' he offered with a sigh.

'Would you mind?'

'I suggested it.'

'Please, and call me straight back,' she said, hanging up.

Knowing she was home alone, Kaidence flicked the switch to light up the hallway as she made her way to the lower floor. She thought a smooth hot chocolate was in order to hopefully soothe the knot in her stomach that was as present now as it had been when she'd fallen asleep.

She hit the light switch as she entered the kitchen and headed straight to the fridge. Removing the milk, she shifted slightly to the right to retrieve the glass jug from the lower cupboard next to it but before she had the chance to pour the liquid into the container, there was a knock at the front door. With a puzzled look, she went to answer it.

'I called the station; no reports of accidents have come in,' Jackson said.

'What are you doing coming to the door?' she demanded.

'Mitchell isn't at home and I saw the lights on, so I knew you were out of bed.'

'Yes, but what if he comes around the corner in a minute? How are we going to explain this?'

'Relax, Kaidence, I'm on the doorstep. There could be any number of reasons for me being here.'

'Give me an example.'

He stuttered, 'A...all right, I don't have one off the top of my head but I'm not really here, I just wanted to tell you that there is no reason to think your beloved was in an accident.'

'Then where is he?' she asked, heading back to the kitchen.

Instinctively Jackson followed behind her, closing the door as he crossed the threshold. 'Maybe he's trying to teach you a different lesson this time,' he suggested, trying to be helpful.

Hearing his voice close, she spun to face him. 'What are you doing inside? You can't be inside.'

'Does it really matter if I'm inside or on the doorstep? The result will be the same, won't it?' he asked rhetorically.

'You should have called me on the phone,' she said, proceeding to pour a cup-sized measure of milk into the jug and moving to the microwave. Placing it inside, she set a two-minute timer.

'Kaidence, calm down, if I hear his key in the lock I'll bolt for the back door and be out of sight before he walks in.' He tried to reassure her. 'Are you making hot chocolate?'

'Yes. I'd make you one but on your mad dash to the back of the house you'd leave evidence of your presence and that would defeat the purpose of you moving that fast.'

He sniggered at her humour.

'I wasn't being funny.'

'And yet, it amused me.'

'Then you need to get out more,' she said, forcing a smile.

'I could always take the cup with me when I escape,' he suggested, hoping to get a drink out of the process.

'Fine. One hot chocolate and then you have to leave.' She caved in and fetched him a cup. She picked up the jar of powder from beside the kettle, opened the utensil drawer and removed a teaspoon before scooping two heaped measures into each mug.

'I'll drink it in double time,' he reassured her.

'This is getting to be a regular thing.'

'It's the second time; that's hardly regular.'

'Twice in a week could be considered regular,' she refuted, removing the milk from the microwave once it pinged.

Jackson watched as she half-filled each cup with the dairy product and stirred in the hot chocolate. She looked beautiful in her pyjamas as she completed the menial task, but he didn't dare to vocalise it. The last thing he wanted to do was make her feel like he was hitting on her. It would add a pressure on the foundations he had put into place and he couldn't have that. She was damaged enough already without him laying any expectations on her. He needed to contain his growing feelings because when she finally did leave her boyfriend, she would need space to integrate back into the life she was living before Mitchell had taken her from it. He couldn't expect anything from her unless it was something she wanted and instigated in the future. For now, friendship was as good as it was going to get.

Amid his observations, he had taken a seat at the dining table, which always looked so empty. 'So, why don't you just call him?' he asked, as she made her way over and placed his beverage in front of him.

'Because that would be checking up on him, and he hates that,' she replied, sitting beside him at the opposite end to the one that she usually sat at when eating any meals with her live-in partner.

'Surely he'd understand you were concerned?'

'Not after I abandoned him for the day. He'd see it as controlling and I'd get a lesson in how superior he is.'

'Wow! So many rules; how do you manage to keep them all straight?'

'Basically, I fight all my natural instincts; it's served me well in the past.'

'Given the state of your face at the beginning of the week I'd have to disagree.'

'I do everything in my power to keep him happy but sometimes I make mistakes.'

'Everyone makes mistakes. You just have unrealistic expectations to live up to so it's only natural you would slip sometimes.'

The air between them thickened with the silence that had fallen on the room. Kaidence was the first one to cut through it, as she shared what had been playing on her mind. 'My sister told me today that I've changed since I've been with Mitchell.'

'Do you think you have?' he countered, not knowing her well enough to have an opinion.

'It's hard to be in a relationship like this one and not. I had just persuaded myself that I was hiding it better.'

'I guess your sister knows you better than you think she does.'

As though a switch had been flicked, she picked up his cup and thrust it in his direction. 'Drink, because you need to leave.'

He smiled as he took the brew from her. 'You're always so welcoming.'

'It's a luxury I can't afford. Now knock back that cocoa mister, like my life depends on it.'

'I will never like the fact you joke about that.' He lifted the porcelain to his lips and took a sip.

'Less talking, more drinking,' she said, gesturing for him to hurry.

Jackson had left the house thirty minutes ago and now Kaidence was lying in bed trying desperately to sleep, but her mind was occupied with all the possible reasons why Mitchell hadn't come home. He'd never stayed out this late and it worried her. What if he had been so angry with her that he had drank the bar dry and was now lying in a doorway somewhere? Or worse, what if he hadn't gone out drinking and instead had left her a dummy note before parking down the street to watch the house? What if he had seen the officer enter and then leave half an hour later?

Although as soon as she thought that, she dismissed the idea because she knew he wouldn't have been able to suppress the urge to storm in and kick the shit out of them both. It was just like him to torture her by not coming home. Still, it didn't change the fact she was lying awake wondering where he was. She was furious with herself. After everything he had put her through, she couldn't believe she was so concerned about his safety. She should be thankful she had a night of freedom and take advantage of the empty bed again. Instead she was awake, mentally listing all the horrible possibilities for Mitchell not being home. She had to stop obsessing. She tried to tune out the echo of what she was thinking as she got into a comfortable position and closed her eyes.

It wasn't until early Sunday afternoon when Mitchell finally walked through the front door. He barely acknowledged Kaidence slaving in the kitchen over the roast beef dinner she always cooked on Sunday's as he dumped his keys and phone on the island on his way to the fridge for a bottle of water. Breaking the seal to open it, he drank it dry and disposed of the plastic in the recycling bin before turning to address her.

'I'm going for a shower,' he stated, without offering an explanation as to where he'd been.

She suppressed her outrage. She had proceeded with the dinner he'd requested Friday on the off-chance he was going to return, even though deep down she had hoped he was gone for good. He hadn't had the decency to make up a reason for why he hadn't returned before now and apart from the one line of communication, he hadn't indicated the anger he had felt in order to punish her with a sleepless night. She was thankful she'd had the foresight to begin the meal he'd pre-warned her that he wanted, otherwise he would have displayed more rage when he'd walked in.

She could surmise that she would never know where he'd been, because he wasn't the kind of man who explained his comings and goings to a mere woman, but she couldn't help being curious. As best as she could guess, he had gone out and got intoxicated; she could smell it on him. But where he'd ended up sleeping it off was up for debate. He'd never spent the whole night out since they'd been living together, not even when he'd been so drunk that he forgot where he lived. He always managed to make it home before the sun came up and now, here he was walking in after lunchtime the following day. This was definitely some form of reprimand; she just had to figure out what kind it was.

She was about to tend to the potatoes roasting in the oven when she heard his phone vibrate on the worktop, causing it to move slightly. Out of curiosity, she got closer to the object in time to read the text that was on his screen. *Thanks for a great night baby. See you soon x*, she managed to read before the screen darkened again. Her brow furrowed. That sounded like a lover's text. Had he been out overnight because he'd been with a woman? She found herself getting her hopes up that he had moved on to his next victim and although she felt a small obligation to let his future squeeze know what she was getting into, she wanted rid of him. But she had to bide her time and not get ahead of herself. What if it wasn't the start of something and it was just a one-night stand? She couldn't build up her expectations. She had to maintain the status quo and wait for him to make the next move.

Once he'd showered Mitchell had taken four beers and a glass into the living room to watch whatever football match was airing and left Kaidence to her culinary domesticity, which had given her space to digest the new information she'd stumbled upon. She was convinced that despite his return to the house he already had one foot out of the door, meaning she moved about the kitchen happier than she usually would.

As much as she didn't want to build up her expectations, she was already anticipating her freedom. She could return to loving all the things that were in short supply while she was being judged for her every move. She could pop out whenever she got bored and wanted company. She could lie in her sweats on the settee after spending all morning in bed at weekends. She could gorge on takeaway and junk food when she didn't feel like cooking. It was going to be something she dived straight into and would possibly delight in for weeks before she decided to go back to living properly.

She was about to dish up dinner when she thought it best to check with Mitchell where he wanted to eat it because, judging from the sounds coming from the room he sat in, he was enjoying the sport on television.

'Do you want to eat in here?' she asked, standing to the side of his line of sight. The last time she had got in front of the flat screen he had kicked her legs out from under her in order to teach her the error of her ways, and she wanted to avoid that for a second time.

'Yes,' he answered harshly without making direct eye contact.

'Okay.' She walked out of the room.

He was angry. She could tell by the way he interacted with her. He was being very short with her and he didn't speak unless she instigated it. She wasn't used to it. He had always let her know his exact feelings when he felt them. He never brooded. Brooding was a completely new experience and maybe that had something to do with the woman he had spent the night with, or maybe the time apart had helped to diminish his rage. So instead he'd opted for the silent treatment. It was a tactic he hadn't used before. Oddly it unnerved her.

She dished up their meal with an air of caution, so as not to let any of the vegetables touch the mashed potato or sit on the sliced beef. She had become an expert at making lump-free gravy and didn't add the Yorkshire puddings to the plate until the last minute, so they didn't get soggy. That was another lesson she had learned one of the first times she had cooked him a roast dinner after he'd moved in.

She headed to the fridge and removed a lager to go with his dinner, although he had taken cans of bitter with him into the living room; she knew he liked the alternative when he ate. She put the bottle on the tray along with his plate and took it in to him. She didn't get so much as a grunt of appreciation before she left to go back to the kitchen to eat her own dinner.

She sat in her usual place at the table, thinking it best to keep to the routine she had regardless of whether he was in the room, and she ate with her own company while she listened to the television from the other room. She was surprisingly hungry despite the anxiety she felt. She was waiting for the other shoe to drop and she knew it would eventually. He wasn't going to stay quiet forever. He would take his time and when she was least expecting it, he would strike, and she planned to be ready for it.

Her thoughts turned to the officer she had asked for help the night before and she removed her phone from her pocket, taking advantage of being alone. *He's home. I'm okay for now,* she quickly punched into the on-screen keyboard and send before deleting the text along with the stored number from her device and returning it to her jeans. She was thankful to have the opportunity to check in with him even if she couldn't speak to him.

Jackson had maintained his position in his car on the street outside the house he had visited in the middle of the night in case he'd been needed. Although Mitchell hadn't returned home in the night, he had stuck around until he saw him. He wasn't sure whether it was a good or bad thing that he hadn't got home until lunchtime, but Jackson had stayed for an hour for good measure and as of yet hadn't had a call from the woman inside – assuming she could get to her phone. He desperately wanted to creep around the exterior of the house to see if she had come to any harm, but he knew the chances of him being caught were infinitely higher in the daylight especially with Mitchell at home, so he sat helplessly watching from his vehicle.

He had resigned himself to spending his whole Sunday parked up watching her property, but he was starting to get hungry and he was definitely tired. He was contemplating having a takeaway delivered to him on the street when his phone went off. Reading the message that had come through set him slightly at ease. He was grateful that she had taken a risk to let him know she was all right, because it meant he could leave and get some food.

Spending an hour cleaning up in the kitchen was Kaidence's idea of heaven even though she knew that she was just prolonging the agony of what was to come. She had peered around the door to make sure he had finished eating before she collected his plate, and now she was just wiping the surfaces down. She still had a pile of ironing to do, which would take up any free time she had before going to bed, and that suited her just fine.

On the off-chance that his mother had dished up a dinner for him, Jackson had shown up at his parents' house on his way back to his quiet apartment. He thought the chances of him falling asleep in the middle of the day would be greater once he had a full stomach. The only disadvantage to showing up when he had was that he hadn't got to see his father because he'd already left for his weekly visit to the pub. However, he had got to touch base with his sisters on their way out of the door to whatever social date they had arranged with their friends and now he was sat alone at the table while he listened to his mother cleaning up in the kitchen.

'Mum, please wait until I'm finished, and I'll help you,' he called to her.

'It's okay, son. This is really a one-person job.'

He was about to put his fork loaded up with food in his mouth when his phone rang, and he jumped to answer it. 'Hello?'

'Jackson, did you get a hold of your abuse victim?' Louisa asked, not beating around the bush.

'Yes. She's okay. The boyfriend didn't get home until about two hours ago.'

'But you spoke to her?'

'No. She sent me a message.'

'So, what are you going to do?'

'I'm going to eat the dinner my mum cooked for me and worry about follow-up tomorrow.'

'We've got to teach a stranger danger class in the morning,' she reminded him.

He groaned. 'Oh God. I hate those.'

'I know. We go through this every time we get one on the rota. They're not as bad as you try to make out.'

'They're not the reason I joined the force.'

'No, but we're getting to the next generation before they have a chance to offend.'

'We have this same conversation before every school assembly.'

'I know. So, can we skip it this time? I've got too much to do before I get into bed tonight.'

'Yes, go, do what you have to do, and I'll see you in the morning.'

———————

Darkness fell before Kaidence realised how late it was. She had been dragging out the ironing since the clean-up after dinner and she hadn't had any interaction with Mitchell at all. She had heard him moving around on the lower floor, though she hadn't laid eyes on him. But it was almost bedtime, so she couldn't put off the unavoidable. He would be coming upstairs soon because he had a set time for bed any night before work. She had allowed him the space he obviously wanted in order to process his feelings about whatever was torturing him but that was about to come to an end. She was going to be forced to be in the same room as him and she wasn't sure how she was going to handle that after forty-eight hours of them not talking.

She was finished packing away the cool iron and the ironing board by the time she heard him locking up the house which meant he was minutes from climbing the stairs. She wasn't sure if she'd be expected to sleep in the spare room because she was being punished like a teenager who had snuck out after her curfew and got caught sneaking back in.

She was changing into her pyjamas when he walked into the room and began doing the same. The air between them was awkward and she could tell that he could barely stand being around her, which was ridiculous since all she had done was spend time with her family. She hadn't stayed out all night like him. But of course, he was allowed to do as he pleased because he was the only one who mattered.

'You don't need those,' he said, gesturing at her night attire.

She frowned. He hadn't so much as said five sentences to her since he'd got back and now he was making demands.

'I sleep in pyjamas,' she said, as though he needed reminding.

'You won't be sleeping when you get in bed,' he stated, letting her know exactly how he planned to make her pay for freedom the previous day.

She wasn't in the mood for sex, not that it mattered. What she wanted wasn't a factor for him; all he was concerned about was his own desires. Not daring to protest due to the threat of the alternative, Kaidence accepted her sentence. She could lie under him for five minutes just to fulfil her obligation as his girlfriend despite her confusion. If he had spent the previous night with another woman, why did he want to sleep with her? Maybe she'd overvalued his feelings about the situation. Maybe the female had simply been a one-night stand in order for him to release some of the frustrations he felt about his relationship. If he had consciously been trying to make a point, surely it made sense for him to parade his conquest under her nose. Unless he suspected that she wouldn't be so broken up about it as he wanted her to be.

Suddenly she felt deflated. Maybe the thing she had focused her energy on for most of the day wasn't as promising a prospect as she'd fooled herself into believing. It made her re-evaluate the expectations she had as she got naked and climbed beneath the covers.

Mitchell wasted no time with foreplay as he joined her. It seemed the only thing he needed to get aroused was to know he was in control, because as he worked her knees apart his penis started to stiffen. Nonetheless he grabbed her hand and forced it onto his manhood. Knowing it wasn't a good idea to not participate, Kaidence stroked him from tip to hilt repeatedly and watched as the ecstasy started to etch on his face. It repulsed her. She was no better than a prostitute, except instead of money she did it for survival.

Unexpectedly he moved, causing her hand to disconnect. 'Get on your knees and turn around,' he ordered.

She always hated doggy style because it wasn't romantic, not that this was romance, although it was easy to disconnect from the situation this way. It was just another technique for him to assert control over her, which meant it was another thing for her to endure. Doing as she was told, she rose to her knees in front of him and spun to face the headboard. At least this would mean she wouldn't have to look at his face as he grunted his way to climax, but she disliked how much power the position allowed him. The last time he had been so enthusiastic he had forced her head into the wall and given her a concussion, which meant more days off work. She so desperately wanted to return to work the following day because she disliked being away from the children in her class; it brought about a disruption to their routine that made learning harder for them.

He didn't even bother to make sure she was sufficiently stimulated before he forced the head of his penis inside her, and the intrusion caused her to clench the muscles that surrounded him as she winced in pain. The tension of her pelvis seemed to kindle extra pleasure for him as he groaned in ecstasy but all she could feel was the irritation between her legs and in her stomach. She felt him withdraw a little before he forcefully sank his full length back into her vagina. It was like sandpaper had been taken to her delicate places and the discomfort resulted in her squeezing her eyes shut while the rest of her face scrunched in agony. She was fortunate that he couldn't see the effect his touch was having on her because he always expected her to play along as if she was enjoying it.

Ploughing into her over and over, he reached out to pull her hair, but it wasn't a loving tug; it was as though he was trying to scalp her with his bare hands and that caused her more pain. He yanked on it as if to get the extra momentum he desired in order to burrow as deep into her as he could get.

Her body betrayed her as she started to feel his movement getting easier; she knew his penetration was stimulating parts of her that she had no control over, and she was furious about it. He got pleasure from hurting her – that much was evident by his constant rough manhandling – but now her body was betraying her too.

She tried to transport herself somewhere else in her mind. But it was proving difficult. Her concentration was set on the invasion of him inside her. Every time he pounded his groin into her back end, she opened her mouth mimicking a scream she didn't dare vocalise because it would be worse if she did.

Without warning he used his grasp on her hair to pull her back towards him so that his torso was touching her back. He used his free hand to reach up around her throat and squeeze her windpipe slightly.

'Remember this the next time you think it's okay to use your sister to spend the day away from me,' he warned in a low threatening voice.

It wasn't worth insisting she had done no such thing because raping her was as mild as it had been for a long time. At least she had no other injuries to contend with at the same time, so the pain was concentrated to one area. So she bit her lip to stop her objection to his allegation and nodded her compliance.

He released his hold on her neck and hair in order to force her to return onto all fours with a push in the back before continuing his sexual assault.

CHAPTER SIX

Monday morning was cooler than the previous days had been. Instead of sunshine peeking out from behind the clouds, rain hung in the sky and the wind blew cold. There was a crisp fresh smell that had been missing during what little summer they had in the months prior.

Kaidence had been up since the crack of dawn making sure she had everything she needed for her first day back at work. In truth, she had barely slept all night, but it had taken until five a.m. for her to decide to give up and get out of bed. She was sore after the assault and sitting down was a challenge if she didn't lower herself into her chair slowly, but other than that she was unharmed. She had organised her bag with her teaching plan, made both their lunches and prepared a fresh pot of coffee ready for when Mitchell got up before she picked out an outfit for the day. She hadn't got time to dwell on the evening's events; she was just looking forward to being back in the classroom with the kids who made her job worth doing.

Kaidence wrapped her coat around her to protect her body from the chill in the air as she made her way to her car. She loved this time in the morning when there was just a handful of people on the street, because it was peaceful. She used to have friends who hated being out of bed before eight a.m., never mind leaving the house, but she revelled in it; especially when she'd been cooped up for so long.

If she'd have been thinking about it, she would have put Jackson's number into her phone, so she could have used the drive to contact him, but she had been too scared to rummage through the drawer with Mitchell in the house.

She cursed herself for deleting his contact information the day before because she knew he'd want her to touch base as soon as possible. She would have to make do with trying the local station during her lunch break and hope he was on shift.

She happily drove towards Ridge Primary School, where she'd been teaching practically since she'd become certified, and turned on the radio. She scarcely got to listen to music these days and she loved the way certain songs made her feel. But Mitchell hated music. He preferred mindless television. The song that played wasn't a particularly good one, however it was enough to get her geared up for the day ahead even though the drive wasn't a long one. The roads had been virtually empty simply because she was so early, which had cut her journey time in half.

She pulled up in a parking space next to the few faculty members who liked to be there early and got out of her car. She was eager to get back into a routine and surround herself with people who may have suspected but had no true knowledge about the life she had to suffer. Six weeks away from work had allowed her the luxury to do as she pleased when Mitchell was at the office, but she was more isolated without anywhere to go and she loved company. Regardless of whether she could share details of her relationship, having someone to talk to about inane things helped with her state of mind.

Walking in through the office door, which was unlocked at seven a.m. by the caretaker, Kaidence wasted no time going to the staff room to get a cup of tea she could take to her desk. The fact that a supply teacher had been into her classroom before her meant that it wouldn't be laid out the way she liked things, and she was a creature of habit.

'Good morning, Emily,' she greeted the thirty-year-old nursery teacher.

'You're back,' she exclaimed. 'Are you feeling better?'

Kaidence dropped her head, feeling a semblance of shame. 'I'm feeling a lot better thanks,' she replied with a smile. 'Who did they get to cover for me?'

'Gayle Edwards.'

Kaidence screwed up her face. 'It's going to take me a while to get my students to forgive me for that.'

'It might take the parents some time too,' Emily added.

Kaidence always made a point of having introductions with the parents of the students she would teach that year before they broke up for the summer holidays, so she knew they'd have been expecting to see her face on the first day of term. She wouldn't have been able to make up for being absent or explain the real reason why; she just had to hope she could regain their trust.

'There wasn't another incident like last year's, was there?'

Emily laughed. 'God no. I'm sure word of her tolerance for tardiness circulated around all the adults in a timely fashion last year and has been filtered down to any new parents since. They just don't like her face to be the first they see in a morning; she's hardly got a sunny disposition.'

'I'll make it up to them on parents' evening with muffins and coffee.'

'Don't you just love the power baked goods and caffeine have on them?'

Picking up the mug she had brought from home, Kaidence turned to leave. 'I'll see you later, Em.'

'See you in assembly.'

With a frown, Kaidence turned back to face her. 'It's Monday. Did Irene change the day of assemblies? They don't usually happen until the end of the week.'

Irene Metcalf had been the headmistress at the school for twenty years and had been the one to hire Kaidence when she'd been looking for her first full-time job. Kaidence had floated about in the district substituting for any teacher who needed cover until she'd heard about the opening at her old school, and the fact she had attended as a student meant she had known Irene as a teacher. She considered that to be an advantage, but it was only after she was hired that she learned that she had been the only applicant.

'I know, but she's decided it's time to bring the police in for stranger danger awareness.'

'Oh. I don't think we've ever had one of those before.'

'No. But since her great-grandson was approached outside his school last week, she's made it her mission to educate every child in the area.'

'He was what?'

'Yes, some man walked up to him and asked for his help finding his puppy.'

'Oh my God! Is he okay?'

'Yes, her daughter taught him about strangers a while ago, so he went back into his school until she got there to pick him up.'

Silence fell on them momentarily. 'Well thank God for that,' Kaidence said.

Emily nodded. 'You know, I saw the male officer who's coming and I have to say, I am a fan.'

Kaidence laughed. 'Of the police or men?'

'Either. You'll understand when you see him.'

'I'll see you in the hall then,' she said, walking out.

Jackson adjusted the tie on his police uniform in front of the bedroom mirror and made his way to the kitchen for the jacket to complete his outfit. Ordinarily he'd leave the tie at home, but he needed to dress formally if he was going to be acting on behalf of the force at the primary school he had once attended as a child. He had wanted the opportunity today to find out where Kaidence worked so he could better put together a plan to keep her alive, and the assembly got in the way of that. He would have to put it off until there was a lapse in his shift, *if* there was one.

He had agreed to drive the cop car to the school alone, allowing Louisa to drop her kids off for the day as usual, then he'd follow her to the station where she'd drop off her vehicle ready for when their shift ended. It was the little favours he did for her because of the sacrifices she made for him whenever he had a strong urge to pursue his gut feelings.

He picked up his phone from the table and had an urge to use the number for Kaidence that he'd saved into his phone, but he fought it. He had no idea if she was alone at home or otherwise, so he couldn't risk revealing their collusion. He slipped the device into the inside pocket of his jacket, took a sip of the coffee that was going cold, and picked up his keys on his way out of the door. He would make sure to get a chance to touch base with her at some point during the day, but for now he had to get to the station to pick up the stranger danger packs he would have to distribute to the kids at the end of the hour.

Kaidence scanned her classroom, satisfied she had laid everything out for her students and got things exactly as she liked them, before she checked the time. It was almost time to meet the children she would have a teaching influence over for most of the following year and she was nervous. She planned to have less time off this year, and be more present for her pupils than she had been for her previous students. It would take great restraint on her part and extra vigilance at home to be sure that happened, but it would be worth it to give them stability.

'Are you ready?' Imogen Fox, the year one teacher, asked, popping her head around the archway entrance to her room.

Kaidence pushed her chair out from under her desk and walked to greet her. 'How bad was Gayle?' she asked.

'Your class was a lot quieter from Thursday onwards.'

'My kids already hate me then.'

Imogen laughed as they made their way to the door to the playground in order to allow the pupils access inside. 'Oh, they'll get over it after a week with you.'

'I hope so.' Kaidence opened the door and turned her attention to the students. 'Good morning everyone, let's all get in nice neat lines please,' she instructed, before a parent in a police uniform signalled to her. Kaidence beckoned her closer and stepped out onto the playground to avoid the stampede of kids trying to get inside.

'I just wanted to touch base with you,' the female officer said once Kaidence was close enough. Kaidence instantly noticed the sadness in the officer's brown eyes. 'I'm Juliette's mum, and she's going through a stage of wanting to be treated like a teenager before she's reached a double-digit age, so she might be a little defiant until she gets to know you.'

'It's okay. I can be patient while she works through that.'

'I just didn't want you to get the wrong idea about her, that's all. She's a good kid, she's just rebelling because her dad and I called it a day last year and it's just caught up with her.'

'That's understandable. Honestly, she's not the first child I've had in my class who has gone through that and I doubt she'll be the last. I'll keep it in mind any time there's an issue with her behaviour. In the meantime, if there's anything you need from me, just let me know.'

'Thank you, Mrs...'

'It's Miss, Miss Hadaway.'

Louisa smiled. 'I really appreciate your understanding.'

'It's okay. She'll come out the other side of this. It'll just take time,' she said, trying to reassure her. 'Now, if that's all, I better get inside before they riot.'

'Oh yes, of course.'

The drive from the station had been quieter than Jackson was used to on a school morning. But he had waited until after usual office hours started before he had begun his journey, so that would account for it. He was now sat in the squad car waiting for his partner to meet him before they entered the building together.

He could understand the need to try and influence the next generation in walking the line, but he knew that children were influenced by their parents and their environment, not by an hour in the presence of the police. Although they were there to raise awareness of strangers, it would only be a matter of time before they were back there for a crime prevention assembly, which was not the reason why he'd joined the force. He felt like it was a job best suited to special constables, who volunteered their time, not officers who were paid to enforce the law, because he saw no benefit in them being taken off the streets.

The passenger door opened, and Louisa bundled in. 'How long have we got until we go inside?'

Jackson smiled. 'About half an hour.' He motioned to the cup holder. 'I got your iced peach green tea lemonade when I got my coffee.'

'Thank you,' she countered, appearing on edge.

'Are you okay? You seem anxious.'

'Do you think it would be inappropriate if I hopped over the fence to have a cigarette or three before we went in?'

'You're not nervous, are you?'

Louisa sighed. 'No, I just had to admit to Juliette's teacher that I'm having trouble with her because Scott and I aren't together any more.'

'Your kids aren't the only ones ever to go through their parents' separation.'

'I know that, Jax, but I've met the woman twice. She did not need to know I was a failure right off the bat.'

'You're not a failure. Those girls haven't gone without a single thing they need since you've been a single mum. They're lucky to have you.'

She turned her head to look at him. 'So you don't think I've screwed them up for the rest of their lives?'

He was tempted to joke with her, but thought better of it because it wasn't often that she showed any vulnerability. 'No. It would've been worse if you had stayed in a loveless relationship just for them, and Scott's still in their lives – he's just not in the same house.'

⁂

Kaidence spent half an hour with her class, getting to know them a little, before the assembly that she hadn't been aware of before arriving at work. Every new school year she liked to acquaint herself with each of their names and at least one thing they liked to do when they were at home. It gave her a sense of what they would be like to teach. The exercise had already given her insight into three pupils who she thought would pose a challenge, and a handful of ones that she thought would be eager to learn; Juliette was one of the latter students, despite the concerns her mother had raised. Although it occurred to her that Juliette might be on her best behaviour because Kaidence was a teacher the eight-year-old wasn't familiar with yet.

She finished explaining the reason for the assembly, which they also hadn't been expecting, and asked them to line up quietly at the door. It was another simple task that would give her handy information about the kind of personalities she had to contend with, depending on who stood quietly and who was disruptive.

Making her way out to the small communal area between the year one and year two classrooms, Kaidence approached Imogen. 'Are we ready?' she asked.

'I'm not sure about the kids, but I am ready to see the officer that Emily hasn't stopped banging on about since she saw him pull up in the police car,' she responded in a hushed tone.

Kaidence laughed, extending her hand towards the hall. 'After you then.'

Jackson watched as the pupils filtered into the hall, form by form. The sheer volume of kids under secondary school age made him uncomfortable, not because he disliked children but because the only ones he encountered regularly were Louisa's, and his ease with them hadn't happened overnight. Over the years that they'd known each other they had built a foundation which had formed a connection naturally. He hadn't forced it. This environment was different. That's why he was glad he had the partner he had because, even though he was the senior officer, he knew she'd be comfortable taking the lead if he froze up.

It wasn't until all the students were sat cross-legged on the floor that he saw her. She was in her natural surroundings and he could see how relaxed she was. Strangely – despite her home life – he could see how commanding she was in her faculty role, and he couldn't seem to take his eyes off her.

'You're staring,' his partner pointed out.

He turned his back to the room. 'That's her.'

'Who's her who?' Louisa asked, a frown etched on her features.

'The woman in the red shirt walking towards us, that's Kaidence.'

'Who's Kaidence?'

'The woman who's being abused by her boyfriend and I had you spy on last week.'

She looked over his shoulder to find who he was talking about and she was shocked when she saw her face. 'That's her?'

'That's her.'

'Jackson, that's Juliette's teacher,' Louisa said, suddenly aware of exactly why he was so intent on helping her. The teacher strongly resembled the woman she'd seen from the reports she had read when researching him once they were partnered up. He knew her death had affected him badly and any residual feelings he had about it were being transferred to this situation. It wasn't healthy, but she had to allow him to work through it and be a support instead of pointing out the damaging repercussions of his relationship with Kaidence.

'Is she?'

Her dark brown hair was tied up in a bun, so it didn't move as she nodded. 'She's being beaten by her boyfriend?'

'This is perfect,' Jackson announced. 'This way you get to see her every morning when you drop off Juliette. This is our in.'

Making sure her class were sat neatly behind year one at the front of the hall, Kaidence's attention turned to the officers, who were stood a few feet from her, and she was somewhat taken aback when she saw their identity. The fact that one of them was the woman who had pulled her aside at the beginning of the day was nothing compared to the shock that the other was the officer who was privy to her secret.

It occurred to her how handsome he looked in his uniform. Although she'd seen him in his official capacity before, she hadn't really taken the time to appreciate him in his police clothes because she'd been distracted by the shock of him showing up at her door. But now that she was more relaxed, she could see how good-looking he was. She had always been attracted to men in uniform, though firemen were her usual predilection, so she wasn't surprised to find herself tempted by the way he was dressed. Previously, at any social encounter between the two of them, she had hardly dared to look him in the eye, let alone study his features, and now that she was so close, she could see a similarity to men she had dated prior to her current partner.

'You're staring,' Emily observed over her shoulder.

Kaidence spun on her heel to face her. 'I know him,' she said in a hushed tone.

'How do you know him?'

'There was a burglary in my street about a week ago and he knocked on my door.'

'So, you don't really know him, you two have just met.'

'No, I know him,' she insisted. 'He has two sisters and one brother. His father has served thirty-four years in the military and he thinks extremely highly of his mother, who kept them together for all the years she was the only parent at home.'

'Whoa, you actually do know him. How is that? Are you sleeping with him?'

'No!' Kaidence answered, outraged. 'Despite appearances, two people of the opposite sex can be friends, you know.'

'Absolutely, but that's a lot of information to obtain about someone in such a short time.'

Kaidence wore a smile as she shrugged. 'For some reason people find me easy to talk to.'

'Are you staying?' Emily asked.

'Uh, no, I've got some catching up to do regarding last week's work so I'm going to be sat behind my desk for the hour.'

Emily nodded. 'Okay, I'll get Imogen to bring your kids back with hers.'

'Thanks Em,' she said before making a conscious effort to walk towards Jackson at the front of the hall on her way back to her classroom. Seeing it as an approach, Jackson stepped forward. 'Good morning.'

Kaidence smiled. 'Morning.'

'So, this is where you teach?'

She replied with a nod. 'For about four years.'

'This is my partner, Louisa Jessop.'

'We've met; her daughter is in my class.'

'That's going to make it easier for us to keep in contact with you.'

Kaidence smiled. 'I thought that might be an option when I saw you both up here.'

'We'll exchange numbers,' Louisa told her as Kaidence scanned the hall. 'Not now; later.'

'Well, the kids will be going out for break after this, so you can find me in my class if you want to.'

'Thanks, we'll do that.'

The room was quiet as Kaidence sat reading through the work her pupils had done the week before with her substitute. Gayle had kept to the teaching guide she had uploaded to the online closed-circuit network all the staff used, which meant the students were up to date with the national curriculum. They'd got much further into the guide than she had expected but given the strictness of the teacher who had taken her class, she wasn't surprised.

She was still sat there an hour later when she heard the kids returning to the room. She got to her feet in order to greet them and as they bundled through the open archway, she called out for them to walk instead of run. But they barely stayed long enough to collect their coats before they made their way outside, which caused Kaidence to smile. Their zest for living was the reason she loved her job.

Her smile held when she saw the two officers enter her classroom. 'Did you have fun?' she asked, walking around her desk and perching on the front of it.

'I did,' Louisa replied before thumbing towards her companion. 'I'm not so sure my partner did though.'

'There was just so many of them,' Jackson countered. 'And they were all looking at me like they were waiting to devour me.'

Kaidence laughed. 'They're kids, not wild animals.'

'It's all the same to me.'

She turned her attention to Louisa. 'So, did you want to exchange numbers?'

'Sure.' The officer removed her mobile phone from the inside pocket of her uniform and unlocked it before handing it to her. 'Just punch your number into the keypad and I'll add it to my contacts.'

Kaidence followed her instructions and added her number before passing it back.

'I'll call you, so you can save my number,' Louisa continued, hitting the phone icon, waiting for it to ring a few times and then hanging up.

'So, now that you two have a way to get in touch with each other – what happened when Mitchell got home yesterday?' Jackson asked, changing the subject.

'He, uh, gave me the cold shoulder,' Kaidence answered.

'So, there was no retribution for spending the day with your sister?'

'I didn't say that.' She dropped her eyes to the floor for a minute before she returned her gaze to his. 'He forced me to have sex with him.'

'He raped you?' Louisa asked, outraged.

She nodded sombrely. 'It's not the first time.'

Jackson motioned to her neck. 'Is that what those bruises are under your collar?'

Thinking she'd done a better job of covering the evidence, Kaidence reached up and fastened her top button. 'That was just a warning not to change our plans in future.'

Louisa looked shocked. 'You can bring charges against him for raping you; it doesn't matter if you're in a relationship or not.'

Kaidence looked to Jackson. 'Didn't you explain to her how I feel about that?'

'She doesn't understand why you're unwilling to file a police report,' Jackson replied with a shrug. 'I'm not sure I understand either.'

'We've been through this. I'm not ready to leave him yet and if he was to find out I'd even thought about pressing charges I would be dead.'

'We can protect you,' Louisa insisted.

'How exactly do you plan to do that?' the teacher asked, folding her arms across her chest awaiting an answer.

Jackson noticed the suit trousers she wore hugged her thighs enough to see definition while the red satin shirt she wore avoided contact with her skin except around the cuffs and the collar. It was a professional look that he wasn't familiar with when it came to her. She'd always been dressed down, so she drew no attention, and he suspected her attire at work was designed to look professional so as not to draw notice in a different way.

'We can take you out of the area and set you up somewhere else,' the female cop suggested.

Kaidence shook her head. 'No. He'll find me.'

'Not if we take you far enough away.'

'You don't know the range of his reach, Officer Jessop. He'd find me.'

'What is he? MI5?'

'No, but he's driven when he wants to be. He wouldn't stop searching until I was back here with him or dead. I've got to set the pace here or you can both walk out that door now and not bother coming back.'

Louisa looked at her partner. 'She's bossy.'

'I've never seen her like this; it must be something to do with the venue,' he responded.

'You said she was determined, I guess I underestimated how much.'

'Are you two finished trying to push me now?' Kaidence asked.

They both nodded slightly in response.

Jackson took a deep breath to prepare to share the plan as he saw it. 'Louisa will check on you every morning when she drops Juliette off and she'll report back to me. You have her number so if you need her, call. We'll always be the other end of the phone and when you're ready to get out, we'll be there to help you; it doesn't matter if it's the middle of the night.'

'Well, if you're calling anyone in the middle of the night please let it be Jacko; I've got two young kids that I'd need to find someone to watch so it'd be more convenient that way.'

Kaidence nodded with a smile. 'I'll do my best to be considerate.'

'And we'll do the same regarding your feelings on pressing charges.'

'I appreciate that.'

But before there was further conversation between the trio the male officer's phone rang. Taking the device from his pocket, he checked the screen and excused himself, moving to the communal area between the two classrooms.

'You know, he's so set on helping you because in his mind he's linked you to the woman he lost while he was undercover,' Louisa said as her partner disappeared.

Kaidence nodded solemnly. 'He told me about her.'

She was taken aback. 'He did?'

'I asked why he was so hell-bent on getting me away from Mitchell and he told me.'

'Usually he doesn't trust so easily.'

Kaidence shrugged. 'I think he knew I wasn't so open to trusting him, so he opened up in order to make me more comfortable.'

'While he was sharing, did he tell you that he only gets to eat home cooking if he goes to his parents at the weekend?' Louisa asked to lighten the mood.

'He did not.'

'He lives on microwave meals and takeaways.'

'Well that can't be healthy.'

'It's not. But I've tried to set him up with women who will cook for him and he won't have it.'

Jackson heard the two women bonding as he approached their position and, although he wasn't happy that he was the subject of that connection, he was content they had something in common to build a friendship on.

'It looks like you two are getting on.'

His partner smiled. 'We've found that talking about you helps with that.'

'Well, before you start conspiring to set me up with any and every woman you both know, we've got to go. A call came over the radio as I got off the phone; there are some kids that have been caught shoplifting across town.'

'Duty calls.'

Kaidence smiled and extended her hand to Louisa. 'It was lovely to meet you, Officer Jessop.'

The other woman reached out and obliged her with the handshake she was expecting. 'I look forward to getting to know you better.'

As his partner released her hold on the teacher, Jackson got closer and reached out to lightly grip her upper arm. 'I am just a phone call away if you want to talk.'

Kaidence nodded. 'Thank you, Officer Chase.'

She watched them walk away and managed to get back to her seat behind her desk before Imogen entered the room.

'What did Officer Handsome want?' she asked, approaching her.

'He didn't want anything.'

'Then why were they in here?'

'The female officer's daughter is in my class, so she just wanted to talk to me about some behavioural issues she's been having with her at home,' she countered, twisting some of the truth to appease Imogen's curiosity.

Imogen frowned. 'Didn't she do that this morning in the playground?'

She laughed. 'Have you ever tried having a conversation in the playground? No, she pulled me aside to say she wanted to talk. I told her to find me when it was quieter, that's what she did.'

'So, the handsome officer didn't want to whisk you away to a deserted island?'

'Sadly, he didn't.'

'Well that's disappointing.'

Kaidence nodded slightly. 'Isn't it? I'm sure Mitchell will be just as upset to be stuck with me.'

By the time Kaidence got home she was exhausted. It had been a long day and it would take her a while to get back into the swing of her routine. She kicked off her shoes at the door, threw her keys on the side table beside the front door and removed her coat. Hanging it on the coat stand on the other side of the door, she made her way into the kitchen and placed her briefcase on the dining table on her way to filling up the kettle for a hot drink.

She had barely placed the jug on its base and flicked it on to boil when her mobile phone started to ring. She rushed to her coat pocket to retrieve it and answered when she saw the officer's first name on the screen.

'Officer Jessop,' she answered with a smile.

'Hi Kaidence, Jackson thinks it's a good idea for us to get to know each other. I think he thinks it will humanise you to me, so I won't treat you like a victim who needs to be convinced to press charges.'

'Officer Jessop, I don't expect you to understand my situation. It never makes sense to someone without experience of abuse, but this is how I need it to be right now.'

'And I promise to try and make my peace with that; but while I'm trying, it won't hurt us to get to know each other.'

CHAPTER SEVEN

It was almost a month later when Kaidence was sat on the phone having her usual Saturday night call to Jackson. She had daily contact with Louisa in her role as her daughter's teacher and weekends were the only time she got to touch base with the officer who had originally decided to make her survival his mission.

Mitchell had spent every Saturday night away from home since the first time he stayed out all night, only to return at lunchtime every Sunday, and he always showered before they sat down to eat. She knew he was washing another woman's smell off his skin because he always got a text to his phone from her. She would be upset if she cared, but she was waiting for him to leave, which he showed no signs of doing. She was happy with the arrangement because she got one full night alone and he hadn't so much as raised his voice to her since he'd started playing around behind her back.

She always used her free night to have a conversation with Jackson without the tension of expecting her housemate back. There had been some nights he hadn't been able to talk for long because he was on shift, and there had been others where they had talked until the small hours of the morning. They had built up quite a friendship without the structure that their initial relationship had set in place, because they were more familiar now. It was easy for her to open up to him and sometimes she didn't even realise she was doing it until the words were out. They even shared jokes that only two people who were familiar enough with each other could use, because they knew the sense of humour of the other.

'So, how was your week?' Jackson asked after they'd been through the usual pleasantries.

'Good, and it's made better by the fact I'll be home alone all night.'

He took a minute in silence to take in the new information she had made him privy to. 'Where's Mitchell?'

'He's been staying out on Saturday nights for about a month now.'

'Did he say where he's been?'

'I haven't asked but I happen to know by way of a text message I saw pop up on his phone that he's been with a woman.'

'Do you know who she is?'

'No, and I don't care. He's not here and might not be for much longer because he's probably getting ready to leave me for her.'

'He has no intention of leaving you; it suits him to have you at home while he's sleeping with someone behind your back. That's his way of getting back at you for defying him.'

'The only problem with that theory is that as far as he knows, I don't know about her.'

'How did you manage to see the text on his phone?'

'He left it on the work surface in the kitchen while he showered.'

'I think it's likely that he left it there on purpose, so you would see the text. I bet he even told the other woman a specific time to send it.'

She sighed. 'I've got half a mind to go out and find someone to have sex with just for payback.'

'Why go out? I can come over and help out with that.'

She laughed. 'That's so selfless of you.'

'Nobility has nothing to do with it; I've been single for a long time.'

Her laughter continued, and he smiled. It was a sound unlike any other he had ever heard and one he'd got used to over the course of their contact. It always made him feel euphoric.

The truth was they had become closer and, if he was honest, he hadn't been that close to anyone since his last girlfriend. He'd told Kaidence things he hadn't shared with friends he'd known for most of his life. He had even made her privy to stories of growing up, which he hadn't told anyone outside his family circle. He trusted her; it was impossible not to. He knew himself enough to know he was involuntarily falling in love with her and he had no idea how to stop it, so he had chosen not to. It could prove problematic when it came to acting officially on her behalf because he was emotionally involved, but he wanted her away from Mitchell for her safety. He hadn't allowed himself to think of a time when she wouldn't need him, because he wasn't sure what he would do without her weekly phone calls. But that was more about him than it was about her and he wasn't about to burden her with an expectation that wasn't coming when she had enough going on in her life. She considered him a safe place to fall, not as a love interest, and that was a boundary he needed to respect.

'Why don't you come over?' she suggested when she finally finished expressing her joy.

He was taken aback. 'What?'

'Not for sex. Just for company. Come over; let's have this conversation in person.'

'Are you sure? What if Mitchell comes back tonight?'

'I always knock the deadlock down on the front door so that'll give you time to escape out of the back and climb over the fence – he'll be none the wiser.'

'What if the neighbours see me?'

'It's eight o'clock on a mid-October night; it's dark. The only thing the hard-core neighbours that spend their evenings curtain twitching will see is a dark figure; as far as they'll be concerned it could be Mitchell coming home. I'll even put the door on the catch if you text me when you're close, so it looks like you used a key.'

'Can you promise me we'll have as much fun if I come over and we continue this conversation in person?'

'If you bring a bottle or two of white wine we will.'

'Would you prefer Chardonnay, Sauvignon Blanc or Pinot Grigio?'

'Surprise me, just don't spend more than ten pounds on each bottle. The expensive stuff is like drinking vinegar.'

'Then I'll drop by an off licence. Do you want me to pick up some food too?'

'Haven't you eaten?'

'I haven't yet.'

'You can forget fetching a takeaway; I'll cook you something.'

'I don't want you to do that.'

'But I want to. I know that you don't get to eat home cooking very often, so I'd like to make you something. What do you want to eat?' She made her way from the living room to the kitchen to check her supplies.

'Please, let me bring a takeaway. It'll save you the effort.'

'I like cooking; it's therapeutic, so tell me what you want.'

'Honestly, I'm starving, so it could be anything and I'd eat it.'

She giggled as she sifted through the ingredients in the fridge. 'I'll throw together a spaghetti bolognaise. I think I've even got a baguette that I can make some garlic bread with.'

'You make your own garlic bread too?' he asked, as she looked in the bread bin for the item.

'Oh, there is no end to the depths of my creativity in the kitchen.'

'Then I can't wait to sample your culinary delights.'

'Great, I'll see you soon,' Kaidence said, hanging up and getting a start on the meal she'd promised Jackson.

Hanging up his phone, Jackson checked his attire and rushed to the bedroom to change. He didn't want Kaidence to see him in the clothes he only deemed good enough to wear at home. Grabbing a pair of jeans from his wardrobe, he threw them on the bed on his way to his chest of drawers to find a shirt. It didn't take him long to get changed and be on his way, finally satisfied his appearance was presentable for the occasion.

The drive from his apartment wouldn't take him long seeing as he was only twenty minutes away, but he had a stop to make so he could pick up some wine as per her request. He was looking forward to spending time with her when he wasn't there officially, yet he had to remind himself that the point of the night was to keep building on their friendship and that it wasn't a date, as much as he'd like it to be.

Music played throughout the house. It wasn't loud because she wanted to make sure she heard her mobile phone when the text came through from Jackson to say he was near, so she could unlock the door, allowing him to walk inside without hesitating on the doorstep. She happily pottered about in the kitchen, preparing food like she had done the day after she'd had her first real conversation with him, when he'd shown up at her door in order to check she was okay. There was something about the male officer that made her feel confident about her future – that she was going to make it out of this relationship alive and not lying on a slab in the morgue.

She had butterflies in her stomach at the prospect of seeing him, as if she was getting ready to entertain a suitor, even though she knew his interest in her was purely professional. She admitted to herself that she had been attracted to him the instant they met, but that attraction had grown over the course of them getting to know each other because of the man he was. He was exactly the type of man she had dreamed of being with for the rest of her life and, if it weren't for Mitchell, she would have already made it clear how she felt. But the scars she had from her current relationship ran deep, so even if she was to leave him now, her confidence had taken a knock and she wouldn't make the first move. Jackson was too valuable in her life now for her to lose him if the feelings weren't reciprocated; and if they were, the risk would be that they could break up and she would lose a man that she considered a friend.

Her mum had always told her that to be friends with a man you wanted to spend your life with was one of the best ways to maintain a successful relationship, because you'd have a bond that was unbreakable before you committed to him. It was what her mother had with her father and, as far as she could tell, it was what her sister had with her husband. She wanted that, and she knew she didn't have it with Mitchell.

Kaidence looked down at the clothes she was wearing and decided in an instant that she was presentable enough in her jeans and T-shirt. It was what she'd usually wear at home, and she wasn't in the habit of dressing up to sit around the house, no matter how attractive she found her visitor.

She was happily adding the gently fried and drained mince to the sauce she'd prepared when Jackson's text lit up her phone screen. It made her smile. *Around the corner*, she read without needing to open the message fully. She instantly made her way to the door and put it on the catch before returning to her phone and replying. *Door's open*, she typed back.

Jackson parked in his usual spot on her street, far enough away that he wouldn't be easily seen yet close enough to see the front of her house, and he climbed out. He locked the car with one press of the button on his key fob, engaging the alarm, and took a look around for anyone watching.

The street was deserted and most of the houses appeared to be in darkness because, he assumed, the curtains were closed, but there were a couple of houses that were lit up like the Blackpool illuminations. However, he couldn't see any figures stood at any of the windows, so he took a chance, walking directly to Kaidence's door.

Reaching the porch, he found the door open like her text had said and he didn't hesitate to walk inside, calling out as he entered and closing the door behind him. 'Hi honey, I'm home.'

She chuckled as she rushed to meet him. 'Hi, go through to the kitchen,' she told him, returning the deadlock in place.

'Mmm, something smells good,' he said, leading the way.

'It's almost ready. I've just got to bake the garlic bread and keep stirring the sauce while the pasta cooks.' She rushed back to the cooker, placing the garlic-buttered baguette in the oven and turning it on.

He placed the bottles of wine on the island in the middle of the room and made his way towards her. 'Let me stir the sauce.'

'Are you sure you can handle that?'

'I can't really fuck it up just by stirring it, can I?'

She couldn't help the laugh that escaped her mouth and filled the room. 'Have you ever tried cooking?' she asked as she reached for two glasses from the cabinet before removing the corkscrew from the utensil drawer.

'I have, and I can burn boiling water,' he replied, causing her to laugh again.

'Would you mind?' she asked, thrusting one of the bottles in his direction with the corkscrew to open it.

Obliging, he took both objects and proceeded to fulfil her request. 'Keep doing that, I like it,' he confessed.

Unsure what he was referring to, she frowned. 'What?'

'Keep laughing. I love the way it sounds.'

'Well, I didn't have much cause to do it before I met you.'

'It's good to know I'm useful for something,' he said, pulling the cork from the neck of the bottle and passing it to her.

She gestured to the bottle in her hand to reference the task he'd just performed. 'This is a nifty skill too,' she said, pouring two glasses and handing him one.

'I'm not sure I should be drinking while I'm in charge of stirring.' He placed his wine on the worktop beside the hob and turned his attention back to the stove.

'You'll be fine. I'm supervising.'

The room fell silent momentarily while Jackson concentrated on the job at hand before he spoke. 'I brought a film with me too.'

'What kind of film?'

'I just picked one from my own collection. I didn't even look at it until I was halfway here.'

'So, which one did you pick out?'

He winced. 'It's a horror.'

'And what were the odds that you'd choose a comedy or a thriller?'

'Slim. Now I think about it, I've got a lot of horrors in my collection,' he replied with a laugh. 'We don't have to watch it. I just thought that if we ran out of topics to talk about that it could be an option.'

'You could have picked something a little more light-hearted.'

'I'm sorry. Like I said, I didn't look at it.'

'I'm just going to have to do everything in my power to not allow the conversation dry up,' she said with a smile as she took a sip of her wine.

'I take it you're a chick flick kind of girl.'

'Not particularly, I just prefer anything other than horror.'

'Then you can select one from your collection.'

Kaidence felt a sense of belonging as she moved around the kitchen to drain the pasta from the saucepan, as if it was natural for her to share that space with him. There was a comfort that came from being around him that she hadn't noticed before. She didn't feel threatened by him, just protected, and maybe that was why she had invited him over. She enjoyed their conversations on the phone but so much of her life was spent absent company that tonight she had sought to have some, and it helped that she felt at ease around him.

Placing the colander on top of the saucepan the pasta had cooked in to drain whatever excess water she hadn't been able to shake off, she moved towards Jackson's position.

'Excuse me,' she said, placing one hand on the oven handle, causing him to take a step to his side, away from her. 'Thank you.' She opened the door and removed the bread that had been cooking inside.

Slamming the door shut, Kaidence turned the dial for the oven into the off position and did the same with the hob the sauce was sitting on. 'That's done now,' she told him with a smile.

'And I didn't burn it,' he said, pleased with himself.

'You really don't do this at home do you?' She relieved him of the saucepan he'd been attending to and placed it with the rest of the food. 'Do you prefer it mixed together or do you want the sauce placed on top of the pasta?'

He shrugged. 'However, it comes.'

He watched her dish up the meal she'd made especially for him and he instantly visualised a life with her. A life of coming home to her after every shift, a life blessed with a couple of kids and of them being happy together for the rest of their days. But that was for a time after this, when they were both free to explore being a couple. Still, it was nice to picture holding her in his arms when she needed comforting and kissing her whenever he felt like it. He wanted to do more than imagine it, but he wasn't about to thrust more expectations on her when she already had enough to live up to. Although it was killing him to keep his feelings to himself, he knew he had to.

She moved about the kitchen, getting utensils for him to eat with and setting him a place at the table before collecting his plate and laying it down in front of him. 'Your dinner is served,' she said, motioning with her hand for him to take a seat.

Grabbing both of their glasses, Jackson made his way over and sat down opposite the chair Mitchell usually sat in as she took a seat beside him. 'This smells divine.'

Kaidence smiled. 'Well, eat it before it goes cold.'

He didn't waste any time lifting his knife and fork and tucking into the food in front of him. It was a little strange for him to be watched but as he nodded his approval with his first bite, Kaidence relaxed back in her chair and sipped at her wine while he continued to eat.

'So, how was work today?' she asked, wanting to break the silence.

'Have we already exhausted all the other topics of conversation?' he asked, amused.

She frowned. 'Is asking about your day that strange?'

'We just never talk about work; yours or mine.'

'That's because I don't know if I should. It's hard to tell by your voice what kind of day you've had but seeing as you're here and seem in pretty good spirits, I thought I'd take my chances.'

He sighed as he chewed what food remained in his mouth before swallowing. 'My days at work involve shoplifters, teenage delinquents who terrorise their community and drunks who think they can fight the world every Saturday night. It's not as exciting as I bet you think it is.'

'Oh, I don't know, it helped you find me.' She smiled smugly.

He nodded, wearing his own smile. 'I can't argue with that, although it's unfortunate that it led me to you in your current predicament.'

'Quite the contrary, I think you found me at precisely the time you were supposed to.'

'Can you really believe in fate even with the hand you've been dealt?'

'It helps to believe in something.'

The room fell silent while Jackson continued to eat and Kaidence drank from her glass. It was a comfortable quiet that felt completely ordinary. But as she sat there, she played over his words.

'Wait, what did you mean by its unfortunate that it led you to me in my current predicament?'

Jackson cursed himself for the slip-up because it had been about his feelings, but he couldn't tell her that. Maintaining a professional relationship was something that she needed right now.

'I mean unfortunate because you're being hurt by him.' He plucked an answer loosely out of the truth.

She seemed to accept his explanation. 'You know, since he's been seeing this woman, he hasn't even raised his voice to me, let alone his hand.'

He put his utensils down on the plate and sat back in his seat. 'Oh no.'

'What?'

'Tell me you're not considering staying with this guy so long as he's sleeping with another woman.'

'God no, but it allows me time to repair and gain the mental strength to figure out a way to leave him.'

'I have a way; pack your bags right now and you can hide out at my place. He can't link us together, so he'll never find you.'

She laughed. 'Officer Chase, are you suggesting that we shack up together?'

He leaned forward and picked up his fork before loading it with food. 'If it means I get more home cooking like this, I'm suggesting we get married.' He smiled, playing off his attraction to her as he filled his mouth.

'Exactly how long have you been single?' She asked, trying to disguise her curiosity in amusement.

She watched him break up the garlic baguette she'd buttered and baked to round off the meal. 'I've been single so long that I'm not sure I remember how to be a boyfriend,' he confessed, taking a bite.

'Oh, I'm confident you'd find your feet.'

'I've got used to being alone. Relinquishing control now would be hard for me.'

'Don't you ever get tired of being on your own?'

'Not really.'

'Well I do, and I'm in a relationship. Granted I don't want to be around him, but still, I like company.'

'I think if I was to find a woman like you it would make relinquishing easier but the women I come into contact with are so superficial and I've got nothing in common with them.'

'You don't necessarily have to have anything in common right away; you can just sleep with them.'

'The problem with that is, I'm particular who I have sex with.'

'Really? That's interesting,' she said, raising her eyebrows prior to consuming the last of the wine in her glass and then getting up to refill it.

He shrugged. 'It's not that big a deal. I just like to have feelings for someone before I sleep with her.'

'Have you ever had a one-night stand?' she pried, taking the bottle to the table and retaking her seat.

He finished his mouthful and shook his head. 'Never.'

'Wow!' The word passed her lips in a whisper, but he still heard the aston-ishment behind it.

'That begs the question, have you?'

'One or two in the days before I knew what love was. But I prefer a deeper connection other than first attraction these days.'

'Then what the hell did you see in Mitchell that made him worthy of sharing your house?' he asked with a frown.

'He wasn't always so cruel, or he'd be homeless rotting on the street somewhere.'

'Why would he be homeless?'

'He lost his job eleven months after we started dating and he couldn't afford his rent, so I stupidly asked him to move in. It was instinct. If I'd have had more time to consider it, I'd have thought better of sharing my sanctuary with anyone, because I like my space. It wasn't until I let him get away with the odd slap that he showed his true colours, and to add insult to injury he's living here without paying a penny for the privilege.'

'So, he's a bum as well as a bastard?' he observed as he finished the last of his meal.

The air thickened around them as the subject they had both been avoiding raised its ugly head and weighed heavy on their shoulders. He tried to keep their conversations cheerful and away from the topic of Mitchell or her abuse. But sometimes his curiosity got the better of him and he had to ask the questions she found it hard to answer, though she did answer.

'Where do you go in your mind when he's laying into you?' he queried, giving her his undivided attention.

Her eyes dropped to the base of the glass that rested in her lap. 'It's so bad sometimes that I can't transport myself anywhere else. He seems to know right where to hit me to exert the maximum amount of pain.'

'Of course he does – he's stronger than you.'

She nodded. 'At first the shock overtook the pain. Then I would scream as loud as I could to try and get him to stop, but that would just make him angrier. Now I bite my lip until it bleeds just to not give him the satisfaction of hearing my pain. I used to try and think of being anywhere else but that doesn't work any more because his punches are too hard to ignore.'

He sighed. 'I will never be all right with leaving you here to endure that.'

She reached out to place her hand on his as it rested on the table. 'And that's why I'm glad you know. My survival matters to you and that's why I want to get out of this alive.'

He squeezed her hand slightly as their skin-to-skin contact sent faint elec-tric currents of euphoria through his body. 'I'll help you out of this.' He paused and applied slightly more pressure to their connection so that she looked at him. 'You matter more than you believe you do.'

Tears built up in her eyes and spilled onto her cheeks as she blinked. 'Do I?'

He shook his head. 'I hate that he's made you believe that you're worthless. I wish I'd known you before you were the person you are now.'

She forced a smile to her mouth. 'I used to dream of marrying a man like you one day, having too many kids and living a comfortable life in a home we made. But now all I dream about is being alive the following day. It's horrible but it's my cross to bear because it's my punishment.'

He frowned. 'What are you being punished for?'

'My parents; they died because of me,' she said, sniffing back the tears, snatching her hand from his grasp and beginning to clear the table as a distraction.

'They died in a car crash. That wasn't your fault.'

'That happened the day after my twenty-first birthday.' She nodded. 'I knew they had to drive the next morning because they had an early flight, but I begged them to stay for one more drink anyway. After all, I only turned twenty-one once in my life,' she said angrily, wiping away the waterfall of emotions soaking her cheeks before supporting herself on the sink.

He got to his feet and made his way over to her. Taking her shoulders in his grasp, he turned her to face him. 'There was a toxicology report done with the autopsy and there was no alcohol in either of their blood.'

'No, but I kept them out late. If my dad had had more sleep...'

He cupped her face with his hand, forcing her eyes to his. 'You couldn't have changed a thing. The truck driver was negligent because he'd been driving all night. It was not your fault.'

'Then why does it feel like I'm paying for it?' she asked, breaking down.

He pulled her close to his chest and wrapped his arms around her as she did the same. She could feel the strength his comfort provided as he held her, and she knew she was safe. Her body shuddered as she sobbed, allowing him to see a side of her that very few got to see. He provided a reassurance that she'd been craving, and she was going to take advantage of it. She squeezed him tighter as she cried because she needed the release. The months of abuse and the guilt she'd been holding on to since she'd heard of her parents' passing came flooding out.

By the time she pulled away from him, her eyes were puffy and red. But he could still see her beauty. If anything, she looked even more beautiful with her emotions out on display than she did when she was fighting them. He could tell she didn't let her guard down for just anyone and he was honoured she trusted him enough to allow him to see behind her defences.

'I'm sorry,' she apologised, drying her eyes.

'You don't have to be. It's probably been a long time coming.'

'I should clean up this mess.' She diverted the attention from her display of vulnerability.

'Let me do the dishes,' he said softly. 'Go and get comfortable with your wine in the living room. I'll come in when I'm done.'

She nodded, accepting his gesture. 'Thank you.'

It was a testament to the man Jackson was that he had offered to clean up after she'd cooked only one meal for him, when Mitchell had always expected her to do it after ten months of meals.

She wished that she had known Jackson before she had made any kind of commitment to the boyfriend she now had, but instead she had to endure his torment while the man who would be worthy of loving was only a friend, and she truly believed he was that, and nothing else.

She was finally ready to share a piece of herself that was hidden behind a combination lock. Heading to the home office, Kaidence removed the picture frame from the wall and punched in the six digits on the keypad of the safe. Reaching inside, she retrieved her journal and grabbed her laptop from the desk before going into the living room to wait for him.

Jackson was just wiping down the hob and the surfaces when he heard the faint sound of music coming from the room she'd retired to, and it brought a smile to his face. He dried his hands and picked up the bottle of wine with his glass before using the melody to guide his way to her. Walking through the doorway, he found her on the settee looking despondent.

'Hey, are you okay?' he asked, putting the items in his hand down on the coffee table and taking a seat next to her. That's when he saw the thick leather-bound A5 journal in her lap and he instantly knew what it was.

'I thought it was time you saw these,' she said, passing it to him.

He took it from her. 'Are you sure you're ready to share them?'

She nodded. 'I trust you.'

Kaidence had already placed the SD card in the slot on her computer for when he was ready to see the evidence she'd collected, but she was forced to be an observer as Jackson began to read through the encounters she'd had to endure. His face gave nothing away at first but as he got further into the pages, she could see his revulsion for the things he was reading etched on his features. She couldn't tell if he was repulsed because of things she had to suffer while insisting on staying or if he was amazed that she was still alive.

Jackson prided himself on being mild mannered and not losing his temper easily but as he read from the pages, he could picture Mitchell laying his hands on the woman he'd become so familiar with and rage built up inside him. He wanted to go out into the night, find the man who had done the terrible things she had detailed in her book and give him a taste of the things he'd put her through, but he was forced to take things at the pace she set because those were the terms she'd set. His heart and his mind were at odds because he wanted to keep his promise to her and yet he wanted the satisfaction of beating Mitchell bloody.

She could hear his breathing get heavier and she assumed he was annoyed. Only she didn't know the signs for his feelings yet. So, she didn't talk, she just waited patiently for him to finish and when he finally closed the book, she waited a little longer for him to speak first. But he stayed quiet.

Kaidence lifted the laptop from the coffee table to her lap and took a deep breath. 'Do you want to see the pictures?' she asked softly.

He was distracted by the things he had read about but he cleared his throat and nodded slightly. 'Okay.'

Her hand poised on the top of her portable computer. 'Some of these are... sensitive.' He nodded his understanding. 'You'll see more of me than you are probably ready for; more than I'm really ready for. Nevertheless, I need you to see them.'

For the third time, he nodded.

She took another deep breath as she opened the lid on her laptop, which sprung it to life. Opening the explorer for the hard drive, she clicked on the memory card and double-clicked on the first picture listed. It was her first black eye. The next was a bite mark on her left shoulder. She flicked through the photos one after the other and each one was worse than the one before. Her injuries ranged from bruises all over the parts of her body that were usually covered with clothes to cuts on parts that she had to mask with foundation. When she got to the images of her more intimate areas, she could see his obvious discomfort.

'Was that the first time he raped you?' he asked, keeping his voice low.

She gulped, remembering that night as if it had just happened. 'I fought him, so that's why there are bruises on my inner thighs and pubic bone.'

'And the cuts on your breast?'

'They're from his teeth,' she answered, clearing her throat.

Suddenly Jackson reached out and closed the lid on the computer. 'I don't need to see any more.'

'I'm sorry. It's one thing to know, it's a different thing entirely to see.' She placed the electrical device back on the table in front of them.

'The only reason you're willing to put up with the way he treats you is because you feel guilty for the way your parents died, but that wasn't your fault, so you don't owe it to anyone to live like this. You're punishing yourself for a crime you didn't commit. You shouldn't be serving this sentence.'

His words brought more tears to her eyes. 'It's too hard to forgive myself when I can't ask them for it.'

He turned in his seat towards her and reached out for one of her hands, which he held in his own. 'You don't need to be forgiven. What happened to them was nothing but a horrible accident.'

'I know, but it still doesn't stop how I feel.'

He shifted closer. 'Believe me – you're worth more than this.'

'The bad stuff is so much easier to believe,' she said, wiping away the stray tear that had spilled onto her cheek.

'I know it is, but you have nothing to atone for,' he said, rubbing his thumb back and forth on the top of her hand.

She sat feeling his touch and for a minute craved more intimacy than he was here for. It would be so easy to lean forward and kiss him just to feel anything but the sadness she'd had in her heart for seven years. She wanted to replace the hate inside with the love she knew she was capable of. She just didn't want to alienate the only person she could turn to by making a pass that wouldn't be reciprocated; she was too vulnerable for that. However, she couldn't deny wanting him.

'You know when you say it, I can almost believe it.'

Her smile made him do the same. 'Only almost, Kaidence? I thought I was more convincing than that.'

'How are you still single?' she asked, amazed.

He shrugged. 'It's no grand gesture like I'm saving myself for someone special; I just haven't found anyone I want to be with yet.'

'But women must throw themselves at you.'

'It's been known to happen, but I'm on the job and they're only really interested in the uniform.'

'Women do love a man in uniform.'

'Tell me about it; in high school I only managed to convince one girl to give me the time of day and now every weekend when I'm on duty every drunk female walking out of a club wants me to take them out.'

'That's not just because of the police clothes; you're a handsome guy.'

'And you're a beautiful woman,' he said, causing her to dip her head, and he could tell it was because she doubted his compliment. 'The bad stuff is definitely easier to believe, isn't it?'

'I've been told I'm a worthless piece of shit in one way or another more times than I can count – it isn't long before you stop thinking its bollocks.'

'If we were a couple, you'd know how beautiful you are because I'd tell you every single day.'

Kaidence didn't take compliments as easily as she used to. They made her feel self-conscious now, not confident like they had when she'd been much younger. She had once thrived on being found attractive and had even been known to use it to her advantage with men she found good-looking, but that was before she decided to settle down. Mitchell wasn't the kind of man who built you up because he wanted you to know your worth, instead he stripped away any confidence and convinced you that you had no worth at all. She was used to being knocked down, so it was a foreign feeling when Jackson tried to instil her with some self-belief.

'Well, I learned a long time ago that I'm not that lucky.'

It was then that she realised they'd been holding hands for the entirety of their conversation and she hadn't noticed because it had felt so natural. Her hand fitted inside his like it was designed to be there. But as she sat relishing the softness of his skin, he must have realised they were still touching and freed his light grasp on her to reach for the full glass of wine he'd been neglecting.

She coughed to clear the air and her mind as she sipped from her own glass. 'That's enough serious talk for one night. Can I distract you with a film from the thriller genre?'

CHAPTER EIGHT

It was Sunday afternoon again before Kaidence had much chance to realise where the time had gone.

Jackson hadn't left until the early hours of the morning and that was only because they were both threatening to fall asleep on the settee in front of the television.

She'd climbed into bed just before four a.m. and had only got up an hour prior to Mitchell's arrival home. Despite her tardiness, she still had everything ready for when it was time to eat. As usual they sat at the table in silence while they ate the meal she'd prepared. But instead of her trying to transport to somewhere far away in her mind, she was sat in the other room with Jackson like she had been the night before. She could picture being snuggled up on the settee with him while they watched a horror film and she hid her face in his shoulder at the scary parts that were too graphic or jumpy for her to watch. It was exactly what she desired, and yet the closest she'd get to it right now was an image in her mind. She hoped one day she would be free to actually act on those feelings but for now she had to hide that passion deep inside because if she didn't, she'd risk a false sense of security and if she lowered her guard she definitely wouldn't survive. She had to deal with one man at a time. She had to get rid of the dead weight before she prepared herself mentally for a normal relationship, if that was what she'd have afterwards.

Suddenly Mitchell's voice penetrated the picture of her and Jackson in each other's arms. 'What did you do last night?'

She was pulled back to the room kicking and screaming. 'I, um, had a bath and an early night,' the lie falling out of her mouth naturally.

'Are you sure? Because Tim said the lights were on over here until gone three a.m.'

She panicked initially because in her excitement to spend time with Jackson, she'd forgotten about the man who was so obsessed with her that he watched the house any chance he got. But then she remembered that the man who had been telling tales about her wasn't someone who Mitchell considered a reliable source. She knew she had to play on that doubt if she was to make it out of this conversation able to go to work the following day.

'I was home on my own,' she replied, trying not to have an attitude. 'I put the timer on the lamp in the living room to turn it off in the early hours in case there was anyone casing the house, because I heard that there have been burglaries in the area, but I was tucked up in bed long before that.'

'He also said that he saw someone coming in about an hour after I'd gone out.'

'Well Tim's lying.' She flat out disputed his account of the evening.

Kaidence was expecting some kind of penalty for the outrage she had let slip out in her statement. But Mitchell smiled instead. 'He's always had a thing for you. Maybe he's trying to split us up so that he can have you all to himself,' he said, letting her know he'd noticed.

'It wasn't going to happen for the five years before you moved in, it's even less likely to happen now,' she said, pushing her food around her plate. 'Do you think he's spying on us?'

'Why? Did you have someone here last night?'

'No, I just think he was watching the house, saw that you didn't come home and thought he'd do some shit stirring to see where it led.'

'I may have to have a word with him.'

She shook her head. 'He's not worth your time. He's harmless. I'll just warn him off when I get back from work tomorrow.'

'That's right; he's scared of you.' He chuckled like the implication was absurd.

'He hasn't been able to look me in the eye since I threatened to feed him his testicles because he thought it was appropriate to slap me on the arse at the Wyatt's Christmas party last year.'

Then it dawned on him. 'Oh God, tell me I haven't got to go to that this year. It sounds so dull.'

She shrugged. 'I've been going on my own since I moved in here, and one more year isn't going to make a difference.'

'You'd go without me?'

'It's expected of me now,' she replied before realising she wasn't talking to Jackson and neither was she free to make her own decisions. 'But I'd only show my face and then I'd come home so we can do something together.'

The party was ten weeks away and she planned to be out of her obligation to him by then. She wanted to be on her way back to her former life, to laugh more than she felt like crying, to have freedom instead of being confined to the house she once loved, to meet a man worthy of everything she had to offer and have the babies she always desired, but most of all, she wanted to be herself again.

'Oh, I won't be spending Christmas with you,' he said, dismissing the idea. 'I'll be going home to my mum and dad's.'

The mention of his parents made her realise that although they'd been dating for two years already, she still hadn't met them, and it occurred to her that now she knew what kind of man he was, she didn't want to. She was thrilled by the idea of not having to be with him for the holidays, but kept it hidden like a secret she was guarding. 'Then would it be okay for me to spend mine with my sister?' She scolded herself for feeling the need to ask permission.

'I don't care what you do, darling, I'll be with my family.'

At least he's honest, she thought, mentally raising her eyebrows. But she left the conversation there. She didn't want to push or set him off by rejoicing at the fact she'd get time to be with her own relatives during the holidays.

It wasn't until much later that afternoon, when Kaidence was putting away the clean clothes she'd spent a few hours ironing, that Mitchell really spoke to her again. He'd been getting together his outfit for the following day at work when he asked a question she dreaded him asking, because of the answer she would have to give.

'So, you haven't asked why I don't come home on Saturday nights. Aren't you even curious?' he asked out of the blue, hanging his suit on the front of the wardrobe door.

She was taken back. She didn't want to tell him that she knew exactly where he was because of a text message she saw on his phone after the first time and that she didn't care because as long as he was sleeping with someone else she could hope that he was getting close to leaving. She had a feeling that wouldn't be the kind of honesty he wanted to hear.

'I thought you were staying with one of your friends.' She shrugged, passing it off as no big deal.

'And why do you think that is?'

'I don't know,' she lied, hoping he wasn't about to catch her out.

'I don't want to be around you because you make me miserable.'

She wanted to insist that it was no barrel of laughs for her either and that he was free to leave any time he wanted to, but she suspected he wanted her to beg. The question was whether she could be convincing, given the new-found strength Jackson had instilled in her through their contact.

'I don't mean to.' She began her defence with less enthusiasm than she would have if she cared.

'You need to try harder to keep me happy.'

Inside her brain was screaming. *Harder! I already cook, clean, don't talk out of turn and pay all the bills without a penny from you. Not to mention I take a beating once in a while. How much harder can I try?*

'What do you want me to change?' she asked, knowing he must have had something in mind to bring it up after four weeks.

'You used to smile more, maybe that would help.'

She couldn't help it, she had to say something. She couldn't just take his suggestion without offering an explanation and it was not going to come out passively.

'Well it's hard to smile with internal injuries.'

'Are you trying to be funny?'

'No. I'm just saying that it's hard to be happy when I'm in pain, that's all,' she answered, thinking it was high time for some honesty.

This was it. This was the fight that was going to end their relationship and she was ready for it, thanks to her temporary confidence boost from the hours spent with Jackson the night before.

'Do you think I enjoy having to point out your many mistakes? I don't. But if I don't teach you, how are you going to learn?'

His stance made it clear that he was in no mood for taking criticism. He was definitely ready to teach her a lesson that she maybe wouldn't make it out of alive, especially given his sudden disinterest in her.

She had forgotten her place. The smidgen of confidence that she had pumping through her veins had made her think that she could talk to him however she wanted to without ramification, but Jackson wasn't here to shield her and if she continued on this course it was going to be costly. Weighing her options, she instantly decided to back down.

'You're right,' she said submissively, dropping her eyes to the ground. 'I need you to keep me on track. I'll try harder to smile more. You just need to tell me if I'm not doing it enough.'

She hated herself for conforming so quickly but she didn't have a choice if she wanted to avoid another possible life-threatening altercation. She wasn't sure if her body was completely healed from the last one, but she didn't want to find out. Just when she thought Jackson had given her a small tool of strength to stand up to the man who had made her his punching bag for the best part of a year, she retreated back to the scared and fragile teacher who hadn't had a fight in her life.

Picking up the clean towels that had been with the ironing, Kaidence headed out to the landing to place them in the airing cupboard where they were kept, unaware of Mitchell following behind her until she turned to make her way back. He caught her off guard and she halted at the top of the stairs to cover her heart.

'Jesus Mitchell, make a little noise so a girl knows your whereabouts.'

'Do you think I'll tolerate being mocked?' he asked, his face contorted in anger.

In an instant she wondered if she'd be able to make it downstairs, fish Jackson's card from the drawer and dial his number before her abuser caught up to her but she knew she wouldn't, and there were no locked doors she could hide behind on the lower floor that would be sufficient to hold Mitchell at bay even if she dialled triple nine to try and reach the officer she'd forged a connection with.

She shook her head. 'No, I didn't... I wasn't...' she stammered.

He grabbed her upper arms in his hands. 'Oh I think you were.'

She could feel herself start to tremble and she hated it, but she was terrified and the more she tried not to be, the worse she began to shake. It wasn't going to take much for him to put an end to her; before she knew it, her boyfriend had turned her ninety degrees so her back was to the staircase. He held her there, hovering over the top step for a second before he released his hold on her and, although she tried desperately to grab onto the handrail or spindles to stop her decent, she fell backwards. Her body bounced down the stairs and each rebound felt like a cricket bat being taken to her ribs and her head until finally, after what felt like hours, she crumpled at the bottom. She lay there listening for his footsteps and she was thankful when she didn't hear them. She considered moving, but she couldn't muster the energy to fight against the pain throughout her body, so instead she lay there. She felt tired, and she knew that meant the repeated hits to her head on the way down had caused concussion, which meant she shouldn't fall asleep, but she just couldn't seem to stay awake. She fought to keep her eyes open but when the lightness around her suddenly seemed to go dark and the noises faded into silence, she realised she had lost the battle.

Louisa stood in her police uniform on the school playground on Monday morning waiting to see Kaidence's smiling face when she handed Juliette over to her for a day of learning, but when the glass doors opened, and it was the unfamiliar member of staff who had taken over the first week of term in September, she knew something was wrong. She waited until all the children had filed inside before she made her way up to the teacher covering the year two class.

'Excuse me, is Miss Hadaway absent today?' she asked.

Gayle didn't allow her stern expression to change, even though she was addressing a parent. 'Did you need to see her about something regarding your child?'

'No, I just like to keep her updated about Juliette's behaviour at home.'

'Well she's not in today,' the teacher said, starting back inside.

Louisa stopped her. 'Will she be back in tomorrow?'

'I don't know. If you don't mind, I need to get inside.'

Louisa nodded her understanding and headed to the front of the school. She needed to know if Kaidence had called in sick and if she hadn't, she had to find out why. She knocked lightly on the open office door of the secretary and entered without waiting for an invitation to enter.

'Excuse me, has Kaidence Hadaway rung in sick today?' she asked, getting straight to the point.

'I'm sorry, who are you?'

'My daughter is in her class, but we actually know each other out of school. I've got her number; I just want to know if I need to use it or not.'

The woman behind the desk looked her up and down, trying to decide whether she was trustworthy, and the police uniform must have tipped the scale in her favour because her face softened.

'She hasn't called in, which is unusual for her. Usually when I get in there's a message on the answering machine from her letting me know if she's not going to be in. But this morning there's nothing.'

'Have you tried contacting her?'

She nodded. 'Her home number just rings out and her mobile goes to voicemail.'

Louisa pulled her phone from her pocket. 'Thank you.' She walked out of the room, searching her contacts for Kaidence's number.

As the secretary had stated, the line the other end rang out until her message clicked in and Louisa hung up without leaving any evidence for Mitchell to find. She immediately hit Jackson's number in her list of favourite contacts as she headed back to her car. Climbing in behind the wheel she waited for her partner to pick up and when he did she got straight to the point of her panic. 'Jax, I'm at the school and your favourite victim isn't so I'm going to her house to check on her.'

'Okay, I'll meet you there.'

'Where are you?'

'I've just clocked in.'

'Then stay there. I'll keep you updated. The last thing we need is a squad car showing up on scene and getting the neighbours all riled up.'

'Oh no, I'm coming. Our cover is that the school got in touch when they didn't hear from her.'

'If I disagree, you're still going to show up, aren't you?'

'You bet your arse I am.'

'Then at least clock me in before you walk out of the station.'

'You got it,' he responded.

Louisa was at the address before Jackson. She didn't wait for him to accompany her; instead she headed to the front door. She used the large heavy knocker to announce her arrival. But when she didn't hear any movement the other side, Louisa dialled Kaidence's mobile number. She could hear the faint sound of the ringing from inside and again the voicemail kicked in. Hanging up, she bent down to peer through the letter box and her heart caught in her throat when she saw her lying motionless at the bottom of the stairs.

'Kaidence!' she called out to be sure there was no response, and when there wasn't, she used her phone to contact Jackson.

He wasted no time answering, 'Have you found her?'

'She's lying at the foot of the staircase. She's not moving.'

'Break down the door,' he ordered.

'Have you seen the door to this place? It's like a barricade. I haven't got the strength to break it down on my own.'

'I'm five minutes away. I've got a key in the boot.'

The key was a shorter nickname for the Big Red Key: equipment formally known as the enforcer or battering ram. It was a steel tubular construction with a steel pad at one end so that the police could break down doors when they needed to gain entry into a property, and Jackson always had one in the boot of his squad car in the event of an occasion to use it.

'Well put on the blues and I'll call for an ambulance – she could be clinging onto life in there,' she said, hanging up.

He didn't need telling twice, and although Louisa could hear the siren down the line, she could also hear it in the distance. It allowed him to use more speed and she needed him there the sooner the better.

Louisa was straight on her radio requesting an ambulance. 'Can I have an ambo to my location straight away? We have a female with a possible concussion.'

The radio cracked with the message back. 'I'm dispatching one to you right now, officer.'

Within a few minutes, Jackson pulled up and the officer already on scene watched him retrieve the equipment from the boot before rushing to her position. He didn't hesitate to use all the strength he could muster in his blind panic for Kaidence's safety and force the battering ram to impact the door at the site of the lock. It usually took a few hits to weaken the point of the blow, but his fear must have given him superhero-like strength because the door flew open, allowing Louisa to rush inside to check her vitals.

'There's a pulse, it's faint but she's still alive,' she said, holding two fingers to Kaidence's neck.

Jackson was straight on his radio, as he checked Kaidence for any signs of broken bones. 'Can you update the ambo that we have a female victim, approximately thirty years old with a faint pulse and shallow breathing, and no obvious contusions.' He looked down at Louisa. 'Check this floor to make sure there's no one else here. I'll check upstairs.'

'I think if he was here, he'd have bolted by now.' His partner dismissed his suspicion.

'We have to follow procedure because if he's here and gets the jump on us, we'll have to explain that,' he insisted.

Louisa nodded. He was right, and he was her superior. She had to follow protocol, even if she was sure the perpetrator was long gone. She removed her taser gun from the holster on her duty belt and poised it ready to use. The kitchen was the first room she cautiously entered, checking all the hidden corners before moving anticlockwise throughout the downstairs doing the same until she was back at her starting point.

Confident there was no one else there, she holstered her weapon and looked down at Kaidence. She didn't know what had happened, but she knew Mitchell had something to do with it. He'd probably beaten her half to death for a workout just because he could, and had then left her for dead while he went to work. It made her sick that Kaidence would live this life just to prove she could. It was going to lead to her demise, if it hadn't already.

Jackson appeared at the top of the stairs. 'All clear up here,' he said, starting on his way down.

'He's long gone,' she said as the faint sirens from the street got louder and louder until they stopped.

Louisa stepped out onto the doorstep to wave the paramedics to the patient. They rushed up the drive, through the open front door, and wasted no time attending to Kaidence while the two officers stood by and watched.

It wasn't until Kaidence was wheeled out on the stretcher that Jackson realised their mode of entry meant that they couldn't leave the house at risk of anyone entering. It was unprofessional, and he wouldn't have her getting out of hospital to find police negligence had led to her being robbed. He got straight on the radio. 'I need an officer on scene to watch the property until we've secured the entrance.'

'Do we know where this scumbag works?' Louisa asked her partner as they watched the ambulance drive away.

'I do. But it doesn't matter; we're stuck here until relief shows up.'

She wagged her finger side to side to signal he was wrong, 'Only one of us needs to stand guard and you've got it covered. So, I'll go and question the waste of an existence and you can stop here until you're relieved,' she said, backing down the drive.

'Do you want the address?' he responded.

'I'll use the on-board computer. Just text me the company name.'

Louisa walked into the warmth of the building and made her way straight to reception. She addressed the receptionist, who didn't look busy despite one of the phones on the desk ringing. 'I'm here to see Mitchell Stevenson. Could you please tell him I'm here?'

'Is he expecting you?'

'I don't expect he is,' she said, smiling slightly.

'Can I tell him what it's in reference to?' the receptionist asked, her hand poised over the handset for what Louisa could only assume was the inside line.

'It's a police matter. I'd rather discuss it with him.'

'Of course, follow me,' she said, getting to her feet and leading the way.

Following the receptionist, Louisa tried to figure out which man was the one who had beaten the woman she'd seen taken off to hospital not half an hour before, but any of the men sat in the cubicles she passed could have been the perpetrator, because often monsters hid behind the faces of normal men. It wasn't until the woman she'd been walking behind stopped that it seemed obvious that this was the one.

Although he didn't stand up, she could see that he was built like he used to lift weights when he had enough energy to care about his physique, and he had thick hands that looked like they could be powerful enough to cause a lot of damage when he wanted them to. His skinhead hairstyle made him appear more intimidating than she expected; in her experience men like him only bullied women because they were trying to make up for something they lacked, whether it was wealth, strength or sexual prowess, and he didn't look the part.

She noticed as he sat back and gave her his attention that although he was dressed in a suit, he was dishevelled and unkempt. Even his facial hair contributed to his untidiness.

'Mr Stevenson?' Louisa enquired, taking her notepad from her pocket. Addressing him formally stuck in her throat when all she wanted to do was forgo questioning and put him in handcuffs for the whole floor to witness while screaming at the top of her lungs about how he treated his women. But she had to maintain professionalism.

'What can I do for you?' he asked, as if he was oblivious of the reason.

'We received a call from the school where your girlfriend works this morning. They were concerned that they hadn't heard from her, so we went to her house and found her lying unconscious at the bottom of the stairs. Do you know what happened to her?' she enquired, trying to keep her cool.

He sat up. 'Is she going to be okay?'

Louisa groaned internally. His attempt at concern was severely lacking. 'She's been taken to the hospital.'

'Which one?'

'Good Hope,' she replied flatly and repeated her question. 'Do you know how she was injured?'

'No officer, I've got no idea what happened.'

She could tell by the subtle micro-expressions that she'd had training in that he was lying. But aside from strapping him to a lie detector, she had no solid proof of his deception. She scribbled his response to her question down on paper.

'What time did you leave the house this morning?' she pushed.

'The same time I do every morning, seven a.m.,' he answered.

Again, she jotted down his response. 'And where was Miss Hadaway when you left the house?'

'She was in the bathroom,' he countered, as if he'd been rehearsing a story in the event she died as a result of his actions.

'Did you two speak?'

'Yes, of course we did. We live together; it'd be strange if we didn't.'

'Did you argue?'

'While we've been together? Sure, what couple doesn't argue?' he asked with a shrug.

'Did you argue today?' she clarified.

His cocky attitude was starting to get on her nerves and she'd only asked him a handful of questions. She didn't know what Kaidence saw in the man sitting in front of her. She hadn't known him for long and already she wanted to strangle him.

He confidently shook his head. 'No.'

Closing her notepad, Louisa smiled. 'I'll be going to the hospital to consult with the doctors, so I could have more questions.'

'Sure. I'm happy to help.'

She could tell by his response that he was confident that the police wouldn't have enough to charge him and at this point he was right. It was all circumstantial. But once Kaidence received treatment and was well enough to be questioned, they would have the evidence they needed to prosecute. What he didn't seem to understand was that the police could press charges regardless of whether his girlfriend wanted to; they just needed to have confirmation of a crime. If they could prove he was a danger to society, they would have grounds to charge him anyway.

'Thank you for your co-operation this morning.' She turned and walked away.

She wanted to punch him hard in his self-assured mouth. He was the most infuriating man she'd ever had the displeasure of meeting and she couldn't see what Kaidence had possibly found likeable about him that warranted a second date, let alone an invitation to move in.

She exited the building and was on her way back to the car when her personal mobile started to ring. It was Jackson. 'I'm on my way now,' she said without waiting for him to speak.

'No need, I'm at the hospital. I just spoke to the doctor and he told me that she's got a cerebral oedema. They've induced a coma and moved her to the intensive care unit.'

'Is she going to be okay?'

'They're hoping the coma will stop any permanent damage to her brain, but they won't know for sure until she wakes, *if* she wakes up.'

'My God, this arsehole is going to get away with it,' she said, unlocking the car and climbing in behind the steering wheel.

'He won't.'

'If she doesn't wake up, he will.'

'We'll cross that bridge when we come to it. And if we come to it, I have a contingency plan for that. But she *is* going to wake up.'

Louisa growled down the line to vent her frustrations. 'If you could see this guy Jackson, he's so cocksure that he believes he's untouchable.'

'Good, then he won't see us coming when we drag him off to jail.'

CHAPTER NINE

Jackson walked into Kaidence's private hospital room in his uniform trousers and the T-shirt he wore under his work shirt and took a seat on the chair beside the bed where he'd spent every spare minute he could. He'd got off duty half an hour ago and, apart from stopping off for a burger, had gone straight to visit her so he hadn't had a chance to change. He didn't want to draw attention to his presence so instead of walking into the intensive care unit in full costume, he had stripped down so he was less recognisable. But all the nurses knew he was a police officer, so permitted him to visit around his shifts.

She had been in a coma for two days and Mitchell hadn't visited once despite knowing exactly where his girlfriend was. Jackson knew that was a silent admission of guilt and that he was hoping she wouldn't wake up. Jackson had driven past her place on his way home from work for a shower every morning and seen her abuser leaving the house where he'd left her to die. Her lodger had the best of things now; he was living in her property rent free and Kaidence's injuries were severe enough that she might not remember the assault even when she was brought out of her coma.

The doctors had summarised that based on the severity of the swelling, Kaidence had been lying on the tiles where she'd been found for longer than Mitchell's initial statement had indicated, so Jackson had accompanied his partner for follow-up questioning at the house he now occupied alone, and he'd been just as vague and self-confident as in his first interview. It made

Jackson just as angry as it had made Louisa, especially given the free ride he was taking advantage of.

Mitchell knew he had left Kaidence lying at the bottom of the stairs all night and he knew both officers knew it too, but he also knew they had no real proof, or they would've carted him off to a cell to await trial. It was Louisa who knocked the smug smile off his face when she informed him that they could charge him with active neglect for stepping over his girlfriend's body on the way out of the door without calling for an ambulance first. But that only worked for a second before he composed himself and confidently announced that they wouldn't be able to pin anything on him. He wasn't entirely wrong. They had to have proof a crime was committed before they could act, and their only witness was unable to give them a statement. That had forced the officers to retreat with their tails between their legs, which had given them a drive to see him pay for what he'd done.

Jackson had taken it upon himself to be Kaidence's company whenever he had enough spare time to dedicate to her because he hadn't informed her sister, as much as he'd wanted to. He assumed Kaidence wouldn't want her to know given that she had kept her abuse hidden. But he was acting as her friend and if he was being professional, her kin would've been his first stop. He didn't know if he was doing the right thing or not. He just had to pray she opened her eyes, so he wouldn't have to make a death notification and explain why Meredith hadn't been informed of her sister's accident.

The room was quiet as he sat there in the low light beaming in through the window from the street. He could see her clearly and she looked fragile lying in the hospital bed. It was something he'd never noticed before. Even though she weighed no more than nine stone and he'd seen her covered in cuts and bruises, it wasn't something he considered her to be. He knew the strong, confident woman she'd once been was still inside her but seeing her like this reminded him of just how delicate she was. It proved that she hadn't been as in control of the situation as she liked to think she was.

He had a sudden urge to talk to her, because he missed her, and he'd heard that coma patients could sometimes still hear what was happening around them so, if it meant getting her to wake up sooner, he was going to try it.

He leaned forward and took her hand in his. 'We'll get him for this, Kaidy, you've just got to wake up first and we can put him behind bars. You won't have to walk in that house and ever feel like you can't be yourself again,' he said, gently squeezing the part of her he held on to.

Louisa reached the doorway of the private hospital room in time to hear her partner talking to the unconscious woman he spent every available minute sitting with. She'd never seen him like this about anyone, let alone someone he wasn't even dating. It unsettled her. He was usually the strong silent type, so this was a drastic change to the man she'd spent the better part of four years with. This side of him was vulnerable and he didn't show vulnerability easily. She felt sorry for him, not just because he was unable to express his undeniable feelings for her but because her situation meant he wouldn't. Knowing him like she did, Louisa knew Jackson would prefer to live in misery as Kaidence's friend rather than put her in a position to force anything she wasn't ready to give. His selfless nature was admirable, but it wasn't going to get him any closer to getting what he wanted, and it was obvious to anyone who saw them together that he wanted her. Louisa just had to find a way to give him a push when the time was right and, while Kaidence was still in a relationship with the monster she'd had the displeasure of questioning twice, it wasn't right yet.

He couldn't bring himself to release her hand. He liked feeling connected to her and this was the only way he could express it without compromising his position in her life. His thumb caressed the back of her hand, like it had at the weekend when they'd spent hours together. Her skin was soft, making him think that she had only used her hands to do the chores to please or avoid the piece of shit that had put her in the position to need urgent care.

He had spent the day at his desk writing reports and filling out paperwork while his partner had hunted down as many of Mitchell's exes as she could find to question about his behaviour during their relationships. She had given him a run-down about what she'd discovered but there wasn't anything significant to report back and without a history of abuse they couldn't pin anything on him until Kaidence told them otherwise. It wasn't enough that he'd harmed her in the past, because she had chosen not to press charges, this time she didn't have a choice.

'How long have you been here?' Louisa asked softly, not wanting to surprise him as she walked into the room.

He released his hold on Kaidence's hand like he was guilty of something. 'Not long. I barely managed to shirk off my uniform.'

'Jackson, I think you can take your time to go home, shower and change,' she pointed out compassionately.

'I know, but I can't stand to see her like this so the more time I spend here maybe somehow she'll know, and it'll make her wake up.'

'I want her to wake up too.' She was sympathetic, but she wanted to lift the mood. 'But you really need a shower.'

When a smile appeared on his face, she knew her attempt at humour had worked. It was something he needed. He'd been downhearted since he'd seen Kaidence lying at the bottom of the stairs and she knew it was because he was scared. He had convinced himself that he was getting through to her and it wasn't going to be long before she walked away from her boyfriend. This incident gave him a reality check because it made him realise that every day she was more at risk than the day before.

Silence lingered in the room; both officers felt the weight of the situation they were dealing with and neither of them had any words of positivity to elevate their frame of mind. Until they had a witness, they were simply waiting to be able to proceed, and she was in no state to help.

'I need her to wake up from this Lou,' Jackson said, breaking the silence in the room.

'We both want that Jax,' she responded compassionately.

'But I... I...' He couldn't get the words out.

'I know how you feel about her.'

'No, you don't,' he sighed.

'No?' she asked, taking a seat in the chair beside him and crossing her arms across her chest as she relaxed back. 'Do you think I don't recognise when you're falling in love with someone?'

He was about to counter when it sunk in what she'd said. His eyes shot up to meet hers. 'How did you know?'

'Jackson, I can count on one hand how many times I've seen you like this about anyone. It's once and it's right now. Even with the three women you've dated over the years, I've never seen you like this, which is precisely how I know how you feel because as much as they wanted it, or you tried to kid yourself, you were never in love with any of them.'

He exhaled in relief. 'I don't know how it happened.'

'It happened because you weren't looking and from what I can tell, dick boyfriend aside, she's a great woman.'

'But it's unprofessional. I shouldn't be falling in love with someone I met because of my job.'

'Well first of all, you met her while you were working but technically, we didn't deal with her in an official capacity until two days ago. So, you can stop feeling guilty about something that isn't even an issue. And secondly, you can't control who you fall in love with otherwise I wouldn't have married my high school sweetheart before I met Scott.'

'Neither of which excuse my behaviour.'

'My God, Jackson, it's not like you're sleeping with her. She doesn't even know how you feel.'

'Are you sure? Because you knew.'

'The difference is I've known you for years. She doesn't know you well enough yet. But I've seen you two together and if she wasn't dating already, you'd be the perfect fit. And if she knew, she wouldn't be trying, like you, to maintain a professional distance when all she really wants to do is start living the rest of your lives together.'

He frowned. 'You think that she feels the same way?'

'Of course she does, you're her knight.'

He exhaled as he leaned back in his chair. 'That's what I was afraid of.'

It was Louisa's turn to frown. 'How do you make that negative?'

'Because what if it's not love and it's just white knight syndrome?'

'And what if your feelings are just Florence Nightingale syndrome?' she countered. 'The only way you're going to know is by giving it time after this Mitchell thing is over and seeing where it leads.'

'I know my feelings are real. She is my first thought when I open my eyes in the morning and she's my last thought before I sleep at night. I can barely contain the urge I feel right now to shake her until she wakes up because I miss her that much. It kills me that she's with Mitchell and that arsehole treats her the way he does but I can't tell her how I feel because she's not ready to hear it, emotionally or mentally, and even when I do get her away from this piece of shit, she still won't be ready. He's seen to that with the life he's sucked out of her and how he's made her live this last year. The chances are that she probably won't ever be over the trauma of this relationship and I might only ever have her friendship, when all I want to do is spend forever with this woman,' he vented.

'Whoa Jackson, you need to slow down. Let's get over this hurdle first, then we can get her away from the man destroying her and we'll see where the chips fall, because I've got a feeling that she's not as broken as you think she is. She's still the woman she used to be and over this last month she's found some strength from the contact she has with you, so I don't think it'll take too much time for her to bounce back once she's free of Mitchell.'

'What did his exes have to say for themselves?'

She sighed, defeated. 'They all say he had a short fuse and that he started arguments over nothing, but he never laid a hand on any of them.'

'So, she really was the first,' he said, remembering back to their first real conversation.

'What?'

He rubbed his brow. 'She once asked me if he had a record for violence against women and when I told her he didn't, she concluded she was the first.'

'Well, I haven't managed to find his last two girlfriends so let's hold off on reaching that conclusion until I've been able to question them too.'

'If she is the first, why is she? What makes her so different to his past conquests that he thinks it's okay to treat her like this?'

'You'd have to ask him.'

'He'll never admit to that because he's arrogant enough to believe he's doing nothing wrong.'

'True, but if I had to guess I'd say it's because she hasn't got much family to tell her he's no good for her.'

'Yes well, now she has us.'

'And that's why every day she gets a step closer to leaving him. You're showing her that she doesn't have to live like this.'

'Except she's lying here in a coma because of something he did, and we can't do a damn thing about it.'

'He'll get his. Like you said – if he thinks he can't be caught he's not going to see us coming when we are able to do something.'

'And what if she dies, Louisa?'

'You told me you have a contingency plan for that.'

'I do, but it won't matter because she'll already be dead and the whole reason I got involved with her in the first place will have been for nothing,' he shouted in frustration.

She shifted forward in her seat and reached for his hand. 'Then you have to hold on to that conviction you showed two days ago when you told me she was going to wake up, because if you don't keep coming here and showing her she's worth something to you, she will stop fighting to stay alive.'

'I'm not even sure she knows I'm here,' he said in a whisper.

'I'm sure she knows,' she said, with a gentle squeeze of his hand before letting go. 'And knowing what I know about that woman, I'm sure she's fighting hard to open those eyes of hers.'

Kaidence walked through the front door of her childhood home and was immediately met with the image of her parents in the kitchen making break-fast. It felt real, although she knew it wasn't. It was a memory, but she smiled anyway. It was great to see their faces after years of living without them and even though she was only a teenager around this time, she watched it play out.

Her father was smiling as he spun her mother around to face him and pulled her in for a kiss. It happened every morning much to her and her sister's disgust. Seeing their affection for one another was something that made their children uncomfortable while they were growing up, but now it settled Kaidence.

It occurred to her then how loving they were and that she should have used their example as a standard to aspire to, instead of forgetting that she was worthy of the same kind of love, and the fact she'd settled for anything less was underestimating her worth.

That's when her seventeen-year-old sister walked into the room behind her, expressing her aversion to the display of affection their parents were engaged in.

'You don't understand this yet Meredith, but when you're married, if you are lucky enough to still be as in love as we are after twenty years, you'll be happy to revolt your kids by kissing your husband,' their mother told her.

'It's still gross,' she countered.

That's when she was transported to another memory.

Twenty-year-old Kaidence stood in the doorway of her parents' bedroom watching her mum get ready for her anniversary date with her dad. She smiled as she leaned against the doorframe. 'You're so beautiful,' she whispered, just loud enough for the woman to hear.

Her mother's eyes connected with hers through the mirror. 'I'm old,' she said, deflecting the compliment as she stood up and walked towards her.

'You don't look a day over thirty.'

'That's because I'm lucky enough to have a good life. Your father has seen to that.' Her feelings for the man she married were evident on her face as she spoke about him and it made her youngest daughter smile.

'I hope I marry my best friend one day.'

'Never settle for less than you deserve, sweetheart, because you are worthy of being treated like a queen by the man you love, the same way your father treats me.'

With a blink that memory disappeared like the one before it and another gathered formation in its place. She could see the officer stood in front of her clearly, as if it had only been yesterday that, hung over, she had stumbled out of bed to answer the doorbell of her shitty apartment. The officer standing there asked her name, and her reply confirmed to him that he'd found the person he was looking for.

Somehow, once the words *I'm sorry* fell out of his mouth she knew what he was there to tell her, and her legs buckled beneath her. The wind had been knocked out of her and she struggled to breathe as she began to sob. It was impossible to imagine them being gone. They hadn't even had the chance to witness any real milestones in her life and she had to find a way to pick herself up off the floor.

Her boyfriend at the time had been the rock she needed to pull herself together enough to function until eventually the pain subsided making it easier to remember them with a smile instead of tears, but she had a few months of drunken debauchery before she was forced to come to her senses. She'd been prepared to drink herself into oblivion until her sister talked her into making their parents proud instead of ashamed, and that had forced her to evaluate her life. So she finished her schooling and became a teacher like she'd always wanted to be. But in her drive to succeed she'd lost the man she thought she loved when he started sleeping with another woman.

The room returned to silence after Jackson had opened up to his partner. He had no idea what had instigated it, he had just needed to tell someone to get it off his chest and out of his head. He hadn't really wanted advice, just a sounding board, but she'd contributed anyway because she was more than just his colleague. They were family, just a different kind of family, and he knew she wanted the best for him.

He looked over at Kaidence in the bed she'd been occupying for too long and his breath caught in his throat when he saw her tears. He jumped up, startling Louisa in the process, and grabbed her hand.

'Kaidence, can you hear me?' he asked, forcing the woman sitting with him to shift to stand beside him.

'What happened?' Louisa asked.

He pointed to her face. 'She's crying.'

'Oh my God, she heard us.'

'Did she?'

'We were talking about her so maybe.'

'I should tell the nurse,' he said, rushing to the door.

'Jackson, she's still asleep.'

'But she could be about to wake up,' he said, darting out of sight.

Kaidence could hear the pull of Jackson's voice as she stood at the cooker in her kitchen. She spun to face the sound to find him sitting at the dining table looking back at her and wearing a smile, and she took a step closer to him. But with every step he moved further away. She started to run but still the distance between them got no shorter. Then suddenly she was in his arms, except he wasn't Jackson any more. His face morphed before her eyes into Mitchell's.

She jumped backwards, and she was thrust back to her spot by the cooker. She stood and watched as his rage built, making him red in the face. He was like an old whistle kettle and he was ready to blow. But as she braced for the impact of the explosion, she felt his hands around her throat getting tighter and tighter until she couldn't breathe. She gasped for air to fill her lungs, but she could feel her windpipe being crushed as he squeezed the life out of her.

Louisa was still staring at Kaidence when the machines she was hooked up to started to screech to indicate a problem. She rushed to the open door of the room and screamed for help. But they had alerts on the screens at the nurses' station and were already running in her direction. The four nurses and one doctor almost knocked her onto her arse in their haste to attend to their patient, but she managed to steady herself with the help of the wall behind her in time for Jackson's reappearance.

'What happened?' he asked with horror written across his features.

'I don't know,' she replied. 'I was standing with her and next thing I know she flatlined.'

'Did you touch any of the wires?' he asked, fearful that he was losing her.

'I didn't touch anything,' she shouted to match his volume.

With his heart in his mouth, Jackson watched as the medical staff did chest compressions and assisted Kaidence's breathing using a manual resuscitator after unhooking the ventilator that had been helping her breathe since she'd been admitted. It was horrifying to witness her life dangling in the balance and being powerless to do anything about it.

The chaos seemed to take forever to die down and when it did, he was relieved to hear the rhythmic beep of the machine monitoring her heartbeat.

Jackson took the opportunity of having the doctor in the room to get some information as the nurses filed out. 'What just happened?'

'Are you family?'

'We're the officers investigating how she ended up here,' Louisa explained. 'She has no family.'

The doctor took a second to consider whether he should waive patient confidentiality to divulge any information about her diagnosis. 'The swelling on her brain seems to be subsiding but she's not ready to come off the ventilator yet or be brought out of her coma.'

'But why did she flatline?' Jackson asked.

'It could be any number of reasons; unfortunately, we can't know for sure.'

'She was crying five minutes before her heart stopped.'

The doctor slowly shook his head from side to side. 'I'm sorry, but that could simply be because she's dreaming,' he clarified.

'What if it stops again?'

'Then we'll do what we can to start it again.'

'Is she showing any signs of improvement?'

He nodded. 'We did some scans earlier today and at the rate the swelling is shrinking we'll be looking to bring her out of the coma in a few days.'

'Will there be any long-term damage?'

'I'm afraid we can't know that until she's awake. It's possible the swelling has affected her mobility or her memory. But there really is no way to tell yet.'

Louisa nodded. 'Thank you doctor.'

Jackson moved back to the side of the bed as the doctor left the room, and exhaled as he exhaustedly lowered himself down to the chair he'd been sitting in before he'd noticed her emotions. He took a second and then wiped a hand down his face to try and shake some of the worry etched there.

'I thought that was it,' he admitted. 'I was sure she was going to die.'

'She's stronger than you think she is.'

He placed his hand over hers on the bed. 'I need you to come back to me Kaidence,' he pleaded, not caring that Louisa was witnessing his vulnerability.

His partner moved across the room to his position and placed a reassuring hand on his shoulder. 'If there's any reason for her to fight to get back, it's you.'

'I want to believe that. But what if she doesn't remember her accident? How am I supposed to help her leave this guy?'

'She might not retain the information of this accident, Jackson, but this isn't the first time he's hit her. Their whole history won't be wiped out by this incident, so if she doesn't remember then we'll have to figure out another way to get her out.'

'We're running out of opportunities to help her get out. In case you haven't noticed she's lying here close to dying already. If she does wake up and she goes home with him, how long do you think we have until he kills her?'

'You keep going to worst-case scenario right away. Don't have us doomed to fail before we really take a run at this. You have to believe that it'll work out.'

'I've got to prepare myself for if it doesn't. I won't make it through losing someone else, *especially* if it's her.'

CHAPTER TEN

Friday came around in what seemed like the blink of an eye. It was Jackson's first day off in five and he planned to spend it at Kaidence's bedside. He'd continued to spend the time that he wasn't at work at the hospital because he wanted his face to be the first she saw if she woke up.

According to the doctor, the swelling had all but disappeared, so they were going to take her off the ventilator and attempt to bring her out of the coma they'd induced by the end of the weekend. The nurses had confided in him that there was a chance that she could wake up sooner depending on how quickly her metabolism processed the remaining drugs in her system, so he sat in her room talking to her hoping that his voice would stir something in her. But it was two days after they'd had to restart her heart and he was still waiting for her to open her eyes.

He'd barely managed to leave her side in case the unthinkable happened, so he knew that Mitchell hadn't got enough of a conscience to visit in a bid to keep up appearances. He was sure that the man was lapping up living in her house like it was his own and hadn't given her or his actions a second thought. It took all his control not to march up to Kaidence's front door and beat Mitchell up a little before putting him in handcuffs, but he knew that without proof his integrity would be called into question, and he needed to follow protocol in order to get the maximum penalty on his conviction so that she would finally be free of him.

Walking up the corridor, he saw a nurse he'd become familiar with during his visits appear from Kaidence's room up ahead and registered that she looked worried. His heart jumped into his mouth as his pace quickened. *Please don't be dead*, he repeated over and over in his head as panic pounded in his chest.

Spotting him, the nurse began to make her way in his direction in a bid to cut him off. 'Officer Chase.'

'Is everything okay?' he asked, his concern evident in his question.

'She woke up about an hour ago.' She responded as if she was delivering bad news.

'That's a good thing, isn't it?' he asked, trying to get around her.

But she pulled him to one side. 'She seems to be suffering with retrograde amnesia.'

He stopped moving and frowned. 'What is that?'

'It means she lacks the memory of events preceding her head injury.'

He couldn't help showing the disappointment he felt. 'Could they come back?'

'It's possible. But there is no way to know how long it'll be before that happens.'

He sighed. 'Can I see her?'

'Of course, but keep it short and try not to push her to remember – it could influence her memories. This needs to come back to her naturally.'

He nodded. 'I understand,' he confirmed, removing his mobile phone from his jeans pocket. 'I'm just going to call my partner and give her an update.'

'Then go outside or use a pay phone – that shouldn't even be on in this ward,' she gently reminded him before she went back to doing her rounds.

'Thank you, Katherine.' He expressed his gratitude with a smile.

Turning to exit the way he'd come, Jackson broke into a sprint. His mood was a little lighter than it had been when he first arrived because, even though she didn't remember the incident, at least she was awake. He was optimistic that after some recovery time, it would come back to her and then he could use the full force of the law to punish the man responsible. For now, he wanted to give Louisa the news so that he could get back to the patient.

Kaidence sat up in her hospital bed feeling disorientated. She'd been trying to force herself to recollect how she'd ended up there, but the memories were fuzzy to say the least. Rationally she knew it probably had something to do with the man she lived with, but she couldn't be certain, and it wasn't like she would tell anyone even if he was responsible, because it was her burden to endure. Although if Mitchell had gone far enough to put her in hospital, she must have really pissed him off, because he was always careful not to injure her too severely, so he didn't draw unwanted attention.

She was still trying to navigate through the fog in her mind when a man walked into her room. He was tall with dark hair and blue eyes, and addressed her by name. That was an indication that they were familiar enough with each other for them to be on first-name terms but for the life of her, she couldn't place him.

'Do I know you?' she asked.

The disappointment was evident on his face as he introduced himself, and she countered with an apologetic expression. But it wasn't until he divulged his profession that she became instantly guarded. She wanted to believe she'd made him privy to her current predicament, but she couldn't imagine a world where that was true because that would mean she trusted someone who wasn't herself. She'd made it this far alone, so why would she jeopardise her safety? Maybe that's how she'd come to be admitted to hospital; because she had told the police and Mitchell had found out. Maybe he meant to kill her, and he just hadn't been efficient enough. Regardless, she wouldn't be telling the officer anything else; she needed to think of self-preservation.

'You don't remember me at all?' Jackson asked cautiously, edging forward.

'No sir.' She responded in such a formal way that he knew she wasn't just playing a role to avoid suspicion.

He offered context to their meeting. 'We met about five weeks ago. I knocked on your door after a burglary in your area and I saw bruises on your face.'

As much as Kaidence wanted to believe him, the idea of it didn't sound like something she'd do because of Mitchell's rule about opening the door when he wasn't home. She was about to protest when he broke the silence to enforce his story.

'I came back a few days later to make sure my visit hadn't meant you were disciplined again, and you told me about the journal you keep in the office safe with the photos you've taken since he moved in with you ten months ago.'

He was accurate with his facts, which made her question if she'd been stupid enough to have actually done the things he was suggesting.

He offered more. 'We're friends, have been for almost as long as we've known each other.'

She shook her head slightly. 'I'm sorry but I don't remember.'

'It's okay, I'm sure it'll come back to you and when it does, we can just pick up where we left off,' he said, not wanting to add the pressure of forcing his memories on her, as the nurse had warned him. 'Do you remember anything about Sunday night? Even the slightest detail might help.'

As she searched her mind for a sliver of reminiscence, the haze unsettled her equilibrium and she slumped down in her bed, so she could rest her head on the pillow. She had only been awake for ninety minutes and she was already exhausted from overworking her brain searching for a thread of something recognisable.

'Apologies if I'm bombarding you with information, I just need something – anything – to use against Mitchell in order to get you away from him.' Jackson relinquished the seat he'd made his own since Monday.

'It's okay. It's just a lot to take in especially when none of it sounds like me.'

'I think you opened the door to me that day because you saw a chance to alert someone to your situation without having to initiate contact yourself.'

'I'm sure if that was true, I'd remember.'

'The nurse says it's some form of amnesia.'

'Did I hit my head?'

'We think so. Louisa found you at the bottom of the staircase so it's likely you fell from the first floor.'

'I probably tripped; I can be quite the klutz,' she offered as an explanation.

'And I'd like to believe that, but I've seen the pictures of what he's done to you. Pushing you down a flight of stairs would be nothing in comparison.'

She knew he was right. But she still didn't know if she could trust him. What if he was a friend of Mitchell's whom she hadn't met, and he was testing her to find out how much she was willing to divulge? But then how would he know about her journal? Mitchell wasn't privy to that information and he couldn't have even stumbled on it by accident because no one knew the combination to that safe but her; she hadn't even written it down. The questions kept coming and she had no answers to any of them.

Her eyes fluttered closed. 'I can't...'

Jackson got to his feet. 'I'm going to leave you to rest for a while but if it's all right with you I'd like to come back later.'

She managed to open her eyes for long enough to give him a silent nod before drifting off to sleep.

He couldn't help watching as the uncomfortable expression on her face relaxed as she stopped fighting her fatigue. She looked so peaceful suddenly, and he found himself just standing there. He was relieved she'd woken up because he could carry on fighting with her to get the life she deserved, once her memories returned – *if* they did.

That's when it dawned on him that if she never remembered him, he had no idea how to proceed. He'd have to start from scratch getting her to trust him, just when they'd got a really good rapport going. By now it was more than him helping a woman he felt deserved better; she was at the very least his friend and he valued that, so having to begin the process again was a bitter pill to swallow. He had to confer with Louisa to work out their next move.

He slowly backed out of her room, feeling less optimistic than when he'd walked in. It was one thing for her not to remember the accident that had put her in that bed fighting for her life, it was another for her to have lost all knowledge of him and the trust they'd built up. It was infuriating. It wasn't as if he could show her proof of their contact because there was none. Every conversation they'd ever had was either in person or on the phone, and he couldn't get her phone bill without a warrant. His word wasn't enough grounds for him to go poking around in her life without something to back it up, and he had no other reason than to prove to her that he was being truthful about them knowing each other, which wasn't enough cause for the department he worked for.

On his way across the hospital car park, Jackson pulled his phone from his pocket and speed dialled his partner. 'It's worse than I thought,' he announced as she answered. 'She doesn't remember me.'

'Maybe she'll remember me,' Louisa countered, trying to be positive.

'That's doubtful. She has no recollection of us meeting or having any discussions about getting her away from Mitchell. So, we're back to square one.'

'Well, not really; you've already established a dialogue about her abuse.'

'Except she denied it – instead she implied that she was clumsy, and her injuries were probably because of falling down the stairs, not being pushed.'

'That's because she doesn't know if she can trust you yet. She's acting on her instincts and covering for him like she probably did all the time before you knocked on her door. She's just being cautious. She can't just take your word that she trusts you, because that could be putting herself at risk,' she explained. 'We'll just have to give her some time and hope the memories come back; forcing them could make her withdraw and we might never get her away from him. We're going to have to be patient, as much as I know you hate to be.'

'I can be patient,' he insisted.

His claim made her burst out laughing. 'Jackson, you have many good qualities but even you can't kid yourself that patience is one of them.'

It was dark when Kaidence opened her eyes. She'd slept another day away but remembering was exhausting. For the life of her she couldn't place the officer who had insisted they knew each other and had facts to back it up. But surely, if they were so close, she would have a vague recollection of him? She couldn't have just lost five weeks of her life with a simple bump on the head.

The questions continued to pile up and she didn't have a shovel to dig her way through them. She even had a feeling that the doctors wouldn't be able to give her answers regarding getting her memory back, because she suspected that recovery time depended on the patient. The only way she could think to try and prove whether the officer was being truthful was to check her journal for a corresponding attack the night before he said they met or better still, to see if she had mentioned him at all. That would go a long way towards her believing all the things he'd claimed.

She forced her body upright in bed. She felt restless, like she had energy to burn and she decided instantly to try moving about the room. Throwing the blankets back she attempted to stand but she was weak, and her legs were like jelly, so when she hoisted herself off the bed, they buckled beneath her weight, sending her plummeting to the floor. She landed with a loud smack as she took the brunt of the fall on her hands and forearms.

She was still lying on the cold laminated floor minutes later, considering how she was going to pull herself up onto the chair without any help from her legs, when she heard an enquiring voice in the room.

'Down here,' she signalled, raising her arm in the air to flag down her visitor.

'What are you doing down there?' he asked, coming into view.

She cursed her unfortunate timing as the handsome officer who had introduced himself to her that morning used his strong frame to lift her into his arms and place her back on the bed.

'I wanted to walk around for a bit,' she said, feeling embarrassed. 'It turns out my legs didn't get the memo.'

'You've been lying down for the best part of five days, you've got to take it slow.' Jackson took a seat in the chair by her bedside.

'It's a bit late for that warning.'

'Why didn't you call for a nurse to help you?'

'I'm not an invalid.'

'You need to work on getting your strength back before you go on any explorations.'

'Thanks Officer Obvious.'

'What if you'd have hit your head?'

'I didn't.'

'You couldn't have known you weren't going to.'

'I'm weak in the legs not stupid in the head.'

'Well, if you want to have a walk around, I can help you.'

'I don't want to go far; I just want to get the blood circulating again.'

He stood and shifted to the head of the bed as she swung her legs over the side. Jackson put his arm around her back and slipped his hand under her arm to take her weight as she pushed herself off the mattress. Instinctively he held her other arm in his hand so that he could be a firm support if her legs buckled again. He could feel her shaking as she planted both feet on the floor and shuffled to take a step.

'How can I be going stir-crazy already? I've only been awake a day.'

'From what I know about you, you hate being cooped up even though you have to sometimes while you're recovering from your injuries.'

'It's one thing to be confined to the house; it's another to be forced into one room in the hospital.' Then another thought occurred to her. 'Does my sister know I'm here?'

'I didn't think you'd want her to know because then she'd have a ton of questions.'

His response made her smile. 'It sure sounds like you know me pretty well despite me having absolutely no memory of you.'

'I'm a lot of things, Kaidence, but I'm not a liar,' he stated. 'Although I'm not sure how I'd have explained not telling her if anything had happened to you.'

'I fell down some stairs – it wasn't life-threatening.'

He stopped moving. 'Kaidence, your heart stopped two days ago.'

Her breath caught in her throat. 'What?'

'I was visiting you, like every night since you were admitted, and you flatlined right after I noticed you were crying.'

She took a minute to process the information he'd given her, her mouth open. 'Isn't there some kind of law that says they can't keep that from me?'

He shook his head. 'I don't think that's included in the Hippocratic Oath. They most likely haven't got around to it yet.'

'Well now they don't need to,' she said, taking another uncertain step forward.

Jackson moved with her. He had probably been wrong to tell her, but he needed her to realise the severity of her situation, and the fact was that she'd been closer to death than she imagined. He knew deep down he was trying to push her into a decision about Mitchell without influencing the memories she had forgotten, because he knew she remembered being abused; no bang on the head was hard enough to wipe out the previous eleven months.

They were a little further through the corridor when she felt strong enough on her legs to release her hold on him and stay upright. He gingerly removed his support and made sure she was steady before he relaxed. He shadowed her movement to the end of the corridor and noticed she was beginning to tire. He had to react quickly to stop her from falling into the wall.

'All right, I think that's enough exercise for today,' he said, giving her the support of his strength again. 'Let's get you back to bed.'

Holding onto him as he spun her in the direction they needed to move in, she laughed. 'That is one hell of a proposition, Officer Chase, but I don't think I know you well enough yet.'

He allowed a chuckle to escape his lips. 'At least you haven't lost your sense of humour.'

'I don't even think a lobotomy would accomplish that.'

He almost had to carry her back, but he didn't mind because it was an exercise in trust. It wasn't until they got back to her private quarters that they realised they had company in the form of his partner.

'Louisa.' Jackson uttered her name as he helped the patient back to bed. 'Kaidence, this is my partner.'

The patient got comfortable on the mattress and covered herself with the crisp white sheets that lay beneath a pale blue hospital blanket. 'You found me.'

'You remember?' Louisa asked, getting to her feet.

'Actually, Officer Chase told me,' Kaidence explained. 'It seems my memory isn't what it used to be.'

'I'm sure it'll come back to you.'

'I hope so, because it feels like I'm missing an important chunk of my life where I made life-changing decisions, and it's weird that it also includes any knowledge I had of you two.'

'Maybe we should spend some time together – it might help.'

'Well my schedule is clear for the rest of the day so if you're not busy, there's no time like the present.'

Louisa checked her watch. 'I've got two hours before I've got to pick up the kids from their dad's, so I've got time.'

'I probably have this information somewhere in my head but I'm going to ask anyway; how old are they?'

'Alicia is five and Juliette is eight,' she said with a smile. 'My eldest is actually in your class at school.'

Jackson smiled. 'All right, I'm going to leave you two to catch up while I do some errands I've spent all week avoiding. I'll come back tomorrow to check on you.'

'Okay, thank you Officer,' Kaidence countered. She was thankful for the company because there was nothing worse than being in hospital alone, even if they were strangers. But she was glad her sister was none the wiser; she could do without having to explain why she had officers visiting her and why they were so set on blaming her boyfriend for her supposed accident. Her life was complicated enough without having to describe the reality of her relationship and why she had kept it hidden for close to a year when she had had plenty of opportunities to divulge the horrific truth while they were alone. She felt guilty whenever she spent time with her sister for having such a big secret and not taking the opportunity to confide in her, but she had to deal with Mitchell her way, because she knew his threats to find her if she ever left weren't idle ones.

Jackson was halfway across the car park when he spotted Mitchell exiting his car and he couldn't resist the opportunity to approach him in order to express his feelings. Somehow it was better to have his say without Kaidence knowing about it, so that he didn't inadvertently cause her any more damage.

'So, you finally got around to visiting,' he blurted out once he was close enough that he didn't need to shout.

Mitchell frowned. 'Who are you?'

'I'm one of the officers who found your girlfriend at the bottom of the stairs on Monday.'

'Oh, of course, you're half of the duo that all but waterboarded me to get a confession for putting her in hospital,' he accused Jackson. 'Is that what you're doing here? Are you trying to get her to put me behind bars?'

'No, I'm here to check on her,' Jackson replied with as much animosity as he received. 'Where have you been all week?'

'I work for a living. I don't go around accusing people of crimes so that I can meet my arrest quota.'

'I don't just accuse people of things; I use my gut instinct and I've seen plenty of women like your girlfriend over the years. Just because she doesn't remember what put her in that hospital bed doesn't mean it wasn't you.'

'And just because you think it was me doesn't mean it was,' he retorted.

'It's pretty suspicious that she had a fall down the stairs that put her in a coma and no one's seen you here until now because she's woken up. I suspect that's because you're worried about what she'll say.'

'One of the nurses I know was keeping me updated. There was no point me being here until she was awake.'

'Lucky for you Miss Hadaway doesn't remember what happened so I can't take any action, but the minute it comes back to her I am going to be ready to slap my cuffs on you. Until then you better strap in because you're going to be seeing a lot of me. I'll be checking in with her and watching you like a hawk waiting for you to fuck up.'

'She's not going to tell you anything, because I didn't touch her.'

'No, she's scared of her own shadow. You've got so far under her skin that without even having any memory of what happened she's covering for you. According to her she's just accident prone and must've fallen, but she came down those stairs with enough force to knock her into a coma, which doesn't happen by slipping. She had to have been pushed.'

'You're speculating because you've got no proof. If you had anything, I'd be in cuffs already.'

'And when she remembers what happened and tells me you had nothing to do with it, you'll be off the hook. In the meantime, if she so much as gets a paper cut, I'm coming after you.' Jackson walked away from the man before he had a chance to reply.

Kaidence and Louisa were mid-conversation when her boyfriend walked into the room, and Kaidence's heart started to beat a little faster at the sight of him. It was like she'd been caught red-handed and she started to panic but tried not to show it.

'Mitchell.' His name passed her lips unconsciously.

'Hi baby.' He greeted her with a smile, rushing over to kiss her on the lips. He immediately turned his attention to the other woman in the room. 'And who are you?'

'This is one of the officers who found me; she just dropped by because she heard I was awake.' She shifted uncomfortably in her spot.

'I've just seen your partner,' he divulged. 'He collared me on the car park and accused me of pushing her down the stairs.'

'He did what?' Kaidence asked, outraged at the thought of what that was going to lead to when she finally left the safety of her private room.

'Apparently, his gut instinct is telling him that this is an abusive relationship and he's going to be watching me.'

Louisa got to her feet. She knew she had to try and defuse the situation so that Kaidence didn't get any backlash from her partner's inability to keep his feelings to himself.

'I'm really sorry, Mr Stevenson. It's no excuse but my partner lost a woman not so long ago because of abuse, so his emotions are running a little high at the minute,' she said, trying to portray diplomacy.

Louisa felt like she was betraying her instinct to back up Jackson, but she had to be smart because he was thinking with his heart, not his head, and they needed to be seen to be maintaining a distance if Mitchell was to believe they were nothing more than the officers who had found her. 'I'm just here to do an informal follow-up for our files,' she continued, trying to reassure him. 'I can guarantee you we're treating this as an accident.'

'Well you better get him in check because if I see him, if he as much as drives by my house, I'll put in a complaint against him for accusing me of a crime I didn't commit.'

Kaidence listened to the threat he issued and knew exactly what Mitchell was doing. The officers were getting close to learning his secret and he needed to force them into maintaining their distance, so he could continue to treat her however he pleased. He couldn't risk being found out; he knew, with the police sniffing around, that his true character was going to be hard to disguise for long. She knew he'd try his best to abstain from hitting her while the eyes of the authorities were on him, but he'd only be able to fight it for so long before his natural impulses breached the surface. He had to protect his reputation; he couldn't have his image tainted when people started to learn the truth about what he got up to once his front door was closed. Jackson's threat wasn't going to be enough to save her if Mitchell wanted to kill her for putting him under the microscope.

Thinking the best course of action was to put some distance between her and the police as a show of loyalty to her relationship so that there was no blowback on her once she got home, Kaidence turned her attention to the woman who had been keeping her company. 'I want you to leave,' she told Louisa through gritted teeth, attempting to say it with conviction.

'Of course, we can finish this some other time,' Louisa replied.

But the patient shook her head. 'No, I've already told you that I have no recollection of what happened. That's it; I don't want you to come back.'

Immediately understanding Kaidence's need to show solidarity, the officer nodded. 'Thank you for helping as much as you could.'

Jackson had just walked through his parents' front door when his phone started to ring. Seeing it was Louisa made him hesitate. He wasn't sure if he wanted to answer it if he was going to get earache over confronting Mitchell, and he knew that a man who was coward enough to hit his girlfriend was a man who was going to tell everyone he could about what had happened on the car park.

'Do you need to get that?' his mum asked, shutting the cold out.

'It's Louisa – if I don't pick up, she'll just keep trying until I do,' he replied with a sigh as he swiped the green phone icon across the screen and put the receiver to his ear. He'd barely managed to greet her before his mother had disappeared out of sight.

'Well done. Your confrontation just got me kicked out of Kaidence's hospital room,' she blurted out accusingly. 'Thanks to your inability to keep your mouth shut, we just took a huge step back.'

'We were back there anyway because she doesn't remember anything,' he clarified with a raised voice. 'I needed him to know he couldn't get away with hurting her.'

'And all you succeeded in doing was pissing him off.'

'Good, if he's angry it means I hit a nerve.'

'And who do you think he's going to take that rage out on?'

'By the time she's released he'll have lost the momentum.'

'He's threatening to lodge a complaint against you.'

'He's just blowing smoke because he's trying to avoid detection. He hasn't got a leg to stand on.'

'Of course he has, you threatened him.'

'I had to try and get him to stop hitting her and that was the only way I knew how. Besides, he needs proof of a crime just like we do, otherwise it's just his word against mine.'

'The validity of his accusation won't matter. Your reputation will be tarnished by it for the rest of your career. I know that means something to you.'

'I won't care as long as she's no longer under his thumb.'

'You say that, but this job is everything to you.'

'Then maybe it's time to put something else first.'

'She's not ready for that kind of commitment. She's determined to end things with him on her own terms.'

Francine Chase couldn't help but listen to her son on the phone. From hearing only his side of the conversation she could tell he was invested in helping someone else get out from the dangerous life they were living, even though last time he had come back to her a broken man. She didn't ever want to see him like that again, but she had raised him to be the kind of man who cared and sometimes that was to his detriment. He wore his heart on his sleeve and she was proud of that, although she wished it didn't come at the cost of his pain. She knew he was good at his job, even if he did make some cases personal, so she had to trust that this time he could keep his distance while still giving the woman the help she needed. But just in case, she planned to use his time there and her influence as his mother to encourage him to do no more than his job required in order for him to make it out the other side with as little damage as possible.

She finished up the brew she'd started upon his arrival and carried it out to where he was in the living room just in time to see him hang up his phone.

'Is everything okay son?' she asked to test if he'd share the weight on his shoulders as she put the cups on the coffee table in front of the settee he sat on.

He sighed to prepare himself for the tale he had to tell. 'I lost my temper with the boyfriend of a woman we had to admit to hospital Monday because he threw her down the stairs and put her in a coma.'

'Did she press charges?' she asked, sitting down next to him.

'No, she didn't remember the accident.' He sighed.

'So how do you know he pushed her?'

'He's abusive.'

'Do you know that for sure?'

He nodded. 'The first day I met her she had been beaten bloody. I've been trying to get her away from him ever since.'

'How long ago was that?'

'It's been about six weeks.'

'And you haven't been able to get her to leave yet?'

He shook his head. 'He's got her so scared that he'll find her if she leaves, so she wants to do it right, but I'm worried that he's going to kill her before she gets the chance.'

'Will you promise me that while you're trying to save this girl you won't lose yourself like last time?'

'This is so much more complicated than last time.' He sighed, raking a hand through his hair. 'I think I'm falling in love with her.'

She frowned. 'That's not like you.'

'She's not like any other woman I've ever met.'

'But you met her on the job. Isn't there a rule against that?'

'She wasn't part of an investigation until this week. I met her because I was knocking on doors after a burglary in her area. I saw how beat up she was, and I've felt this pull towards her ever since.'

'Are you sure that isn't just because you want to save her?'

He pushed his body from the edge of the settee to relax against the back. 'I thought that at first but she's in my head. I think about her all the time – from the minute I get up to the minute I go to sleep, and I miss her whenever I'm not with her.'

His mother stayed quiet. She knew he had more that he needed to get off his chest, so she was going to let him talk.

'You should see her, Mum, she's amazing. Even though she's in this terrible relationship right now, she still finds humour in things and her laugh is a sound unlike anything else I've ever heard. It's infectious. It makes me want to keep her laughing.' He sighed, trying to form thoughts that would make sense in words. 'She hasn't got much family, so I feel protective of her, but it's more than just professional concern; I get angry at the sight of the boyfriend who thinks it's acceptable to lay his hands on her when he's living off her good nature.' He growled under his breath. 'I want to tear his head off his shoulders for the way he treats her because every new bruise I see on her face is a step closer to her dying on my watch, and I don't think I could live through that again. I just want her to be safe.'

His mother reached out to place her hand on his forearm. 'You've got such a big heart and I love that about you, but please make sure you're not more invested in getting her away from this guy than she is, because it sounds to me like she's not sure she wants to leave.'

'No, that's not it. He's got her believing that he'll hunt her down and kill her, so she's scared. She just wants to have a plan and do it right.'

'I can understand that. I only want to make sure you don't invest so much of yourself that you can't get it back once you've got her away from this man, because it's possible that she just sees you as her way out and once that happens, she expects you'll go back to your separate lives.'

'But I don't want that.'

'Maybe not, but that might be all she's capable of.'

'And I don't expect her to fall into my arms the minute she's single, but I can't just walk away from her. I want us to at least be friends.'

'And if that's not what she wants?'

'I guess I'll have to deal with that if it comes to it.'

CHAPTER ELEVEN

Kaidence was awake to see the sunrise out of her hospital room window on Monday morning. Knowing she was being released was weighing heavy on her mind because she was worried about what awaited her at home when she was finally alone with Mitchell in an arena he was used to dominating.

They'd barely had any contact since she'd woken up in the hospital on Friday despite it being the weekend, and she suspected that he was taking advantage of having her house to himself. She knew it was likely that she'd have to clean up after him once she got back because she had never seen him so much as swill his cup out after his coffee in the morning. But at least if she was at home she wouldn't feel so alone.

She hadn't seen either of the police officers since she'd ordered Louisa out of her room two days ago, which she'd only done to protect herself and keep her boyfriend from detecting any familiarity between them. She hoped she'd have a chance to explain that to her at some point once she returned to work now that she knew her child was in her class. Though somehow Kaidence had to explain her absence to her employer while having no details of what had landed her in hospital, and hope they understood. Still, she had some experience with coming up with a plausible story for her injuries.

She disliked being isolated in a private hospital room, but she supposed it was preferable to being at home where she'd see no one; at least here she got to see her nurses and doctor. However, she had spent her weekend staring out of the window from her hospital bed because she was on strict bed rest, and having no visitors meant she couldn't request any items to occupy her boredom.

She was lost in watching people outside when she heard someone in the room behind her. She spun to face inside and saw the nurse who had been taking care of her for most of her stay. 'Good morning Katherine,' she greeted her.

'You're up early,' the nurse observed, checking over her chart. 'I bet you're excited to be going home.'

She nodded with lacklustre enthusiasm as she headed back to bed. 'I'll be glad to sleep in my own bed.'

'Have you remembered anything yet?'

Her question made Kaidence hesitate. Mitchell had told her on Friday – once they were alone – that he had a nurse keeping an eye on her, so she had to be mindful of how much information she shared, because she didn't know who his inside source was.

She shook her head. 'Still nothing as of yet.'

Technically Kaidence wasn't lying. She'd had a few flashes of memories she couldn't put into context, but it was nothing substantial enough for her to remember what had happened.

'Unfortunately, we can't tell if or when those memories will come back to you; it depends on how damaged your brain was by the fall, but we have had a patient who woke up one morning with all her memories after a whole year without them, and another simply walked through her front door and they all came flooding back.'

'Have you ever had anyone who hasn't got their memories back?'

Katherine nodded. 'A few have never got back what they lost but they find a way to live without knowing. There's no real way to know which you'll be.'

'Do you know any way to speed the process up?'

'I'm afraid not. Memories can be triggered by anything; a scent, a voice, a taste, a song or even familiar surroundings. I'm sorry I can't give you something more definitive than that. It's different for everyone and unknown territory for us.'

Silence filled the room while the nurse placed the blood pressure cuff on her bicep and secured it in place. Pressing the start button on the machine, Katherine checked her watch for the time, so she could jot the results on her chart.

'Do you know what time the doctor is doing his rounds today?' Kaidence asked, trying to make conversation as the nurse started the same routine they went through every morning.

'He just got in, so he'll probably be on the floor by nine o'clock.'

'Have you got any idea what time I'm likely to be released? I need to call Mitchell at work to fetch me.'

'Is that your police boyfriend?'

'He's not my boyfriend. The man that showed up Friday afternoon is.'

'Oh sorry, the cop was here so much while you were in your coma that I just assumed.'

'No harm done. It's an easy mistake to make under the circumstances. I think the officer just felt an obligation because he didn't think I had anybody.'

'Have you got any family?'

'I've got a sister, but the police probably couldn't make the connection between us because she's married so she's got a different surname.'

'Wouldn't your boyfriend tell her?'

'They don't get on.'

'Would that really prevent him from telling her you were in a coma?'

'You underestimate the hatred they have for each other.' She laughed. 'We've been living together for a year and they've only met twice. I'm not even sure he knows *how* to find her.'

'Now I think about it, I don't think we have a next of kin on file for you.'

'Then it's probably a good job you were able to revive me on Wednesday.'

A slight frown presented itself on Katherine's brow, 'How do you know about that?'

'Our friendly neighbourhood policeman couldn't help but let me know just how serious my injuries were when I tried to pass it off like it was no big deal.'

'He seems to really care about you? Are you two friends?'

Despite the officer telling her otherwise, she could answer with honesty because she didn't remember knowing him. 'No. But he found me so maybe that's why he kept visiting,' she answered, keeping in mind that she could be reporting back to Mitchell.

'Well we didn't know you had a boyfriend until he showed up five days after you were admitted.'

'He probably saw no point in being here when I wouldn't have known, so he went to work to try and distract from feeling helpless.'

'Some people still find comfort in talking to their loved ones while they're in a coma; it makes them feel like they're keeping them connected to the world.'

'Mitchell isn't spiritual.'

'Neither are half the people that come in here, but that changes pretty quick. It just makes them feel like they're helping.'

'He channels his emotions into his work.'

The nurse shrugged. 'Some people do that too.'

'So, if you had to guess?' The patient revised her original question. 'What time do you think I'll be released?'

'I shouldn't think it'd be before lunchtime,' the nurse said, turning off the machine and removing the cuff from her arm. 'But you'll have a chance to call whoever you need to after he's been round and given you the once-over.'

'Thank you,' Kaidence said, watching her exit the room.

Then she was alone again. Her eyes instinctively moved in the direction of the window to the world. She could barely see anything beyond it, but she could imagine people going about their day without drawing attention to the issues in their own lives, because she'd done that herself. None of her colleagues knew what was happening in her home life because she hid it so well, even though sometimes she wished one of them had seen through her poor excuses and come to her rescue.

She'd barely got used to the silence before she could sense that someone else had entered the room. Turning her head, she saw Jackson gingerly step further into the room with his hands up in an act of submission.

'I come in peace,' he surrendered.

'You shouldn't be here, Officer Chase. If Mitchell finds out...'

'I won't be here long,' he assured her. 'Are you being discharged today?'

She considered answering his question, but she had something she needed to get off her chest. 'Why did you have to confront him the other day? Why couldn't you just leave it alone?'

'Because I've been waiting to confront that piece of shit since the first day I laid eyes on you and saw the bruises he had inflicted.'

'I wish I knew that, but I don't remember you, and all your macho head-to-head accomplished was to piss him off.'

He nodded. 'Louisa gave me the heads-up.'

'You knew, and you still came? What if he was here?'

'Then I would have walked right by and he would've been none the wiser.'

'He said that a nurse was keeping an eye on me. What if she sees you and reports back to him?'

He pulled a face that portrayed doubt. 'He hasn't got anyone reporting anything to him. Louisa overheard a couple of the mothers talking in the playground; she's a nurse here and her husband works with Mitchell. She probably mentioned in passing that the coma patient woke up without realising her other half knew him, and he acted like a go-between, relaying the message to Mitchell. He lied to you to make you think you were being watched.'

She raised her eyebrows. 'Then it worked; I've been second-guessing the nurses all day.'

'That was his way of controlling what secrets you told people when he couldn't be around to make sure you weren't divulging details that could taint the perfect image he likes to portray.'

She rested her head back against the pillow she was propped up with. 'Why are you here?'

'I came to see if any of your memories had returned, but based on the fact that you addressed me formally when I walked in, I'm guessing they haven't.'

She shook her head. 'No, there are still months of my life that are missing.'

He sighed. 'So Mitchell's visit didn't bring them all back?'

Again, she shook her head. 'Not even a little bit.' Suddenly she sat upright. 'Wait, how do you know the nurse's husband works with Mitchell if she didn't know?'

'Louisa heard her talking with one of the other mothers about where her husband worked, and she recognised her from the ward. He has no friends that you don't know about because no one else would put up with his bullshit.'

She sighed. 'You obviously don't know about Dale, John and Alan.'

'He has *three* friends?' he asked, perplexed.

'Yep, and they're bigger arseholes than him.'

'I guess that makes sense; the only friends he'd have are ones that would be.'

'Well at least he has some. I haven't seen any of mine since he drove them away.'

'You've got friends.' He tried to argue when he knew better. But she seemed to lose her temper in an instant and her voice was raised when she spoke. 'Then where are they? I'm here; have been for a week and the only people I've seen are nurses and coppers.'

It was the first time Jackson had seen her angry and he suspected it had more to do with being cooped up in a hospital room alone for days than anything he'd said. 'Hey, I'm sure they'd be here if they could.'

But she shook her head wearily and her voice regained normality. 'No they wouldn't. I made the mistake of driving them away a long time ago.' She sighed. 'I'm sorry, I'm just frustrated.'

'I get it, you've been in this room staring at the same four walls all weekend; you're pissed off. But you're bound to get out of here, soon right?'

Her eyes dropped to the bed. 'Today. I get to go back to the prison of my own making.'

He frowned. 'Hey, you didn't ask for this. You thought you were doing the right thing and helping out someone in need.'

'And look where that's got me.'

'I will get you away from him, trust me.'

'That's just it, I don't trust you. I don't know you,' she said, her frustrations edging up the volume of her voice again.

'You'll get your memories back.'

'Will I? Because every day that passes, I wonder if that's true.'

'Well if you don't, we'll start building our trust from here and eventually we'll be back where we were before you were in a coma.'

It was almost dark by the time Kaidence was on her way home. She had been dressed and packed ready to leave the hospital practically as soon as the doctor had released her, and she'd put in a call to Mitchell. But it was just like her boyfriend to make her wait until he was ready to fetch her just to remind her who was in control of the relationship. She wasn't in any hurry to return to the hell he tortured her with practically every day, but she was happy to be free of the confines of hospital life. At least at home some form of normalcy might help bring her lost memories into focus. It was annoying that they were just out of reach when she could sense them waiting to be discovered. It was like having a word on the tip of your tongue that you just can't spit out.

The car ride home was travelled in silence as she watched the scenery whizz past and tried to feel relief that she had some measure of freedom back. But she couldn't fathom what tomorrow would hold because if Mitchell had caused the injuries that led to her coma, it was only going to be a matter of time before he reminded her of the reason why, and she wasn't sure she'd survive another battle so soon after her head trauma.

Climbing out of the car once it had stopped on the drive, Kaidence took a deep breath of fresh air to fill her lungs with before she was forced back inside the house. She reached into the back seat to collect the bag Jackson had put together for her and followed Mitchell to the front door. But even in the dimming daylight she could see the damage.

She frowned. 'What happened to the door?'

'The police had to break it down,' he said with a tinge of accusation as he opened it with a key. 'It's secure but you might want to get a new one.'

As she stepped up to assess the harm done by the police entry, she got a waft of the stench coming from inside and it turned her stomach. It smelled like a bachelor pad, so she was expecting the mess she found when she got beyond the threshold. She didn't recall it looking that bad even before he lived there, and she wasn't quite the clean freak she'd turned into. The tiled floor was dirty from a week of trampling in the outside because working out how to use the steam mop was beyond his capabilities, the kitchen bin was over-flowing with takeaway containers and the sink was piled high with crockery because he didn't know how to use the dishwasher. She knew it was more likely that he considered the chores to be tasks that were below him. Or he had just got used to her cleaning up after him. She was aware that the shock on her face was evident when he broke the silence in the room.

'I thought you'd need something to do this week while you were *recovering*,' he said, using air quotes for the last word of his sentence before he retrieved a bottle of beer from the fridge and disappeared from view.

She knew he'd retired to the living room because regardless of her being in hospital an hour ago, it was just an ordinary night for him. With a sigh, Kaidence made her way upstairs to shower and change. She needed a good shower in order to feel human enough to deal with the mess her house was in and she wasn't about to attempt cleaning it before she'd had a full night's sleep. She was sure she wouldn't be expected to cook because Mitchell had been finishing off a portion of chips from the local fish shop when he pulled up at the hospital entrance and she'd had a sandwich in the cafeteria during her wait for freedom, so she wasn't hungry.

The old familiar feeling of fear crept up on her as she started to get undressed. Just knowing Mitchell was downstairs and could choose to invade her space at any time put her on edge. At least in hospital she had been afforded the luxury of relaxing, even if it had only been for the weekend. Now she was back to checking over her shoulder and that would only hinder her recovery, if she was given the chance to. She tried to push the thought of Mitchell's temper out of her mind as she stripped down to her birthday suit and turned on the shower before climbing beneath it. She allowed her shoulders to relax a little as the water cascaded over her head and down her body. She was at home, and that was all that mattered right now.

―――――――

The next morning when Kaidence woke up, she was alone in bed. She had climbed under her duvet after cleansing herself of the hospital smell and hadn't felt him get in beside her. She had been so exhausted she had barely stirred all night. It wasn't until she checked the clock that she realised the day was well under way and Mitchell had left for work hours ago. Throwing the blanket off her body, she headed over to the doors to the small balcony that overlooked the back garden and opened them to stare out. It was nice to see that view again even if the bright summer colours had faded into autumn.

Standing there taking in all the fresh air her lungs could manage, she allowed her mind to wander without steering it in any way, hoping that somehow it would lead to a memory she desperately wanted back. But all she got were flashes of pictures she didn't recognise.

She took another few minutes of breathing in the crisp air before she closed the doors and got dressed. She didn't put on anything glamorous, just slouch trousers and a T-shirt because she didn't need to put on good clothes if she was just going to be cleaning the house, and that's exactly how she was about to spend her morning. She ventured downstairs and headed straight to the kitchen; she needed a cup of tea for motivation before she attempted to make her house resemble a home.

It was hours later by the time the kitchen looked like one, and she could finally put her feet up. Making her way to the study, Kaidence headed to the safe in order to corroborate Jackson's claims with her abuse journal. If there had been an incident on the second Sunday of September, she could be sure that the stories he had filled her head with were true. But when she opened the secure door, she found two books where she expected to find one. She removed both of them and sat in the chair behind the desk. Taking a deep breath, she opened one and the date on the first page was from September the twelfth; the day she'd met Jackson.

A policeman knocked on my door today. There had been a break-in on the street, and he wanted to know if I'd seen anything. I told him I hadn't.

He didn't seem to react to the cuts and bruises on my face at first, like they were normal. But when he did draw attention to them, he seemed to feel an instant need to save me. He's a police officer; saving people is probably in his DNA. But I know Mitchell would find and kill me if I disappeared because he's got it too good living with me.

The policeman couldn't believe I was willing to stay. I guess it is unconscionable to accept someone would choose to stay in this life. But I just can't go yet. I need to have a carefully laid-out foolproof plan before I take that leap. I've got to know I'll be safe once I'm out of it because I'm not ready to die yet and if I was to do it the way the officer wanted to, feet in with no real planning, I'd be dead inside a week. Nowhere would be far enough away.

He left me his card after he made his best sales pitch and told me I could contact him whenever I needed to, so at least now I have a means to get help, if I need it. But I've got a feeling today isn't going to be the last time I see him. There's just something about him that makes me sure he won't be able to just walk away.

. . .

She turned the page to read the second entry, dated the fourteenth.

Saw the officer again today. He showed up on my doorstep to check that his visit had gone undetected by Mitchell. I assured him it had but that it wasn't a good idea for him to keep coming back. The last thing I want is one of the neighbours to tell him that I've been having a strange man visiting after he's gone to work. Although I suppose at least the officer wasn't in uniform today, so no one would know it was the same man who was here two days ago.

I invited him in for a drink and I explained to him as best as I could why I'm willing to live like this for now. He doesn't understand. I didn't expect he would. But he seemed to accept my wishes as much as he was capable of. He couldn't fathom my unwillingness to involve the police either despite my two hospital visits during the last year.

I found him to be extremely invested in my situation even though today was only our second meeting. It felt like his interest ran deeper than just police protocol. In any other situation, I'd welcome his concern because he looks exactly like the men I used to date but there was a reason why those relationships didn't get off the ground – usually they loved themselves more than they loved me. I'm not sure if he's the same, he seems genuine enough, but his attention is driven by his need to save me. I'm the only person who can do that and I'm just not willing to uproot my whole life because I picked the wrong guy to shack up with.

I did find out that Mitchell hasn't got a police record. So, I'm either the first woman he's treated this way, or the others didn't file reports either. I can hardly blame them; after all I'm not willing to do it. But he has spent time in cells at the local station for fighting in pubs, so that's one strike against him.

The officer asked me if I remembered the woman I was before, and I do. I even remember a past conversation with a friend when she claimed she would never put up with any man thinking it was okay to lay his hands on her in an act of violence and she truly believed that. But I'm not that woman; I haven't been for a very long time and I won't ever be again.

She read over the entries one after the other, each one filling in pieces of the puzzle that had been lost to her. Reading the words put down on paper in her own handwriting gave credence to what Jackson had told her. Although she didn't have an emotional connection to the things she had written, she could visualise them and by the time she got to the last entry she could feel how important her connection to Jackson was.

Getting to her feet to place the journals back into her hiding place, she returned the room to the way it was before she'd entered and headed to the kitchen to find the business card she'd read about in her entries. After a short search, she found what she was looking for and picked up her mobile phone from the worktop. She hadn't had it with her at the hospital; it had been sat there all week slowly losing battery power so when she tried to turn it on, there was no life left in it. Cursing, she headed to where she kept the power lead and plugged it into the only socket she had free. Leaving it to charge while she toasted some bread for breakfast and boiled the kettle for another cup of tea, she hoped it would have enough battery life for her to connect a call to the officer who spent time by her hospital bed. She could barely contain her impatience as she ate her first meal of the day and sipped at the scalding hot drink. She checked the clock. The phone had only been charging for ten minutes, but she was sure she'd have enough power to make the call.

She rushed over to the phone and punched in the number from the card onto the touch screen dial pad without unplugging it from the charger. Hitting the speaker icon, she rested the device back on the surface and waited for the call to connect.

'Hello?' Jackson asked, not wanting to assume it was Kaidence when it could quite as easily have been her boyfriend.

'Yes Jackson, it's me,' she confirmed. 'Can you call me back on my landline? My mobile is dying.'

'Is everything all right?'

'Yes. I just wanted to talk.'

'Oh, okay. Yes sure, I'll call you right back.'

'Thanks,' she said before the line went dead. It was only a moment later when the other phone in the house started to ring, and she instantly picked up. 'Hello.'

'How are you?' he asked, unsure of the purpose of her call.

'I'm better now I'm home,' she replied. 'Are you all right to talk?'

'Yes, I'm not at work until later. You called me, so does that mean you've got your memories back?'

'Unfortunately, it doesn't. But I did find a second journal.'

'Is it another abuse journal?'

'It's actually about you. It's got entries from the first day we met right up until I was admitted to hospital.'

'That sounds interesting.'

'It's not as sordid as it sounds but it does mean I know I can trust you and that's why I'm calling; to let you know I'm still on board with the plan.'

Her words agitated him. 'The plan where I do everything the way you want because you hold all the cards?'

'Is that what you think? Because the impression I got from my journal was that you would allow me to choose when and how I leave him.'

'That was before he put you in a coma,' he spat back, annoyed.

'We don't know that he did.'

'C'mon Kaidence, stop protecting him, you know he did.'

'I admit it's likely, but I can't just accuse him when I don't remember if he did it.'

'What about the other things he's done to you? Don't you think he deserves to be held accountable for those?'

'Of course he does. But I've already told you how I feel about that.'

'Kaidence, you can't let him keep getting away with hurting you, because he almost succeeded at killing you this time. Next time you might not survive.'

She'd had enough of his lecture and decided to bite back. 'Well, not if you keep antagonising him like in the hospital car park the other day.'

'You don't get it; every time I lay eyes on that sorry excuse for a man, I want to rip his head off his shoulders for doing what he's done to you and it kills me to stay professional. I needed him to know that I'll be watching him.'

'Except all you've done is given him a reason to take out his frustrations on me.'

'He's not going to hit you so soon after putting you in hospital. He won't want to risk being put under the microscope by other officers when he needs the element of doubt if he wants to claim I've got a vendetta against him.'

'If he gets mad enough, he won't care about that.'

'Isn't that all the more reason for you to get out?'

'I called you because I thought I could trust you, but if you're going to push something on me that I'm not ready for, I shouldn't have bothered.'

'Kaidence, don't hang up. I'm sorry. I'm just frustrated that you won't let me take action against this arsehole because what he's doing is getting more serious than a slap when you talk back or a punch when you don't do things the way he likes them done.'

'I know that, but I thought we had an understanding.'

'We do,' he was forced to admit with a sigh. 'I promise to keep my opinions to myself and let you set the pace so long as you promise you won't put up with his bullshit for much longer.'

'I know how serious it's getting; I won't put up with it for much longer,' she said, consciously not making any promises.

'You know, I notice when you do that,' he countered.

'What?'

'When I ask you to promise something, you never actually do. You say words that sound like you are, but you bypass the word completely.'

'I don't make promises, not since my parents died.'

'I'm sure there's a story behind why that you won't want to get into right now, so I'll shelf it for later, but I can't play the waiting game regarding you leaving him forever.'

'It won't be forever. It's just until I figure out a safe way to do it.'

CHAPTER TWELVE

After a fortnight of being at home, it was apparent to Kaidence that things had changed between her and Mitchell. She knew he couldn't afford for her to get seriously injured so soon after her coma, so he'd reverted to being non-violent and instead opted to ramp up the mental abuse he'd started once they were living together. Every day she heard how worthless she was often enough that she could recognise the words before he said them. His frustration at not being able to lash out at her made him find new and inventive ways to torture her. It started with him making her iron his shirts for work a couple of times more than they needed which meant she was standing at the ironing board into the early hours of the morning. Then he'd decided to make her clean the kitchen floor and the three bathrooms in the house with a toothbrush. But more recently he'd made her sleep on the floor at the foot of the bed at night.

It was apparent that he no longer had any feelings for her because he didn't even care enough to disguise his hatred any more. As little as two months ago, there would still be days when he'd kiss her as he was going out of the door or hold her as they both drifted off to sleep. But all evidence of his feelings had gone since she had left the hospital. He was either mad and couldn't touch her for fear he wouldn't be able to fight the urge to discipline her or he just didn't care enough to keep up the façade of their relationship. She suspected it was more the former than the latter although they were both probably true.

Every day, despite Mitchell's attitude, Kaidence felt stronger as piece by piece the memories she lost came back, and although she'd been deprived of contact with Jackson because her boyfriend had barely left her side, she remembered him. The only thing she was struggling with was remembering the accident that had landed her in hospital. It was as though her mind was trying to protect her, even though she was confident Mitchell was responsible for it.

Despite being home, Kaidence was more isolated than ever. Before the accident, she had begun to rely on her contact with Jackson and Louisa but in the fourteen days since her release she'd only been able to see them each once, because Mitchell was cautious enough to not let her out of his sight, with the exception of his work hours. He'd stopped going out drinking with his buddies so hadn't been staying out overnight at the weekend and the resentment that he exuded for needing to be sure she had no contact with the police affected his desire to make conversation with her or even sit with her for any length of time. The meal she slaved over was taken to the living room and eaten in front of the television while she sat at the dining table. The only upside was that she had her appetite back, which was helping her regain her strength, and she needed something to help her remain strong because the lack of human contact was getting hard to tolerate.

It had been a few days since she'd seen or spoken to Jackson, and the last time was only because he'd jumped her garden fence once she'd been left alone. She hadn't been expecting him, so she had been scared to death when he rapped on the back door trying to gain access. But they'd managed to spend a few hours talking before he escaped the same way he'd arrived to avoid detection. That had given her a bit of a pep to get through the weekend, but after two days spent with the man whose life's purpose was to make her miserable, she was ready to commence the new week in her own company.

She had hoped to be back at work by now, however the dizzy spells she was having had caused her physician to advise against it as well as prescribing medication to try and get it under control before her usual schedule resumed. As much as she hated being kept away from civilisation, she didn't want to end up back in hospital so thought it best to follow her doctor's advice. Sleeping on the floor the night before hadn't exactly helped her recovery, but she couldn't afford another fight so had obeyed, as she had so often during her relationship.

Kaidence was so submissive now that she feared the lengths she'd go to in order to appease Mitchell, and that was also a concern of Jackson's; he'd told her so much during their recent rendezvous. He was driven more than ever to get her out of the life she felt it acceptable to stay in so long as Mitchell was keeping his hands off her, but she had maintained her pig-headed need to bow out of the relationship without Mitchell coming after her. She was almost ashamed of how stubborn she was being, but she knew a life on the run wasn't going to be like it was in the movies, where her abuser would find her and she would use the self-defence training she'd taken upon first leaving to turn the tables on him. Instead they'd find her body in her new apartment after he'd silently gained access while she was keeping up appearances at a new job she was overqualified for in some misguided attempt to be normal.

Using her dominant hand, Kaidence reached across her body and grabbed at the muscle slightly to the left of the base of her neck and did her best to relieve the tension there as she walked out of the bathroom. Setting eyes on the king-sized bed tempted her to climb beneath the sheets and grab a few hours' sleep to refresh her body from the harshness of the floor, but the sound of her mobile phone ringing downstairs made her rethink her instinct. She didn't rush given that at the best of times she was unsteady on her feet; instead she made her way towards the ringing that echoed throughout the house as quickly as she was capable of. By the time she got to it, the ringing had stopped, and she was unable to return the call because the number had presented as private. But she didn't have to wait long for the caller to try again. This time she answered by the second ring.

'Hello?' she questioned down the line, unsure of the identity of the person on the other end.

'I've just pulled up outside, can I come in?' a female voice asked.

'Louisa?'

'Yes, it's me. I've just dropped the kids at school and thought I'd pop in for a quick cuppa before I do the one hundred things on my to-do list.'

Kaidence laughed. 'Sure, come in; I'll stick the kettle on.' She headed to the door and opened it before going back to the kitchen.

By the time she'd filled the kettle and put it on to boil, Louisa had joined her.

'Morning.' The female officer greeted her wearing her civilian clothes.

The occupant turned and smiled in her direction as she reached for two cups from the cupboard. 'Morning,' she replied.

Louisa enquired after her welfare. 'How are you today?'

She focused closely on the task she was performing as she replied. 'A bit sore. Mitchell has taken to making me sleep on the floor.'

Louisa was outraged. 'He's making you do what?'

Kaidence raised her eyebrows in silent agreement with her disgrace as she stepped to remove the milk from the fridge. 'At least he's not using his fists.'

Louisa shook her head, lifting herself up onto one of the bar stools. 'The fact you're still willing to put up with his bullshit baffles me, Kaidence, and I know we agreed not to push, but this guy has no power over you any more.'

'Of course he does. Just because he hasn't hit me since I came home doesn't mean he won't. It just takes me to refuse an order and he could fly into a blind rage, forgoing his restraint, and I'm back in hospital; either on a ventilator or a morgue slab.'

Her visitor rubbed at the frown lines on her forehead. 'The things you're willing to accept from this guy flummoxes me beyond belief. You'd be so much better off looking over your shoulder on the run than stuck in this house where he has you pinned down.'

Kaidence shook her head as she filled the cups with boiling water and stirred the coffee. 'Changing address every month is no kind of life, Lou. At least here I have people. On the run I'd have no one.'

'I'm sure Jackson would go with you,' Louisa muttered unconsciously.

Her mutterings didn't go unheard by her host as she fished around for the tea bag in her cup with a different spoon, 'He's pretty determined to get me away from Mitchell, isn't he?'

Louisa nodded and changed the direction her comment had originally been focused on. 'It takes all his restraint not to drag you out of this house and lock you up in his apartment, just so he can beat the shit out of the guy. I daren't tell him about this latest development because he'll want to pay the arsehole a visit and Mitchell's already threatened to report him. I'm sure he'd follow through on that and I could do without losing my partner.'

Kaidence smiled as she joined her at the island in the middle of the room and placed both their drinks down on the breakfast bar before sliding onto the bar stool beside her guest. 'What's he doing with his day off?'

'He's working. I've got this week off as holiday, so I can catch up with Christmas shopping I say I'm going to start every summer and never do.'

'Oh. I thought I might have got to see him later,' she responded, revealing her disappointment.

'No such luck. I'm sure he's pulling a double shift just so he can catch up on paperwork.' Louisa dashed even her smallest of hopes that he would still find a way of popping in before her boyfriend got home.

'We could always drop by and see him.'

'I'm not sure that's a good idea.'

'Sure, it is. You could file a restraining order while we're there; kill two birds with one stone,' she joked, with an underlying optimism.

Kaidence reached to rub the aching in her neck. 'If I'm going anywhere today it's to the massage parlour to sort out this bloody kink.'

Louisa threw her head back. 'Oh a massage sounds like bliss. I can't remember the last time I had one.'

'I'll ring my regular place and see if I can get us an appointment.' Kaidence reached for her mobile phone and scrolled through her contacts.

Her companion looked apologetic. 'Kaidence, that's money I just can't afford to spend.'

'My treat.' She shrugged.

'I can't let you do that.'

'You don't have a choice. Per doctor's instructions I'm not allowed to drive. You play chauffeur and I'll pay for the treatment,' she said, putting an end to Louisa's protest by connecting the call.

It was early afternoon by the time the women emerged from the massage parlour feeling relaxed and refreshed. The kink in Kaidence's neck had been worked away and she felt suitably prepared to go on with her day.

'Do you fancy going for something to eat?' she asked the woman who'd shown up on her doorstep a few hours before.

'I'd love to, but my to-do list isn't getting any shorter.'

Kaidence tried to persuade her as they made their way back to the car. 'I'm sure that list will be better tackled tomorrow.'

'Feeling a little starved of human contact?' Louisa asked, seeing through her desperation.

'It's that obvious?'

She shrugged. 'I suppose I could eat. I just have one request; let's pick up Jackson on the way. I know him and once he gets stuck into filing reports, he'll forget to eat.'

'That sounds doable.' Kaidence smiled as they climbed inside the vehicle. 'As long as we go somewhere remote in case someone Mitchell knows sees us.'

'I'm assuming that rules out most of the spit and sawdust kind of places.'

Kaidence laughed. 'There's actually nothing wrong with slumming it occasionally; you should try it.'

'Oh, I've slummed more than you can imagine. I think it's time for an upgrade.'

'Are we still talking about pubs?'

'We weren't using them as a metaphor?' Louisa laughed, starting the engine.

'There's nothing wrong with bad boys. I've dated a few of them in my time.'

'Surely one of those would've been a better option for you to settle down with than Mitchell.'

'Actually, he masqueraded as a good guy, so I was caught off guard when he turned sour,' she admitted. 'But I did date a guy before him called Cam, who rode a motorcycle and whisked me away on a whim anywhere in the country to try new things. I've sky-dived because of him, among other things. He was a good kind of wild and the sex was out of this world.'

'He sounds perfect. So how come you two split up?'

'I wasn't the only one he was having sex with, and monogamy is a deal-breaker for me.'

Louisa nodded. 'Whereas bruises are an acceptable downside.'

Jackson almost choked on the coffee he'd taken a sip of when he saw Kaidence walking towards him at the desk he'd been sitting at for the better part of the day. He seemed oblivious to Louisa, who'd led her in, as he put his mug down and headed in their direction.

'Kaidence, what are you doing here?' he asked, looking around to see if any of his colleagues were watching.

Louisa answered his question, alerting him to her presence. 'We came to take you for something to eat.'

But he addressed the woman standing beside her, who was obviously on edge. 'Do you think it's a good idea to be walking into a police station if you don't plan to press charges?'

'I didn't have a choice,' she replied meekly, with her arms wrapped around herself for comfort.

'That's my fault,' Louisa said. 'I knew that if I came in here alone, I wouldn't be able to get you to come with me. But if I brought in Kaidence that it wouldn't be an issue.'

Her partner looked her in the eye and spoke under his breath. 'So you thought risking her security was the right course of action when he could be having her watched?'

Her brow furrowed at his subtle reprimand. 'It didn't cross my mind to think like a spy, Jackson,' she countered, slightly angry with herself rather than at him.

'You should be more cautious,' he scolded her, still at a muted volume. 'Look at her; she's so petrified she's shaking.'

'All right Dad, I'm sorry. I should've left her in the car outside where every passer-by could have seen her, instead I took pot luck that someone wouldn't see her during the minute or two it took her to walk in.'

'What if he knows someone on the force?'

Despite his undertone, Louisa answered him at her usual volume. 'My God, you're more suspicious than she is. If he knows someone on the force, it's already over partner,' she said, lightly tapping him on the chest. 'Now go and get your civvies on so we can all be seen out in public together.'

***

Kaidence was relieved to be sat in the back seat of the car, which was travelling far enough out of town for them to go unseen by anyone who knew her or Mitchell. The fear she felt on the walk into the police station ten minutes before was slowly subsiding but had enveloped her whole body at the time. When Louisa had pulled up at the station, she had wanted to stay put in the car, even though it would probably make no difference if she was spotted, but Louisa had made a convincing argument for her to go inside. With each step she had taken towards the building with two-foot-high lettering announcing the occupation of the people inside, she had become shakier and sweatier, and neither symptom eased until she was back outside. But she didn't hang around by the entrance for fear someone would spot her; instead she rushed to the car and as soon as it was unlocked, she climbed into the back seat out of sight.

Sensing her unease, Jackson twisted in his seat, so he could look back at her. 'Are you okay?' he asked.

She nodded. 'I'm getting there.'

He let her know he'd noticed her discomfort. 'You looked like you were going to pass out.'

'It felt like I was going to have a heart attack.'

Their conversation provoked a feeling of guilt in Louisa. 'I'm sorry Kaidence, I didn't think it through.'

'It's okay. I just hope no one he knows saw me.'

'Well, where do his friends work?' she asked, trying to help Kaidence eliminate her worries.

'Dale moved two counties over six months ago and only comes back once a week to go drinking. John is a mechanic on the outskirts of town and doesn't do breakdown calls, but Alan spends his day in the pub at the top of town so depending if he was on his way in or out, he could've seen me.'

Jackson checked his watch. 'It's just hit half past one. It's likely that he was banging on the door at opening and I doubt he'll be leaving until closing if he's an alcoholic, so you're probably safe.'

She shrugged. 'I guess I won't know until I go home.'

'Your head was on a swivel, Kaidence, you would've seen him if he was there to see,' he insisted, in an attempt to calm the nerves that were on display.

'I suppose there's no point me worrying about it until there's something to worry about.' She shrugged. 'I just want to enjoy being out of the house for the first time in weeks.'

'Right, where are we going?' Louisa asked, changing the subject as they stopped at traffic lights.

'There's a pub about ten clicks north from here if you want to go somewhere remote,' Jackson suggested.

'And for those of us who weren't in the military?'

'Six miles.'

'Sounds perfect.' Kaidence smiled as the lights changed and Louisa started moving again.

It took them about twenty minutes to reach the public house, which was situated in the middle of what seemed to be nowhere; essentially, it was just surrounded by beautiful countryside and hidden at the base of a hill popular with hikers. It was picturesque to say the least.

Having two small children, the back of Louisa's car had the child locks implemented on the back doors, making them inoperable from the inside, so Kaidence stayed seated as Jackson climbed from the front passenger's side and opened her door. Getting out, she took in the beautiful peacefulness of her surroundings. The nature was on such a grander scale than what she had access to behind her house. It was astounding and immediately calmed her.

'Are you okay?' Jackson asked lightly, placing the palm of his hand on the small of her back.

His touch caused her to suck in a breath sharply. It had been a long time since she'd felt such tenderness in someone else's fingertips, and it caught her off guard. But Jackson took it to mean something else.

He retracted his hand quickly. 'Sorry, I didn't think...'

But before his thoughts spiralled out of control, Kaidence spun and took his hand in hers. 'It's okay. I'm just not used to how gentle affection can be, that's all.'

'Play your cards right and he'll show you just how gentle his affection can be.' Louisa hinted at the extent of his feelings.

'Take no notice of her. She doesn't understand that a man and a woman can have a platonic friendship,' Jackson said to detract attention. Even though he had at first found it difficult to separate his feelings for her and his duty as an officer, he had forced his emotions on the back-burner knowing it was in her best interest for him to maintain his professionalism, and now the last thing he wanted was for Kaidence to feel any extra pressure from his partner's insinuations that there was more between them than she was capable of.

Kaidence smiled, despite his sentence hitting a core in her. She'd felt an attraction to Jackson since meeting him so had romanticised that at some point in the distant future there could be a relationship between them. Hearing him verbalise only a professional interest in her disheartened her somewhat, because she liked the feeling she got whenever he was affectionate. Although at least she was sure where she stood now, and that made things less complicated. Knowing there were no expectations from Jackson apart from getting her away from Mitchell would help to focus her.

'I'm sure she was just joking,' she said, almost through gritted teeth as she followed the two of them inside.

Walking into the public house, she was struck by how much the inside reflected the outside, with exposed beams that gave it a cottage-like feel. The dark wood furniture and log burner in the fireplace were features that set off the idyllic sanctuary. It was her idea of perfection.

'I'll get us some drinks,' Jackson said, breaking her focus on their surroundings.

'I'll just have a lemonade,' she replied.

Louisa laughed. 'It's ironic that we're in a pub and I can't drink because I'm driving, you can't drink because you're working, and she can't drink in case Mitchell smells it.'

Jackson completely ignored the mention of the man they would all rather forget about. 'Why don't you two grab us a table and I'll ask for menus.'

It wasn't until they sat down that Kaidence noticed the time on the huge clock hanging close to where they were sat. 'Is he going to have time to eat? It's already been half an hour since we left the station.'

'Working a double shift can be pretty exhausting so the superintendent likes us to take both of our hour breaks together. That way he can get a good eighteen hours' work out of us,' Louisa answered.

'You do ten-hour shifts?' she asked, astonished.

She nodded. 'On a four day on, three days off rotation.'

'No wonder you have no time for a social life.'

Kaidence placed her knife and fork side by side in the centre of her plate and relaxed back in the booth she shared with her lunch companions. 'That was quite possibly the best pub grub I've ever eaten.'

'It's not as good as your cooking,' Jackson pointed out, making her smile.

Louisa frowned. 'Wait, when have you cooked for him?'

Kaidence looked to the man between them to confirm her answer. 'A couple of weeks ago,' she replied, unsure of her timeline.

He nodded. 'It was the night you were going to go out and find someone to have sex with just to get back at Mitchell and I offered to come over to save you the job.'

'Wow. I think I underestimated just how close you two are,' Louisa commented, leaning back and folding her arms across her chest.

Kaidence took the opportunity to laugh. 'I'd almost forgot about that proposal.'

'I do love that sound.' Jackson smiled.

Louisa watched as the two people in her company flirted with each other without realising that that's what they were doing, and she could envision them having a future together. She teased her partner sometimes about his feelings for the woman they'd formed an unlikely friendship with, but she'd never seen him as alive as when he was around her. It was almost like she flicked a switch in him that no one else had been able to reach since his time undercover. It was a part of him she hadn't witnessed before Kaidence; he seemed so serious all the time, but she liked this lighter side.

'You say that a lot,' the teacher pointed out.

He shrugged. 'Because I prefer to build you up instead of putting you down. Besides, you have many good qualities; it doesn't hurt to remind you of them.'

'I'm not so sure about that,' she said, tucking a few strands of wispy hair that had escaped from her pulled-back ponytail behind her ear as best she could.

'I know compliments make you uncomfortable, but that's just because you're not used to receiving them.'

It amazed her how well he knew her already, despite only meeting her a few months ago and them barely spending any time together. But he was right; compliments made her squirm, they always had. Not that he would know that. She suspected Mitchell's constant barrage of put-downs didn't help her self-confidence, but it wasn't all down to him. She laughed to cover her embarrassment. 'I don't suppose you're free this weekend, are you? I could do with a few days of compliments while Mitchell's at his work retreat.'

Louisa leaned forward and rested her elbows on the table in front of her. 'He's leaving for the weekend?'

She nodded. 'Friday to Sunday.'

'Then why don't we pack his shit and change the locks while he's gone?'

She sighed. 'We've discussed you pushing this issue.'

'But it's the perfect opportunity.'

'Except I'd still be in the house when he got back.'

'Even with the enforcer we had trouble getting through that front door.'

'But I just have a UPVC fire door around the back and there are two huge windows on the front that he'd think nothing of breaking just to get to me,' she argued. 'Things just aren't that urgent right now; he's barely looked at me let alone raised his hand.'

'So that justifies letting him stay?'

'No, but I need somewhere to go before I leave.'

'We could probably figure out a safe house,' Louisa said, looking at her partner for confirmation.

But Jackson grimaced. 'Between now and the weekend? That'll be a tough ask.'

'Hell, you could stay with me. I just want you out of his grasp.'

Kaidence reached out and gently gripped her forearm. 'And I love you for it. But now isn't the right time to uproot my life.'

'No, that was a couple of weeks ago when he put you in hospital,' she said. 'And if I'd had my way you wouldn't have gone back to that house.'

'It's *my* house.'

'A house you could live in without him if only you'd press charges.'

But she shook her head determinedly. 'He wouldn't let me.'

'You could get a restraining order.'

'A piece of paper that says he has to stay a certain distance away from me? That's not going to do shit to protect me.'

'It would mean you get a priority response when you dial nine-nine-nine.'

'I'd be dead before anyone got to me.'

'You don't know that.'

'Don't you get it Louisa? I'm scared,' she blurted out as tears escaped from her eyes out of nowhere. 'If I stay, he could kill me the next time I piss him off but if I leave, I'm dead for sure.'

'We can protect you.'

'But you can't. When I close that door behind me, I'm alone. There's no one there to get between us when he decides it's time to teach me a lesson because he thinks I've done something wrong or he just wants to vent some frustration. It's just me versus him and I'm no match. If he wanted to kill me, it'd take no effort at all and I'm worried he's getting so irritated at playing nice for appearance sake that it's not going to be long until he snaps. I just don't know how to leave without making him determined to find me, and he has people that will help him. I just can't risk walking out without having measures in place that would ensure my safety.'

Jackson observed the women interact. He wanted to back up his partner and insist that she used the weekend to put as much distance between her and the boyfriend who didn't appreciate her, but he could feel Kaidence's fear as she rationalised why she couldn't. His life revolved around getting the woman he was falling in love with away from the man who threatened her life every day, but he'd grown to realise that her terror was the reason she stayed, and he didn't want to push her to do something she wasn't ready for, that might ultimately get her killed. His instinct was to reach out for her hand and assure her that he'd be with her every step of the way, but the reality was that she was right; her survival was all on her shoulders. He couldn't promise her that he'd be there to save her when he wouldn't know when that would be.

'Three days is more than enough time to pack up your whole house and set you up somewhere else,' Louisa said, as if reading his mind.

'And what about my sister; what would I tell her?'

'Maybe it's time she knew the truth,' Jackson softly suggested.

Louisa was astounded. 'How doesn't your sister know?'

'It's not exactly something I want announced to the world,' Kaidence said, dropping her head.

'Hasn't she seen the bruises?'

'I don't see her after a fight and when we do get together, the last thing I want to do is upset her.'

'But she's your family. She'd want to know.'

'And that's precisely why she doesn't.'

'We're all guilty of hiding certain truths from the ones closest to us, but you're isolated enough, you need a support network,' Jackson said.

Kaidence nodded as she wiped her eyes. 'That's why I have you two.'

Louisa sighed. 'We'll be here for you, whatever you need.'

'Will you stop trying to get me to leave until I'm ready?'

'I won't apologise for wanting you far out of the life you've got, but I'll do my best not to mention you leaving again unless you mention it first.'

'So, when does he go away?' Jackson asked, not really changing the topic.

Kaidence relaxed at the thought of having the weekend to herself. 'Early Friday morning.'

'Have you got any plans for your freedom?'

She shook her head. 'Not really. It's enough knowing I can do what the hell I like for the better part of three days, and that doesn't include housework.'

'It just so happens that Jax has the weekend off so maybe you could cook for him again.' Louisa was keen to encourage them to spend time together. She knew Kaidence was having a positive impact on her partner and that he was doing the same for her. She liked the look of them together and hoped that once they were out of the current situation their friendship could blossom into something romantic – but only when they were both ready for it. Still, she had to lay the groundwork now if her wishes were to be granted in the future.

Jackson cut his eyes at the woman he worked with. 'I'm sure Kaidence doesn't want to have company if she can spend time relaxing.'

'Actually, I'd love to cook for you properly instead of just throwing something together,' she countered.

'Well I'm not one to turn down a home-cooked meal.'

Kaidence smiled. 'Then it's a date.'

CHAPTER THIRTEEN

Kaidence walked in through her front door and hesitated to listen for any noise coming from inside, unconsciously holding her breath. Finding the house in silence, she allowed herself the luxury of relaxing as she closed the door behind her. The stillness inside meant that if Alan had seen her, he hadn't contacted Mitchell to tell him otherwise he'd be home already, to catch her in the act of returning. It made her hopeful that she hadn't been discovered.

She removed her coat and hung it with her handbag on the stand behind the door before venturing into the kitchen to make a cup of tea. She'd had an unexpected good day out with people she now considered friends, which gave her a boost of positivity that she'd needed after weeks of limited social interactions, especially given that Mitchell had taken to ignoring her. Her outing had meant she'd been able to eat and fully enjoy the meal that had been prepared for her. But now she was home, she would go back to having no appetite and forcing the food she cooked down her throat just to keep up the appearance of happiness.

She hadn't got a lot of time before her boyfriend returned from work, but she had a contingency plan for exactly this kind of occasion: bulking up on her measurements whenever she cooked in the week and freezing the excess. She lifted a chicken curry from the bottom compartment while she waited for the kettle to boil and placed the container in the microwave to defrost. By the time she finished her beverage it would be thawed and ready to heat through, meaning Mitchell would be none the wiser about her day out.

That's when it dawned on her that she was still wearing her shoes. Heading back to the entrance, she forced the flat footwear off her feet and put on her slippers before going back to the kettle. She wanted it to look like she'd been home all day. Luckily the house remained in a constant state of spotlessness, so it wouldn't be immediately noticeable to Mitchell that she hadn't done any cleaning.

A couple of hours passed before she got the obligatory text from Mitchell to say he was leaving work, which he'd taken to sending once her dizzy spells had started and she'd needed to lie down when they were bad. It was his warning to her that his meal should be cooking so he didn't have to resist his urge to punish her, because she could tell it was getting harder to do. The longer he went without lashing out at her, the shorter his fuse seemed to get. But she could handle him shouting in her face because it was easier to recover from than the physical injuries. She replied with her usual two-word response and knew she only had half an hour before he was walking in through the door.

Placing her mobile phone back on the work surface, she went about stirring the curry heating up in a saucepan on the hob, only to get notification of another text. She rushed to read it in case it was from either officer she had spent her day with, but found instead that it was a follow-up to her reply to Mitchell informing her that they weren't going to be alone for the whole evening because he'd invited his three friends round for drinks.

Kaidence sighed and rubbed at her forehead. 'Fuck in hell!' she spat out angrily into the empty house. 'That's all I need.'

It was seven o'clock before Louisa sat down in her living room. She hadn't got a single errand she planned to complete that day done and yet she was happy with the outcome of the day. It was rare she got to take a day for herself and it was even rarer to spend it in the company of friends. The few hours she'd spent with Kaidence and Jackson had given her a different perspective on them both. She was a step closer to understanding how Kaidence felt about her current predicament and she'd seen a side of Jackson that he usually kept hidden despite them being partners for years.

She'd managed to settle her daughters down for the evening with only a minimal amount of resistance from Juliette, who lately insisted she was too old to be in bed at the same time as Alicia. But this evening she deflected the kicking and screaming tantrum by agreeing to allow her to read for half an hour before going to sleep. The everyday battles between her and her eldest had only started after her eighth birthday, but after ten months they were easy to see coming. But she still had to negotiate with her like the drunks who didn't want to leave the town streets at kicking-out time, so it felt as if she was constantly on duty.

It was difficult being a single mum, having to deal with everything yourself and always questioning whether you were doing right by your kids. As much as their father was a part of their lives every other weekend and when she needed help during half term, he had no input in the day-to-day raising of their daughters. Besides, she'd heard somewhere that children learned more from their same-sex parent and if there was anything she wanted her girls to get from her, it was her strength and ability to provide for them regardless of the circumstances. Although she suspected Juliette was going to test her every day until she reached adulthood, she wouldn't have it any other way.

Once she was finished eating, Kaidence didn't hang around cleaning up. She planned to be out of the way by the time Dale, John and Alan knocked the door and busy herself upstairs doing anything to avoid being around them. They had a habit of treating her like a topless waitress with no regard for her personal space and Mitchell never stopped them man-handling her because his relationship with his friends was more important to him than she was.

But as she exited the kitchen and was about to take a step up the staircase, Mitchell appeared in the hallway. 'I want you to be hostess tonight,' he announced.

'Oh, I've got some ironing that really needs to be done,' she said, trying to get out of any obligation he expected of her.

But he wasn't going to let her off lightly; he needed to torture her, and this was the only weapon he had at his disposal for the evening. He took a step towards her to enforce his intimidation. 'And I *need* you to fetch beers and snacks tonight.'

She dropped her eyes to the floor. 'Would it be okay if I get changed first?'

He shot her down. 'No, you look fine.'

She slowly nodded. 'I'll just go and get a crate from the garage.'

'That's a great idea.' He smiled, puffing out his chest, feeling empowered by his domination over her.

Kaidence felt like she was being punished for having such a good day with Jackson and Louisa. She mentally told herself off for bowing to his orders as she disappeared through the back door to enter the double garage that was barely used for its purpose and instead stored a large chest freezer on the far wall. Buying it was a decision she made once she wasn't living alone so she could buy enough food to feed them both for the month. She hadn't considered that the freezer could also be used to store her body until after Mitchell had hit her for the first time. But every time she went into the garage, for whatever reason, she always side-glanced the freezer as though it was biding time until it was her coffin. She'd considered getting rid of it so he wouldn't be tempted to kill her and hide her body inside, but she knew that'd make him suspicious and she could do without giving him ideas for how to keep her body from being detected until he was far enough away to avoid capture by the authorities.

Heading to the corner of the outer building, she exhaled loudly with the effort it took to pick up a twenty-four pack of bitter from the small tower that was six crates high and made her way back inside. She knew it wasn't going to take the trio long to consume them all and she'd have to do the journey at least once more that night before they'd had their fill. She struggled to lift the cardboard tray of cans above her waist, so she could use the door handle that would lead her out of the garage. This wasn't the first time she'd been required to do this chore, so it was something she'd got used to struggling with no matter what the weather. She had sworn, once she bought the house, to have the garage made accessible via a door inside the kitchen, but had never got around to it, which she regretted every time she had to make her way out to the garden and around to the entrance at the back of the side building. Propping the heavy load against the wall, Kaidence turned the key to lock the door for the separate building before hoisting the cans back into her arms and making her way to the kitchen. The beers were cold, but they needed to be unloaded from their packaging into the fridge so they stayed that way.

She was in the middle of filling up the bottom shelf when she heard the patterned knock on the front door that was attributed to Dale and she rolled her eyes. Her peace was over. But she was steadfast where she stood. The only time Mitchell answered the door was when he was expecting company. That's when she heard the familiar buddy call of the four men she'd had the misfortune of spending too much time with.

'Kitty Kat.' She heard John use his nickname for her as he rushed over and scooped her up in his arms.

She had repeatedly told him that it wasn't short for her given name and that she disliked it, but it didn't seem to matter. Alan was another one guilty of not caring to learn her name, instead opting to call her 'doll' and breathe his alcoholic fumes all over her. The only one of the foursome that was always courteous was Dale, even though he was just as sexist as the others. He would always call her by her name. There was a possibility that he had a soft spot for her, because despite the pack mentality he partook in when he was with his friends, when it was just the two of them in a room, he'd apologise for it, almost as if he was embarrassed by his behaviour and was only keeping up appearances for the sake of the other three men.

She happened to catch sight of Mitchell as she was spun around by the man who deemed it appropriate behaviour to treat her like a little girl to find he was smiling. Ordinarily, if a man were to even look at her, he would feel a need to prove his masculinity and claim her like a possession but when it came to his friends, they had carte blanche because he knew how she hated them.

Finally, having being put back on solid ground, Kaidence continued the job she was doing as if there had been no interruption. She wasn't allowed to protest if they touched her inappropriately or were depreciating when they spoke to her because she'd be embarrassing Mitchell, and she was never allowed to do that. She was expected to put up and shut up, which was getting harder to do. They had escalated from the odd slap on the arse at first to full groping of her boobs, which Mitchell never objected to. It made her feel more worthless than he had already, but she knew there was no point in fighting to maintain her dignity because it would only fall on deaf ears and she'd be put in her place once they were alone. He'd always choose to teach her a lesson in private, which led her to conclude that even his friends didn't know about his abuse.

Being sure to keep four cans out ready for the males, Kaidence finished loading up the fridge and disposed of the packaging. Knowing that they liked to snack while they drank, she went to the cupboards and removed the snacks she always kept stocked up.

'Bring the beers in,' Mitchell ordered her as the four of them retired to the living room.

She rolled her eyes; they could have picked up the drinks she'd left out by the refrigerator to save her the extra journey, but Mitchell wasn't about to make her life easy. Dropping what she was doing, she walked across the kitchen to retrieve the cans and took them into the room.

'I'll be right back with the munchies,' she informed them.

'You've got her trained,' Alan said to the man of the house.

'She knows her place,' he countered.

'She knows how to treat a man, that's for sure.' Dale winked at her.

'Put some music on, Kitty Kat,' John ordered as he slapped her backside on her way out of the room.

Without missing a beat in her disgust, she spun on her heel and headed over to the stereo. 'What do you want to listen to?'

'It doesn't really matter, doll, it's just for background noise,' Alan answered.

Opting to hit play on the CD that was already in the machine rather than look for an alternative, Kaidence was back in the kitchen loading up bowls of Twiglets, crisps and jelly babies. From experience, she knew they'd snack until they got to the second crate of beers and then they'd need something more substantial, so she'd have to ring for whatever takeaway they wanted. Taking a plastic serving tray from the side of the microwave where they were kept, she placed the bowls onto it with four more beer cans and took them in to her unwanted guests. She was careful not to bend over in front of any of them; instead she faced them to place the tray on the coffee table and empty it.

'Thank you darlin',' Dale said with affection.

But as she was about to pass Alan, he grabbed her hand and pulled her down into his lap. She tried to fight him and stand but he held her around the waist to restrict her.

'That's it sweetheart, wriggle for me,' he laughed. 'I'm getting off on it.'

'C'mon Al, let her go.' Dale tried to relieve her torment.

'In a minute – I'm nearly done,' he said, causing Mitchell and John to laugh, finding amusement in her struggle.

One final fight against his hands and Kaidence was free to stand. Stepping backwards, she put as much distance between her and Alan as she could before taking her leave. She tried to steady her trembling hand as she reached the kitchen but the fear she felt had consumed her whole body, so it was proving difficult to regulate her breathing. She was having a panic attack. She had started having them after her parents died and it took her a year to find a coping mechanism that worked for her. It had been six years since her last attack, so she was out of practice at coming out of it. Using the worktop for support, Kaidence talked herself through the exercises the doctor had taught her and slowly the panic subsided, leaving a frightened child in its wake. She could handle the odd grope and slap on her backside because, as much as they were unwanted, they were momentary. But being restrained and held somewhere she didn't want to be with men she had no trust in was frightful.

She considered, for a split second, making a cup of tea to get her nerves under control and quickly dismissed it. She needed something stronger. Bending down, she reached into the back of the cupboard where she kept the saucepans, knowing Mitchell would never find it, and pulled out a small bottle of whisky. She had it in reserve for emergencies and this situation constituted one. Screwing off the cap, she took a swig of the alcohol inside and replaced the lid before returning it out of sight. It was just the right measure to bring her shakes under control and give her the courage to face the rest of the night.

She was limited as to what she could do while still being on hand to play waitress, so she opened her laptop, which she'd been using prior to Louisa's phone call, and it woke up straight away. She'd forgotten to shut it down, expecting to go back to what she was doing once her visitor had left but had impulsively made plans instead. Still, the beauty of not shutting down properly meant she could pick up exactly where she left off. But as she looked over the teaching plan she was trying to lay out, she saw someone enter the room, which caused her to look up.

'Is there something you need?' she asked the man who'd joined her.

Dale shook his head as he walked over and sat in the chair opposite her at the table. 'I just wanted to check you were okay.'

She nodded. 'I'm okay.'

'Sorry about Al. He's harmless; he doesn't realise when he's pushed the joke too far.'

'It's all right.' She brushed it off as less than it was.

'Okay,' he said, pushing the chair out from beneath him and standing. 'I'll let you crack on. I just wanted to make sure you were all right.'

Feeling somewhat guilty for her lack of interaction, Kaidence called out to him before he disappeared out of sight. 'Dale, thanks for checking on me.'

He forced a smile in response before going back to his friends.

Watching him leave, Kaidence was perplexed by his need to check on her. She had been subjected to worse in the past and he'd never showed concern before. But she had heard he was dating so perhaps he was now looking at it from the perspective of a man who'd dislike his woman to be treated the way she had been. Whatever it was, it was a side of Dale she'd never been privy to before. She only hoped that if the other men got out of control during the night – her boyfriend included – then he would come to her aid and not wait until after they'd ended their torture before checking on her well-being.

Kaidence had about ten minutes' peace before she was called into action with the request for more beer being shouted from the living room. She didn't hesitate to get up and take four cans from the fridge before rushing them to the waiting men. Her interaction with them this time was painless. Learning from her last mistake, she gave Alan a wide berth. Instead of walking past him, she went behind the settee to place the drinks on the coffee table before collecting the empties and disposing of them in the kitchen bin.

Sitting back behind her laptop, she started inputting her teaching plan for the following term in case she wasn't well enough to go back to work and her silenced phone vibrated once to signal an email had come through. Picking it up, she clicked on the screen notification to view the correspondence, only to find it was from Louisa. Curiously she read the words and a frown etched itself on her features. There was nothing specific in the email to warrant sending it, but she had a feeling it was a way of checking in without alerting her other half like a text message or phone call would. It was a smokescreen. The content was regarding Juliette's behaviour and her theory about why – all information she already had. She hit the reply icon and her fingers tapped a reply that was just as distant as the reason for it. Sending the correspondence of reassurance, Kaidence put her phone face down on the table beside the laptop and glanced at the clock. Her undesirable guests had been there for only three-quarters of an hour and she had been wanting them to leave for just as long. Any ordinary night she'd be heading to bed for half past nine, but that was ninety minutes away and she knew the evening had only just started for the men. The prospect made her sigh heavily and rest her head in the palm of her hand as she rested her elbow on the table. Trying to concentrate with the noise in the other room was proving difficult. But she needed to be in the kitchen so she would be on hand to serve.

Forcefully closing the lid on the portable computer, she got to her feet, driven by the fire that had been growing in the pit of her stomach all night. She needed to work out her aggression somehow and the only way she knew to do that was to knead dough. She went to the cupboard where she kept her baking supplies and got out the necessary ingredients for making bread. It wasn't often she made her own because it was a lot of work, but tonight was the perfect opportunity for her to kill some time. She enjoyed a slice of freshly baked bread and somehow it tasted better because she'd made it herself. Her efforts weren't appreciated by Mitchell though; he didn't understand why she would make something when it was easier to buy it from the shop, and she couldn't tell him that it helped her work through her frustrations regarding her relationship unless she wanted to get smacked about.

The kitchen light inside the house allowed Jackson to see Kaidence through the window, busying herself, and he exhaled from deep down inside, relieved to see she'd come to no harm following their lunch date. When he'd got home from work twenty minutes ago, a sudden feeling of dread came over him and he had an overwhelming need to check on her for his own peace of mind. He knew better than to knock on the door or send a text to her phone, so instead he'd parked around the corner and sneaked up to the front of the property to catch a glimpse of her. He'd known not to expect to see her boyfriend because she'd be in a different room simply to be away from him, but he was glad to see she was safe.

Taking a cigarette from the packet on the kitchen table, Louisa placed it between her lips and dragged hard on the filter as she lit the other end with the engraved petrol lighter her ex had got her for Christmas while they were together. She hadn't been able to relax, not knowing if Kaidence had been made to suffer for spending time with her and Jackson, so she'd sent an email hoping it wouldn't draw any negative attention to the female in danger. She was now waiting for a response and it was making her anxious; smoking was her way of keeping her distracted until she heard from her.

She was halfway through her cigarette when she heard her phone notify her of an email and she wasted no time picking it up to read the reply. She breathed a sigh of relief, satisfied that Kaidence was okay, and finished her cigarette before going upstairs to check on her daughters before she treated herself to a bubble bath.

She was hesitant as she pushed open Juliette's bedroom door beyond the crack she'd left it at when she'd put her to bed because she didn't want yet another argument about respecting her privacy. But as her daughter's bed came into view, Louisa found her fast asleep with the book she was reading open across her chest. Images like this compensated for the difficulties she had every day as a single parent. She made her way inside the room, lifted the reading material off the bed and placed it open face down on her bedside table before kissing Juliette on the forehead. She took in the picture of her daughter again as she reached inside the shade of her lamp and turned off the light.

Kaidence was up to her elbows in flour when Dale joined her in the kitchen for the second time that night as he headed for the fridge.

'Did you call, because I didn't hear anything?' she asked, panic-stricken in case she'd been beckoned and hadn't responded.

'No one called. We were finished, and I offered to fetch the beers. I didn't want to bother you because I thought you were working,' he replied.

'I was, but I got an urge to bake so I decided that work can wait until tomorrow,' she said, starting to knead her dough.

He smiled her way as he retrieved four cans from the fridge. 'I better get these back to the guys before they riot.'

She didn't respond. She just concentrated on the task she was performing. Even though she hadn't been called on to fetch that round, she knew Mitchell would make his disapproval known somehow and sure enough, two minutes after Dale had returned to the living room he was in the kitchen.

'So, you are still here,' he said rhetorically, alerting her to his presence.

Instant dread built in her stomach. The fact he hadn't physically abused her since she'd been home had lured her into thinking she was safe. But she had a feeling he was about to prove otherwise.

She spun around so her back was against the counter she'd been working at. 'Dale said I didn't get called.'

'You didn't,' he said calmly as he got closer. 'But my friends shouldn't be doing what I asked you to do.' He put his hand on top of hers on the worktop and pushed down with all the weight he could.

After weeks of no contact, she felt the pain as intensely as the first beating he'd subjected her to. But she maintained her blank expression, not daring to give him a hint of anguish to get off on.

'So instead of pissing about in here, pay attention to what *I* need from you,' he warned.

Kaidence nodded her compliance. That fear had never gone away. But she realised now that she'd become complacent about her safety since her release from hospital – while he was waiting for the eyes of the law to be diverted away from him, she had convinced herself that he felt some anxiety about hospitalising her. She should have known that the mental abuse wasn't about restraint but about self-preservation. He was always going to hit her again; it was part of who he was, and he wasn't about to stop when she'd given him permission to treat her that way every time she didn't report her injuries to the police.

'I'm sorry,' she apologised, the words sticking in her throat. The small amount of confidence she got from spending time with Jackson and Louisa always made her hate herself for apologising to him so readily when it wasn't her at fault.

He lifted his hand from hers and still she didn't react. But she gasped, caught by surprise when he reached up to grab her by her throat and squeezed slightly.

'Never forget who's in charge,' he insisted, adding pressure to her windpipe.

Through the window, Jackson could see Mitchell's proximity to Kaidence, but it wasn't until he shifted a little to the side that he saw exactly what kind of torture he was subjecting her to. His instinct was to bang on the front door, wait for it to open and then barge in to grab Mitchell around the throat so he'd know what it was like to feel in danger of his life. But Jackson knew the chances of him showing any signs of vulnerability were slim and ultimately, he'd be putting Kaidence in more danger, so he swallowed down his urge to dish out some personal justice and continued to watch in case the need to intervene was unavoidable.

The wait for Mitchell to release his hold on her throat seemed to take a lifetime. But when he did Kaidence couldn't help gasping for air. She could already feel the bruises forming around her neck where his fingers had been. For a split second her instinct was to pick up the glass bowl she used to prove her dough and smash it over his head before running out of the front door to freedom. But she wasn't brave enough, and she knew if she reached for the bowl, he'd do more to hurt her.

She kept her eyes on the ground as he stepped away from her and went back to his friends. She didn't know if they knew what he was like, or if they cared, but she assumed Mitchell didn't want them to witness him punishing her, so his attack had been swift and effective. Somehow, though, whether it was a five-minute encounter or an hour-long one, it always had the same effect on her.

Kaidence took a minute to pull herself together. Her heart was beating quickly, her breathing was shallow, and her hands were shaking. It had been weeks since she'd felt this way, so she'd almost forgotten how fearful he made her. But this refresher course was the drive she needed to focus her plan to leave. She would need more time than his weekend away would allow but she wanted out. She was sick of living in fear or pain, and the excuses she told herself weren't enough to keep her there. So, what if he hadn't raised his hand to her while he was sleeping with some woman who he'd spend Saturday nights with? That just proved he was an abusive cheat. And so what if he'd left her alone since she'd been released from hospital? That just proved he didn't want to get caught. He wasn't going to change; being violent was a part of him that had developed long before he'd started dating her. It had just taken her acceptance of his behaviour for him to keep using it against her.

Having the company of Jackson at the weekend would be the opportunity she needed to work out a step-by-step plan that they could put into action immediately, because she didn't want to be here for a minute longer than she had to. It was as if Mitchell's outburst had woken her up, and all she wanted was to be as far away from him as she could be.

She'd always known he wasn't the man he initially portrayed himself to be, but tonight had triggered her lack of tolerance for that. It was as though his hand around her throat made her realise any feelings she'd once had for him were gone. She didn't care to make excuses for his behaviour any more, and the thought of him touching her turned her stomach, whether it was violent or otherwise. She was suddenly desperate to be rid of him.

Her anger drove her as she kneaded her dough, working her aggression out. But time moved fast and before she knew it, the raw ingredients had developed enough for her to put it in the glass bowl and cover it with cling film to prove. Not wanting a repeat performance of Mitchell's evening lesson, Kaidence washed off her hands and took more beer to the men in her living room. As she placed the cans on the coffee table, Mitchell caught her eye. The smarmy expression on his face made her want to fly at him and knock it off but her problem had always been that she was no match for him. He was stronger and knew just where to hit for maximum effect. So she tried to swallow down her rage as she collected the empties and returned to the kitchen. But once out of his sight, Kaidence paced the tiles to try and calm her temper. She took a few deep breaths to focus, and something clicked in her mind to tell her she had to make a trip to the garage because they had almost finished the first crate.

Sucking up her irritation, she headed to the back door to get access to the garage. But as she turned the key in the lock, she heard a *pssttt* sound on the other side of the fence and realised someone was trying to get her attention. With a frown, she got closer to the six-foot gate and gingerly unlocked it before opening it, only to find Jackson stood the other side.

Her heart started to thump in her chest as she frantically checked that no one inside was watching. 'What are you doing here?' she asked in a whisper.

'I needed to check on you,' he replied, staying on his side of the boundary.

'What if he sees you?' she asked, staying alert to her surroundings.

'He hasn't yet, and I've been here for at least an hour,' he replied in the same hushed tone.

'Well I'm fine so you can go?'

'Are you? Because I saw what happened in the kitchen.'

'He was just flexing his muscles. But it's under control.'

'It didn't look that way, Kaidence. It looked like he was hurting you.'

'And we will deal with getting me far away from him at the weekend. But right now, you have to leave and trust that I've got it under control.'

Jackson did a double take. 'You're finally ready to leave him?'

She nodded. 'I'm ready to start putting together a plan to put into immediate effect.'

But he was suspicious. 'Are you just telling me what I want to hear in order to get rid of me?'

'I guess you'll find out Friday,' she said, gently pushing him backwards to clear the gate, before closing and locking it.

She'd already been out of the house longer than the task usually took her, so she spun on her heel and rushed inside the garage to retrieve another case of twenty-four cans. Seeing Jackson had forced her to concentrate her focus on getting through the evening, because then she'd only have to put up with Mitchell for one day until she had a weekend without him.

Once in the kitchen, Kaidence restocked the fridge ready for when she was called on to be waitress again, and then went back to the laptop that was sitting on the dining table. She would waste time doing the job she was paid to do, because she wouldn't be able to focus with the endless possibilities of getting free running through her mind. So instead she shut down the computer and sat at the breakfast bar waiting to be called into action.

CHAPTER FOURTEEN

It was almost midnight when Kaidence climbed into bed. The three men Mitchell had invited over had left an hour ago and when she'd gone to clean up after them, she found her housemate fast asleep on the settee and decided to leave him there. Her eyes had been heavy as she cleaned up the cans and takeaway cartons from the Chinese food she'd had to order towards the end of the second crate, but she managed to get the room looking tidy before the dizziness got so bad that she was forced to stop. Plummeting the place into darkness, she made her way into the bedroom, sure that she would have the bed to herself. Regardless of how much alcohol he consumed, the stairs always seemed like too much effort for Mitchell and so she was guaranteed a good night's sleep.

She lay on her back for a short time, listening for any noise, but she could only hear Mitchell's snoring. Satisfied he was out cold, she turned on her side to get comfortable and it didn't take her long to drop off. But it seemed like only a short time later when she was waking up in the morning.

The clock was the first thing that caught her eye. Her late night had meant a just as late lie-in. It was almost lunchtime, so she was sure Mitchell had already left for work, but she had to get out of bed to be certain. Deciding not to get dressed before heading downstairs for her first beverage of the day, she grabbed her dressing gown off the back of the door and slipped it on at the top of the staircase.

There was no noise from the house, other than what she created as she stepped on creaky floorboards on her descent, so she knew she was alone. Reaching the ground floor, she went straight into the kitchen to boil the kettle before checking the living room to be sure her worst half had made it out of the door.

The smell of stale beer and cigarette smoke hit her as soon as she walked into the room and it turned her stomach. She didn't smoke and neither did Mitchell, but she wasn't surprised he'd allowed his friends to light up inside the house rather than being made to go outside. She walked over to the windows, unlocked them and threw them open as far as they would go. She needed to air it out if she was to clean in there and it needed it. Never had she known four grown men to make as much mess as a bunch of two-year-olds, but they had no regard for anyone but themselves.

Turning her back on the living room until she'd had her first cup of tea of the day, she closed the door and hoped by the time she walked back into it that the strong smells would've dispersed somewhat. She returned to the kitchen as the kettle reached full boil and wasted no time making a strong drink, which she sat at the dining table with. It was going to be a long twenty-four hours until she was free for the weekend, and the only thing she had to occupy herself with was the plans to put Mitchell in her rear-view mirror.

Jackson opened his eyes and took time to focus them. Usually it was still dark outside when he woke up because it was so early, but this morning it looked like he'd managed to have a lie-in. He checked the clock to find it was a few minutes shy of midday and he relaxed. It seemed hearing Kaidence say she was ready to leave her abusive boyfriend was just what he needed to ease his mind. He hadn't had an unbroken night's sleep since he'd knocked on her door two months ago, because he was constantly expecting a call to attend a homicide at her address.

The morning Louisa had found Kaidence lying at the bottom of her stairs had been one of the worst days since knowing her. He had been sure that was the call he'd been dreading, and he hadn't been around to protect her like he'd promised. It had happened before, and he was petrified that it was to be her fate too. Only her death would be harder to take, because he was in love with her and he couldn't help that even though he tried to keep himself at arm's length. He'd been relieved when the doctors had told them she was in a coma, because at least she was alive, and he could still help her. Now he was getting that chance.

He swung his legs out of bed and grabbed his phone off the bedside table. He needed to call his partner and let her know there'd been a development regarding Kaidence, so they could start brainstorming how they were going to help her.

———

Louisa could hear her phone ringing from her pocket as she packed her monthly shopping at the checkout of the supermarket. Whoever was calling would have to wait until she got back to her car. She couldn't answer without holding up the queue.

She'd spent the morning making her way through the to-do list she had compiled knowing she had booked time off work, and so far, she'd only managed to check one thing off. But she had five more days of holiday to complete it and she knew at the rate she was moving that she'd use them all before the last chore was marked off.

Her phone rang twice more before she got out of the supermarket so when it rang while she was pushing the trolley back to her vehicle, she fished it out of her pocket and answered it.

'Finally! What have you been doing?' Jackson asked as soon as the call connected.

'Jackson, do you even know the concept of annual leave?' she asked, ignoring his question.

He disregarded her counter question. 'Kaidence has finally said she's ready to leave Mitchell.'

Reaching her car, Louisa stopped the trolley and unlocked the boot. 'When did she tell you that?' she asked, starting to load her boot with the monthly shop.

'Last night when I went over to check on her because I was worried.'

She stopped unloading her shopping. 'You went to her house, while Mitchell was there?'

'He didn't see me.'

'How do you know?'

'I stayed out of sight,' he replied, not wanting to divulge that he'd been spying through her window like a stalker.

She started loading her boot again. 'How did you get her to agree to leave him?'

'I didn't. She was the one who brought it up.'

'But there has to be a reason for her sudden change of heart; only yesterday she was determined to stay,' she said, trying to understand as she finished emptying the trolley and closed her boot.

'I think she'd fooled herself into believing that he was done hitting her, and when he grabbed her around the throat last night, she realised that wasn't true.'

'You saw him hit her? And you're not locked up in a cell? Blimey, that must've taken great restraint.' She locked her car and returned the trolley to the nearest bay.

'It did. But if I'd interfered, she would've had worse than a bruised windpipe.'

'So, what's the plan?' she asked, walking back to her vehicle, unlocking it and climbing inside.

'We haven't had a chance to talk about it yet. I don't suppose you've got any ideas?'

'Well, she's got money, so we could pack her up, change her name and ship her off to Ireland. That way we can keep an eye on him using his passport.'

'That's not a terrible idea. But I don't know how ready she is to leave her family behind.'

By the time Kaidence had finished her clean-up in the living room it smelt a whole lot fresher than when she'd first walked in. There was still a hint of cigarette musk on the fabrics but removing the curtains from the windows took more effort than she was willing to put into housework today. The wind blowing in from outside was going to have to do for now. She wanted to get a few things down on paper regarding her leaving before Mitchell got home.

Heading to the study, she took an unused notebook from the locked third drawer down in the desk and sat behind it. She had begun to formulate a plan the minute she'd made her decision to leave the night before. She knew Jackson and Louisa would likely want to go at it like a bull at a gate and not work out the finer details, but she needed to have something more concrete if she was going to attempt something that would kill her if it went wrong.

She knew she'd have to change her name, which would be hard for her because it was all she had left of her parents. Without the surname they brought her into the world with, there'd be no evidence that her family even existed, because her sister had married hers away and they had no brothers. That would be the first hurdle she'd have to jump, and something she would need to come to terms with. Then she'd need to find a location to move to that was far enough for Mitchell to be unlikely to trace her. Next would be her confession to her sister. That would surely break Kaidence. But if she could navigate her way through that conversation, she'd be ready for what was to follow.

As difficult as it was going to be to start over somewhere new, keeping her distance from Meredith and not being able to see her nephew grow up in case Mitchell used any contact between them to find her was going to test her, because family meant everything to her since losing both of her parents. A possible silver lining was that she could stay in touch with Jackson and Louisa, because there was nothing to connect them, which would make the transition a little easier.

She was guilty of not liking change, and it was going to be tough not to be able to pick up her phone when she felt vulnerable and lonely to call the sister she could always depend on to help her feel less cut off from everyone she knew. It may be impossible for Mitchell to locate her from a number, but she couldn't take the risk that he could. At least being able to talk to the officers that she now considered her friends would mean she could pass messages through them, which was some consolation.

Kaidence was scribbling the possibilities that she'd thought of regarding where she'd be happy to live and suggestions of names she wouldn't mind going by for hours before her stomach growled to remind her she needed to eat. She placed her pen down on the paper and headed into the kitchen to find some food and while she was there, she decided to ring Jackson. She dialled his number from the card he'd left her and waited for him to answer. 'Morning,' she greeted him as soon as he did.

'You're still with us then?' he asked rhetorically.

'Did you really doubt I would be?'

'After what I saw last night, I wasn't sure.'

'That was mild compared to what I've had to endure.'

'Yeah well, it's one thing to know you're being abused, it's another to see it. You wouldn't believe what restraint it took not to bang down the door, just so I could give him a taste of his own medicine.'

'You'd have got more than you bargained for if you had because he had his idiot friends over last night.'

'So, he did that with witnesses?'

'Oh no, he was careful not to let me make any noise, so they didn't hear him crushing my windpipe.'

'Then they obviously don't know he's an abusive arsehole.'

'I doubt it. I'm sure Alan would've done more than just hold me on his lap to get off otherwise.'

'He lets his friends treat you like that?'

'He treats me how the hell he wants. Don't tell me you're surprised he lets his friends do the same.'

'I just wouldn't have thought you'd put up with it.'

'The last time I followed my instinct to slap John around the face for grabbing my arse, I got a lesson in reacting with repeated kicks to my ribs.'

He exhaled so hard she heard it. 'I am really not okay with how blasé you are about him hitting you.'

'I know it seems that way but it's just what I've got used to.'

'The sooner we can get you away from that waste of air, the better.'

Kaidence could hear the desperation in his voice. She knew all he'd wanted since the minute they'd met was to free her from Mitchell's clutches and make sure he never lay his hands on her again. But she'd been resistant, making excuses out of fear of what he'd do when he caught up to her, and she knew he would eventually catch her. He had the power to paralyse her whenever the switch went off in his head so even if she wanted to fight back, she lacked the mental capacity to think rationally and ultimately did nothing. She wanted to stand up to him, to demand she was treated better, but she could never build up enough courage. Now it was too late to do anything except leave.

'You'll be pleased to know I've been jotting down a few ideas that we can discuss at the weekend to begin that process,' she said.

'So sleeping on it hasn't changed your mind? You're still on board with leaving?'

'There's no going back now I've made the decision.'

The hours alone seemed to pass by more quickly than Kaidence was prepared for. The obligatory text from her housemate to prepare her for his return interrupted her scribbling down plans for her future and forced her into girlfriend mode. After speaking to Jackson, she'd prepared a bolognaise sauce and put it into her slow cooker on low so that she didn't have much to do to complete the meal.

Locking away the journal she'd been writing in, she headed to the kitchen and measured out the pasta she needed. She hadn't felt any dizziness throughout the day, and she wondered if it had something to do with impending freedom. Since making the decision, she felt like a weight had been lifted from her shoulders and could sense her tolerance for his violence was changing. But she knew she wasn't clear yet, so she had to maintain her mouse-like behaviour despite already being gone in her mind.

Placing a saucepan of water on the hob to bring it to the boil, Kaidence awaited the return of Mitchell. She seemed to be acting on instinct because once he was home, she stuck to the same routine and before she knew it, they were sitting at the dining table eating.

'What did you do today?' Mitchell asked to break the silence of the room.

It made her paranoid, as if he knew exactly what she'd been doing. But the logical part of her brain knew that was impossible. Any plans she had for leaving were locked away in the safe he didn't know about. Yet her heartbeat quickened, and her mouth ran dry at the thought of being found out.

'I just did some cleaning,' she replied, being half truthful.

'I suppose you've got nothing better to do with your day, have you?' he asked, and she could tell it was a put-down, but she didn't care because she wouldn't have to listen to his critical remarks for much longer.

She shook her head. 'No. All I've got these days is cooking and cleaning. I'll be glad when I can go back to work.'

'You don't need to go back to work, you have all the money you need.'

'I don't have to go back, but I want to.'

'I can think of better ways to earn a living that don't require pandering to other people's brats all day.'

'It's not that bad, they make every day interesting.'

He picked up his beer. 'I find that very hard to believe,' he said, taking a swig from the can. 'I hope you're barren because we're never having kids.'

Hearing him being derogatory about her fertility made her blood boil, especially given that she'd already had a miscarriage that he obviously didn't care to remember, so she couldn't possibly be sterile. As much as she wanted a child of her own, she'd been taking contraception because he refused to use condoms and she wasn't prepared to bring a baby into her current situation. Now she understood what his trigger was the first time he'd beaten her; it centred around her pregnancy and he'd been punishing her for that mistake ever since. Not that it excused his behaviour, it just explained it. But they'd never actually had a conversation about having a family, so she wasn't to know he would react so badly to news couples were usually happy about.

She let his statement slide. She just had to get through tonight without incident and she'd have three days to organise her escape. First on her to-do list would be handing in her notice at work, then finding somewhere to go before changing her name. Tomorrow would be the first day of the rest of her life.

'Talking of baby making, I'm going to bed early tonight and you'll be joining me,' he ordered. 'I need a release before I go away.'

'You might be able to do the job better than I can at the minute because of the dizzy spells,' she said, trying to get out of any obligation he thought she had.

'Well, you haven't got to do anything, you just have to lie there.'

She sighed inwardly; she was never allowed to just lie still and not partici-pate. He didn't get off on her doing an imitation of a sex doll, he required more input than that.

'Can you not just wait until you get back?'

'Are you really going to deny me my rights as a man?'

She knew better than to refuse him anything. 'No, I'm just asking if you'll mind waiting until Sunday.'

'And I'm telling you, you're giving it up tonight.'

She was going to pay for challenging him; for daring to think negotiating was a viable option when it never had been before. It was because of her impending departure. She'd got some fight back. But she was sure that slip-up was going to cost her an incident-free night.

Kaidence behaved like a kicked puppy for the rest of the evening. Since his announcement at teatime, she had considered every possibility to get out of the commitment he held her to but short of stabbing herself in the abdomen she hadn't come up with anything. So she'd sat on the other end of the settee watching the pictures move on the television waiting for her impending punishment. It wasn't as if this would be the first time she'd allowed him to do what he wanted with her body without complaint. But being a reluctant participant was better than being violently raped, like so many times in their history.

The minutes until bedtime passed so slowly that it was bordering on torture. But when he turned off the television, she knew her time was up. She had to climb the stairs and put on a convincing performance despite not wanting him to touch her.

Once in the bedroom, she removed her clothes and slipped on a sexy negligee that she knew he had a particular fondness for. She got beneath the covers and watched as he stripped off. The sight of his naked body revolted her, but abuse had a way of doing that and what she'd once found attractive now turned her stomach. The anticipation was enough to make her nauseous because it had been building for hours, but she forced it down as he got into bed beside her. She was about to reach over and douse the light when his voice filled the room.

'Leave it on,' he said. 'I want to watch you bouncing on top of me.'

Instinctively she responded before thinking it through. 'I thought you were doing the work tonight?'

He grabbed her hair in his hand and pulled her towards him. 'What did you say to me?'

'At dinnertime you said...'

'I don't care what I said, plans change, and you should know by now how to roll with the punches,' he said, twisting his fist, so her locks wrapped around it.

With her head forced back her movement was restricted so she couldn't fight his hold on her; instead she had to hope he would release her without causing her more damage. But that was too much to hope. Using his grasp to his advantage, Mitchell made a fist with his free hand and punched her in the mouth.

'Don't *ever* talk back to me. You know better than that,' he said, shifting to position himself above her. He used his weight to pin her to the mattress and pried her legs apart.

His dominance over her aroused him and she could feel it pressed against her pubic bone as he released her hair. She was thankful she didn't have to stimulate him because she didn't think she could bring herself to. But she had to tune out her current situation and imagine someone else in his place in order to be sufficiently ready for his intrusion into her body; it was Jackson's face she saw. She imagined him kissing her and running his manly hands all over her skin, which helped to adequately lubricate her. When Mitchell slipped his penis inside her it was less painful than it usually was but there was still some discomfort. She tried not to show any evidence of that distress as he moved back and forth, not because he cared if she was in pain but because she didn't want another punch for dampening his enjoyment.

He forced her knees up towards her chest, so he could get deeper penetration, and slammed his pelvis into hers repeatedly. The impact hurt as he grunted his way to climax, but she kept from calling out by biting on her bottom lip. She knew it would only be a few more strokes until he ejaculated because they hadn't been as active in the bedroom since she'd left hospital as they had been in the month before. But as he pounded into her, she bit down so hard that she drew blood. She could feel the bruise forming on her vagina and she knew she was going to suffer for his over-enthusiasm tomorrow.

She stared at the ceiling, waiting for it to be over and when it was, he momentarily collapsed on top of her like he always did before he rolled off. Usually he gave her an 'attagirl' for her efforts but tonight he didn't even grunt her way before he started snoring.

Kaidence gave it a few minutes before she threw the duvet back and went to the bathroom. Although she knew it was unlikely that he'd wake up before morning regardless of any noise in the house, she pushed the door that separated the two rooms into the frame, so it made as little sound as possible, and proceeded to run the taps slowly to fill the bath. She needed to wash him off her skin; she always did. However, no amount of scrubbing ever seemed to be enough because she could still feel him there.

She was about to sit on the closed toilet lid when she felt a trickle of liquid making its way down the inside of her leg. Looking down she saw it was blood. Mitchell had been too rough again but this time he had caused her some internal damage. She only hoped it wasn't too serious and would heal itself; or maybe the trauma had just brought her menstrual cycle on earlier than expected.

By the time the morning came Kaidence was in chronic pain from the injuries she'd sustained the night before. She could barely walk upright, and sitting was extremely uncomfortable. But despite her agony, she had forced herself to get up, so she could watch Mitchell leave. She needed to see it with her own eyes in order to believe he was really gone. Still, once she'd waved goodbye, she headed straight to her laptop to track his phone. It was a handy tool she'd been clued into by Louisa a few weeks ago and had put into action while he was passed out drunk on the settee. It was her way of making sure he wasn't spying on her when he was supposed to be at work. Confident he was getting further away, Kaidence decided to take full advantage of having the house to herself and headed straight to the living room. She wanted to blast out music loud enough to express her mood regardless of the hour. But before she had the chance to turn on the stereo, her phone started ringing in the kitchen. With a disgruntled groan, she moved as fast as she could to get to it. Luckily, she got to it in time.

'Hello,' she answered, recognising the number as Jackson's. She'd punched it into her phone so many times that she'd learned to identify it even though she wasn't confident enough to dial it without the card yet.

'It seems I don't need to ask my question because you already sound lighter somehow,' he responded.

She smiled. 'Are you coming over? I can make breakfast.'

Hearing how happy Kaidence was brought a smile to Jackson's face that she couldn't see. 'I'll be right over,' he replied, unable to refuse her infectious mood.

'Great! I'll start cooking,' she responded enthusiastically.

He had got up early on his day off because he knew Mitchell was leaving at his usual time and he wanted to ring her to make sure he'd gone. But Jackson didn't expect her freedom to have such an instant effect on her. It was like a switch had been flicked and her zest for life was screaming at him. It was something he wasn't used to experiencing, but he wanted to be around her for as long as it lasted.

CHAPTER FIFTEEN

Even though Kaidence had met him at the door wearing a smile, Jackson had immediately seen the bite mark underneath her bottom lip and noticed her walking gingerly as she led him to the kitchen where she was cooking. But he hadn't questioned her. Instead he sat at the breakfast bar watching her move about the room enjoying her liberty. He had a feeling that this was as close to the old Kaidence as she'd felt in ten months, so he didn't have the heart to question her about the injuries that would force her back down to reality just yet.

The way she carried herself was different enough that he noticed; she seemed lighter somehow. Even with her obvious injury restrictions she was happier in her movement. He knew she was most content in the kitchen, but this joy went beyond that and he was convinced that if she could dance, she would.

Kaidence felt her freedom way down in the depths of her soul and having Jackson there just cemented her confidence in her security. She was looking forward to not feeling that she had to be careful about what she said or did. In fact, she was looking forward to doing what the hell she liked when she liked and not fearing any repercussions for it. She wanted to live as close to ordinary as she could in preparation for when she was permanently away from Mitchell. It sounded so simple and yet she was out of practice.

She finished dishing up the full English breakfast she had wanted to make for her guest and smiled as she walked over to place it in front of him before climbing up onto the bar stool next to him.

He watched her wince as she sat down and realised which area was causing her discomfort. 'This is great,' he said, picking up his cutlery. 'But are you going to tell me what happened last night?'

'It was nothing.' She brushed it off.

'It's not nothing Kaidence; your movements are laboured and I saw you grimace when you sat down. So, what did he do to you?'

She sighed, knowing from experience that he wasn't going to let it go until she told him. 'He made me have sex with him.' She shrugged.

'You mean he raped you.' He put it bluntly.

'It's nothing he hasn't done before.'

'That doesn't make it okay. Rape is rape even if you're in a relationship.'

'I know, but it was either let him do that or die for resisting.'

He exhaled his anger at the thought. 'Don't think that split lip has gone unnoticed either,' he said, putting a forkful of food in his mouth.

'I'm leaving him, so can you table your disapproval until after the weekend please?'

'I'm not going to stop asking questions when I see that you're injured, Kaidence.'

She sighed as she chewed on the food in her mouth and swallowed. 'He was rougher than usual, that's all.'

He shook his head. Hearing how vulgarly her boyfriend treated her when he was supposed to be expressing his love disgusted him. It didn't surprise him, because he doubted that was the emotion he felt regarding her, but he didn't like to hear her recount how rough Mitchell was with her at a time when she was most vulnerable.

'Sometimes I wish I didn't need to know every single detail.'

'Well, that's probably the curse of the job.'

He raised his eyebrows to agree with her as he chewed another mouthful of food. 'My relentless determination to uncover every detail is precisely the reason why I chose to be a police officer.'

She smiled. 'Then you shouldn't complain when all I'm doing is giving you what you want.'

He chose to drop the subject. 'So, what's the plan for the rest of the day?'

'Have you got anywhere you need to be?'

He shook his head. 'I am all yours.'

Her smile grew. 'Fantastic! I have a few indoor activities we can do.'

'Kaidence, you can do anything and that includes going outside.'

She nodded. 'Baby steps, Jackson. Let's not run before we can walk.'

He laughed. 'All right, what is the first thing on your list?'

'We are going to make the dessert we'll eat tonight: a banoffee cheesecake.'

He tilted his head. 'Interesting. And then?'

'Then you're going to help me chop up vegetables while I make noodles from scratch for our stir-fry. When that's all done, we can go out for a walk.'

'A walk?'

She nodded slightly. 'I miss fresh air and walking always helped me clear the cobwebs before I stumbled into enemy territory. Now I'm lucky if I get to sit in the garden for an hour taking in the nature.'

'You know it's the middle of November though, right?'

'That's why coats were invented.'

'Then a walk sounds good.'

She laughed. 'You suck at lying, Jackson, but I do admire your commitment.'

'Well this is your weekend, so you get to do whatever you want.'

Kaidence knew he was trying to just open her eyes to the liberation she'd feel once she was single, but he'd made it sound like he was preparing for the end of her life, not the end of her relationship. 'Bloody hell, I'm not terminal. You don't have to grant all my last wishes in case I change my mind about leaving. I still remember what freedom is like, I don't need to be reminded.'

'I just want to spend two days witnessing you in your element, so I get a glimpse of how you'll live once you're safe.'

She reached out to place her hand on his forearm as it rested on the worktop. 'Trust me, you'll get plenty of examples with what I've got planned.'

'Then we'd better get these dishes cleared away, so we have a clean kitchen to dirty,' Jackson said, getting up and taking the empty plates to the sink.

The hours he spent watching Kaidence in the kitchen made Jackson realise that even if she wasn't restricted to the confines of her house, she'd be in there anyway because she actually enjoyed being creative. He could tell she thrived on showing him how to make a two-course meal from scratch and although he was sure he wouldn't retain any of the lessons she'd taught, watching her confidence in the kitchen was a glimpse of what could blossom once she was given the space to remember who she'd been before.

'That's all the preparation for our dinner done,' Kaidence said, as she finished bagging up the vegetables and noodles in zip-lock bags, so they wouldn't spoil before she got to cook them. 'Guess it's time to bundle up for our walk.'

'I've had an idea about that,' Jackson said.

'You're not getting out of it.'

'No, I don't want to. I saw your eyes light up the day we went to that pub for lunch, so I thought we could drive out there to take our walk.'

'I like that idea.'

She smiled; she hadn't been aware of the attention he paid to the littlest detail and yet it didn't really surprise her. He was precisely the kind of man who would make a point to notice even the smallest thing, so he had information available to make any number of gestures pertaining to the person in question. It was part of his job, sure, but she suspected it came in handy when he was dating.

'Then you'd better get your walking shoes on,' he said, reflecting her expression.

But she held up her finger to stop him going for his jacket. 'We have to make some sandwiches to take with us.'

'You want to take a picnic?'

'Not a summer's day picnic but we're going to need something to eat if we're walking for a while. Besides, by the time we get out there it'll be lunchtime.'

'My God, you're a feeder,' he said as it suddenly dawned on him. 'I didn't see it before but every time we see each other, you feed me.'

She held up her forefinger. 'Not always. Sometimes you only get coffee,' she said, removing the margarine and sliced chicken from the fridge.

He laughed. 'Rarely.'

She defended herself as she took a few slices of bread from the bag sitting on the side. 'Well Louisa told me you live on TV dinners and they're a crime against edible food.'

'Like I said, feeder.'

She found the humour in his depiction and it showed with a smile. 'I'm just trying to make sure you eat right, seeing as you don't.'

'What we've done this morning, it's too much effort to put in when I get home from a shift,' he said, watching her retrieve a knife from the cutlery drawer and begin to butter the loaf.

'You don't have to do that much. I can give you some twenty-minute recipes that are easy to put together.'

'And I wish I could tell you I'd change the way I eat if you did that, but I doubt anything would change.'

She shrugged as she finished making up the sandwiches and wrapped them in cling film. 'At least you're honest.'

'I don't know any other way to be.'

Kaidence bundled in through the front door with a laugh. They were both wet through because it had started raining while they were walking and, although they'd done their best to shelter under a large tree until it had passed, the rain had still found them between the branches. So they had decided to make their way back to the car, ducking beneath tree after tree to shelter as much as possible. But the last part of the journey had no cover, so they had to make a mad dash to the vehicle. Despite the heater being on full during the journey home, they were still soaked.

'Getting drenched was not part of today's plan,' Kaidence said, removing her coat and forcing her walking shoes off her feet.

'It's a good job I keep a spare set of clothes in the boot of my car just in case,' he said, holding up the duffle bag in his hand. 'Where's your bathroom?'

She pointed down the hall. 'It's on the right by the back door.'

'I'll be right back.'

She nodded. 'I'm going to go and get some dry clothes on too,' she told him as she instinctively reached out to deadlock the front door before heading upstairs.

Despite the weather, Kaidence was happy as she dropped her wet clothing into the laundry basket and went to the bathroom to fetch a towel to dry off her hair. She had to strip down to her underwear in order to shed anything touched by the rain but despite her scars and how ashamed she was of her body now, she wasn't nervous about Jackson being downstairs. She trusted him, and that meant knowing he wouldn't venture upstairs without an invitation.

Opening her wardrobe, she looked inside for an outfit that would be comfortable but wouldn't look like she was making too much of an effort to entertain a friend, and settled on a pair of black leggings with a long grey top. The reality was that Kaidence had come to think of him as more than just a friend and she relied on him more than she felt she should. He was the back-bone that gave her the confidence to leave. He injected her with a belief that she could get her old self back, or at least a semblance of it somewhere new. He made her want to be single, and she knew that was because of her attraction to him; but it didn't matter why she wanted it, just that she did. Even if she was never supposed to have anything more intimate with him than the friendship they shared, at least she had one person she could rely on whenever she needed to talk to someone who knew her.

The thing about starting over in a new place was that she could be someone completely different if she wanted to be, but she liked who she'd been before Mitchell had turned her world upside down. She wanted to be her again, but it was going to be hard to find that person when she'd be isolated from the only family she had. Despite keeping her abuse a secret from her sister, Kaidence depended on their family ties to help her feel a sense of belonging, and without that she wasn't sure how she was going to fit in to her new life as her past self.

When she got back down to the ground floor, she found Jackson making his way towards her from the bathroom she'd sent him to, shoving his wet clothes inside the bag he'd retrieved from the car.

'Don't put them in there. They're wet. Give them here and I'll put them on the radiators to dry,' she said, reaching out for them.

He handed her the bag. 'And I'll put the kettle on; make us a nice brew.'

'Perfect!' she said as they went their separate ways to complete each task. 'Then we'll put dinner on.'

Jackson checked the clock on the kitchen wall as he lifted the kettle from its base. 'It's not even four o'clock yet.'

'Aren't you hungry?' she shouted back at him.

'I'm always hungry,' he countered, putting the small appliance on to boil.

'Then when we've finished our cuppa, we'll start cooking,' she said, appearing in the kitchen. 'Are you ready to show me your culinary prowess?'

'No, but I am ready to assist while you demonstrate how it's actually done.'

'One of these days I will get you cooking for me,' she said, taking a seat at the dining table.

'You've got to be around for that, and if you're serious about leaving Mitchell, you won't be,' he said, joining her with the drinks he'd made.

'There'll be nothing stopping you coming to visit me wherever I end up.'

He dashed her hopes. 'Once you're in the witness protection programme, we won't be able to have any contact – it's designed that way to keep you safe.'

'So I won't even be able to call you?' she asked, as the reality of what she'd be leaving behind came to light.

He shook his head. 'You won't be able to contact anyone from your old life Kaidence, that's the point of the programme.'

'But I thought, because you're the officer on the case, that I'd at least be able to communicate with you.'

'I'm afraid not.'

'Well, that puts a different spin on it.'

'Oh no! You're not doing that; you're not changing your mind.'

'I don't want to, but I didn't know I'd be cut off from everyone and expected to start over from scratch.'

Suddenly she wasn't sure it was worth being alive if the cost of living was sacrificing the life that had been the driving force behind leaving. Being completely on her own was a frightening prospect.

'There'll be an adjustment period but you're strong enough to get through it. Deciding to leave is half the battle.'

'And apparently the other half is to be fought on my own,' she said, taking a sip from her cup.

'Kaidence, don't make that change your mind. Please. You need to get away from this arsehole before he kills you.'

'I know, I know that. But I didn't expect to have to do it alone.'

'You'll have people from the UK Protected Persons Service to help you transition.'

'But I don't know any of them.'

He leaned forward in his chair and reached out to grab her hand. 'I'll up sticks and move with you if that's what it takes, but you cannot stay in this house with him.'

She liked the feel of his skin on hers. Although his tender touch was unfamiliar, it felt like their hands belonged together. It was comforting and almost enough to make her forget her anxiety concerning their current topic of conversation, but only almost.

'I don't want to be here, Jackson, but I can't just leave everyone behind. That's punishing me when I'm not the one at fault.'

'I know it seems like that, but it really is for your protection.'

'And I realise I wouldn't be able to visit because he could follow me back to my new home, but he won't be able to trace a phone call.'

'Can you say that with absolute certainty?' he asked, retracting his hand.

She leaned back in her chair. 'Yes, he's not a spy.'

'But are you sure he doesn't know someone who could?'

'Well, I haven't met *everyone* he knows, I've never even met his family; but I can't imagine he associates with any tech-savvy people.'

'But you can't know, and that is precisely why it's done that way. So any unknown threat doesn't tell the person you're trying to get away from where to find you.'

She couldn't stop tears forming in her eyes. 'I understand why, I just know I can't do it on my own.'

'You won't be on your own for long, you'll make friends.'

'Except I won't. I don't have the confidence for that, and my self-esteem issues won't improve if I'm isolated in a strange place.'

'Then I'll look into seeing if it's possible for me to be there while you get settled in.'

Relief transformed her expression. 'Do you think they'd let you do that?'

He shrugged. 'They might take some persuading, but the fact I already know the protocol can only help.'

There was a beat of silence, and Kaidence frowned. 'Won't that mean you'll have no contact with your family?'

He nodded. 'I'd be willing to sacrifice a few phone calls and home visits if it means you'll be as far away from here as you can possibly get.'

'You'd really be willing to do that for me?'

'Yes. If it gets you away from Mitchell, I'd be willing to do anything.'

'Then I guess this conversation is best had after you speak to the agency that runs witness protection,' she said, ending the topic. She got to her feet. 'In the meantime, let's get dinner on.'

He stood up and spun to face her as she busied herself by getting the ingredients they'd prepared before leaving the house. 'That's it, end of subject?'

'Well there's really no point in me fighting you about something that a; you have no control over and b; I might not need to fight at all. You've said you'll ask if you can come with me, so I'll have to wait to figure out my next move. There's no reason the uncertainty should ruin our weekend.'

'Then I'll go and get us some wine,' he said, fishing the car keys from his jeans pocket.

'You could do that, or you could walk to the garage and get the two bottles I got with my shopping and hid for this weekend once Mitchell said he'd be gone.'

Jackson put his keys down on the work surface nearest the kitchen archway, 'A walk it is.'

By the time they were done cleaning up after their meal, Jackson and Kaidence had already finished off one of the bottles of wine and had cracked open the other. Being safe in the knowledge that her boyfriend wouldn't be home until Sunday had loosened her inhibitions and he liked seeing the side of her that wasn't so careful to avoid saying or doing something wrong.

'So, what's next on your agenda?' he asked as they retired to the living room.

Placing her wine glass on the coffee table, she grinned from ear to ear. 'I thought we could watch one of my favourite films,' she said, going to the DVDs on the shelves beside the television stand.

'And which film is that?' he asked, sitting down.

She turned to him, holding the case up so he could see the title. 'This one.'

'Oh God. I've heard about this film, but so far I've managed to avoid it.'

'It's great, you'll love it, I'm sure.'

'I'm not so convinced it'll be as thrilling for me as it'll be for you, but you can put on whatever you want. I'll just keep drinking.'

'Then you better go and fetch the other bottle I stashed in the spare tyre well in the boot of my car,' she said, loading the DVD player with the disc.

'Did you hoard alcohol all around the house so you could get drunk this weekend?'

'No, just the three bottles. It's just been so long since I felt comfortable drinking at home that I thought I'd take advantage of it.' She shrugged as she sat down beside him.

'I'll be right back,' he said, reaching out and touching her knee.

Kaidence enjoyed how affectionate he was with her. They'd fallen into a natural rhythm of acting like a couple even though they weren't one. But she didn't want to analyse the reason why, she simply wanted to appreciate it while she could. It was a reminder of how a relationship between a man and a woman could be, of how two people of opposite sexes could enjoy each other's company without any expectations or fear and of how comfortable she was with the man who vowed to save her. It felt natural, like they had known each other a lifetime and if she was honest, leaving her sister behind was going to be hard but leaving Jackson was going to be harder, because she had come to rely on him and she didn't see a future without him by her side, whether that was romantically or otherwise.

The film had started by the time he returned to the room and placed the unopened bottle on the coffee table as he sat back down next to her. He'd positioned himself closer to her on the three-seater settee so there was barely a foot between them, something she had only noticed because his hand had brushed her shoulder as he placed it behind her along the back of the seating. Neither of them spoke. Kaidence slyly glanced over at him. She was tempted to shift closer and rest her head on his chest in order to settle down to watch the pictures moving on the television but those were the actions of a woman in love and she wasn't; she was just contented around him, so she continued to stay upright, looking ahead.

During the hour they sat there she restrained herself from interlocking her fingers in his just to feel how it felt and bask in the much-needed human contact she desired. But she had unconsciously lessened the gap between them, so their upper arms were touching.

'I want a love like that,' she said, referring to the chick flick they were almost at the end of.

He pried his eyes from the screen. 'You could have it any time, once you're away from the arsehole you're currently shacked up with.'

'But do you think that kind of love really exists?'

'I've never experienced a love like it, but I'm sure it does.'

'Maybe it did a decade ago, but I'm not sure it does now.'

'Why do you say that?'

'My mum and dad had an overwhelming kind of love; you could see it when they looked at each other. But in all my relationships the feelings have been slow developing and none of the men I dated would go to great lengths to make sure I knew just how deep they felt. That kind of thing only happens in the movies now.'

'I'm sure it happens somewhere in the world; you just haven't met the kind of men that are comfortable making grand gestures that's all.'

'I've probably met a few, it's just that they're already in relationships.'

'Well maybe wherever you end up they'll have better men who are single.'

'God, after Mitchell I want to be single for a long time,' she countered.

'If that's what you want then that's what you'll do.'

'Maybe if I'm not looking, Mr Right for me will find me.'

'What if you've already met him and he's passed you by because you're off the market?'

'Then hopefully we'll have an opportunity in the future to have more of an impact on each other's lives,' she replied. 'I refuse to settle for just anybody once I'm free of Mitchell.'

He removed his arm from behind her and placed his hand on her knee. 'You should be treated like a queen.'

That's when a memory of her mother sprang into her mind and she smiled. 'My mum told me that once, but I didn't really understand what she meant by it until he hit me the first time. I know I should have walked out then, but I stupidly believed his promises that he wouldn't do it again. I listen to people who say they wouldn't stay in a violent relationship, but I defy them to leave when the person abusing them is someone they have feelings for.'

He moved his hand to his leg. 'I've seen too many women stay because they think they can change their abuser, but sadly they always learn the hard way that they can't. Sometimes it takes them wanting to protect their children, but often it takes being beaten within an inch of dying for them to finally walk away; nevertheless it's a lesson that's always learned too late. I never wanted you to be one of those women.'

'And you're the reason I won't be. If you hadn't knocked on my door when you did, I'd already be dead; I'd have died at the bottom of those stairs,' she said, pointing in the direction of the entrance before wrapping her hand around his. 'I owe you my life.'

He deflected his importance. 'It's part of the job description.'

She shook her head. 'You've always gone above and beyond what the job requires, Jackson, and I'd like to think our relationship goes deeper than that of officer and victim.'

'Of course it does. But ultimately, I'll have to do my job when you decide it's time to report him and in order to do that I have to be seen to be maintaining a professional distance, because we don't want any familiarity between us to obstruct the national crime agency giving their permission for me to go with you when you're relocated.'

'Can we at least maintain our non-professional distance until then?' she asked with a cheeky smile as she gently squeezed the hand she was still holding.

'Oh, I insist on it,' he replied, smiling back at her.

As the credits rolled on the second film Kaidence had talked Jackson into watching with her, the off-duty police officer placed his empty wine glass down on the coffee table with a sigh.

'It's getting late, so I better get off,' he said, getting to his feet.

Kaidence followed suit and stood up but she wasn't ready to be alone in her own home when she was so used to having someone else there, because she hadn't been on her own overnight since she'd been discharged from hospital a little over a fortnight before.

She gingerly followed him to the door, her mind a whirl with possible ways she could raise the subject of him staying without seeming so desperate not to be left alone.

'Jackson,' she blurted out as he reached down to slip on his shoes. He looked up at her. 'I don't suppose you'd be willing to stay the night in the spare room, would you? It's just that I'm so used to having someone else here that I don't like being alone.'

'Sure, I can do that as long as you think it's a good idea.'

She frowned. 'Why wouldn't it be?'

He shrugged. 'Well, what if Mitchell comes home?'

'He's not going to come home. He can barely stand to be here when he has to be; he's hardly going to travel back when he can spend the night far away from me at someone else's expense,' she said. 'Besides, this place is like a fortress at night. He wouldn't be able to get in if he tried.'

He removed his footwear. 'Then point me in the direction of my bed.'

She stood in the doorway of the room she'd given him for the night and watched him sleeping. Knowing he was lying in the next room had meant she hadn't been able to drift off, especially after the day they'd spent together. Her urge to feel his skin touching hers was overwhelming and compelled her to move closer to him. He looked so peaceful. She couldn't seem to stop herself as she climbed into the bed beside him. Her heart thumped in her chest, expecting him to wake up, but he didn't stir. She covered her body with the duvet and got close enough to feel the heat of his skin on her own. Still he didn't rouse. She leaned into him and placed her lips on his. That's when he responded.

His eyes opened, and she came into focus as he felt her lips on his. Instantly it registered what she was initiating. He reached up to place his hand on the back of her head, making their connection more certain and silently communicating his approval of her intentions. The kiss intensified as they both released any inhibitions they had about maintaining a certain distance while she was still under the roof that she shared with her current partner.

Jackson raised himself up off the mattress and flipped Kaidence onto her back, so he could control the situation. He wanted her to set the pace, but his need of her was fuelling his actions. While he had the opportunity to express the passion he felt for her, so that she knew she didn't have to settle for the way her boyfriend chose to use sex, he was going to take it. He needed her to know there were men who valued the connection of making love for what it was; an expression of love.

She could feel him on top of her, pressing her into the mattress as he kissed her with a passion she reciprocated wholeheartedly. She had forgotten she could be important to someone and how it felt to be wanted, but all those familiar feelings came back as he ran his hands over her body. Her senses started to slip, her concentration was on Jackson's tongue as it massaged her own and she tingled with her desire for him.

He used his sense of touch to explore her form on top of the satin night-dress she wore, and his body reacted to it. He'd wanted her for a long time and all those feelings came rushing to the surface as she slid open her legs and allowed him to slip between them.

Kaidence could feel his rock-hard member pressed against her inner thigh as he nestled himself in position to penetrate her. She was impatient to feel him inside her and arched her back towards him in order to relay the message. Reaching down between them, she slipped her hand beneath the waistband of his boxers and connected with his erection. She heard the sound he tried to bury in the back of his throat with the skin-to-skin contact and smiled against his mouth. Releasing her hold on him, she stretched to pull his underwear down, only to have him assist in her mission to have him naked. Jackson ducked beneath the covers to remove the one item of clothing he was still wearing before throwing them on the floor and returning to his position above her.

She smiled, gently pushing him over onto his back, and got up on her knees. She watched the hunger grow on his face as she slowly lifted her night-dress up her thighs. She raised it to her waist, revealing her vagina, and then up over her chest before removing it entirely. He reached up to cup her right breast in the palm of his hand and rub his thumb over her nipple. She bit her lip as the warmth of her arousal spread throughout her body, creating suffi-cient lubrication for what was to come next. Effortlessly she shifted to straddle his pelvis and lowered herself down onto the part of him that made them fit together.

Feeling him between her legs created a release she hadn't realised she was desperate for. Human contact was one thing, but sexual contact with true emotional connection gave her something else. She moaned in ecstasy as she took his full length and held him there. This feeling was long over-due, and she wasn't going to rush it. She moved herself to his tip before sinking him fully inside again, the sensations of pleasure completely over-whelming the pain she should be experiencing. She repeated the action over and over, battling to suppress the orgasm quickly edging towards the surface.

He allowed her the control she needed but he could feel himself getting closer to climax and he wanted to be completely connected at the time of release. He couldn't do that while she was on top. He pushed into her as she lowered onto him and lifted himself off the mattress, so he could roll her beneath him.

Her legs automatically moved to wrap around his waist and, as the pene-tration deepened, she called out with the heightened pleasure it caused. He moved back and forth inside her, gradually building to the crescendo of his own orgasm and noticed she was biting on her bottom lip to contain her need to scream out as she was reaching climax.

He lowered his lips to her ear. 'Don't hold it in. I want to hear how I make you feel,' he whispered.

And just when he thought her release would never come, he felt her muscles tighten and contract. She screamed out in ultimate pleasure and that caused him to roar as he ejaculated.

———————

Kaidence bolted upright in bed. She'd been dreaming, and her screams had woken her. It had been so vivid, which was evident by the knot in her stomach, the shortness of her breath and how extremely horny she felt. She took a minute to compose herself, but the feeling stayed with her. Needing to shake it off, she headed downstairs to get a glass of water.

———————

Jackson stirred. Something had disturbed his sleep. But it wasn't immediately evident what that was, so he lay still and listened for any signs of what it had been. He didn't have to wait long before he heard movement, which forced him into action. It wasn't until he edged out of the bedroom and onto the landing that he saw the light coming from the lower floor. He relaxed, realising that it was Kaidence moving about the kitchen, so he made his way down to her.

'Can't sleep?' he asked, walking into the room and inadvertently startling her.

She covered her heart to try to steady it as she spun to face him. 'Jesus Jackson!'

'Sorry, I didn't mean to scare you.' He smiled.

Her eyes dropped to the floor as she tucked her fringe behind her ear. 'It's okay. I just had a dream that woke me, that's all,' she said, instantly cursing herself for her need to be honest.

The fact she couldn't bring herself to make eye contact with him didn't go unnoticed. 'Was it a bad dream?'

She shook her head. 'Quite the opposite.'

'Oh, who was it about?' he asked, already having an inkling.

'Please, don't make me say it,' she pleaded with a smile.

He laughed. 'Oh go on, humour me.'

She covered her face with her hand. 'Don't. I'm embarrassed enough.'

He teasingly put his arm around her and tucked her head into his chest. 'You don't need to be embarrassed; we've all had dreams like that about someone we know.'

She looked up at him. 'Really?'

He screwed up his face. 'No, not really. But you almost believed me.'

CHAPTER SIXTEEN

The morning broke through her curtains before she was ready for it. Although contented from her company the night before, she hadn't slept very well; the embarrassment she felt over her dream had seen to that. Jackson was as gracious as he always was and tried to help put her at ease while they'd been sat in the kitchen in the middle of the night drinking hot chocolate, but knowing he knew where her unconscious mind had taken her made her uncomfortable at the thought of facing him over breakfast. Still, she pushed the feeling down. She wasn't about to be a prisoner to her mortification when it was something she'd get over almost as soon as she started cooking.

She climbed out of bed and headed to the bathroom to relieve her bladder. Having only woken once during the night – after her dream – instead of a handful of times like she usually would, meant that she was desperate. Sitting on the toilet, Kaidence realised the pain she had felt between her legs the previous day had subsided somewhat. It was still obvious she'd got an injury, but it wasn't immediately detectable.

Going back to her bedroom, she picked up her dressing gown and slipped it on as she made her way downstairs. She could feel the chill in the air around the house and she wanted to make breakfast before getting dressed. She didn't want to do a full-plate breakfast like the day before, but still wanted to give Jackson something substantial to eat to give him enough fuel to start his day. Entering the kitchen, she made the decision to do a stacked bacon, egg and sausage sandwich before waking him. She had no idea what kind of morning person he was so hoped the offer of food would soften the blow of having his sleep interrupted, but she was halfway through the task when she heard movement upstairs. The smell of food had obviously roused him, so she filled up the kettle and put it on to boil.

By the time Jackson entered the room, Kaidence had finished his beverage and was placing it on the breakfast bar where he usually sat. She looked at him in time to catch sight of his torso as he slipped on his T-shirt. He was built like she expected him to be, with a lightly defined six-pack that matched the defined biceps she had noticed the first time she'd seen him out of uniform, and she found it hard not to stare. She forced her eyes to look anywhere else and cleared her throat to speak. 'Morning,' she said, pushing away any embarrassment she felt. 'Did you sleep okay?'

He nodded as he perched on the stool he claimed whenever he visited her. 'That was the second-best night's sleep I've had for a long time.' He was honest.

He didn't tell her that she was the reason he'd had so many sleepless nights, because he didn't want her to feel that guilt. It was his own burden of not wanting to repeat his mistake while he'd been undercover, that was the truth behind it, and he was certain he'd only slept so soundly under her roof because he knew she was safe.

Kaidence allowed his response to sink in as she turned her attention to the bacon under the grill. 'Do you fancy trying your hand at a curry today?' she asked, putting out feelers for the day's activities.

'I thought I'd head home for a shower and a change of clothes first,' he said, sipping from his mug.

In the pit of her stomach she worried that her dream confession had caused him to think better of their closeness and that leaving was his way of pulling back, but he soon put her fear at ease.

'How about we order in tonight – my treat?' he suggested. 'I don't want you to spend all weekend cooking.'

She shrugged. 'I like it.'

'I know you do, but I'd like to break you away from what you'd ordinarily do and branch out into new territory.'

'Well, cooking with you is brand new territory.'

He shook his head. 'That's not an acceptable answer.' He paused, considering whether to allow the words for his next suggestion to leave his mouth. 'I don't suppose you'd let me take you out to a restaurant.'

His proposition caught her off guard and she responded instinctively. 'Like a date?'

'You're not single yet,' he stated, implying that it would be if she were. 'It'd just be a treat from one friend to another.'

Kaidence saw the opportunity to tease him, like he had done the night before when she'd divulged vague information about her dream. 'I don't know, that sounds like a date to me.'

But she wasn't prepared for his comeback. 'You're not dreaming now,' he said with a chuckle at the back of his throat. He'd got to know her enough that he knew gentle teasing was something she would take the way it was intended and not be offended.

She felt her cheeks flush red with embarrassment and covered it with bravado. 'Hey, you opened that door first; offering to come over and help me get back at Mitchell for sleeping with someone else. I was unconscious last night so I can't be held accountable for what I dreamt.'

Jackson cleared his throat. 'Well...'

She smirked. 'Don't like it when the boot is on the other foot, do you?'

'No, I don't mind. I just thought you had forgotten about that.'

Kaidence threw her head back with laughter. 'I forget nothing.'

He decided to shift the focus back to his original thought. 'So, I take it ordering in is where we've landed on food tonight.'

She gave a slight nod of regret in his direction. 'You can take me on as many dates as you like once Mitchell is out of the picture, but until then I think it's best we're not seen out in public together looking like we're dating.'

Jackson nodded as he mentally reprimanded himself for forgetting what he was trying to achieve by befriending her in the first place. Of course, she didn't want to be seen with someone who wasn't her boyfriend and have their relationship be misconstrued, especially in an intimate setting, because she'd likely pay the price with her life. He didn't want that. He simply hadn't been thinking straight and instead of being level-headed, he'd allowed his heart to hope for something that wasn't available yet.

'Of course not.' He confirmed his understanding. 'It seems that while I was sleeping so soundly last night I forgot about your boyfriend.'

'Well, if my dream is anything to go by, apparently I had done the same by the time I went to bed last night,' she said, poking fun at herself to detract attention from the stupidity he felt about his idea.

Although he hadn't meant it to sound like he was asking her out on a date, Kaidence had to think of every angle and if Mitchell, or anyone who knew her, were to see them sharing a meal – even just as friends – it would be perceived as such. She appreciated that not everyone thought the way she did, but she was forced to be prepared for every eventuality because her life could be on the line if she overlooked even the slightest detail that could be misunderstood.

Jackson laughed, not because he found what she'd said particularly funny

– he knew she was just trying to deflect – instead it was to cover his embarrassment for inadvertently acting like they were a couple. He sipped from his cup as he watched her assemble the breakfast double-decker that had finished cooking and put it on the counter in front of him.

'Thanks,' he said, ignoring the awkward feeling that hung in the air.

Approaching the seat she always sat in beside him with her own sandwich, she could see the discomfort on Jackson's face regarding their last conversation, so as she climbed up onto the stool she changed the subject.

'You know while you're out today, would you mind going to the shop and picking up a few things?' she asked.

He raised his eyebrows in amusement. 'So in a matter of minutes I've gone from dream lover to personal shopper. That's quite the demotion.' He laughed.

She shrugged. 'I just thought that, seeing as you're going out anyway...'

'Write me a list,' he instructed, as he took a bite of his sandwich.

Jackson escaped out of the back door to avoid detection and left in the car he'd parked on the street at the side of her house. It was one of the advantages of the house being on the corner; no one who overlooked her property would see where he had emerged from so wouldn't report back to Mitchell that she'd had a man inside. It had been just another precaution she had to consider when she started having him over.

But now she was alone, Kaidence found herself gravitating towards her usual routine of cleaning up any evidence of having company. Granted she only had to load the dishwasher, but it was habit. It wasn't until she felt a bit of a chill that she realised she was still in her pyjamas and dressing gown and instead of continuing to follow her instinct to cleanse the house of the other man in her life, she headed upstairs to shower and get dressed. It was a change for her to feel so relaxed, knowing that no one would be able to get inside her weekend sanctuary unless she let them in, and she took full advantage of it.

Walking into her bedroom, she headed over to the stereo on top of the chest of drawers opposite her bed and pressed the power button. She wasn't sure when she'd used it last so didn't know what CD was inside but pressed play anyway, and was pleasantly surprised when she heard swing music. She took no time discarding her clothing and entering the bathroom, leaving the door wide open as she showered. It was novel for her to feel secure while she was naked with the door open, but she did; it was amazing how being alone was strangely liberating. She sang along with the lyrics as she washed her body from head to toe, taking less time than she usually would because she didn't want to miss Jackson's return.

She dried off and wrapped towels around her hair and her body as she moved to stand in front of her wardrobe to decide on an outfit. She sighed in frustration because all the hanging garments were so similar. They kept her body completely covered so no one could see her scars or any bruises she might have. But today she felt like wearing some of her old clothes. Clothes that Mitchell wanted her to get rid of, that revealed too much skin or were sexy enough to draw male attention, so she'd boxed them up and put them in one of the other two bedrooms; they'd smell musty, and she wouldn't be able to freshen them up in the time it would take for Jackson to return. Then it dawned on her, she had washed one of her dressy tops the month before in preparation for chaperoning the Halloween disco at school, which she never got to go to. She rooted to the back of her wardrobe where she'd hidden it from Mitchell under one of her work shirts and removed it from the hanger. It wasn't inappropriately dressy for being home all day and it was long sleeved, but the neckline was lower than she was usually allowed to wear because her cleavage would definitely be visible. She gave it a sniff just to be sure it smelled fresh enough to wear and placed it on the bed.

Removing the towel she'd wrapped around her wet hair, she rubbed at the long locks to get rid of any excess water before she went to her dressing table and sat on the stool to blow dry it. Ordinarily she didn't care about her appearance, but something made her want to look nice for Jackson so that his lasting memory of her when he left her in witness protection wouldn't be as a victim. She happily groomed her mane and when she was completely satisfied with it, she moved onto her face, using the compact mirror hidden in her dressing table to apply a light dusting of make-up. It was just enough to notice she was wearing some without it looking like she was making too much effort.

She removed the towel that covered her naked form and returned it to the bathroom, where she hung it on the towel rack to dry before going back to the bedroom and beginning to dress. It had been a long time since she'd been on a date, but that's what it felt like despite their agreement to maintain a professional distance. He'd seen her at her lowest, and because of that she'd allowed him a glimpse behind the curtain of the woman she used to be; now she wanted to impress him. He'd brought so much to her life in the short time they'd been friends that she wanted to give him something back and she had the perfect thing in mind.

She smoothed down her top; having no mirrors beyond the small compact mirror in the house made it impossible to check her reflection so she hoped she looked acceptable.

As satisfied as she could be with the energy she'd put into looking less damaged, Kaidence made her way downstairs. It had been a long time since she'd cared enough about her appearance to put in any effort, but she knew it had everything to do with the man she'd been sharing her weekend with. She was about to take the last step on her descent to the ground floor when she heard the back door unlock and open. She peered over the stair rail, expecting it to be Jackson, who she'd given her key to, but wanting to make sure.

He smiled upon seeing her face and held up the plastic bag he was carrying. 'Hey. I brought some more wine.'

She jumped down the one step to the ground floor and smiled as he reached her. 'That'll be perfect for when we get back.'

'Where are we going?' he asked with a frown.

'I thought you could take me to the station to file a couple of reports.'

'I know just the officer to file those,' he said, taking the wine to the kitchen and returning to find her putting on her shoes.

Although it had been her suggestion, the closer they got to the station the more nervous Kaidence got and apparently, she was wearing that worry on her face.

'You'll be fine,' Jackson said, reaching over to lay a reassuring hand on top of hers.

She used her thumb to rub his fingers affectionately. 'Will you stay with me?'

'Of course,' he assured her, placing his hand back on the steering wheel.

She glanced at the road as silence fell between them before her eyes shifted to watch the hands she'd dreamed about touching her, as they controlled the vehicle. There was something sexy about a man driving and she needed to focus on anything other than what she was about to do, so she allowed her mind to drift. She envisioned him pulling over somewhere secluded, of her climbing into his lap and kissing him until she fulfilled the need inside that she'd had for a while. But he caught her daydreaming as he pulled up in the parking lot behind the station.

'Kaidence!' he said repeatedly, getting louder and louder each time until he got her to snap out of the fantasy she was distracted by.

Her eyes shot to his. 'What?'

'We're here,' he announced, turning off the engine.

'Oh.' She looked up at the building.

He frowned. 'Where were you?'

She shook her head to dislodge the image of them kissing from the fore-front of her brain. 'It's not important.'

Removing his seatbelt, he turned towards her. 'Are you ready to do this?'

She was less than convincing as she nodded. 'As ready as I'll ever be.'

Kaidence felt sick as she got out of the car and followed Jackson towards the building she'd been petrified to be near just days before. She didn't notice but her pace had progressively slowed on her walk across the car park. It was only when Jackson made his way back to her that she realised he'd been significantly further ahead of her.

He reached for her hand. 'I'll be by your side the whole time.'

'I know.'

'Are you sure you still want to do this?'

Almost like she'd only just felt his hand, Kaidence's grip tightened around his fingers. 'I'm here now. I'll be all right once I get inside.'

'Then let's get you inside.' He tried to encourage her into moving.

***

Phillip Valentine was easily ten years her senior as far as she could tell but Kaidence felt almost as safe telling him her story as she had with Jackson all those months ago. She was sure she'd seen him before at one of the stranger awareness assemblies they held at school, but she didn't want to ask. Still, his dark chocolate eyes seemed familiar somehow.

'I'll get these typed up and put into the system,' he said, gathering the papers for the reports she was filing. 'I suggest you file for a restraining order the minute the courts open on Monday so that we can serve him with papers and advise him of what happens if he violates it. We'll wait until that's done and bring him in for questioning regarding the two incidents you've filed about today.'

'How do I get him out of my house?'

'Officers can be there while he gets his belongings.'

'And what's to stop him coming back to the house?'

'Nothing, but with an order of protection you'll have a priority response if you have to call nine-nine-nine.'

'Except it's just a piece of paper. If he wants to get to me, he will.'

'Believe me, units are sent immediately. They'll be there to stop him.'

'I hope so,' she said, trying to be optimistic.

Officer Valentine addressed her in a serious voice. 'Just make sure you file with the courts first thing Monday.'

'I'm working the late shift Sunday, so I'll make sure she gets there,' Jackson said as they all stood up.

Valentine continued to speak to Kaidence. 'Deciding to get help is the hard part, you've done that. Just be sure to follow this through.'

She nodded. 'Thank you Officer Valentine, I will.'

Jackson reached out to shake his colleague's hand and he countered with the same. 'Thanks Phil.'

Valentine nodded and picked up the report papers before walking away.

'Shall we?' Jackson asked, bending his arm in her direction, inviting her to take it.

She linked her arm in his. 'I think I'm ready for that bottle of wine now.'

He laughed as they headed to the exit. 'Then maybe we should get another one on the way back.'

'Maybe we should get two.' She laughed as they exited the building.

To get through the doors, Kaidence unhooked herself from Jackson's arm and stepped outside in time to barrel into a passer-by, resulting in them both being knocked backwards. Although each of them managed to maintain their equilibrium, they lost their grip on the bags they were holding.

'I'm so sorry,' Kaidence apologised, scrambling to pick up the things that had fallen from her handbag.

'No harm done,' was the response from the other woman as she grabbed the backpack she had been carrying.

'Taylah?' Jackson asked, recognising the woman as his youngest sister.

Her face lit up with a smile at the sight of him. 'Jax,' she said, throwing her arms around his neck in a hug.

As they broke apart, Jackson turned to address Kaidence. 'This is my sister.'

Taylah bore a close likeness to her brother, though her blue eyes were a slightly darker shade than his. She stood not much shorter than him, and had an ample bust for her size.

She smiled at his younger sibling. 'Hi. I'm Kaidence.'

Taylah raised her eyebrows at her brother. 'Is this your girlfriend?'

He shook his head. 'No. We're friends.'

But Taylah ignored his denial and turned to Kaidence. 'So you're the reason I haven't seen much of my big brother lately.'

Kaidence looked at Jackson for confirmation of her accusation but he gave none. 'I had no idea...'

'No, it's good. It's great in fact. It means that he finally has something better to do than to meddle in my life.' She laughed. 'I've lost count of how many boyfriends he's driven away.'

He held up his hands defensively. 'It's not my fault that they fold under a little bit of pressure.'

'You're lucky to have someone that cares enough to look out for you the way he does,' Kaidence interjected.

Taylah's smile held. 'You two might not be dating but you're definitely more than friends.'

Jackson chose to change the subject. 'Where are you going?'

'Dance class,' she responded.

'You go to dance classes?'

'Yes, they help to keep me fit.'

He frowned. 'What? You don't go for fitness.'

'All right, the teacher is hot,' she admitted. 'Talking of, if I bring new people to class with me it'll get me extra brownie points.'

'Trust me, making me tag along will not get you brownie points.'

'You're not as bad a dancer as you think you are.'

'And you're not as convincing at giving compliments as you think you are.'

'The first lesson's free,' Taylah almost sang as a means of persuasion.

Listening to them made Kaidence smile; it reminded her of her own relationship with her sister. 'I wouldn't mind taking part in a dance class.'

'See Jax, not everyone is as opposed to having fun like you,' his sister teased.

'Do you really want to go?' Jackson asked Kaidence.

She shrugged. 'It'll be fun, and it could help your sister with her crush.'

Taylah smiled and wiggled her eyebrows. 'I like her.'

'I'm in jeans and trainers,' Jackson said, looking down at his clothes.

'It's an amateur class. You don't need to be dressed like you're appearing on Strictly Come Dancing; you're wearing what everyone else will show up in.'

He sighed. 'Okay, we'll come. But I don't know why you're bothering to try and impress this guy; he's just going to be one more that I have to drive away because he's not good enough for you.'

She began to lead the way. 'Not every guy I meet is as bad as you expect them to be.'

'It's my job as a big brother to make sure they're worthy of you. I'm just weeding out the time wasters.'

'They're not all time wasters.'

'If they weren't, I wouldn't be able to chase them away.'

Kaidence laughed. Witnessing the siblings interact made her affection for Jackson deepen. She didn't think it was possible to find him even more attractive than she already did, but seeing the side of him that came out when he was with his family made it possible.

Jackson nudged her playfully. 'What are you laughing at, Kaidy?'

Although it was the first time she'd heard him use the nickname, she liked it and it sounded strangely familiar.

'I like seeing you in big brother mode,' she replied. 'It's *way* more protective than Officer Chase's approach.'

'That's because it's family and they will always come before the badge.'

'Come on you two, we're going to be late,' Taylah said, hastening the pace.

Jackson turned to Kaidence. 'I guess we better hurry.'

'Definitely, because I don't want to miss the chance to see you bust a move,' she responded with a twinkle in her eye.

He smiled. He had a feeling it had been a long time since she felt devilishly playful, but he was willing to indulge her while she was. 'Are you truly ready for this?' he asked, holding the door to the building open for her. 'Taylah can be very persuasive but don't feel like you have to do this just to please her.'

'Oh no, you're not wriggling out of this, it sounds like fun,' she said, following his sister inside.

'I'm not trying to get out of anything, I'm looking forward to seeing you cut loose.'

'Well, you've had a taste of it already this weekend.'

'But this is so different; it's you outside the house, dancing.'

'You might be surprised to learn that I'm a good dancer.'

'Au contraire, mon amie, I can tell by the way you move about the kitchen.'

Her eyes almost popped out of their sockets hearing him speak French. 'Well, that's new.'

'And that's the extent of my French, so don't expect any more.'

She allowed a small laugh to pass her lips. 'It's probably for the best because that's the extent of my understanding.'

'You know neither of us have asked what kind of dance is being taught in this class,' he whispered over her shoulder and into her ear from behind. 'We could be walking into something we're not prepared for.'

Kaidence shrugged. 'I assume it's salsa,' she countered, turning her head back to him to continue their hushed conversation.

'God, I hope it's ballroom.'

'She's your sister, which is more likely?'

'Damn, it's going to be Latin of some kind, isn't it?'

'It's highly probable. Women in their early twenties tend to find Latin men perfect for fun and frolicking. It's only when they're ready to settle down that they look closer to home.'

Jackson rolled his eyes. 'Please, let's not talk about my little sister *frolicking*. It makes me want to lock her in a tower for the rest of her life,' he said as they entered the dancehall only to be met with half a dozen pairs of eyes inquisitive about the interruption.

Taylah held up her hand apologetically. 'Sorry I'm late, Giovanni, I was almost taken out on my way over here.'

The small, neat man wearing tight trousers and a shirt open to his navel at the front of the room was understanding. 'It's okay, Miss Chase, I haven't started teaching yet,' he replied, making his way over.

'This is my brother, Jackson, and his friend, Kaidence. Is it okay if they join us today?'

'Yes, the more the merry,' he said, loosely translating his understanding of the well-known English saying from Italian.

Kaidence removed her coat. 'So what dance will we be attempting?'

'The cha-cha-cha, Bella,' he happily answered, leading her by the hand towards the rest of the group.

She looked back at Jackson to find him following behind with his sister. She didn't like that her question had got her the attention of the teacher, and she was looking to him for rescue. Thankfully her liberation came when Giovanni stepped away from her to address the whole class, so she took the opportunity it created and joined the man she'd arrived with, because he was her comfort blanket and that meant she felt safest by his side.

'Okay dancers, can I have your attention?' Giovanni asked, clapping his hands to silence the room. 'For today's lesson I want you in pairs. I shall have Miss Chase to be my partner.'

Although she downplayed it, Kaidence could see Taylah's delight as she joined her teacher at the front of the room. As far as she could tell, the young woman was the only one who had shown up alone, which was probably the reason for her being singled out, but she doubted Taylah would see it that way. Unconsciously, while she'd been watching his sister, Kaidence had wrapped her arm around Jackson's, staking her claim to him.

He felt her touch and, even though her affection came as a surprise, it felt natural. He didn't draw attention to it, he just enjoyed it while it lasted; which wasn't long because Giovanni encouraged them into hold facing each other.

Taking the chance it afforded him, Jackson took in the details of her face. She was much more beautiful than he knew she believed. Her piercing green eyes were brighter than they'd ever been before, and the amber flecks were much more noticeable as a result. The subtle make-up she wore made little difference to how he saw her, because anything was an improvement on the bruises that he'd once seen there. But the light covering of cosmetics must have added a hint of confidence, which could explain her agreeing to his sister's request.

It wasn't until the instructor gently eased them closer together and placed their hands in the right positions that he noticed a flash of colour in her cheeks. It caused him to smile, especially when he caught her briefly biting her bottom lip. He found it endearing and it reflected in some small measure his own feelings about their closeness. These were the moments he treasured the most and when they started moving in synchronisation with the music, he felt the wall she had built to protect herself slowly lowering.

―――――――

Kaidence was exhausted after the hour of exercise that she wasn't used to, but it felt good to have fun without fear of repercussion. She'd always loved to dance so it hadn't taken much for her to be persuaded to join Taylah, and she knew Jackson had only agreed to it for her sake. He'd as much as given her permission to do anything she wanted, and she'd taken advantage of that. But she could tell he'd enjoyed himself as much as she had once the dancing started, and she had to agree with his sister; he was a good mover.

Taylah made a beeline for Giovanni as the rest of the class dispersed so Kaidence and Jackson retreated to the hangers to put on their coats. They'd got more enjoyment out of the experience than either of them was expecting and somehow sharing that time so carefree had brought them closer together.

'It's been nice to see you have so much fun today,' Jackson commented.

'Honestly, it was nice not to have to think about anything other than where my feet should be,' she replied.

'Then I'm glad we ran into Taylah.'

She laughed. 'Literally in my case.'

'I'll just wait to say goodbye to her and then we'll get you back home to that bottle of wine.'

'Yes, please.'

It was ten minutes before Taylah joined them and that was only because the man she was besotted with had excused himself so he could be on time for his next appointment.

'Right, are we ready to go?' the young woman asked as she slipped her arms into the sleeves of her jacket.

It struck Kaidence then that Jackson's sister was dressed more for fashion than for the weather, because her skinny jeans and short-sleeved cropped belly top would be more suited for spring.

Jackson frowned. 'Where are *we* going?'

'Home.'

He shook his head. 'I'm not a taxi service.'

Taylah shrugged her shoulders. 'Fine. But what do you think happens when I tell Mom that you let me walk home alone?'

'It's the middle of the day, T.'

'Do you think that'll make a difference to her?'

With a sigh of defeat, Jackson addressed Kaidence. 'Do you mind if we drop her off at home? We can get food on our way back to yours.'

The fact he'd been so easily manipulated by his sister made her smile. 'I don't mind.'

They travelled to the Chase house almost in silence except for the odd question Taylah threw at Kaidence about her relationship with her brother, which Jackson answered instead so she didn't feel like she was being interrogated. Jackson knew it was coming from a place of curiosity because his family hadn't seen him with a girl since high school, but he didn't want Kaidence to bear the burden of the spotlight.

Taylah fished for details. 'So, you didn't tell me how you two met.'

'Come on T, that's enough questions now,' Jackson pleaded.

'It's your fault,' she claimed, leaning forward between the two front seats. 'I've got no idea what kind of women you're interested in.'

Kaidence turned her upper body in the passenger's seat to better look at his sister. 'Haven't you ever met one of his girlfriends?'

'What girlfriends?' she exclaimed.

Jackson rolled his eyes. 'I've had girlfriends.'

'That might be true, but you've never brought one home before.'

'I'm not bringing one home now because, a, Kaidence isn't my girlfriend and, b, we're just dropping you off,' he said, pulling up to the kerb outside his parents' house.

'Jax, if Mum knows you dropped me off and didn't come in, she's going to be upset.'

'Then don't tell her I brought you back.'

'I'm not going to lie to her.'

'You don't have to lie, just don't mention it.'

'She knows what time I get home after dance class; she's going to ask how I got home so quickly.'

Kaidence smiled at him. 'You should go inside.'

Jackson unclipped his seatbelt. 'I'll pop in for five minutes.'

'I'll be waiting,' Kaidence said.

'Oh no, you're coming in too,' Taylah announced, gathering her things.

'Come on T, she doesn't have to do that,' Jackson said, trying to discourage her request.

'You can't let her sit out here in the cold,' his sister said before addressing Kaidence again. 'You're coming inside.'

Kaidence shrugged and smiled at Jackson. 'I guess I'm meeting your mother.'

'You should probably prepare yourself for more family members than that,' he countered, not wanting her to be overwhelmed if that was the case when she got inside.

They all climbed out of the car and Taylah ran up the steps ahead while Jackson kept Kaidence company in her calculated walk towards the front door. He could tell she was worried about what she was walking into, so he tried to ease her fears by placing his hand on the small of her back.

'If you don't make any sudden movements, they'll barely even notice you,' he said, attempting to make her laugh.

She felt a surge of assurance from his delicate touch and straightened her back to portray confidence she didn't feel. 'I've never met someone's parents before, never mind the parents of a guy I'm not even dating.'

'I'll make sure they know we're just friends.'

'Are we friends?'

'You want to ask me that now?' he asked as they reached the door.

She smiled. 'What we are is pretty hard to label, isn't it?'

He nodded. 'That's a job for another time. Right now, we're friends,' he said, unconsciously reaching down for her hand as they walked inside.

'Mum, Dad, I found a stray while I was out, and he has a friend,' Taylah announced to the household as she closed the door behind them.

Kaidence's instinct was to snatch her hand back before anyone noticed but she liked the way it felt around hers so instead she gripped a little tighter until his family came into view. The shock of being face to face with them then made her involuntarily let go of her hold on him.

Francine Chase seemed to appear from nowhere and embrace her son before looking at his companion. She was roughly the same height as the stranger with auburn hair and she had a twinkle in her turquoise eyes as she greeted her with a one-arm hug.

Richard Chase was where Jackson got his defining features from. He wasn't much shorter than his son in height, with dark hair and intense blue eyes. But his military background was evident in his welcome; unlike his wife, he was slightly colder and only offered a nod of acknowledgement.

Jackson's mother wasted no time linking Kaidence's arm in hers and guiding her to the kitchen. 'Let's get you a seat, my dear, and then you can tell me all about how you know my son.'

'Oh, we're just friends Mrs Chase,' she was quick to counter.

'Well you're the first girl he's brought home since high school so you two have to be more than *just* friends.'

'I wasn't bringing her home,' Jackson clarified. 'Taylah made me drop her off and then forced Kaidence to come inside; she was going to wait in the car.'

'Oh, it's freezing out there so I'm glad she came in.'

'And I'm sure that as long as you don't give her the third degree, she won't regret that decision.'

'A few questions are not the third degree; we just want to learn a little about your *friend*,' Francine said, filling the kettle with water and putting it on to boil. 'So, Kaidence, is it?'

She nodded. 'Yes ma'am.'

'That's an unusual name. Where is that from?'

'I think the original spelling of it is Latin and derived from an English word meaning rhythmic flow of sounds, but my parents adapted the spelling a little when I came along.'

Jackson found it interesting to watch her interact with his mother. He knew she was aware of how important his mum was to him, so it was good to see them trying to get to know each other.

Francine continued her line of questioning. 'And what is it you do?'

'I'm a teacher,' she replied.

'So, is that how you met Jackson?'

Not wanting to go into the complicated details of the reality, Kaidence considered telling a different truth for a second but she didn't want her relationship with his family to begin with a lie. She took a deep breath to prepare to be honest with the woman he held in such high regard. 'Actually, he's helping me get away from my abusive boyfriend.'

Instantly his mother knew who she was because she'd heard him discussing her over the phone with his partner. She had tried to discourage him from getting too close, but she could see that he hadn't heeded her advice and, although she didn't know much about the stranger in her house, she could already tell they were mutually involved with each other. She was worried for her son even though it was obvious Kaidence reciprocated the feelings that were evident in him.

'We were just coming out of the police station when we bumped into T,' Jackson added to fill her in on the developments since they'd last spoken, without Kaidence realising he'd divulged details about her in a previous discussion.

'So, you two aren't friends?' his mother asked, trying to get her head around the conditions of their relationship.

'No, we are,' Kaidence was eager to confirm. 'It just started as a rescue mission for Jackson. But over the last couple of months, we've spent a lot of time together and that's how we got so close so fast.'

'She even feeds me,' Jackson added.

Francine offered her a seat at the dining table. 'That makes me so happy. I hate those microwave meals he eats.'

'I've tried to persuade him to let me teach him a few twenty-minute recipes, but he said he wouldn't use them so any time I have the chance to invite him over to eat, I take it,' Kaidence said.

'You are fast becoming one of my favourite people,' his mother said, preparing cups for hot beverages.

Her distance created an opportunity for Kaidence to look across at the man who always did his best to reassure her and found him smiling back. She took that as a good sign and reflected his expression. It had been so long since she'd been in the presence of a mother a similar age to what her own would have been if she was still alive, that she was sure she'd forgotten how to properly interact with one respectfully, but she had just fallen back on her instinct. It seemed that she was doing okay – although she wouldn't know for definite until Jackson was alone with her. Still, she took it as a good sign that she hadn't been thrown out after the initial introduction.

The early afternoon passed in the company of not just Mrs Chase, but her husband and the two children that still resided at home. Riley only joined them once they moved into the living room and instantly Kaidence noticed he was the spitting image of his older brother, apart from being a few inches shorter and having arms covered in tattoos. She couldn't imagine their strict army father was happy about his inked display of expression, but she could tell he'd learned to live with them.

They drank tea and talked about nothing of importance and everything that mattered, giving them all a better understanding of each other. Sometimes Richard contributed very little and other times he was the only one that spoke. Witnessing the family dynamics made Kaidence miss the times she and Meredith had spent with their own parents; something she'd never focused on before.

She'd been reluctant to divulge the untimely death of her mum and dad but when it came up in conversation, she couldn't evade it and the usual look of empathy followed. She hated it but had realised over the years that although it was unintentional, it was unavoidable. As a defence mechanism, Kaidence had redirected the topic onto the family she still had, and that had sparked curiosity about her sister's knowledge of the abuse, which had led to another uncomfortable discussion. But by the time Jackson made excuses for them to leave, Kaidence felt like she knew him better and had been accepted by the people closest to him.

CHAPTER SEVENTEEN

Kaidence sat in the passenger's seat of the car while Jackson was inside the takeaway getting their food, feeling more like the person she had been before she'd been unfortunate enough to pick the wrong boyfriend. Spending time with his parents had reminded her of how much she missed her own, something she hadn't allowed herself to feel for as long as she had needed the strength to make it through every day. During the last year she hadn't given herself permission to visit any of her memories of them; she'd barely even been able to look at the portrait she had hanging in her hallway above the ones of her and Meredith because she knew they'd be ashamed of her tolerance of her current situation. What her mother told her about being treated like a queen by anyone she dated only really resonated the first time Mitchell lay his hands on her, but by then it was too late. She had let him into her heart as well as her home and she knew getting rid of him wasn't going to be as straightforward as asking him to leave. It had escalated from there and she only wanted to fight for her freedom once she had someone who had stumbled upon her abuse by chance.

So many times, she had wanted to tell her sister, but the words wouldn't form and any explanation she had for putting up with it so long seemed pathetic, so she had carried the weight of it alone, until Jackson found her. It had been easy to let him see the bruises because he was a stranger, regardless of being a police officer; she just hadn't expected him to become a friend and she really did consider him to be her friend. Although she believed her feelings went deeper than friendship, she couldn't trust them while she was vulnerable because they might just be gratitude for him wanting to rescue her.

Once she was in witness protection and there was some distance between them, she would know for sure. Their relationship wouldn't be based on him being the knight in shining armour or her the damsel in distress, which would give her the chance to understand her feelings from a fresh perspective. She didn't relish not having him around while she lived in isolation, but she knew that it would help her to get her independence back.

Her thoughts were interrupted as she watched Jackson emerge from the takeaway across the street. She had never really noticed before that he had a pretty great walk. But she barely had a chance to appreciate it before he was back in the car and handing over the bag of hot food to her.

'Did you remember the dim sum?' she asked, peeking inside the carrier.

'Yes, I got your appetizer,' he replied, starting the car. 'I also treated us to a banana fritter.'

'Ooh, then let's get home and crack that bottle of wine,' she said with a little laugh.

He saluted. 'Yes ma'am.'

'Drop me here,' Kaidence told him as he pulled onto the street that led to her own.

He pulled up to the kerb. 'I'll see you at the house.'

'I'll take the food, so you don't reduce it to a mess as you jump the fence,' she said, climbing out onto the pavement and closing the passenger door.

The walk back to her front door gave her the opportunity to reflect on the day. It had been one of the best she'd had in years, because it was the closest she'd been to her old self in just as long. She'd almost forgotten what it was like to be so carefree and make spur-of-the-moment decisions. It felt good. Being around Jackson always lifted her spirits so this was hardly surprising. However, meeting his family had really helped her get a better understanding of the man he was. It was obvious that he got his drive from his father and his compassion from his mother. They were a perfect well-knit family, just like she and her sister had been with her parents. Being around them magnified how much she disliked her isolation. Despite still having her sister in her life, she didn't get to spend as much time with her as she used to before Mitchell. She missed their closeness. She missed telling her every single detail of her life, including sexual encounters. It was foreign to keep anything from her, especially something as life-threatening as the abuse she had to endure. In that instant she decided to carve out some time the following week to visit Meredith and reveal the horror she'd been living so that when the time came for her to leave, it wouldn't be such a shock.

As she made her way up the steps to her front door, Kaidence saw Tim's net curtain twitch and she internalised her eye roll as she slid the key in the lock. She let herself inside and as she closed the door, she instinctively knocked down the snib button on the latch to deadlock it before heading to the back of the house, so she could give Jackson access.

'For a minute I thought you were going to keep me outside until you'd eaten all the food and drank all the wine,' he joked, walking inside.

She closed and locked the door behind him. 'If I did that, you'd spend all night out there. My tolerance for alcohol isn't what it used to be; a bottle of wine would comatose me until morning.'

'You seemed to manage it last night,' he commented as they made their way into the kitchen and she put the carrier of food on the island.

'And we both know what kind of dream that inspired,' she countered, reaching up to take two plates from a cupboard and then two glasses from another.

Jackson removed the takeaway containers from the bag she'd put on the counter, before moving to get the cutlery and placing them on the dining table where they usually sat, while Kaidence lay the plates down. He swung to move the food between the two place settings as she grabbed the bottle of wine and the glasses. They moved like a couple who'd been going through the same routine for years even though it had only been twenty-four hours.

'I'm going to miss this,' Kaidence said, thinking out loud as she scooped a portion of fried rice out of the container and onto her plate. 'It's been so long since I've been this comfortable with someone without any effort at all.'

'Well, I've never been this comfortable with anyone before, so you've got one up on me,' he said. 'Besides, we'll get to do this again.'

'Not once I'm in witness protection. I'm going to be completely cut off from everyone I know,' she reminded him.

'But you'll be alive.'

'Alive and unable to cook for you ever again, bear that in mind,' she teased.

'But if PPS allow me to come with you, we'll have plenty of opportunities to eat dinner together.'

'The witness protection people?' she asked to clarify they meant the same thing.

He nodded. 'Protected Persons Service.'

She passed him the wine bottle. 'And if they say no, we'll never see each other again.'

He made his way to the utensil drawer and uncorked it with very little effort before returning to his chair. 'Well let's not prepare for the worst until we've asked the question and got an answer.'

'But I need to plan for every eventuality, it's part of who I am. I don't like surprises.'

'I have faith that you can take whatever is thrown at you.'

'I'm glad you do, because I'm not sure I can live without you in my life even when I don't need rescuing any more.'

'You won't be alone for long.'

'But how do I trust a man again after this?' she asked, mixing her food together. 'My judgement cannot be trusted; I think we've established that.'

'Not all men are like Mitchell.'

'They're not all like you either.'

He let her statement linger as he started eating. 'You can't stay single for the rest of your life. You know the warning signs, so you'll use your experience to weed out the bad ones.'

'But I picked Mitchell; I can't be relied on to make decisions about my love life,' she insisted, scooping up a forkful of food and putting it into her mouth.

'Your judgement is fine. You just had a lapse is all,' he said. 'Mitchell's the first boyfriend who thought it was okay to treat you this way, isn't he?'

'I'm not so tragic that this kind of relationship is a pattern.'

'You don't always see abuse coming.'

'Exactly, which is why my judgement can't be trusted.'

'The first time you don't see it until it's too late, but you'll know how to spot it in the future should you meet someone who has the same tendencies.'

'Oh, I think I'm done with dating.'

Her declaration made him hesitate for a moment. At least if she didn't plan to date, he wouldn't have to hear about her being with another man. But swearing off men for life wasn't the point of what he was trying to achieve by giving her back her freedom. He understood there would be a transition period while she recovered from the trauma Mitchell had inflicted but he didn't expect her to be celibate forever.

'C'mon, don't let one arsehole ruin you for the rest of us.'

'I fear it may already be too late.'

He shook his head. 'I am proof that you're not a lost cause just yet.'

She shrugged. 'I just don't think I'll be able to date without having someone to run the guy past first.'

'Did you run Mitchell past anyone first?'

She chewed her food and pondered his question. 'I think my friends approved of him until he started to disapprove of them.'

'So, if friends weren't any help before, why would they be in the future?'

She raised her eyebrows. 'You'd have a point if one of my few friends these days wasn't a policeman. You'd be able to sniff out any threat in seconds.'

'The problem with that is that I won't be *in* witness protection with you, at least not when you'll be ready to date.'

She threw herself against the back of her chair with a loud sigh. 'Witness protection sounds like it's going to get old fast.'

'You'll adapt,' he offered.

'So, in addition to shredding my baggage from this relationship, I'll be expected to vet my own suitors? Being a normal functioning adult is going to be exhausting.'

'I have faith you'll make it through.'

'Let's stop talking about me being alone, I'm getting depressed.' Kaidence scooped up more food and put it in her mouth.

———

The temperature had dropped, and it was dark by the time Kaidence led Jackson to the living room with the bottle of wine they'd opened with their food. He had insisted on helping her clean up despite her protests to the contrary, but it had meant that they could make the most of their last night together before Mitchell's return.

'So what movie are you delighting me with tonight?' Jackson asked, sitting on the end of the settee he'd sat on every time he'd been there.

'I thought we could talk for a bit and listen to some music first.'

He frowned as she went to the stereo and started sifting through her collection of CDs. 'Haven't we *been* talking?'

'Yes, but I feel like I know you so much better now that I've met your family,' she said, deciding on what she wanted to listen to and putting it into the disc tray.

He hung his head. 'Oh.'

She hit play with a smile and sauntered over to plant herself beside him on the settee. 'I now know where you get your thirst for details from.'

'I'm sorry about my mum's Spanish inquisition, I tried to curb it but that's what I get for taking you inside.'

'Actually, that's what you get for me being the first woman you've taken to your parents' house.'

He shrugged. 'No woman has been up to the task.'

'And you thought I was?' She laughed.

'I didn't want to take you inside,' he pointed out.

'Well it's a good job you did, or you would've had an earful for leaving me in the car.'

'It's all Taylah's doing. She knows exactly how to play me.'

Kaidence couldn't help but laugh. 'She really does. But that's what being a younger sibling is all about.'

'Do you do it with your sister?'

'You bet I do, any chance I get.'

'If it's any consolation, you held your own during questioning.'

'Well, I've had practice. Mulling over an answer for too long is dangerous in my relationship so I've got used to thinking on my feet.'

He repeated his concern. 'It really disturbs me how flippant you are about that.'

'I know, you keep telling me.' She shrugged. 'It's a coping mechanism.'

Jackson sipped from his glass. 'So interrogation aside, did you have fun today?'

Kaidence mirrored his action. 'Yes, I like your family.'

'Well, an extra half an hour might have changed that.'

She fell silent briefly. 'Question; have you talked to your mum about me?'

He hesitated. 'I might have mentioned you once, why?'

'Nothing, I just thought there was a flicker of recognition on her face when I told her how we knew each other.'

'I was at home while you were in hospital when Louisa called to berate me for confronting Mitchell on the car park and she overheard me on the phone. Naturally she asked questions once I hung up and she could see I was angry, so I told her about a woman who'd been in a coma because of her abusive boyfriend. I never mentioned your name, but she would've put two and two together.'

'It's okay. I'm not mad about it. I was just surprised I didn't get more of a reaction, that's all.'

'Trust me, my dad will have reacted once you left. He despises abusive men.'

'Sure.' She shrugged. 'He's a military man.'

'He would've just kept that to himself while you were there. He probably vented to my mum once we left.'

'You don't make a habit of taking domestic abuse cases home with you so it's to be expected.'

'I can tell they liked you though.'

She giggled. 'How?'

'If they hadn't, they wouldn't have asked so much. Dad would've excused himself to his office after saying hello and Mum would've gone into the kitchen to start dinner once she had found out how we knew each other.'

'Maybe it was because you've never taken a woman to meet your parents,' she said with a laugh that echoed off the surrounding walls. 'It's hard to believe that you've never taken a serious girlfriend home.'

He shrugged his shoulders. 'I've never *had* a serious girlfriend.'

'I find that inconceivable.'

'It's not like I've never dated, I've just never been serious enough about someone to introduce her to my parents.'

'And you thought starting with me was a good idea?'

'In my defence, I wasn't taking you home.'

'You keep saying that, but I didn't hear you protest when your sister insisted on my going inside.'

'Because I knew the earache I'd get off my mum if she knew I'd left you out there.'

'You can admit that you wanted me to meet your parents. I won't hold it against you,' she joked.

'I'll admit I wasn't dead set against it. I know meeting them probably did you some good, no matter how unconscious it is.'

Silence fell on the room. He was right. Spending time with his family had reminded her of her own and forced her to consider how her own mother and father would feel about her current situation. The tightening of Richard Chase's jaw when she mentioned her boyfriend's treatment didn't go unnoticed, and she imagined her father would have had the same reaction before escorting her home and turfing Mitchell out of the house. Her mother, despite her need to protect her, would have allowed her husband to take the lead in dealing with the situation. Of course, if her father was still alive, Mitchell probably wouldn't have dared to treat her the way he had.

'I don't let myself miss my parents,' she said sombrely. 'But meeting yours reminded me of how much I wish they were still here.'

Jackson shifted slightly to place his arm around her shoulders. 'You need to use the love they surrounded you with to help drive you through what's to come.'

'I won't be able to do it without you, I know it.'

'Not with that attitude, you won't.'

'I'm serious, Jackson. I rely on you far too much, I know that, but I get so much strength from you and without that I know I'm going to crumble.'

'You're stronger than you give yourself credit for.'

'Strength isn't going to get me through all the nights I'll be on my own in the middle of nowhere.'

'You're not going to be exiled. There'll be people wherever you end up. You'll just be away from here.'

'Which amounts to the same thing and I hate the idea that I'm being punished for picking the wrong man to get in a relationship with.'

'It's not a punishment, it's to keep you safe.'

'All I hear when you say that is *"you picked him, so you have to shoulder some of the blame"*.'

He still had his arm around her, so he affectionately rubbed the shoulder his hand rested on. 'That's not what I'm saying. It's just sometimes sacrifices have to be made, and we can hardly hog-tie him and send him to Timbuktu, so those sacrifices fall on you. It's not fair, but that's the way it's got to be. You'll make friends. You're *really* outgoing.'

'I used to be.'

'I am proof that you still are.'

'That was a happy accident.'

'Aren't all the best friendships?'

'But we're more than just friends, aren't we?' She revisited the question she'd asked as they were about to walk inside his childhood home.

'The way we spend our time together would suggest so, yes,' he answered, being very careful with his response.

She frowned. 'Is that not what you think we are?'

Her question made him momentarily uncomfortable and he drew his arm back as he half turned in his seat towards her. 'Of course we are. We just have to be careful about how close we portray ourselves to be.'

'I understand how cautious we have to be in public, but it's just us here.'

He sighed. 'We're comfortable with each other, which is better than being just friends. But I've come to rely on having you in my life as much as you have with me and I don't want things to get weird between us.'

'Why would things get weird?'

'If I say something that ruins what we have.'

Her brow furrowed again. 'What could you say?'

He rubbed at his forehead. 'Kaidence,' he whispered, and immediately paused to contemplate how to express himself. 'Please drop this. I have to be seen as being professional, I can't afford to let my emotions get in the way.'

She shifted slightly away from him to mask her disappointment. 'I promise to maintain a professional distance.'

'See, I knew this was dangerous territory,' he said, noticing her cold front.

'I'm just respecting your desire for professional distance,' she said with an edge of insolence in her voice.

'Please don't be like that with me.'

'I don't know how else to be Jackson. We've spent two effortless days together, but I ask you one question and you're acting like I've offended you.'

'Because I want to be honest with you, but I shouldn't say anything that could be interpreted as crossing the line.'

Her eyes darted around the room. 'To whom? It's just us here.'

Out of nowhere he relented. 'I like you.'

She took a minute to process the words that had come out of his mouth and when she spoke, she felt like she owed it to him to be just as candid. 'I like you too.'

The shock was evident on his face as he met her eyes with his, but he instantly questioned whether she understood what he was trying to convey. 'Do you know how unethical it is that I have feelings for you?'

'It's not like you set out for this to happen.'

'I doubt that detail will matter to my superiors.'

'How would they find out?'

'I'm not that great at hiding it,' he pointed out. 'Louisa figured it out.'

Kaidence could feel his anxiety and scooted closer as she lay her hand on his forearm. 'Relax. I know these aren't pursuable feelings. No one else will find out.'

He turned his head to take in the sight of her. 'We're definitely more than friends.'

'That's what I thought,' she said with a smile. 'That said, can I ask you something?'

He placed his hand atop hers. 'Anything.'

'How inappropriate would it be if I kissed you right now?' she asked, making her eyebrows dance with suggestion.

He laughed. 'Really inappropriate.'

'I just found myself wondering what it'd be like to kiss you is all, and seeing as I'm sure I'll never get to find out, I thought I'd test the waters,' she said, attempting to seem nonchalant as she got up to draw the curtains in a bid to mask the ache of his rejection. 'You can't blame a girl for trying.'

Jackson knew he'd hurt her feelings; his own weren't exactly untouched. But he was doing the right thing, at least he hoped he was. He couldn't allow his emotions to diminish his responsibility as an officer. Although he hadn't been acting in that capacity around her for a long time and still, he'd achieved so much. He hated that he always felt the need to do the right thing, because all he wanted to do was kiss her now that she had opened the door to the possibility.

He barely heard her excuse herself to get some nibbles because he was so preoccupied mentally fighting what he wanted against what was right. But as she left the room, he realised he couldn't let this opportunity pass without seizing it. He loved her, he was as certain of it as he was of his name, and he knew he'd have no contact with her once she was in witness protection, so if he was ever to express how he felt it had to be now. He could deal with his moral dilemma tomorrow.

By the time she walked back in the room, Jackson was standing. He wasn't entirely sure why – he just felt like he should be. He watched her put a couple of dishes of crisps in the centre of the table and mumble something about popcorn before turning to walk back out again.

'Kaidence,' he said over his shoulder, stopping her at the doorway. He moved on instinct, his determination evident in every stride he took towards her, and when he reached her, he didn't hesitate in his mission. Cupping her face under her jaw, he drew it closer to his and dipped his head slightly to join their lips. She was caught off guard and her heart began to thump in her chest. But her brain quickly engaged, and she slid her hands up his sturdy arms, feeling the slight bulge of his biceps beneath her fingertips. His every sense was consumed by her mouth against his as he felt her snake her arms around his neck in response. Her lips were soft and inviting, encouraging him to slip his tongue delicately inside, kissing her in a way he'd only imagined. His arms moved on impulse and wrapped around her, gently pulling her closer to his body as he lost himself in their connection. Now that he'd already crossed the line, he was going to make sure it was worth the sacrifice of his own moral compass.

The passion rose in his chest and he unexpectedly reached underneath her buttocks to lift her onto his waist as she automatically wrapped her legs around him. He turned to press her against the wall as their mouths collided repeatedly, getting lost in the moment. But Jackson forced himself to pull away before things escalated to a level of intimacy he couldn't withdraw from and lowered her back down on the floor, causing her to reluctantly release her hold on him. He looked down on her face, taking in the sight of her beauty which reached to the depths of her soul and smiled as he caressed her cheek as a parting gesture. But just as with their connection, their separation took Kaidence a minute to register.

She smiled. 'That was a good kiss,' she said eventually, still feeling the tingle on her lips where his had been.

He nodded as if to agree. 'That's going to make it a lot harder to be around you from now on.'

'I think it's actually going to make it easier for me because now I don't have to imagine what it'd be like; I already know,' she said, sitting back down in her spot and picking up her wine glass.

He turned to face her with a frown. 'Weren't you going to get popcorn for the film?'

Still flustered from their connection, she placed her drink on the coffee table and got to her feet. 'I told you that was a good kiss,' she said, rushing out of the room.

Jackson laughed and returned to his seat. Kaidence was right; it had been a pretty great kiss and he knew that – although he was glad to have the possibility of it out of the way – it would be harder to not kiss her whenever he wanted. He'd found it difficult enough to resist the urge before he knew what it was like, now he was going to have to be extra vigilant whenever they spent time together because of how close and comfortable they were.

He paid particular attention to her as she walked back into the room. She seemed even more laid back than she usually was around him and he suspected that was because she'd been carrying around her affection for him for a while and was thankful to have it off her chest. He watched her place a large bowl of popcorn on the table as she lowered herself down next to him and picked up her wine glass again. She gave the impression of being distracted, staring at the blank screen of the television, and he didn't have the heart to break her out of the lasting effect of their kiss before she was ready to return to reality. He sat in silence and watched her sip her drink. There was something heartening about her reaction to what he hoped would be a meaningful connection because it meant he hadn't made a mistake despite his intention to remain professional.

He knew in his capacity as a police officer he shouldn't have allowed himself to become as friendly with her as he had, but he'd been so dedicated to getting her away from the abuse that he'd allowed her to set the pace of their relationship. It just happened that she'd needed a friend, not another person in her life to order her to do things against her will, so he'd happily filled the role. It was inevitable that he'd get emotionally invested given his history, so it was hardly surprising that he ended up falling in love with her.

Kaidence sat replaying the kiss in her head. The touch of his lips. The way he smelled. The strength of his embrace as he pressed her against the wall. The intensity of their longing for each other. It made her head swim with distraction. She ran on autopilot, sipping her wine as her desire for him simmered in her gut. She didn't hear him enquire about the film she planned to make him sit through or if she wanted her glass refilled. It wasn't until he touched her shoulder that she snapped out of the repetition in her head.

She looked over at him. 'Yes?'

'Film?' he asked again.

As though she'd been switched on, Kaidence jumped up to her feet. 'I hadn't decided what we were going to watch,' she said, heading to the DVDs, and took the opportunity to turn off the music.

She plucked a random film from her collection, removed the disc and placed it in the player before proceeding to put the case on the coffee table, pick up the remote and return to her spot on the settee while it loaded. She wasn't really paying attention to what she was doing and when the menu screen loaded, she instinctively pressed play. But her lack of awareness was immediately evident to Jackson because of the kind of film she'd selected.

'Um, Kaidence, I don't think you meant to pick this film,' he pointed out.

But she waved away his concern. 'It'll do.'

'It's a horror.'

'Is it?'

He nodded with a short laugh. 'It's a pretty graphic one too.'

'Is it that bad?'

'Yes, I don't think you want to watch this.'

'Sorry, I'm still barely functioning here,' she said, getting up and ejecting the disc from the player.

He smiled. 'I can tell.'

'It's your fault,' she claimed, returning the DVD to the shelf she'd taken it from. 'You've given me really unrealistic expectations to go out into the dating world with now.'

He laughed. 'I doubt that.'

'You don't think so? Well let's examine the evidence, officer; you've kissed me unexpectedly, even after telling me how wildly inappropriate the suggestion was, and since then I haven't been able to function properly. So exactly what would you attribute to that lapse of concentration?' she asked teasingly.

'Oh, it was definitely the kiss, but that was your fault,' he teased back.

'How?' She feigned outrage.

'You asked for it.'

She laughed; she couldn't argue with that. 'And you deemed it to be unsuitable behaviour considering your role as an upstanding officer of the law.'

He shrugged. 'I changed my mind.'

'Oh, you just changed your mind?'

'I saw an opportunity to seize a moment I could revisit whenever I miss you and can't be with you.'

His admission gave her a confidence boost; knowing he felt that fondness for her was enough to make her feel like a schoolgirl. 'Believe me, I'll probably reflect on that memory a few times over the course of the rest of my life.'

They felt closer somehow; the kiss and their admission of feelings had bridged the gap of their differences. It was easier to speak freely without fear of recrimination now they knew the direction they'd want their relationship to go in if it weren't for the obstacles in their path.

Jackson looked across at his film companion to find her finishing off the last of the popcorn and smiled. 'You know, for such a little person you sure can eat your body weight in popcorn.'

She looked in the bowl to find the contents were gone. 'Well, I rarely get the luxury of having the TV to myself, so I like to indulge when I do,' she smiled. 'You know, my sister complains that she's put on weight since having her baby boy and all I can think about when she does is how much I'd love to be carrying that around because it would mean I was a mum and that's the one thing I've always wanted to be.'

'You'd be a fantastic mother.'

'It's the only thing I was sure I wanted, then I met Mitchell and I had to re-evaluate because bringing a child into this environment would be the absolute definition of cruelty.'

'Well, it's not too late for you to still fulfil that role now that we're going to get you away from him.'

She nodded. 'I've just got to find a man who is worthy of the dad title first.'

'Not necessarily,' he said. 'There are sperm donors.'

'They're great as a last resort but I prefer the old-fashioned way of making a baby, which will only prolong motherhood. It'll take me years to find someone to share that experience with.'

'You're not even thirty yet, I think you have time to find the right man for the job.'

'That's easy for you to say. You haven't been irreparably damaged by one man.'

'No, but you haven't done a double tour with Louisa, that could damage you too.'

Kaidence laughed. 'She's not that bad.'

'She's nice to you. But I've been unfortunate enough to ride around with her for four years, so I've seen her at her lowest and her most vulnerable, which makes her angry because she hates it.'

'She comes across so strong and put together.'

'She is now. But a year ago it was a different story.'

'What happened?'

He took a deep breath. 'Her and Scott split up.'

She nodded knowingly. 'She told me about that because she was worried about Juliette's behaviour.'

'Juliette took it really hard.'

'All kids do, it's just about how they choose to release those emotions. Sometimes it's hitting out at all authority figures and sometimes it's just the parent left behind that bears the brunt of it, which is what I think Juliette's doing because she's a joy to teach. I've seen no evidence of the attitude Louisa told me about. So she's just got to ride it out until Juliette figures out that her parents are still there for her regardless of their relationship status.' She hesitated. 'What's Scott like?'

He exhaled nosily. 'He's a good guy, they just weren't right for each other. They're still on friendly terms, but it's hard for Louisa to raise those girls alone.'

'Doesn't he help?'

'He has them once a fortnight from Friday to Monday but she's still doing it alone the majority of the time, which is why I like to go around occasionally to gently remind them that they have someone else to rely on.'

She smiled. 'That's how I know you'd be a good father; you're the dependable type.'

'I've never thought much about it.'

'Never?' she repeated, wearing a frown.

'Well, I haven't met anyone worth considering becoming one with so yes, never.'

'Regardless, I can tell you'd make a great dad.'

'Yes well, I don't envisage me getting that job title; I work far too much to find a potential mother.'

'I'd offer my services, but we've established my advances make you uncomfortable and act irrationally.'

'Oh no, they just catch me off guard. I'll never be uncomfortable around you.'

'Then after this maybe we should make an arrangement to have a baby. That way you don't have to find a woman in your busy schedule who is worthy of spending the rest of your life with and I don't have to live mine cautious that every man will turn out to be abusive like Mitchell before I get to become a mother.'

'That would require us having sex.'

She laughed. 'Hopefully. Remember, I like the old-fashioned way of making a baby.'

'It would affect our friendship.'

'I should imagine so.'

'Except when you find out how bad I am at that, you'll never want to see me again.'

'I find it really hard to believe you're bad in bed.'

'Why?'

'Because I've kissed you and men that kiss like you aren't as bad in bed as they think they are.'

'Oh, I'm not playing coy; I thought I was okay in that department, but I've been told I'm no good.'

'Yes well, women will say anything after a break-up.'

CHAPTER EIGHTEEN

Jackson opened his eyes and stared up at the ceiling of the room he'd spent two nights in. Kaidence had asked him to stay under her roof for a second time and because he hadn't wanted to return to reality, he'd agreed. But now he was faced with having to leave because of Mitchell's impending arrival, and he wasn't sure he could walk away, knowing he would potentially be exposing her to danger. It unsettled him in much the same way that he had felt when he was undercover because he'd had exactly the same feeling of dread the day he'd been presented with the dead body of the woman he'd befriended; but there was more for him to lose this time.

It was barely seven a.m. but the knot in his stomach meant he wasn't going to be able to fall back to sleep, so he peeled himself off the mattress and, being sure to stand well back from the window in order to remain undetected, he looked beyond the glass onto the street she lived on. The room was situated on the opposite side of the house to the master suite, so it overlooked the street where he'd parked his car, but he could see enough of the surrounding dwellings to know there wasn't a single soul around. For him this was the perfect time of day. The calm before the storm. It was when people were still safe behind their front doors, preparing for what the day had in store, and as an officer he knew that criminals were doing exactly the same.

Today would be his first back on shift after the weekend of living in a bubble; as much as he enjoyed his job and wanted to get back to work, he hated the idea of walking away from her. So he planned to make the most of their last day together.

He headed to the bathroom to empty his bladder and take the shower Kaidence said it was okay to have. He'd been prepared to travel home but she'd insisted he use the amenities the room offered, so he was going to take advantage of the convenience.

The bathroom was crisp and clean with white floor tiles and black oblong tiles cladding the walls. The white porcelain suite stood out against the opposite-coloured background and the bright red accessories set the room off. There wasn't a bathtub in the area, just the shower, which he suspected was because it wasn't the main bathroom of the house.

Trying to push down the anxiety of what the day was going to bring, Jackson stripped to his birthday suit and climbed into the spacious cubicle. He wanted to be ready for the day and do something nice for his hostess before she got out of bed.

—————

Kaidence groaned when her alarm clock woke her from the deep sleep she'd been in. She had set it in the early hours before she'd climbed into bed. Knowing it was her last full day with Jackson, she had wanted to make the most of it, but now the idea of getting out of bed at eight a.m. on a Sunday morning when she'd only got in it six hours ago was less appealing than it had been when she was intoxicated.

She hit out at the top of the radio alarm clock and stopped the loud bleeping before it caused a headache. She reluctantly wasted no time wishing she could stay there longer and climbed from beneath her duvet. As the chill of the morning air hit the bare skin of her arms, she hugged herself and rubbed her upper arms to cause enough friction to warm up. It didn't really work. Instead it resulted in making her more desperate for the toilet, so she rushed into the bathroom to relieve her bladder. That's when she heard noise being generated from downstairs and she realised her weekend companion was already awake.

—————

Hearing the alarm clock ringing throughout the house, Jackson knew he could put his plan into action, because Kaidence would be downstairs soon. He put the kettle on to boil, knowing she only drank tea, and pushed the spring-loaded button on the toaster down to lightly cook the bread. It wasn't much of a breakfast, but it was a small gesture to let her know he appreciated her.

By the time he'd poured the hot water into her mug, allowing it to steep while he buttered the toast, the homeowner had joined him in the kitchen. He half turned his body to say good morning and shortly after presented her with his attempt at the first meal of the day.

She smiled as she sat down. 'Wow! No one's made me breakfast before.'

'It's just toast,' he pointed out, turning his attention to the tea he was making her.

'Still, I'm impressed that you didn't burn the house down,' she said, taking a bite of her first slice.

'Well, if I'd had my way, I would've presented you with a full English but...'

'You can't cook,' she said, finishing his sentence as he put her drink in front of her.

'Sadly, it wasn't a skill I picked up, but my mum is an excellent cook and she has invited us over for dinner today. Is that okay with you?'

She nodded. 'That would actually be nice. It's been a long time since someone cooked for me – this breakfast aside – and I really like your family.'

He laughed. 'Yes well, dinner might change your opinion. It's been a long time since we've all been around the same table at the same time, so we'll probably descend into chaos, but it's worth the risk, right?'

'It is for me. I like the idea of being around a table with a family again, even though it's not mine, you know. I miss that.'

'Well, after today I might let you adopt them,' he joked, which made her laugh.

'There's a reason why you can't pick your family.'

'That's because no one would pick their own family,' he said, lifting his coffee from the worktop and taking a sip as he moved to sit next to her.

She shrugged. 'I'd happily choose mine, if it meant they were still here.'

'I'm sorry. I keep forgetting that while I bitch about mine, at least I still have them,' he said, reaching over to lay his hand on top of hers.

She crossed her arm over her body to place her free hand on top of his. 'I don't ever want you to feel guilty for talking about your parents.'

'I'll try not to be.'

She took her hand back. 'So what time is your mum expecting us?'

He checked the clock on the wall. 'I said we'd be there for about eleven, but she won't serve dinner until an hour after that.'

'Perfect! That gives us enough time to bake a dessert to take with us.'

'That would save my mum a job.'

'Then maybe you should ring and tell her not to bother making one,' she said, drinking from her mug.

'I don't need to; she doesn't usually start baking until after we've eaten. I think it's her way of keeping us at home longer because she rarely gets us all together since we grew up. I heard someone refer to it once as empty nest syndrome and, even though it's been years, I'm sure that's what she's still suffering from.'

'So, do you have any suggestions about what we should make?'

He shrugged. 'Um, well, you can't go wrong with chocolate, can you?'

'Then let's make a batch of brownies and a devil's food cake with chocolate filling and frosting.'

'Wow! Chocolate overload. I like it.'

'Well it does increase endorphin levels in the brain that makes you feel good, so maybe it'll help to stave off the chaos that you're sure will ensue.'

Jackson marvelled at her ease and confidence when it came to being in the kitchen and couldn't help thinking that if she could apply that attitude to her relationship, he wouldn't feel such anxiety about having to return to his life. He'd tried to dispel the unease he'd felt at the beginning of the day but instead it had gained momentum and increased to such a stature that it was affecting his mood. He couldn't seem to convince his mouth to fake a smile and, although she hadn't mentioned it, he knew Kaidence had noticed. She would look over when she thought he wasn't watching because he could feel her stare burning into him. But he didn't dare to meet her gaze. He just waited until she moved in his peripheral vision before he raised his head to continue watching her.

She was adding the finishing decorative touches to the devil's food cake she'd baked as an offering when she broke the silence of the room with her voice. 'Are you going to spend the whole day acting like someone stole your lunch money or will seeing your mum inject a bit of pep in that step of yours?'

'You just had to mention it didn't you? You couldn't just carry on in blissful ignorance so that we didn't have to address the elephant in the room?'

'So, this mood is a direct result of the fact that Mitchell's coming home today?'

Jackson held on to his response, fighting to keep his concerns from her because he didn't want her to be distracted by his fears when she had to be on her guard. But she wasn't going to let him clam up now.

'Jackson!' she said, loud enough to startle him. 'Talk to me.'

He downplayed his feelings. 'I just don't want to leave later, that's all.'

'Well, you're welcome to stay but I don't think Mitchell would appreciate that,' she joked.

He rolled his eyes. 'Please don't say his name. It makes the idea of leaving worse.'

She sighed. 'I've survived this long, I'm sure I'll make it through one more night until I get that protection order and he's escorted from this house. You don't need to worry, especially if it's going to have this effect on you all day.'

'It's my job to worry, especially when you're so blasé about it.'

'I'm not blasé, I've just got good at not poking the bear. I only have to avoid pissing him off before I climb into bed.'

'What if he's itching for a fight because he's been away from you for days?'

She shrugged. 'I won't get sucked in.'

'If that was so easy you wouldn't have taken so many beatings over the past twelve months.' He couldn't help but spit the words out.

Lowering her tools, Kaidence responded with the same amount of impatience. 'Maybe that's true. But you don't know how many sacrifices I've had to make to hold on to a semblance of who I used to be either. I have had to bite my lip, so I don't aggravate a situation sticking up for myself any more than I already had, I've had to remain silent while I took those beatings just so he didn't hit me any harder, and I've had to play the dutiful loving girlfriend pretending I don't hold him accountable for laying his hands on me while being helpless to change my situation. After this long, I've learned when to keep my mouth shut so I don't provoke him into teaching me a lesson. So, I'd appreciate it if you had a little more confidence in my ability to avoid a confrontation and snap out of your misery because I plan to enjoy today, which is going to be difficult to do if you've got a face like thunder.'

'And that fight right there is what I wish you'd have when it came to your boyfriend.'

'That would be the quickest way to ensure my removal from this mortal coil.'

'Obviously I don't mean now, I meant the first time he laid his hands on you.'

'Then we might have never met.'

'If we were meant to meet, the universe would've found a way.'

'Huh, I never would've taken you for a guy who believed in fate.'

'Well, everyone believes in something.'

'True, but you don't give the impression of someone who leaves anything to chance.'

He smiled. 'Even fate needs a helping hand sometimes.'

Kaidence walked to the front door balancing the plastic cake platter on the palm of her left hand as she grabbed her coat with the right and then gestured with the cake in Jackson's direction to encourage him to take it from her. Reading her signs, he placed the airtight container of brownies he held on top of the one she was holding and took the dessert from her, so she could slip on her extra layer of clothing.

Scooping her hair from under the collar of the newly applied garment, she reached for the tubs he held. 'Why don't you go out of the back and bring the car around to the front?'

He frowned. 'What about your neighbours?'

'If Mitchell gets to hear about a strange car picking me up before he's turfed out of my house, I'll tell him I went to my sisters for dinner and my brother-in-law picked me up. He's never met Cole, so he'll never know any different.'

'Okay then, I'll go and fetch the car,' he said, making his exit out of the back door.

Kaidence followed him and turned the key in the lock to secure the house before turning off lights on her way to the front. She waited for the sound of the horn outside and walked out of the front door into the daylight with her head held high. This was her first step towards taking her power back.

This time when they walked through the entrance of the Chase household there was no greeting party like the day before. Jackson called out to announce their arrival before they made their way straight to the kitchen where he knew his mum would be preparing dinner and found all three of his siblings there too. Sat around the small circular breakfast table staring at their phone screens, they barely acknowledged their arrival.

'Good morning you two,' she smiled upon seeing them.

'Morning Mum.' Jackson walked over, laid a kiss on her cheek, and presented her with the baked goods he was carrying. 'Kaidence has been baking.'

'Wow! You didn't have to do that,' she countered, inspecting the cake with a small measure of disappointment evident on her face.

Kaidence tried to lessen the expression with an explanation. 'I didn't want to come empty handed after you'd so kindly invited me for dinner.'

'Depending on how good this tastes, you might get an invite to dinner every week.'

Jackson and his guest exchanged a knowing look. 'That'd be nice if she could actually *be* here every week, but we've got a schedule to stick to,' he shared.

'A schedule regarding the boyfriend?'

Kaidence nodded. 'Tomorrow I am petitioning the courts for an order of protection.'

'Will the police be able to get him out of her house then?' His mother addressed her son.

He nodded in response, but it was Kaidence who spoke. 'And after twelve months of living in fear, I'll finally be safe behind my front door.'

'Once more with conviction please,' Jackson commented.

'It's just hard to imagine right now.'

'Well, if there's one thing I know about my son it's that he's good at his job,' Francine interjected.

Kaidence agreed with her. 'Absolutely, if it weren't for him, I wouldn't be looking at freedom. I'd still be living in a never-ending prison of abuse.'

'Is Dad down the pub?' Jackson asked, forcing a subject change.

'He wouldn't dare, he knows better when we have company for dinner.'

The afternoon flew by quicker than Kaidence and Jackson were ready for. The newcomer had helped out in the kitchen, despite the protests of his mother, while the eldest son watched and daydreamed of a future that wasn't possible. He loved to see her shed the weight of her home life and was grateful he could give her that freedom. But it wasn't until they were sat around the table as a family that he saw a glimpse of what her future could be, and he wanted her to have it.

It wasn't long after they'd eaten dessert that the clock on the wall caught Jackson's eye and he sighed. He had to put an end to her fun and return her to the prison he was trying to break her from.

'It's time we got going,' he announced to the room.

In turn, everyone else except his mum got to their feet and dispersed as if they'd finally gotten permission to go.

'Thank you for dinner,' Kaidence said, trying to put on a brave face.

Francine stood up and embraced her in a hug that wasn't unlike one from her own mother. 'You're welcome here any time, sweetheart.'

'I plan to hold you to that,' she responded, returning the affection.

'And I look forward to seeing you once you're a free woman,' she said with a smile as she pulled away and turned her attention to her son. 'I expect you to be here next Sunday Mister,' she said, pulling him in for a cuddle.

'I'll go and get our coats.' Kaidence excused herself to give them a minute.

Jackson expressed his gratitude. 'Thanks for this today Mum. I think she really needed it.'

'It's an unfortunate situation she's caught up in but she's a good girl,' Francine said, releasing her hold on him.

He sighed. 'I'm really worried about leaving her alone because I know he's coming home.'

'He's going to be arrested tomorrow though, isn't he?'

'Yes, but he'll still have tonight to do some damage if he wants to.'

'Do you think he'll attack her tonight?'

He shrugged. 'He's been away for three days, he might want to give her a refresher course and I've got a bad feeling that's exactly what's going to happen.'

She reached out to rub his arm affectionately. 'You can only be there when she needs you, son.'

He rubbed at his forehead to try and remove the worry that had collected there in the past five minutes. 'Mum, if you could see the pictures of her injuries, you'd know how close he is to killing her. I'm just worried that he's going to do that before I get her away from him.'

'That's your past talking,' she responded sympathetically.

'Maybe, but my gut is telling me something is very wrong.'

His mother didn't have a chance to explore his anxiety any further before they were joined by Kaidence, who passed Jackson his jacket.

'I managed to say goodbye to your dad on his way out of the door,' she said.

'We're lucky he stuck around long enough to eat,' Jackson joked.

'I couldn't find anyone else.'

'They always disperse right after dessert, so they're definitely gone by now.'

'It was hard enough to get them here, making them stay when the reason they were made to show their face is leaving would be impossible,' Francine added.

'Well, I'm grateful they showed up, it's been a long time since I've had a family dinner.' Kaidence smiled. 'I look forward to being able to do it again.'

'Until then, you take care of yourself because the world is a brighter place with you in it,' she said with a smile as they made their way to the front door.

'Drop me off here,' Kaidence announced into the silence of the car.

'Are you sure?' he countered with a frown. 'I can pull up closer to the house.'

She shook her head. 'I don't know what time he's getting home; I can't risk him being there already and seeing me get out of the car.'

Her demeanour had changed since leaving his parents' residence. She had blown cold suddenly, and he knew it had everything to do with their impending separation. But he couldn't resist his urge to call her on it, just like she'd done to him earlier.

'Does the cold shoulder help?' he asked, letting her know he'd noticed her distance as he pulled up to the kerb.

She answered honestly, keeping her eyes forward as she removed her seatbelt. 'It's the only way I'm going to make it to goodbye.'

'So, you're not going to look at me?'

'Not if you want me to get out of this car.'

'I don't want you to go; I'll happily drive you far away from here. But you're the one calling the shots.'

She sighed to try and prepare herself for walking away. 'All I've got to do now is get out of the car.'

He sat in silence waiting for her to act but ten minutes later, she was still sat there. He wanted to allow her the time she needed to mentally prepare for what came next, but he had to get ready for a shift at work.

Removing his own seatbelt, Jackson turned in his seat to face her. 'Kaidence, look at me.'

She shook her head. 'I can't.'

He reached over for her hand and squeezed it slightly. 'You are strong enough to do this.'

'I don't think I am,' she said, as tears spilled onto her cheeks.

'Then don't. You haven't got to go in. I can drive to my place.'

She shook her head and swatted her tears away. 'I know I have to go inside. I've just got to motivate myself to actually do it.'

Still he held her hand. 'You've just got to make it through a night and my colleagues will be there to arrest him in the morning.'

She nodded repeatedly. 'I've just got to keep my head down.'

'For eighteen hours at most,' he affirmed.

'And I'll be asleep for ten of that,' she thought aloud.

'Maybe he won't get home until teatime – that'll whittle it down to five hours contact.'

That's when she finally gave herself permission to look at him. 'I think I can make it through five hours.'

He retracted his hand. 'Does that mean you're ready to get out of the car?'

'No, but I'm going to,' she said, leaning towards him as she slid her arm across his shoulders and pulled him into a hug.

He smelled of deodorant and aftershave with a subtle hint of the day. It settled her in a way she wasn't prepared for and she lingered there longer than she should, but holding him gave her the boost of determination she needed to walk away. Without planning it, she released him and planted a kiss on his cheek before climbing out of the vehicle onto the pavement.

'Come see me tomorrow after he's been picked up if you can,' she said before closing the passenger door behind her.

Kaidence's feet pounded the tarmac with a determination that Jackson had helped build up in her, but she could feel the distance growing between them and the closer she got to her street, the weaker her resolve became. She'd been so lost in freedom over the past three days that she hadn't considered how difficult it would be to return to her usual life, albeit temporarily.

By the time she reached her front door, she was shaking. The prospect of Mitchell being inside instantly made her revert back to the nervous woman she was always reduced to around him. She put her key in the lock and took a deep breath to prepare for what she might find beyond the barrier. But when she got inside, she was surprised to find the place was as empty as she'd left it. She wasted no time in heading to the bedroom that Jackson had slept in to cleanse it of any evidence that he'd been there.

Rounding the corner at the bottom of the stairs, Kaidence walked into the kitchen to find Mitchell rifling through the bill drawer and her heart jumped in her mouth. She'd been in the shower, so hadn't heard his return. But she tried to play it off cool. 'Oh, you're back. What are you looking for?' she asked, keeping her voice calm.

'My contract went out of the bank and they've overcharged me, so I need to find the bill to find out why,' he said, continuing to search for proof.

'Can't you log in to your account online?' she asked, hoping to deter him from rummaging.

'I never set one up, that's why I still get paper statements.'

She approached slowly so as not to appear too eager. 'Why don't you let me look for it?'

He didn't respond and by the expression on his face, she knew why. He'd found the thing she'd been hiding for months; her lifeline.

'What's this?' he asked, holding up the business card to draw her attention to it.

She thought on her feet and tried not to panic. 'One of the officers that found me after my fall gave that to me. I just threw it in the drawer when we got home.'

'Why didn't you throw it in the bin?'

'I didn't think about it.' She shrugged.

He frowned. 'I don't believe you.' She gulped in reaction to his honesty. 'I think you've been using this card to talk to them about our relationship, which is our private business. It has nothing to do with the police.'

She shook her head frantically. There was that feeling again. The fear. The hate. The pain in her chest as her heart sank. He'd snapped and there was no coming back from it. That's when the frightened little child within her came out in full and forced the woman in her on the back-burner. 'No. I didn't. I haven't.'

He didn't hold back. Almost instantly he pulled his balled-up fist back and jabbed it into her jaw, causing a spray of blood to land on his face. The force of his anger unbalanced her, so she fell into the stove and pulled the saucepan that was awaiting dinner preparation down on top of her.

She screamed as she bounced off the appliance and landed on the floor, causing a loud smacking sound to bounce off the surrounding walls. She could feel the blood oozing from her mouth, her nose and her left eyebrow. But this time she wasn't going to let him beat her. This time she was going to fight back, even if it meant he'd kill her for it.

Sucking in a deep breath for courage she hoisted herself up onto her feet and when she looked at him, fire clouded her vision. 'That is the last time I let you get away with putting your hands on me.'

He seemed to get a kick out of her combative words and cocked his head to the side. 'Oh yes?' He spurred her on.

'Yes,' she said, reacting immediately with a fist to his jaw.

His head whipped round to the side, but still he stood strong and when he shifted to look at her, he was smiling. 'You're going to have to do better than that if you think you're going to hurt me, sweetheart,' he boasted as he swung to hit her again.

She reacted quickly, dipping to a crouch she picked up the pan that had fallen with her and jumped back up to hit him around the head with it. He dropped to the tiled floor, his blood beginning to coat the pristine clean porcelain. She stood over him for a second to take in the glory of getting in an attack; she didn't care if it'd be her only one, because at least she had attempted to fight back.

She heard him groan and was stricken with panic. She had to make it out and get help. She turned towards the front door to escape but he reached out and grabbed her ankle, making her lose her stability and land on the floor in front of him. She instinctively knew he'd got to his feet as she crawled on her stomach towards the exit. He was going to kill her this time; she could feel it. She forced herself up onto her knees as she saw him out of the corner of her eye by her side. She knew she wasn't going to make it to her destination as she watched him draw his foot back. Using all the strength she could muster, she clambered to her feet and instead of heading out of the kitchen she changed direction, making her way around the stationary island in the middle of the room. He would have to go around it in order to get to her and that would give her time to avoid him. She watched as he stepped in her direction and she moved further around the worktop away from him.

'You can barely move fast enough to get away before I catch up to you,' he taunted her, wearing a smile on his face.

'You're probably right. But you're not getting away with this any more.'

'Who's going to stop me?' he asked, being deliberately deprecating.

She was stumped for a minute while she fished around in her head for a comeback. Her eyes landed on the drainer and she thrust forward to retrieve the knife drying there. She pointed it in his direction but instead of instilling fear in him, it made him laugh because of how shaky she was.

'You'll have to steady that hand if you want to use that blade against me,' he goaded her as he took another step around the island towards her.

'If you get close to me, I will use it,' she threatened. 'You're not going to hit me any more.'

'It's going to be easy for me to get that out of your hand and when I do, you're going to pay for picking it up.'

'You need to leave, Mitchell, or I'll call the police.'

'You'll be dead before they get here, darling,' he announced boldly as they stood frozen, her in front of the sink, him behind the bar stools.

The only way out of the room was past him. She was trapped. She tried not to panic but she couldn't find a way out of this situation with her life intact. She kept the tip of the blade pointed at him as she tried to build up the courage to make a dash for the exit. But she couldn't talk herself into being brave enough. She wavered on the spot, not daring to look in the direction she wanted to escape to, so he wouldn't have any warning about what she had planned. She needed him to believe she was ready for a battle, so she could get away. She would deal with getting him out of her house once she was free.

She bode her time and when she saw him step towards the refrigerator, creating more distance between him and the archway, she made a run for freedom. But her legs weren't fast enough to carry her far before she felt his hand wrap around the wrist of her trailing arm. He yanked her back, causing her limb to pop out of its socket as she whipped around to face him. She screamed out in pain and instinctively used her good arm to thrust the knife into his chest with a rage that had been building for over a year.

He released his hold on her and filled the room with a pained cry she had longed to hear as he tried desperately to stop the blood pumping out of his chest. It didn't stop him. Lowering his hands, he looked down at his red palms and he lashed out, punching her in the face. She felt her nose break from the impact and felt her own blood erupt from her injury. He didn't give her a chance to react before he swiped at her again, bringing his fist up to connect with her jaw. She dropped the knife she'd used on him to the floor as she braced herself for the hard landing and the smack of her face hitting the tiles bounced off the surrounding walls.

She groaned, lifting her head from the floor and began to crawl towards the front door. But he wasn't done with her yet. He grabbed her by her hair and she knew what was coming. She reached for the knife and managed to grasp the handle tight as he hoisted her up to her feet. Determined to not be his punching bag any more and survive the night, she didn't hesitate to use the eight-inch blade against him again, plunging it into any part of his body she could connect with. She hit his shoulder, retracted the steel and countered with a blow to his upper pectoral muscle. He couldn't help but let go of her, which freed her to attack him a third time. This was the injury that counted. As she pulled the blade out of his chest, Mitchell dropped to his knees struggling to breathe. She jumped out of the line of fire in time for him to land in a heap at her feet. That's when it hit her; she'd really hurt him.

Shell-shocked, she stood over him, trying to decipher whether he was alive. But when he didn't move, she panicked. Dropping the knife, she clambered for her mobile phone, which had been on the work surface but had been knocked to the ground in the fight. She had no idea where the business card was that he'd confronted her with so dialled triple nine instead. The wait for the call to connect seemed to take forever and her anxiety grew with every ring.

She kept her eye on the man she'd done her best to injure as she waited for the emergency call to be answered, and it wasn't long before she heard him groan. Panic gained momentum inside her, causing her breathing to quicken as she prayed for someone to pick up the other end.

As if her prayers had been heard, the ringing stopped, and she heard the click of connection. 'Help me, please. He's trying to kill me,' she stated hysterically, witnessing Mitchell hoist himself up onto his forearms and get to his knees.

'Who's trying to hurt you?' the operator asked to try and focus her.

'My boyfriend; he's trying to kill me.'

'Okay, I've dispatched officers to your location. Is there a room you can barricade yourself in until they get there?'

'No, I can't get past him. I stabbed him, but he's getting back up.'

'The officers are on their way. You should hear the sirens any second.' The dispatcher tried to keep her calm.

Louisa was in the middle of running through her weekend drama with her daughters when Jackson heard the call over the radio. It was the one he'd been expecting and dreading since he'd met Kaidence.

'Was that Kaidence's address?' his partner asked.

'This is it; this is the night I've been dreading,' he replied, stepping on the accelerator. He reacted without hesitation to inform dispatch they were going to join the response team and immediately switched on the sirens to aid in getting there as fast as possible.

'She got to the phone to call for help. She's fighting to stay alive.'

'Hopefully she stays that way until we get there.'

Kaidence held onto the phone for dear life as she watched Mitchell gain on her. The voice on the other end of the phone was going to do nothing to protect her but still she grasped it tight. She hoped the police were seconds away from breaking down her door and closed her eyes to block out what was coming, which meant she didn't see him standing over her. She screamed as he knocked the phone out of her hand and instinctively balled herself up into the foetal position to brace for impact but instead of punching her, Mitchell pulled her to her feet by her hair. She fought his hold on her, kicking and punching any part of him she could connect with until her foot found his crotch. The pain he felt from the impact forced him to release her and she ran to the front door. She fumbled with the lock with her one good arm, not daring to look over her shoulder at where he was. One twist and she was free, although he was hot on her heels. She could practically feel him breathing down her neck as she stepped out beneath the night sky in time to see three police cars pull up at the kerb. Relieved the cavalry had arrived, she ran halfway down the steps and dropped to her knees as she broke down. But Mitchell's temper wasn't so quick to subdue. He chased her down and ignoring police instructions to drop his weapon, raised his hand to blindside her with one last attack, only to be tasered into submission by the first officer on scene.

———

Jackson pulled up in time to see Kaidence fall to her knees. Things seemed to move in slow motion as Mitchell appeared behind her with his arm raised. He saw the glint of the blade beneath the streetlights and a feeling of dread washed over him. He climbed out of the police cruiser knowing there was no way to get to her in time, but his instinct had always been to protect her and that ran strong through his veins as he rushed towards her. He barely registered Mitchell being immobilised by his colleague's taser as he locked eyes with Kaidence, and he saw the relief when his face registered with her.

Seeing him, Kaidence released a breath she didn't realise she'd been holding. She was safe because he was here. He was going to make sure Mitchell's attack came to an end. She started to sob as Jackson reached her and scooped her up in his arms. She rested her head on his chest as he carried her towards the paramedics. She was finally free.

CHAPTER NINETEEN

Kaidence's mind raced a mile a minute. She was replaying the night in her mind and suddenly felt the need to defend herself. 'He found your card and came after me,' she blurted out hysterically. 'I had to stab him. He wouldn't let me go.'

'It's okay. You're safe now.' Jackson tried to calm her as he lowered her to her feet on the road next to the ambulance.

She took a deep breath as she ran a bloodied hand through her hair. 'I told him I was leaving, and he attacked me. He broke my nose and pulled my arm out of its socket, I panicked and picked up a knife. I only stabbed him so I could get away.'

'The first officer on scene will go through all that when you're interviewed – right now I need you to let the paramedics give you the once-over.'

Kaidence nodded as Louisa joined them. Jackson turned his attention to his partner: 'Stay with her, I'll help secure the scene.'

The female officer approached the injured woman. 'Bloody hell Kaidence, are you okay?'

Kaidence shook her head frantically. 'I thought this was it. I thought he was going to kill me this time,' she said, as she started to shiver in the cold night air. The adrenaline that had been running through her veins had now diminished and all that was left was the shock of what she'd managed to survive.

Jackson approached the spot where Mitchell had dropped and quickly realised that the taser wasn't the reason for his need of medical attention. Seeing blood coating the paramedic's latex gloves, he knew Kaidence had really put up a fight to survive this time and had seriously injured him. He was frozen in fear. He didn't want her to face manslaughter charges when she'd been the one who had spent a year being abused.

He turned to one of his colleagues, who had already been watching the scene unfold. 'What's his status?'

'He's got a weak pulse and shallow breathing,' he responded.

'Is he likely to make it?'

The officer shrugged. 'They want to stabilise him before they move him.'

Jackson turned to the officer guarding the doorway of the house. 'Are the detectives on their way to process the scene?' The officer nodded a response. 'Who was first on scene?'

'Outterridge.' The officer gave the name of a colleague Jackson knew well.

He scanned the area for the officer he'd named and found him making his way towards Kaidence. He tried to appear nonchalant as he strolled towards the ambulance, where his partner was still standing.

The officer introduced himself to Kaidence as she was being assessed by a paramedic. 'I'm Officer Outterridge. What's your name?'

'Kaidence Hadaway,' she responded, still shivering.

'And do you live here, Kaidence?'

'Yes.'

'And who's the man that attacked you?'

'My boyfriend... um... Mitchell Stevenson,' she answered as Jackson joined them.

Outterridge took a minute as he wrote the information down in his A6 police issue notepad. 'Can you tell me what happened tonight?'

She nodded and swallowed hard to prepare to vocalise the torment she'd had to endure to someone else, something she'd been groomed not to do. 'He came home and found the card Officer Chase had given me and accused me of talking to the police. He punched me in the mouth and threatened to kill me. I told him I wasn't going to let him hit me any more and he said I was too weak to stop him. I told him I was going to ring nine-nine-nine and he said I'd be dead by the time you got here. I only picked up the knife to protect myself.' She started to sob. 'But when I made a dash for the front door, he grabbed my arm and pulled it out of the socket to stop me. I had to use the knife to try and get free, but he got back up. He picked me up by my hair, I only managed to get away by kicking out at him. If you hadn't been here, he'd have killed me.'

'So, he's attacked you before?'

She nodded. 'I have a journal and pictures of all my injuries.'

'Have you previously reported any abuse?'

Again, she nodded. 'I filed two reports at the weekend. I was going to file for a restraining order tomorrow.'

'He was going to be brought in for questioning once he got back from his trip,' Jackson interjected.

Outterridge turned towards the officer he knew. 'Have you been to this address regarding a domestic incident before?'

'Yes, but we didn't know that's what it was at the time.'

He frowned. 'Who called it in?'

Louisa cleared her throat preparing to take responsibility for their connection to Kaidence. 'She teaches my daughter, so we've become friends. She confided in me a couple of months ago that she was in an abusive relationship so when she didn't show up to school one morning and wasn't answering her phone, I popped round to check on her. There was no response at the door and when I looked through the letter box, I saw her lying unresponsive at the bottom of the stairs. We broke down the door and called an ambulance. She was in hospital in a coma for a week because he threw her down the stairs the night before.'

'When was that?'

'Uh, about a month ago.'

The lead officer turned back to the civilian. 'Miss Hadaway, we need you to come to the station to get a more detailed account of what happened.'

She tried to stand. 'I need to get my journal. It's got evidence of all the abuse in it.'

Louisa prevented her from rushing towards the house. 'We'll get it. You can't go back inside yet,' she said, calming her enough to return to her pew.

'It's in the safe hidden by the picture opposite the door in the office. The code is eight, eight, six, zero, four, two.'

'Officer Chase and Officer Jessop will escort you to the hospital so that you can receive treatment, but I'd like you to come to the station afterwards.'

She nodded. 'Okay.'

Outterridge again addressed the officers he'd tasked with babysitting duty. 'Can you collect her clothes as evidence? It'll help the investigation.'

As he turned to walk away, the paramedic who had been working on Mitchell rushed him to the ambulance on a stretcher with the help of officers. 'We need to get him to the hospital.'

His colleague stopped attending to the cuts on Kaidence's face. 'She needs to go too. I've called for a second ambo but there aren't any available.'

'Well, we can take Kaidence,' Louisa suggested. 'If she doesn't need medical attention immediately.'

'Her injuries aren't life-threatening, so you could transport her to Good Hope.'

As Kaidence got to her feet to walk the short distance to the squad car, she took in the sight of Mitchell. He was hurt; really hurt. She instantly started to panic.

'Is he okay?' she asked the paramedic who had stabilised him.

'He's stable. It doesn't look like you hit any organs or arteries, so he should make a full recovery,' the paramedic assured her.

But his assurances fell on deaf ears. After spending so much time taking whatever punishment Mitchell felt she deserved, Kaidence had used the build-up of all her frustration to fight back and now it could backfire. If the police compared each of their injuries and decided she was the aggressor, she could face prison time. She wondered if it would matter that she'd spent a year logging every beating he'd given her and just lost the tolerance for it.

Louisa, seeing Kaidence had frozen at the sight of her boyfriend, encouraged her towards their cruiser. 'Let's get you to the hospital,' she said to try and snap her out of her daze.

Supporting the arm of her dislocated shoulder, Kaidence took a few steps in the direction Louisa was guiding her. 'What if he dies? What happens if he dies? I'll go to prison for defending myself, won't I?' she asked frantically.

But Jackson rushed ahead of her and stopped in her path. 'Kaidy,' he said, causing her to focus on him. 'All you need to concentrate on right now is getting to hospital. The investigation will reveal the truth of what happened tonight, and you have enough evidence to show what kind of man he is. Trust in the law.'

His words had worked to calm her, but Jackson had delivered them with more conviction that he actually felt. He knew Mitchell's injuries were serious; he just hoped that he made a full recovery, so he could be held accountable for his actions.

Kaidence sat in the back of the squad car in silence. All she'd been thinking about was getting free of Mitchell; she hadn't even considered what would happen as a consequence of how she managed to do that. Picking up the knife was meant to be a deterrent, not a challenge. She had no intention of using it on him, but her survival instinct had kicked in when he pulled her arm out of its socket and the pain of it had caused her to react the way she had. It hadn't occurred to her that defending herself might lead to a prison sentence until she'd seen how badly she'd injured him. She was sure the paramedics' response to her concern was a lie designed to prevent her from reacting negatively before she was at the station. How could he possibly survive a knife to the chest? She couldn't recall how many times she'd stabbed him – panic clouded her memory – but once could be enough to kill him. *My God, what if he's already dead? What if the trip to the hospital was misdirection?* The thoughts rolled around in her head and tortured her in a way she hadn't been prepared for. She expected to feel relief because finally his true colours had been revealed to someone other than the two officers she'd confided in, but instead she was petrified that the rest of the police force would see her as the aggressor.

'Are you okay back there?' Jackson asked, glancing back at her through the rear-view mirror as he drove towards the hospital. She'd been silent for a while and he was worried about her mental state.

She barely looked up from staring into her lap to respond to his question and he could see the shock on her as if it was a layer of clothes. He wanted to pull over and reassure her that once all the evidence was discovered she wouldn't serve any time. But he knew he couldn't guarantee anything and the body cam he wore restricted his interaction with her. He knew any footage would be reviewed to check its relevance to the case, so he couldn't be seen to be treating her any differently to anyone else he'd be transporting in the line of duty.

Louisa silently exchanged a look with her partner as he moved his eyes back to the road. She could see the concern seeping out of his pores and she knew not being able to do anything to comfort Kaidence was killing him. She wished she could be the reassurance Kaidence needed, but the same restrictions applied to her. She knew she could feasibly explain any concern as female allegiance, but she'd worked so hard to be seen as an equal among her colleagues that she didn't want to use it as an excuse, so she refrained from too much familiarity when she spoke to her.

'Kaidence, how are you feeling?' she asked. 'Are you in pain?'

When Kaidence looked up to answer Louisa's question, she was crying. 'Yes, but it just means I'm still alive and for a minute there I didn't think I would be.' She released a suppressed sob. 'I thought I was going to die tonight.'

Kaidence was emotionally numb as the nurse led them to a private room. The last time she'd had to visit Accident & Emergency she had to wait hours to be seen. The only advantage to having a police escort was that this time she wouldn't have long before she was treated. The lack of adrenaline that had been pumping through her veins earlier had left the pain of her broken nose and dislocated shoulder in its place. Admittedly, she had felt worse pain but the fact it was mixed with relief of impending freedom was probably why she felt it so much.

The nurse passed her a gown. 'If you could put that on, the doctor will be right with you.'

Jackson raised his eyebrows in his partner's direction as the nurse walked out. 'We've heard that before.'

Putting the gown on the bed, Kaidence attempted to remove the jumper she was wearing, but having use of only one arm made it impossible. Still, she tried. But her struggle didn't go unnoticed by the female officer.

'Here, let me help you with that,' Louisa said, reaching inside her back pocket for the pair of latex gloves she always carried with her. 'I just have to put these on because I don't want to contaminate any evidence,' she explained before assisting her to remove her good arm from the item of clothing. 'Uh, Jackson, can you go and get an evidence sheet from the squad car?' she asked, hoping that he'd understand that she was trying to get rid of him so that Kaidence would be comfortable stripping down to her underwear.

Louisa could tell he was dazed. Usually he wouldn't need to be told to leave the room, but his closeness to Kaidence meant he was still working his way through his emotions. He frowned. 'What evidence sheet? We're not part of the forensics team.'

'Okay, well, why don't you *go* and *get* something for her to *stand on* while she gets *out* of her *clothes?*' she said, trying to convey her meaning through the emphasis of certain words.

It took a second for Jackson to register the message she was trying to get across. 'Uh, yes, I'll uh, do that,' he fumbled awkwardly, exiting without so much as another sound. He knew Louisa's suggestion was just a wake-up call to get him to leave the room, but it wasn't a bad idea to get Kaidence to stand on something to catch any evidence that dropped from her clothing, because she was as much a part of the crime scene as the scene itself, so he went about his mission.

Louisa teased Kaidence's head out of the neck hole, making it easier and, she hoped, less painful to ease over her dislocation before removing the knitwear completely. But there was a T-shirt underneath, which was going to prove more difficult to remove.

'I think we're going to need some scissors,' she said. There was no response from Kaidence. That's when she realised that she hadn't reacted to anything since stepping foot in the hospital.

Jackson walked back into the room and held out a sheet of folded plastic in her direction. 'This is all they had.'

'Something's wrong,' his partner said, not acknowledging his find.

He draped the plastic on the back of the chair beside the hospital bed. 'What's wrong?'

'I think she's in shock; she hasn't spoken since we got her out of the car.'

'Well, that's to be expected.'

'No, she fought to be free. I thought she'd be...' Louisa trailed off, trying to think of an appropriate end to her sentence. 'Relieved?' She was unsure it was the word she'd been searching for.

'Well, she expected to get a restraining order first thing tomorrow morning and that he'd be picked up for questioning. Instead she was forced to defend her life because he found the card that had been in her possession for months and had gone undetected.'

His partner immediately picked up on the undertone of frustration in his voice. 'No, you don't get to do that. You're not to blame for what he did to her. He's the arsehole, not you.'

'But he didn't give her a card that was supposed to be her lifeline only to have it be the thing that could've killed her tonight.'

Louisa turned to him and when she spoke her voice was low and stern. 'Listen to me, *he* did this! *He* put his hands on her over and over and over again. *He* was the one who hurt her. *You* did nothing wrong. *You* were trying to help her get away from him so he couldn't hurt her any more.'

His guilt about the situation had given way to a momentary memory lapse of the body cam he was wearing, but his partner's reclarification of who was at fault had forced him back to remembering. He cleared his throat and grabbed the plastic sheet he'd retrieved. 'Get her to stand on this.'

Louisa nodded. 'We need to find her some clothes to wear. She can't go to the station to be interviewed in a hospital gown.'

He thought for a second and realised he had an alternative. 'I keep a spare set of clothes in the boot of the squad car in case I want to get a workout in. I'll go and get them.'

As he left the room, his colleague laid out the sheet of plastic on the floor and placed the jumper she'd removed on top of it, while still leaving room for Kaidence. 'Step onto the sheet and we'll take off your bottoms,' she said. 'I'm going to have to photograph these injuries as we go, okay?'

Kaidence gave a slight nod and did as instructed, barely looking at Louisa as she reached into her breast pocket for her mobile phone. She unlocked her personal device, launched the camera and photographed the injuries on her face before placing it on the table positioned over the bed. She then took the elasticated waist on Kaidence's trousers and eased them down to the floor. As she lowered them to Kaidence's feet, Louisa was presented with the bruises from her battle on the surface of her skin; they were mostly purple in colour and looked painful. It made her angry. It made her want to dish out her own form of punishment. It also made her realise what Kaidence had been dealing with. It was one thing to know it was happening, it was quite another to see the aftermath. She sniffed back the tears that had involuntarily started to fall as she eased her free of the item of clothing and placed it with the jumper. She took a second to wipe her tears on her sleeve and then reached for her phone to take more photos. She needed to remain professional, detached. But she considered them to be friends, so she wasn't even close to separating herself from her emotions.

Jackson got to the squad car in double quick time. He'd gone through a range of emotions in the short time since the radio crackled for assistance at Kaidence's address: fear, relief, anger, guilt and frustration. His anger had driven him to his destination, barely paying attention to anything that passed him along the way, but his guilt was what haunted him. He knew his partner was right; he wasn't at fault for what Kaidence had gone through that night – Mitchell was. Still, it didn't ease the responsibility he felt.

He retrieved his sports bag and headed back inside, hoping the walk would help to calm his rage. He wasn't sure how he'd react if he saw the true extent of the damage Mitchell had inflicted but he knew he had to swallow down his instinctive reaction and respond as if she was a stranger. It would test him, but if he didn't want to compromise the investigation, he would have to wear his best poker face.

Jackson still wasn't thinking clearly as he knocked briefly, and didn't wait for a response before walking into the private hospital room. Little did he expect to catch Kaidence naked, except for her underwear, having her upper body photographed. His partner's attention was drawn to him, but the victim didn't even flinch; it was as if she hadn't heard him enter. He was so stunned by the sight of the scars on her back that it delayed his reaction to turn away.

Although Kaidence had previously shared with him photographs of her injuries from the days after each fight with Mitchell, which were graphic and hard to look at, seeing the residual marks that she would carry for the rest of her life was enough to make him stop in his tracks. He suspected it had been a while since she had felt beautiful, let alone been told she was, despite the marks her live-in boyfriend had inflicted on her skin. But he'd been trying, in his short time of knowing her, to instil in her a confidence that she was worthy of so much more than she was willing to settle for and finally, when he'd got her to believe it, and she felt able to demand better treatment and walk away, she'd had to endure her worst attack yet.

Her scars told a story of the last year of her life, but he saw past them to the woman she used to be and could be again. She just had to get over this hurdle first.

Jackson stood with his back to the other occupants of the room until his partner assured him that it was safe. Spinning slowly to face them, he was relieved to find Kaidence was now wearing a hospital gown. He noticed the demeanour Louisa had alluded to before he'd gone to the car. There was a definite distance in her eyes, as if she'd forced herself to dissolve her emotional attachment to the situation as protection against what was coming. But he knew he needed to try and make her reconnect. He didn't want her to lose her fight when it was pivotal that she used it to push back against all the wrong she'd endured at the hands of Mitchell.

'Why don't you sit on the bed while we wait for a nurse or a doctor?' Louisa suggested. She turned to Jackson and spoke under her breath. 'So what are we going to do? She can't be interviewed if she won't talk.'

'She's probably just trying to process what's happened. Maybe she'll be more receptive when we get to the station.'

'And if she doesn't?'

'We'll cross that bridge when we get to it.'

The three of them were sat there for almost fifteen minutes in complete silence before a nurse entered the room with a tray of instruments and dressings to treat the patient's cuts and broken nose. She didn't address the officers; instead her attention was on Kaidence.

'Okay, Miss Hadaway, I am going to clean up the cuts on your face,' she said, laying the tray and the paperwork on the table. 'Are you having any trouble breathing through your nose?' Kaidence shook her head slightly. The nurse immediately assessed the damage of her broken nose with a squeeze to the bridge. 'It doesn't look like it's out of alignment and it isn't bleeding any more, so there's no treatment needed now. But if it does start to bleed again, you can come back in.' Kaidence didn't react, causing the medical professional to turn and address the officers. 'How long has she been this catatonic?'

'Uh, since we got to the hospital,' Louisa answered.

'But she was responsive straight after the incident?'

'Yes, she gave an account of what had happened,' Jackson confirmed.

'Well, she's not completely catatonic, she's just not talking.'

'Which'll make interviewing her interesting,' Louisa countered with a short laugh.

'I'm sure the shock will wear off when she's feeling a little more like herself.'

'She's got some pretty bad bruising on her abdomen; I'm worried she could have internal bleeding.'

'We'll get her X-rayed while she's here to double-check her internal injuries and that dislocation,' the nurse assured them. 'Doctor Logan wants to make sure there's no fractures or tissue damage before he resets it.'

'Any idea how long it's going to be?' Jackson asked.

'Sorry, I don't. But we are busy tonight. The doctor already has four patients. My advice is to try and get her to rest while you're waiting.'

Kaidence could hear the voices in the room but they were muffled, as if she had cotton wool in her ears, and the more she tried to concentrate on them, the quieter they got. Her vision was impaired too; she knew the blurs in the dark clothes were her police escorts and that the blue-wearing blur in front of her was the nurse, but she couldn't see her face. Her legs felt weak, even though she was sitting down and her hands, although shaky, felt like they belonged to someone else. She was almost as detached from this situation as she got whenever Mitchell was heaving his way to climax on top of her. She always seemed to dissociate in this way when she had no control over the horrible positions she found herself thrust into.

She knew she needed to try and pull herself out of it. To tell her side of what had happened, she needed to be articulate, and she couldn't bring herself to speak. She wasn't even sure she should. She had so much rolling around in her head that she was scared to say something that would incriminate her rather than exonerate her actions.

As the nurse cleaned the cuts on her face, she tried to distract from the sting of the antiseptic by wiggling her toes, so she knew she still had control over her body. She stared down at them as they moved, and she was relieved that she still had the ability.

'Kaidence,' the nurse said, to focus her attention. She forced her eyes upwards and the stranger continued to talk. 'Swing your legs up on the bed, lie back and try to get some rest. There's a bit of a queue for X-ray but the porter will take you as soon as it's your turn.'

She moved as if on autopilot, doing as she'd been told, and although she was injured, she didn't feel the pain of her dislocation until she tried to get comfortable. It was as if she'd been woken up as the agony radiated from that point throughout her whole body, causing her to scream out in pain. All her senses came back in an instant. She could see the people in the room as clear as day and her ears seemed to pop, clearing out the blockage. She was back in the room, not strangely separate from it.

She rethought her initial idea of leaning against the elevated head of the hospital bed with her good arm, giving her the wrong shoulder alignment, and repositioned to rest her back against it so that her injury was supported.

'I'll get you a strong painkiller to take the edge off that,' the nurse said, exiting the room.

Louisa stepped over to the bed. 'Kaidence, do you need a pillow?'

She shook her head and, wanting to know if she could speak, tried it. 'No, thanks.' It was only two words, but at least her temporary dumbness was gone.

'You're talking again.' Jackson pointed out the obvious.

'There's nothing like bone-wracking pain rippling through your body to wake you up.'

Jackson was relieved that Kaidence was finally interacting. It meant that any shock she had been under the influence of was gone and he knew from experience that the dispersal of the adrenaline from her fight to stay alive would have depleted most of her energy, leaving her exhausted. He watched her as she got comfortable against the bed and fought to keep her eyes open.

'Rest, Kaidence, we'll wake you when they need you,' he said gently.

She heard his sentence and was too tired to contest the instruction he gave. She couldn't even keep her eyelids from sealing shut. Soon the noise in the room faded out and she could feel herself getting deeper into much-needed sleep.

It was half an hour later when a porter walked into the room. 'Kaidence Hadaway?' he asked, making sure he had the right patient.

Louisa nodded her confirmation. 'We told her to rest while she was waiting.'

'That's okay. But the radiologist is going to need her to be awake for her X-ray.'

The female officer moved closer to the bed and lay her hand atop the sleeping woman's hand. 'Kaidence.' She nudged her softly so as not to startle her. But she jolted awake regardless.

'What?'

'Time for your X-ray,' she said, gesturing towards the stranger among them.

'Oh,' she said, attempting to pull her top half off the bed.

The porter stopped her. 'It's okay, you can stay there. I'll just take you down in your bed.'

'I'll escort you,' Louisa assured her friend as the hospital worker pulled up the side panels and prepared to move the bed.

'I'll just stay here,' Jackson said as she was wheeled out of the room.

Being left alone with his thoughts was a recipe for disaster. All he could think about was Mitchell. It was only concern on behalf of Kaidence, because if Mitchell was seriously injured and died, he knew she'd almost certainly face charges. He was sure she wouldn't survive a prison term and the confidence he'd tried so hard to build in her would take a nosedive.

Getting up from the chair near the door, he made his way out through the emergency department to try and get some information about the other patient. He approached the station in the centre of the area and addressed a nurse sat behind a computer when she looked up at him.

'Is there any news on the condition of the man brought in at the same time as the woman I'm with?' he enquired.

'He's been X-rayed; there's been no damage to any of his organs, so he'll be kept under observation and X-rayed again in three hours to make sure he doesn't develop pneumothorax, haemothorax or tension pneumothorax.'

Jackson frowned. 'They sound serious.'

'They are. Any blood or air in between the lung and chest could change his prognosis. But he's stable for now, so there's no reason to believe he won't make a full recovery. The X-rays are just a precaution.'

He nodded. 'So, he's stable?'

She confirmed the diagnosis with a nod of her head. 'The wounds in his chest missed anything vital so we'll probably keep him in for a few days just in case there are any complications and then he'll be released.'

'Okay, thanks for that,' he said before returning to the private room he'd emerged from.

Once she returned from radiology, Kaidence eased back into an exhausted slumber. Jackson waited until he was sure she couldn't hear him before sharing with his partner the information he'd got from the nurse about Mitchell.

'So she'll be all right.' Louisa confirmed her translation of the news in a hushed tone.

He nodded slightly and kept the volume of his voice a little above a whisper. 'As long as no air or blood gets into his chest, he'll live. But that still doesn't mean she'll walk away scot-free. She stabbed him.'

'Yes, she did. After almost a year of being beaten because she didn't do something the way he thought she should, after losing a child and living every day in fear in case she pissed him off, she fought back. I'm surprised she didn't stab him straight in the heart. But he's alive and with any luck he'll stay that way so he can serve time for the horrible things he's put her through.'

He rubbed at his forehead. 'As long as he makes it to trial.'

'Oh, he'll make it to trial, on principle. He'll want to brand her a liar because he doesn't know about her log or the photos. But he can protest his innocence all he wants; those pictures will leave no doubt about what kind of man he is.'

'Have you seen them?'

'No. You?'

He nodded. 'The things he's made her suffer because he couldn't keep his temper in check are unconscionable and he deserves to be locked up for them.'

Louisa lowered to one knee in front of where he sat and lay a hand on his forearm. 'And if there's any justice, he will be.'

Kaidence was awake by the time the doctor entered the room. She was a little bit groggy because the small amount of shut-eye she'd managed to get wasn't enough to sustain her. But her eyes were open.

'All right Kaidence...' the doctor started and unexpectedly trailed off. Seeing her, he frowned. 'Sprinkles?'

Hearing the nickname she hadn't heard since high school ended woke her up a little. She only knew one person who had called her that, and she hadn't seen him since he left to study in London.

Lifting her head, her peridot green eyes met with the deep and warm brown ones she had known from her childhood. 'Cupcake?' she countered, recognising him as a friend she'd been close to years ago. 'You're a doctor?'

He nodded and laughed. 'If I'm not, I'm in the wrong place.'

There was no mistaking that her childhood friend was handsome, with a perfectly symmetrical face, kind eyes, a square jawline and plump lips. But, so far as she could tell, he was still the scrawny boy she grew up with, no matter how much time he spent in the gym working on strengthening his upper arms.

'I mean, you're a doctor here. You moved to London after high school, I didn't expect you to come back.'

'I was practising down there after I got my degree, but I was always coming home.'

'How long have you been back?'

'About eight months ago, fully qualified.'

'I bet your mum and dad are proud.'

'Dad – the surgeon – is, but mum wanted grandkids and presumes that me being a doctor means that she won't get any.' He paused. 'It's weird, mum and I were only talking about how inseparable you and I used to be last week.'

'Really?'

He nodded again. 'She wanted me to look you up, and here you are.'

'Yep, here I am.' She responded less enthusiastically than she had before.

That's when he focused his attention on the other two people in the room and a frown formed on his brow. He decided not to question it, but it did encourage him to do his job. 'So, how did you manage to dislocate your shoulder?'

Her eyes dropped to the floor momentarily, feeling immediate shame. Telling someone who knew her when she was bubbly and carefree that she'd been living with abuse for a year was going to be hard, but she took a deep breath and spat out an explanation.

'My boyfriend... he tried to stop me leaving.'

And there was the look. The one she'd seen a few times now. The look of pity that always made her feel like she was an idiot. Jackson had given it to her the day she'd answered her door to him, Louisa had used it when they'd been in the assembly hall at school and then Francine Chase had used it when she realised who she was. It was the reason she hated telling people, apart from admitting she'd given someone permission to treat her that way.

He looked over her medical records which he had to hand and brought up each point as if to remind her. 'I see this is the fourth time you've been here over the last twelve months. A year ago, you were admitted for a miscarriage, then back in February you had to have fifteen stitches in the back of your head and just last month you were admitted to intensive care where you were in a coma for a week.'

She nodded and explained each in turn. 'The miscarriage was the first time he beat me because I told him I was pregnant, the stitches were because I was putting on make-up in the bathroom mirror and the coma was from him throwing me down the stairs because I didn't smile enough.'

'Jesus Kaidence, I had no idea.'

'No one did. I kept it to myself.'

'I take it you've got a police escort because you're leaving him, right?'

She took a deep breath. 'That's what I was trying to do tonight.'

'Well, your X-rays show no tissue damage so I'm going to be able to reset that shoulder. But I'll need to X-ray it again to make sure it's back in the socket before we can get you out of here.'

'I don't want to be a pain in the arse, but have you got any idea how long that's going to take?' Louisa asked, not wanting to wait around any longer than necessary. 'She still needs to be interviewed.'

'It shouldn't take longer than half an hour,' Matthew replied before turning back to his patient. 'Have you been given a painkiller?'

'I had some after my X-ray,' she replied.

He placed his tablet on the table over the hospital bed. 'Great. I'm just going to lay the bed flat and I'll rotate your arm around the shoulder joint until it goes back into the socket, okay?'

'If it gives me back the use of my arm, that's okay.'

Jackson saw the way Matthew had looked at Kaidence and knew he had a fondness for her from the time he'd known her growing up. He wondered if he'd carried that affection all the years since undetected, and walked around with it every day, and whether that was the reason he'd returned home. He was jealous, which was unprofessional, but that hadn't exactly bothered him up to this point, so he didn't suppress the feeling as it ran through his veins. He resented the history the doctor had with her because he'd known her before the tragedy of her parents' death had damaged her spirit, before she'd fallen for a man who hurt her every day for his own pleasure, and he only knew her as the woman she was now.

He didn't react as Dr Logan re-entered the room and announced she was clear to leave. But as soon as the words were out of his mouth, Jackson got to his feet. It had been a long night since pulling up outside her house and he couldn't wait to get back to doing his job. Even for her, waiting for treatment at the hospital was one of the least favourite elements of what he did.

Seeing her emerge from her private room dressed and ready to leave, Matthew called out to Kaidence as he hurried towards her. 'Call me sometime,' he said, thrusting a scrap of paper into her hand. 'It'll be nice to grab a coffee.'

She smiled. 'Okay.'

'If you're done flirting, we've got an interview to get you to,' Jackson said.

'Of course, sorry,' Matthew said, clearing his throat. 'It was nice to see you Sprinkles; I only wish it wasn't like this.'

'You too Mattie,' Kaidence replied.

CHAPTER TWENTY

The doctor stood watching his old high school friend leave through the emergency department door and was taken back to their close friendship, which started almost three decades ago. They had been inseparable. If he wasn't at her house, she was at his. Their parents had been friends, so all their school breaks were spent together, and they even had a few holidays abroad. But when he'd made the choice to be a doctor and moved away, they'd lost touch.

He'd been meaning to reach out to her when he'd learned of her parents' deaths, but he was working hard to provide a future for himself and hadn't got around to it. Seeing her now, it was obvious how much she needed a friend, and that made him feel guilty for not contacting her sooner. When he'd left for college, she was surrounded by friends, so he assumed she had the support she'd needed to deal with her loss, but it was apparent now that she'd been alone for a long time. It made him sad that the life she had once been so full of seemed to have disappeared, leaving fear in its place.

One of Matthew's colleagues caught him watching Kaidence leave. 'Somebody you know?' she asked over his shoulder.

'Yes,' he answered absent-mindedly before snapping out of it and turning to her. 'I used to, a long time ago.'

'What was she here for?'

'She's being abused by her boyfriend.'

'That explains the police escort.'

'Unfortunately, it doesn't explain how she lost her way so much that she got to the point of needing one to protect her from a man she was dating.'

'How long has it been since you last saw her?'

'Um, I moved away when I was sixteen, so twelve years.'

'You've kept in touch though, haven't you?'

He shook his head. 'No. I thought she had friends looking out for her.'

'Isn't that what you were?'

He sighed, externalising his regret. 'She was more like a sister to me. I should've made more of an effort to stay in touch.'

'At least you've got a chance to put it right now.'

Kaidence's head swam. Seeing Matthew again had thrown her into a tailspin. They'd known each other since they were born and, until he'd left to become a doctor, she thought they'd be tethered to each other forever. But studying took up so much of his time that the distance between them provided an excuse for them both to detach from their family-like connection. It was only now that she remembered how important he was to her, and that brought back memories of the parents she'd done her best to forget during her relationship, because she knew they'd disapprove, and she couldn't stand the thought of disappointing them, even though they were gone.

She was still dazed from her surprise reunion when she was led into the police station she'd visited twice before. It was the same entrance she'd walked through on both previous visits but she paid more attention to the interior this time.

The walls were painted a basic magnolia, cold and uninviting, with posters relating to crime and the treatment of staff and detainees pasted all over them. She barely paid attention to the officers' workstations as she was escorted to one of the more comfortable interview rooms.

As Jackson swung the door open, Kaidence noted that the decor was the same but the walls were blank. There was a three-seater settee directly opposite the entrance with two armchairs against the wall on the left and a small coffee table in the middle, but that was all. She'd seen interview rooms on reality police shows and this looked nothing like those, so she suspected this was where they got statements regarding more sensitive cases.

'Take a seat on the settee, someone'll be in to take your statement in a minute,' he said, talking to her like he would anyone else in her situation.

She nodded and did as instructed. 'Okay. Thank you.'

'Can I get you a drink?' Louisa asked as usual.

She shook her head. 'No thanks.'

'All right, well, you shouldn't be waiting long,' she replied as she and her partner left her alone in the room. But as they turned to head back out on tour, Louisa stopped Jackson. 'Don't you think that was a little much back there?'

Jackson frowned. 'What?'

'The doc hasn't seen her since high school, they were catching up. I don't think they were flirting.'

'That doesn't matter. It was taking up time and we'd been sitting around long enough.'

'Man, I forgot how cranky you get after babysitting duty.'

<hr />

Kaidence sat in the room, waiting, replaying the night in her head. She wanted to be sure she remembered the right order of things so that she didn't cast any doubt about her need to use force in defending herself. If even one detail was wrong, that would cast uncertainty over her whole statement and that could be the difference between Mitchell being prosecuted or getting off scot-free. She hadn't been able to remember how many times she'd stabbed him straight after it happened, but now, the details were crystal clear. But she barely had a chance to run through things once before she was joined by the detective.

'Miss Hadaway, I'm Detective Jensen and I'll be taking your statement tonight,' the detective said, walking in and sitting down in one of the armchairs. 'Just so you know, you're not under arrest and you have the right to seek legal advice at any point during this interview.'

She nodded her understanding. 'It's okay. I don't need a lawyer.'

'All right, well before we start, I just want to let you know that this is being recorded,' she said, pointing out the video camera in front of them in the opposite corner to where they sat. 'But the tape is only going to be used in connection to this investigation, so we can accurately get your account of what happened.' She paused and consulted the notepad she'd brought in with her. 'Why don't you start by telling me about your relationship with Mitchell Stevenson?'

'We met over two years ago in a pub while I was out with friends. Eleven months later, in August of last year, he lost his job and I let him move in with me because he didn't have any money to pay his rent,' she stated matter-of-factly. 'That's when he started to control what I wore and who I saw. But it wasn't until two months later, when I found out I was pregnant, that he hit me for the first time.' Recalling how it all began made her relive the emotions of it. Tears immediately sprang to her eyes and spilled onto her cheeks freely. 'He beat me so badly that night that I had a miscarriage and he's been hitting me ever since,' she said, using the sleeve of Jackson's zip-up hoody to wipe away the tears. 'I've been keeping an abuse journal and taking photographs of my injuries as a record. Tonight, I just reached the end of my tether and I wasn't going to let him hit me any more.' She snivelled.

The interviewing officer reached down to the floor beside her chair and retrieved a box of tissues, which she offered to Kaidence. 'And what happened tonight?'

She dropped her head and took a deep breath, 'He'd been away on business, I was in the shower when he got back so I didn't hear him come in. I came downstairs to find him going through the drawer I'd hidden Officer Chase's contact card in after a burglary in my street. He found it and accused me of using it to talk to police about the things he had done to me. I told him I hadn't been, but he didn't believe me.' The tears began to flow again. 'He hit me and knocked me into the cooker. When I got to my feet, I told him I wasn't going to let him hit me any more and I punched him in the face. But it didn't do anything; he just stood there,' she said, wiping her runny nose. 'He tried to hit me again, but I picked up the pan that had been knocked off the cooker and hit him with it. He dropped to the floor, so I tried to get to the front door, but he grabbed my ankle to stop me and I landed face first on the tiles.' She paused between sobs to dry her eyes. 'He got up and came after me as I was crawling towards the door, but when I saw him draw his foot back to kick me out of the corner of my eye, I went to the kitchen instead because I knew I wouldn't make it outside before he got to me. I was petrified but I used the island in the middle of the room to protect myself. Any time he tried to get to me, I moved the other way, away from him. That's when he threatened me; he said I couldn't move fast enough to get away before he caught up to me. I told him to leave or I was going to call the police...' Her body was wracked with the emotion she was feeling. 'And he said I'd be dead before you got there.' She took another tissue and attempted to dry away the tears, but they just kept coming. 'I picked up the knife off the draining board to try and scare him into letting me go but he laughed at me because I was shaking. He said I'd have to steady my hand if I was going to use it against him and that I was going to pay for picking it up. I told him if he got close, I was going to use it, but I had no intention of using it, I just wanted to get away.' She broke down.

'Okay, take a minute to calm yourself down.'

'I swear I just wanted to scare him into letting me go, but he wouldn't.'

'It's okay. Just take a few deep breaths before you carry on.'

Kaidence tried to compose herself. She wanted to make her statement as accurate as she could, but reliving the attack was forcing out the feelings she couldn't show at the time because Mitchell would've seen it as weakness, and she had needed him to believe she'd found the confidence to fight back.

A few minutes later, when the sobs had subsided a little, the detective spoke to her, softly. 'Are you ready to continue?'

She nodded. 'I bode my time until he stepped away from the archway and ran for the front door, with the knife still in my hand, but I couldn't move fast enough. He grabbed my wrist and pulled me back, which dislocated my shoulder. I spun around with a scream and stabbed him, in the chest, but I didn't realise that's what I'd done until he released me. I froze, and he punched me in the face, breaking my nose. Then he hit me in the jaw, knocking me to the ground and I dropped the knife. I tried to crawl to the front door, but he grabbed my hair to pull me up to my feet and I managed to grab the knife before I left the floor. I stabbed him again, which made him let me go. He dropped to the floor and I knew I'd really hurt him.' Again, she started to cry. 'I don't know why but instead of leaving, I grabbed my phone and dialled nine-nine-nine. I was on the phone to the emergency operator when he got back up and came after me again. He knocked the phone out of my hand, and I balled up into a foetal position, but he picked me up by my hair, so I kicked out until he let me go. That's when I made a run for the front door and when I got outside, there were officers there.'

'Why didn't you leave before, Kaidence?' The detective asked sympathetically.

'Because when he told me he'd find me no matter where I ran to, I believed him.'

'When did Officer Chase give you his card?'

She thought back. 'Uh, it was mid-September.'

'And what precipitated that?'

'There was a burglary in my street, and he knocked on my door to find out if I saw anything. When I opened my front door, he saw my bruises and the aftermath of what had happened the night before, so he gave me his card.'

'Had you been in contact with the officer?'

'Yes, he was trying to get me to leave but I needed to do it at the right time.'

'I saw you filed two reports yesterday; one for pushing you down the stairs, putting you in a coma, and one for raping you a few days before he left on his business trip.'

She nodded. 'That was my first step towards getting away from him.'

'So, let's go through your statement again, slowly, so that I can better understand what happened, okay?' the detective asked. Kaidence nodded her head. 'So, he hit you after he found the officer's card?'

'I fell into the cooker and pulled a saucepan down on top of me.'

'Was there anything in the saucepan?'

She shook her head. 'No, it's too big to go in the cupboard so I keep it there.'

'What happened then?'

'I landed on the floor. I could taste blood in my mouth and feel it coming from my nose and eyebrow. I stood up and told him that was the last time he was going to hit me, and I punched him in the jaw. His head whipped around to the side, but it didn't affect him.' She paused to remember. 'He smiled and told me I'd have to do better than that to hurt him. He called me sweetheart; he was taunting me. He swung at me again, but I dipped to pick up the pan and hit him around the head with it. He fell to the ground, bleeding from a cut on his head. I froze. Then I heard him groan. I headed to the front door. But he grabbed my ankle and I landed face first on the floor.'

'What did you do then?'

'I started to crawl towards the front door to escape but he got to his feet and I saw him out of the corner of my eye pull his foot back to kick me. I forced myself up to my feet and ran to the kitchen instead. He followed me, but I stood behind the island in order to keep him away from me and every time he took a step towards me, I took a step away.'

'So, how did you get your other injuries?'

Silent tears spilled onto her cheeks. 'He told me I couldn't move fast enough to get away from him and I knew he was right, so I waited, trying to build up the courage to make a run for the front door without him knowing that was my plan. I saw the knife on the draining board, and I grabbed it, hoping it would be enough of a deterrent for him to let me escape. But he laughed because I was shaking. He said I'd have to steady my hand if I was going to use it against him and I told him that if he got close to me, I'd use it because I wasn't going to let him hit me any more. Then he told me he was going to get the knife off me and make me pay for picking it up.' She dried her eyes with a new tissue and continued. 'I told him to leave or I'd call the police and he said that I'd be dead before they got there.'

'Where were you?'

'I was by the sink in the kitchen and he was opposite me by the bar stools. It took a while, but when he stepped away from the archway towards the fridge freezer, I made a run for it. Only I wasn't fast enough; I was barely out of the room when I felt his hand around my left wrist. He yanked me back towards him, popping my arm out of the socket. I screamed, and I still had the knife in my hand, so as I turned towards him, I stabbed him in the chest.' She started to sob. 'I didn't mean to, but the pain in my shoulder made me react the way I did. I just wanted him to let me go.'

'And then?' the detective asked, keeping her voice low and compassionate.

'He cried out and released me to cover his wound with his hands. When he moved his hands away and saw the blood, he punched me in the face, which broke my nose. I felt it collapse on impact and start to bleed. Before I could move, he punched me in the jaw again.' She took a second to remember what happened next. 'I dropped the knife so I could brace myself for the hard landing on the floor. I crawled towards the door and when he reached down to grab my hair, I fumbled to grab the knife as he pulled me up to my feet. I stabbed him and kept stabbing until he released me. But when he dropped to his knees, struggling to breathe, I knew I'd really hurt him. So, instead of getting out, I picked up my mobile phone off the floor and dialled nine-nine-nine.'

'You said that you knew you'd really hurt him, but when you rang nine-nine-nine you made no mention to the operator about his injuries until after you mentioned he was trying to kill you.'

'Because I needed you to know that I was defending myself when I stabbed him.'

'You stabbed him four times, Kaidence.'

Her frame crumbled, like she'd been deflated. 'I didn't know.'

'So, when you stabbed him, what was your intention?'

'I just wanted to stop him hurting me.'

'Did you intend to do him serious harm with the knife?'

'No. I just wanted to get free. He was going to kill me, and I didn't want to die,' she said, breaking down. 'I swear I only used the knife because he wouldn't let me go.'

'So, after you called the police, what happened?'

'He got back up; came after me again. He knocked the phone out of my hand and pulled me off the floor by my hair. I kicked and punched out until I caught him between the legs with my foot. I only know that because he doubled over in an instant. I didn't hang around, I bolted to the front door and he was breathing down my neck as I managed to get it open and escape.'

'He had the knife in his hand when he followed you outside.'

'So if the police hadn't been there, I'd be dead.'

'Why didn't you leave or report the abuse earlier, Kaidence?' the detective asked, barely audible.

'Because he convinced me that no one would believe me. That's why I started logging everything and every time he hurt me – he told me there was nowhere I could run that he wouldn't find me. I was scared.'

'So, the book that you wrote in about the abuse, where is that?'

'In my office in a safe behind the picture on the wall. The code is eight, eight, six, zero, four, two.'

'I'll get one of the officers guarding the scene to bring that to me,' she said, jotting something down on the spiral notepad sitting on her lap. 'We've got your statement now and photographs of your injuries, but if I have more questions after interviewing Mitchell Stevenson, would you be willing to come back in?'

She agreed straight away. 'Yes, whatever you need.'

'Right, I've got your name, date of birth, address and national insurance number. Do you have any questions before you go?'

She shook her head. 'No.'

The detective passed her a business card. 'That's all my contact details. If you think of anything you want to ask or remember any details you haven't disclosed in your statement, you can ring me.'

'Okay.'

'Do you have somewhere to stay?' the detective asked. 'You won't be able to go home because it's a crime scene.'

Kaidence exhaled nosily. 'I suppose I could go to my sister's.'

Jensen detected an undercurrent in her sentence and her brow furrowed. 'Does your sister know about the abuse?'

She shook her head. 'I guess she will when I show up on her doorstep.'

'I'll see if Officer Chase is free to drop you off,' she said, getting to her feet. 'It might be a short wait though, is that okay?'

'Yes, thank you.'

As Detective Carla Jensen exited the interview room, she was joined by her partner, Danny James. He'd been watching Kaidence give her statement and taking more extensive notes than the senior officer who had been in the room. He had taken custody of the clothing evidence that had been collected at the hospital but had yet to collect the body cam footage from the officers who had escorted her to have her injuries treated; still, they had enough to start the ball rolling on the investigation before they visited the scene.

'I want to interview the officers who were with her tonight and review their footage before we visit the scene and retrieve the journal she talked about,' she said, as they started walking back towards the office. 'I just hope the uni's haven't contaminated the bloody scene.'

'I called Chase and Jessop back to base fifteen minutes ago so we could get their body cam footage,' Danny informed her. 'They should be back in five.'

'Has there been any word on the boyfriend?'

He shook his head. 'Not yet.'

'Well, let's hope he makes it. I don't really want to prosecute a domestic abuse victim for manslaughter if I can help it.'

***

Having given her account of what had happened leading to her being at the police station, Kaidence felt a weight had been lifted off her shoulders enough for her to relax. She sat back in her seat and replayed the statement she'd given. To the best of her recollection, she had relayed the events of the confrontation step by step accurately. But she didn't know if it'd appear like a vengeance attack or reasonable force to escape with her life. It was in the hands of the police now, and she had to trust that the abuse evidence she'd collected herself in the last fourteen months would be enough to show a pattern of behaviour that would point to the latter rather than the former.

The relief she felt seemed to expel the last of her energy. She closed her eyes for a second to try and give herself enough energy to function until she managed to find a bed to climb into. She knew her sister would want to know why she was being dropped off by the police and, if she was to explain her reasons for hiding the way she'd been living for over a year, she'd need the strength for it. She briefly thought about how she was going to start the conversation, but every beginning was inadequate and every reason for not sharing sooner sounded feeble. She could see the disappointment on Meredith's face already and she imagined that her parents would have had the same expression if they were still alive. She could barely stomach the idea of being honest with her sister after all this time, because she knew she would put her dislike for Mitchell down to knowing there was something *off* about him and she really couldn't stand the 'I told you so' speech. As much as she loved her older sibling, sometimes she could be so righteous, and she could really do without that when she was functioning on no sleep.

***

Carla got out of the seat behind her desk as she saw Jackson walk into the room. She stuck out her hand in his direction. 'Officer Chase, I'm the investigating detective – Carla Jensen.'

He reached out and shook her hand. 'What can I do for you?'

She gestured to the seat on the opposite side of her workstation and sat back down. 'I've just got a few questions about your relationship with Kaidence Hadaway.'

'Sure, anything I can do to help,' he replied, sitting down.

'You first met her, when?'

'Uh, on the sixteenth of September this year.'

'And what were the circumstances of that meeting?'

'There had been a burglary in the area. I was canvassing for witnesses.'

'She said you gave her your card.'

He nodded. 'I saw her black eyes and the bruises on her face. She was scared I'd be seen on her doorstep and it would be reported back to her boyfriend, so she pulled me inside. I saw evidence of an altercation inside and asked her about it. She seemed reluctant to press charges, so I handed her my card and told her to use it when she decided to stop being his punching bag. Then I left.'

'When was the next time you encountered her?'

'Two days later on Monday morning.'

'Who initiated contact?'

'Me. I wanted to follow up with her.'

'And what happened on that visit?'

'She invited me in and made me a cup of tea. I got a dialogue going about the abuse and she told me in no uncertain terms that she wasn't ready to leave. I told her she could ring me at any time, and she confided in me about the journal she'd been keeping. I left feeling like I'd built a rapport with her.' He paused. 'When I realised my partner had another connection to her, I tasked her with reporting on her status.'

'What was that connection?'

'Kaidence teaches one of her daughters at Ridge Primary.'

'Then when was your next interaction with her?'

'A month later, when she was admitted to hospital,' he said. 'Officer Jessop dropped her daughter at school and Miss Hadaway wasn't present. She enquired about her absence with the secretary and was informed she hadn't called in. When Jessop couldn't reach her on her mobile phone, she called at her home address. She couldn't get any answer there either. But she could hear the phone ringing out inside, so she opened the letter box and saw Miss Hadaway lying at the bottom of the stairs. We gained entry using the key, called for a bus and cleared the house. Mitchell wasn't home, so my partner went to his place of work to question him. He denied all knowledge of her injury; said he'd left her in the bathroom on his way out of the door to work.

When I got to the hospital, the doctor informed me she had a cerebral oedema and they were inducing a coma to try to decrease the swelling.'

'How long was she hospitalised?'

'For a week.'

'Did she make a statement about what led to her injury?'

'No, she claimed not to remember. But as soon as she woke up, the boyfriend was at the hospital, so I think that contributed to her reluctance to recall what had happened.'

'She did make a statement regarding that incident on Saturday though.'

'Yes, she contacted me. She had finally made the decision to leave him and wanted to file two reports for the most recent abuse.'

'Is there anything else you think will be pertinent to the investigation?'

'I can't think of anything off the top of my head, but I can consult my notes and get back to you.'

'That would be great. Thank you,' she said, getting to her feet, inspiring him to do the same.

He turned to leave, and almost as quickly turned back. 'Oh, did she tell you about the journal she's been keeping?'

'Yes, and we're going to collect that from the scene.' She frowned. 'Have you read it?'

'No, but I've seen some of the images of her injuries,' he confessed. 'They're not easy to look at.'

'It sounds like you've built up quite a connection with her if she trusts you enough to share them.'

'I think she just wanted to show me the extent of what she's had to endure.'

'Well, we're all done with her now so you can drop her off with her sister.'

Kaidence felt the pain in her shoulder and then the knife in her hand. She gripped the handle tight enough to know that her knuckles were white. She spun to face him and brought the blade up to eye height. Without a conscious thought passing through her mind, she struck. The thirteen months she'd been taking his punishment compounded in the attack because in that moment – in that split second – she wanted to stop him hurting her. She wanted the life she had before him back. She wanted to be free.

Opening the door to the interview room, Jackson saw Kaidence curled up on the settee the detective had left her sitting on. He couldn't help the smile that crept onto his face. She was so exhausted she hadn't been able to stay awake long enough to get to a bed now that she'd unloaded about the abuse of that night. He walked inside and reached out to nudge her. It was a few minutes before she roused with a start.

'It's just me.' The officer tried to ease her panic, holding up his hands to ward off any defensive attack.

She rubbed at her eyes to focus as she raised herself into a seated position. 'Sorry, I didn't mean to fall asleep.'

'It's okay. But why don't we get you to your sister's, so you can get a good night's sleep?'

She followed him out of the room and through the corridors, barely taking in anything because she was so tired. It wasn't until they got to the car that she realised Louisa wasn't with them. Regardless, she slipped into the passenger's side of the squad car when he chivalrously opened the door for her. She instinctively reached behind her for the seatbelt and clipped it into place before Jackson climbed in behind the wheel. She didn't have the strength to muster a question about his partner's whereabouts. She just sat staring forward.

'How did the interview go?' he asked, putting on his own seatbelt.

'Okay, I think,' she answered. 'I had to go through everything a couple of times.'

'That's just to detect any inconsistencies.'

'Well, it felt like I was being interrogated.'

'They're just doing their job and making sure you haven't attacked him for no reason.'

'I have evidence.'

'But they haven't seen that yet,' he pointed out, turning the key in the ignition and bringing the engine to life. 'They will, and then they'll know what you've been dealing with.'

The rest of the journey was travelled in silence, mainly because Kaidence had expelled the energy she had built up in her station catnap in her walk to the car. She was past fatigued; she felt like she could sleep for a week and still not be rested enough for everyday living. Watching the scenery go by lulled her, and her eyes closed. It was only when they reached their destination and Jackson gently woke her that the panic hit. She wasn't ready to admit to her sister that she'd been lying to her since Mitchell had moved in; first for cancelling plans because they didn't fit in with his, and then for any bruises she had seen.

'Do you want me to come in with you?' Jackson asked when she made no effort to move.

She shook her head. 'It's going to be bad enough telling her what I need to tell her, without her having questions as soon as I walk through the door.'

'She might already have seen me pull up.'

'Then I better get out of the car and get it over with,' she said, unclipping the restraint across her chest.

'Are you sure you don't want moral support?'

'No, it's best that she doesn't think anyone else knew, otherwise she's going to think it somehow reflects on our relationship.' She sighed. 'I don't need that headache adding to the pressure of the situation when all I really want to do is get you to drop me at a hotel instead.'

'I could do that if you're not up to this tonight.'

She rubbed at her furrowed brow. 'I can't. I haven't got my purse, so I couldn't pay for a room. I haven't even got my phone. At least here I've got access to my own clothes.'

'Did you used to live here?'

She nodded. 'When my parents died, and I started drinking every day, my sister saw it as her responsibility to set me straight and staged an intervention. If I was living with her, at least she could ensure my sobriety.'

He frowned. 'How exactly could she do that?'

She raised her eyebrows. 'I had an allowance and a curfew. It was like being a teenager again. I hated her for it, but now, I realise she was doing it to save me. If it wasn't for her, I probably would've been dead long before Mitchell got his hooks into me.' She sighed. 'I don't know how I'm going to do this, Jackson. My sister is the one person I've always been able to tell everything, but how do I tell her this? How do I start trying to explain the last year of my life?'

'You'll find a way. There's no use in planning what to say, you'll just have to say it however it comes out.'

She took a minute before turning towards him. 'How bad does my face look?'

He twisted in his seat to look at her. 'It's not that bad, but it is noticeable.'

'Then I know exactly how the conversation will start,' she said, reaching out and pulling the handle. 'Thanks for dropping me off.'

'I'll check on you in a few days.'

Jackson watched as Kaidence walked in front of the car and made her way down the double drive towards the front door. He was relieved he hadn't been required to wear his body cam to drop her off considering how personal and familiar their conversation had been, because having to explain that after divulging only a professional connection to her would have possibly called his reliability into question.

He watched her disappear inside and put the car into gear before pulling off. He hadn't really had a moment to process exactly what had happened because he'd been overcome with fear when he'd heard the call come over the radio, only to be thankful to find her still alive when he got to the scene. He knew the chances were that if her life was in danger he'd be on duty because that was just his luck. But at the same time, he felt better being on the inside of the investigation rather than being kept separate from it. He knew that he wouldn't have much access to any developments but at least he'd be privy to some details. He drove back to the station to clock off, wondering how things were going for Kaidence with her sister.

The door opened to reveal Meredith dressed ready for bed. Kaidence knew it was nearing the middle of the night, but the chances were that she hadn't interrupted her sister's sleep because she'd been up feeding five-month-old.

Her sister rubbed her eyes and frowned. 'Kiki? What are you doing here?' she asked, extending the door and silently inviting her inside.

'I needed somewhere to stay,' she replied, stepping in under the light of the hallway so her sister could better see her face. But she didn't look in her direction; instead she closed and locked the door behind her.

'What's wrong with your house?' Meredith asked.

'It's a crime scene,' she replied, leading the way to the living room, switching on the light as she entered.

Her sister followed her. 'A crime–' she started in a questioning tone but stopped upon seeing the cuts and bruises. She cupped her chin to inspect them. 'What the hell happened?'

'I don't want you to freak out and get all judgemental when I tell you this, I just want to say it so that you know,' she said, taking a seat on the settee, which encouraged her sister to perch next to her. She took a deep breath in preparation. 'For about a year, Mitchell's been hitting me and tonight, he tried to kill me.'

'My God, Kaidence. Why didn't you tell me?' Meredith asked, her heart breaking.

'It's not something you just slip out casually over coffee.'

'I knew you were hiding something; you're withdrawn, you've lost weight and you never wanted me over at the house,' she ranted.

'I didn't know *how* to tell you.'

'You should know you can tell me anything.'

'But how was I supposed to admit to you that I'd picked a man who thought it was okay to take his frustrations out on me? And that I was letting him?'

'If you'd have told me, we'd have got you away from him.'

'He said he'd kill me if I left and I believed him.'

'How the hell did it start?' she asked, her volume reflecting the rising anger she felt.

Kaidence took another deep breath, for the energy to share rather than the preparation of confessing. 'I told him I was pregnant.'

Meredith shot up to her feet with a rage that made her start to pace. 'Of course he wouldn't want you to have a baby! That wouldn't fit in with his plan to control you! Because a baby would be all-consuming, so you wouldn't have time for him! What a bastard!'

The younger sibling rubbed at her forehead. She knew this was going to be a hard conversation to have but she was tired, and she knew her sister wouldn't let her rest until she had every detail of every confrontation.

'Well, thank God you didn't have his baby. At least you're not tied to him for the next eighteen years.' Meredith found the silver lining.

'That was hardly the way I wanted to find out what kind of man he was.'

'I knew there was a reason I didn't like him; I must've had a sixth sense.'

Kaidence sighed. 'And that right there is why I didn't want to tell you! I knew you'd imply that on some level you knew he was an arsehole, and how stupid I was for not seeing it? That I could be in a relationship with a man and not know and yet, you – perfect, all-knowing you – could sense there was something not quite right about him! Well, newsflash, he wasn't wearing a *"beware of the arsehole"* sign around his neck. He was charming and caring when we first started dating.'

'But the first time he hit you; why didn't you leave?'

'Because I already had feelings for him! I believed he was sorry and that he wouldn't do it again.'

'And the second time?'

'It wasn't like he hit me every day. It was months later when he did it again and he made me believe it was my fault.'

Meredith frowned. 'You're an intelligent woman, why did you fall for that?'

'I don't expect you to understand, you can't unless you've lived through it,' Kaidence answered, agitated. 'It started with comments about the clothes I wore or the friends I hung out with, and before I knew it, I was dressing down to prevent being noticed and cancelling plans with anyone he disapproved of.

It wasn't something that happened overnight. He spent months chipping away at my confidence until I was isolated and petrified. So by the time he first lay his hands on me, I had no one to confide *in*.'

'You had me!'

'You were pregnant! I wasn't going to jeopardise that! Not after it took you so long to conceive.'

'But I'm your sister!'

'Which is precisely the reason I *couldn't* tell you.' She broke down. 'I didn't want to let you down again.'

Her sister sat next to her and wrapped an arm around her. 'You shouldn't have had to go through this alone.'

Kaidence thought about divulging that, more recently, she hadn't, but there had been enough shouting tonight and she didn't have the energy for more. 'Look Meredith, I'm exhausted and barely thinking straight; I promise to answer any questions you have tomorrow, but I need sleep.'

'Sure, the spare room is made up.'

Kaidence got to her feet and leaned in to kiss her on the cheek. 'Thanks Mimi.'

Meredith forced a smile to her lips as her younger sibling walked out, leaving her alone. She was in shock. She couldn't believe her sister had been hiding something as serious as abuse from her. She'd noticed a change. She'd seen her slowly step into the shadows, which was unlike her, and yet she hadn't questioned her about it. Before becoming a mother, she would have made it her business to get to the bottom of what was going on with her. But her focus was divided.

'Are you okay?' her husband Cole asked, appearing in the doorway her sister had walked out of.

'Did you hear any of that?'

He walked across the living room towards her. 'It was hard not to, there was a lot of shouting.'

'How didn't I know?'

'You never truly know what happens behind someone's front door,' he said, sitting beside her and reaching for her hand.

'But *I* should have known. She's been different since Mitchell moved in. I should've made the connection.'

'Come on, you can't put this on yourself.'

'I missed it, Cole, and I'm supposed to look out for her.'

'You haven't got a crystal ball, darling. All you can do is be there for her now.'

CHAPTER TWENTY-ONE

The knife was in her hand. The pain echoed throughout her whole body from the dislocation of her shoulder. She felt the boil of the rage inside her chest and thrust the blade into him. She needed to get away from him. She could hear screaming. She didn't know whether it was her or him.

Kaidence woke up in a cold sweat to find her sister sat on the bed. She was disorientated; unsure of where she was. She took a few deep breaths to try and calm her heart thumping in her chest and focus her attention.

'Meredith?' she questioned. 'Why are you here?'

'You were screaming in your sleep.'

The younger woman looked around the room and seemed to remember where she was. 'I was dreaming?'

'I assume so,' her older sister replied, reaching out to rub the top of her arm, detecting her confusion. 'Do you remember what happened?'

She nodded. 'My painkillers are wearing off,' she said, diverting the conversation away from any details that she hadn't yet given her and reaching up to gently hold her injured shoulder.

Meredith jumped up. 'I'll go and get you some. Is there anything else you need?'

She shook her head. 'Just the painkillers.'

Kaidence watched as her sister left the room and rolled her eyes. She could do without her hovering over her like she was going to break, but she knew it was inevitable. She lay in the darkness, staring up at the ceiling feeling the dull ache of her repaired shoulder, waiting for Meredith's return, and searched her mind for what she'd been dreaming about. She hadn't been thinking of anything when she closed her eyes, but maybe it had something to do with Mitchell.

It was only a minute later when her older sibling re-entered with a glass of water and the medication she had requested. 'Here you go.'

She forced herself up into a seated position using only her good arm and reached out for the items she offered. 'Thanks.'

Meredith sat in silence watching her take the tablets. But curiosity got the better of her. 'What happened tonight, Kiki?'

Kaidence placed the glass of water on the bedside table and reached up to rub her brow. 'He got back from a work retreat and found Jackson's card in the drawer.'

'Who's Jackson?'

'The officer that knocked on my door when there was a burglary in my street.'

'You've got to know him better than that; you called him Jackson.'

'He took it upon himself to check in on me from time to time after he saw the bruises on my face.'

'So, he knew about the abuse?'

She sighed and rolled her eyes. 'He's a police officer, he was helping me. Now do you want to know what happened or do you want to give me more shit for not telling you?'

Meredith sighed. 'I want to know what he did to you.'

Carla Jensen closed one of the three journals she'd retrieved from the scene with a sigh. She was one of only a few detectives left on shift and she wanted to get a jump on the investigation. She'd spent an hour going through the written testimony of the victim and had flicked through the photos on the SD card as they pertained to each attack. They were hard to look at. But she had a better understanding of the relationship.

She was rubbing her eyes so didn't see her superior approach her desk until he spoke. 'You're working the self-defence case, aren't you?' he asked.

'Yes sir. She's got physical evidence of abuse. She's covered in cuts and bruises; her nose was broken, and her arm was dislocated.'

'That doesn't mean she didn't initiate the attack.'

'I've just been reviewing the journal she kept and the photos she took; she's got a strong case. This man has been abusing her since he moved in with her,' she answered.

'That doesn't entitle her to get away with stabbing him four times.'

'It might if she thought she wouldn't make it out alive.'

'If the police weren't there when I opened the front door, he'd have caught up to me and...' Kaidence trailed off, reaching the end of her story.

Her sister reached out to rest her hand on top of hers. 'That doesn't bear thinking about.'

'Then why is it all I can think about?' she asked with a sigh.

'Because you have spent the last God knows how long preparing for every outcome, but you're safe now. He can't hurt you any more.'

'Yes, he can Mimi. Do you think he's going to take this accusation lying down? Do you think he's just going to hold up his hands and admit defeat, to me?' She shook her head. 'No, he's going to draw this out as long as he can, to torture me.'

'And that's why you have me. I can help you to be strong. When you feel like falling apart, I'll hold you together. That's what big sisters are for.'

Tears started to fall involuntarily from her eyes. 'I'm going to need a lot of holding together,' she said, sniffing back her emotions as she wiped at her nose with her hand. It wasn't until she removed her hand that her sister jumped up.

'Your nose is bleeding,' she declared, reaching for the box of tissues on the dressing table and handing them to her.

Instinctively Kaidence leaned her head forward and pinched her nose above her nostrils. 'The nurse said it might bleed but I'm not going back to the hospital unless I have to,' she said, wiping her nose free of blood.

'I'll get some ice,' Meredith said, turning on her heel.

'No, don't. It'll stop, just give it a minute.'

The older woman sat back down on the bed. 'I guess a nosebleed is the least you've had to endure.' Kaidence nodded as best she could. 'Do I dare ask what other injuries you've had?'

'Do you really want to know?'

'I don't know, do I?'

She took a deep breath; the next confession she had was going to be harder to hear. 'About a month ago, he pushed me down the stairs and I was in a coma for a week.'

Outraged, her sister bolted up to her feet. 'So why am I only hearing about this now?'

'Because if I told you, I'd have to explain why, and I wasn't ready to make that confession.'

But something occurred to her. 'Why didn't the police contact me when it happened?'

Kaidence sighed. 'Because it was Jackson and his partner who found me, and they knew you didn't know about the abuse so used their discretion.'

'And what exactly would have happened if you had died?'

'I guess they would have crossed that bridge if it came to it.'

Meredith lowered to the bed beside her again. 'How have you managed to put up with this for so long?'

Kaidence gave her nose a temporary reprieve to check if it was still bleeding and looked at her. 'I didn't have a choice, I let him move in.'

'But the police would've helped you get him out.'

'I told you, he said he would kill me if I tried to leave and tonight, he almost proved it.' It hurt to admit how close she'd come to death.

Hindsight provided her the luxury of wishing she'd taken Jackson's advice and left long ago. But she thought she could control leaving and take back some of her power. It was only now that she realised Mitchell was the one with all the power, even now that she was out from under him. He was going to continue to upset her life for as long as he could, providing he was still alive.

She could still feel the knife in her hand. Deep down she knew the anger she'd harboured about the abuse he'd subjected her to had helped to drive the knife into his chest. But she would never say out loud that she wanted him dead. He'd already taken enough of her life without her confession causing her to serve a prison sentence. She told herself she hadn't meant to hurt him, but how could she not want to inflict the same pain he'd put her through? If she was truly honest with herself, she wanted him to suffer and, in the moment, she wanted him dead. But she didn't want to kill him, that was true. She just wanted to hurt him. Even now, she remembered the very first time he'd laid into her and her hatred of him had slowly grown from there.

She looked down at the pregnancy test and couldn't help but smile at the positive result it showed. Ever since her sister had announced her own pregnancy the month before, she had been consumed with thoughts of her own future as a mother. So, although she had only been dating Mitchell for coming up to a year, she was happy about the new development in her life.

He'd moved in with her two months ago, after losing his job, so he didn't have the means to contribute towards living expenses, but things were going well between them. She wasn't completely sure yet whether he was the man she wanted to spend the rest of her life with, but her inheritance would afford her the ability to raise a child alone should she need to.

'What's that?' his voice asked from the doorway of the bathroom.

She showed him the object in her hand. 'I'm pregnant,' she responded with a smile.

'Who's is it?' he countered as she walked past him out into the bedroom.

She spun back to face him outraged by the implication. 'Excuse me?'

'I know it's not mine because you wouldn't be that stupid.'

'It takes two people to make a baby,' she pointed out.

'You're on the pill, or was that a lie?'

'The pill isn't a 100 per cent guarantee.'

'Well, you're getting rid of it,' he ordered.

'Abortion isn't a precaution. You should have used a condom.'

'I don't like them, and I don't like kids either so you're getting rid of it.'

'And if I want this baby?'

'I don't care what you want. You either have an abortion or I'll kick that thing out of you.'

Her jaw dropped open in shock. 'I can do this without you.'

'There's no way you're having this kid to come after me later. So, you're getting rid.'

'You have no right to make that decision.'

'That kid is mine and I'm telling you, you're not having it.'

She laughed. 'You don't get a say what I do in this situation. If you don't want to be involved, you're welcome to leave. I won't come after you for anything, I can raise this baby alone.'

He advanced on her and before she understood his intention, he clenched his fist and hit her in the stomach with all the strength he could muster from his mighty stature.

She was winded as she buckled in front of him and immediately started to cry. She was in shock that he'd laid his hands on her, but she had to let him know that it was unacceptable. She found the fortitude to stand tall in front of him.

'You can't do that!' she demanded in her best stern voice.

'Oh yeah?' he asked, raising his fist and punching her in the face.

She fell to the ground and her location afforded him the opportunity to lay into her with his foot, kicking her in the stomach repeatedly until she could force herself into the foetal position. He still found a way of getting a *few blows to her core as she screamed at him to stop, but her cries fell on deaf ears.*

When he was finished proving his point, and walked away, Kaidence lay there feeling every bruise developing internally. She knew right away that her baby hadn't survived the trauma like she would, and her heart broke. She had one dream growing up – to be a mother – and just when she thought she was getting what she wanted, it had been snatched from her. It was obvious to her now that Mitchell was not the man she wanted to spend the rest of her life with; she wasn't even going to be with him the next day once she got up off the floor and rang the police. She just had to get up off the floor first. She gritted her teeth. The tension in her abdomen intensified the pain. But she had to get up.

As she got up to her knees, using the bedside table to assist her, she felt her mobile phone beneath her fingertips. She pulled it off the surface and unlocked it.

His voice came from above her. 'You're not about to do something stupid are you?'

'I'm losing the baby so I'm calling the police.'

'You know it could be worse; you could lose your life.'

'I need to go to the hospital.'

'I'll take you to the hospital, but you won't say a word about what happened. Remember, you're coming home with me, and think about how much worse it could get when you do.'

Knowing she needed medical attention, she nodded. 'I won't say anything.'

And that's how his manipulation had started.

It was hard to admit she had succumbed so easily to his death threats, but she wanted to live so badly that she'd given herself permission to accept the things she didn't have the courage to change. At least until she met someone who gave her the strength to believe in a future that didn't involve him.

'It looks like it's stopped bleeding.' Her sister's voice brought her out of her self-pity.

She used the tissue she held to wipe away any excess blood and placed it on the bedside table. 'Thanks Mimi.'

'For?'

'Being my big sister.'

She smiled. 'I had no control over that.'

'I mean, for being here for me.'

Meredith reached out and affectionately stroked the top of her arm.

'Always,' she said, standing up and making her way to the door. 'I'll let you get some sleep before your nephew wakes you at four a.m.'

Kaidence nodded. 'I love you.'

'Love you too,' she replied, closing the bedroom door.

Jackson climbed into bed at the crack of dawn after his shift, feeling like he could sleep soundly knowing Kaidence was finally safe. The only full nights' sleep he'd had since meeting her were ones he spent under the same roof as her. Knowing that she was free of Mitchell made him feel much more settled than he had in a long time, even though it could mean she'd face charges.

He had to have faith in the law he upheld, and he was relatively certain that in the unlikely event she served a prison sentence, she'd survive, because she'd survived worse. He wanted her to be vindicated in defending herself after all the abuse she'd lived through, but there was always a small chance that she'd be convicted of intent. Still, he had to have faith in the law he spent his life upholding.

Kaidence lay in bed curled up under the duvet to counter the cold of the night air. She was trying to fall asleep but she could still feel that knife handle in her hand. She could still hear the pained cry as she drove the blade into his chest. She could still see his body lying at her feet. The images were vivid, and she knew it would be a long time before they dispersed. Regardless, she lay with her eyes pressed closed, trying to think of anything else to assist her in falling asleep. She needed to sleep. She thought about the last time she felt safe and Jackson's face sprang to mind. His image provided a comfort in the darkness and eventually she fell to sleep, not deep enough to provide her with the true rest she needed but enough to recharge.

The daylight beamed into the room from the undressed window, waking Kaidence before she was ready. She tried to open her eyes but her left one was swollen, which limited her sight out of it, so she relied on her good eye as she climbed out of bed, still dressed from the night before in Jackson's workout clothes. They were clean, but they smelled of him. It was comforting. She hoisted herself upright and immediately felt the ache in her side, which made her wince. Once she was sat on the edge of the bed, she lifted the side of her shirt to reveal a deep purple bruise she didn't know she had. She gritted her teeth as she forced herself to stand and walked out of the bedroom that was to be Justin's when he was old enough to leave his parents' room. She made as little noise as possible as she made her way to the bathroom. She locked the door behind her and, as she turned towards the toilet, she caught sight of her reflection in the mirror.

This was the first time she'd seen her reflection since being in the hospital and it wasn't pretty. The cut on her lip meant it had swollen slightly. The left side of her face was bruised from the jaw up to her cheekbone. Both of her eyes were black beneath the sleep-deprived bags that had developed over the last twenty-four hours. She could even see some of her scalp where there used to be hair, lost when she was pulled up to her feet.

She got closer to the reflective glass and examined her swollen eye. It didn't look as if it would leave permanent damage once it had recovered from the trauma and returned to its natural state. She sighed; it looked horrible and she knew Meredith would take the sight of it badly because it was the first abuse she'd seen evidence of, but she'd had worse to overcome.

She struggled with the agony in her side and shoulder to lower her bottoms in order to relieve her bladder and had to fight even harder to pull them back up. She flushed the toilet and washed her hands in the sink before venturing downstairs. The aching throughout her body meant the descent took her longer than it ordinarily would, and her face scrunched up against the stabbing pain when it hit her. But she made it to the ground floor without waking anyone else in the house.

Reaching the kitchen, she checked the clock on the wall, to see it had barely graced seven thirty a.m., and she cursed the sunrise for forcing her out of bed. She shuffled to the kettle and flicked on the switch for it to boil. Without thinking about the effect on her battered body, she reached into the cupboard overhead for a mug only to be crippled by the pain it brought on. Thinking better of causing herself any unnecessary discomfort, she looked around the room for an alternative and quickly realised there were clean cups on the draining board. She picked one up and continued making her first brew. Then, armed with her hot drink, Kaidence took a seat at the six-seater dining table and looked out beyond the large French doors into the back garden.

Although she couldn't hear any of the sounds outside, she knew the birds would be singing and the air would be crisp. The natural noises surrounding the sunrise were some of her favourite and she would open the door to hear them if she had the energy, but she just sat staring instead.

She was sat nursing her second cup when her brother-in-law joined her with Bailey, the family dog, in tow. Cole was momentarily startled but smiled at her regardless, as the German shepherd sauntered over to her for affection.

'How are you doing this morning?' he asked, his diluted Irish accent breaking the silence of the room.

'Sore,' she replied, sure he didn't need any more details than that. She returned her focus to the canine who wasn't quite satisfied with her level of commitment to the fusses she was dishing out.

'You need another?' he asked, motioning to her cup.

'Please.'

He walked over to pick her cup up off the table. 'He did a number on you, didn't he?'

'He always knew exactly where to hit to do the maximum damage but keep the evidence of it to a minimum, until last night.'

'You should have told us. We're your family.'

She sighed. 'And that's why I couldn't tell you.'

'I want to kill him, K, for what he did to you, for isolating you from the one person you should be able to tell everything to. I want to hurt him the same way he's hurt you.'

'And I appreciate the sentiment, but I won't have you exact your own version of revenge on my behalf, Cole. You've got a family to take care of.'

'A family that you're a part of.'

'I'm still alive, CJ.'

'Barely,' he said, placing the cup of tea he'd just made in front of her.

'I'll heal,' she countered flippantly.

He leaned against the counter momentarily and she noticed how lean he was despite spending his working hours behind a desk. But she knew his athleticism was down to the weekends spent in his home-made gym and the daily protein shake he drank.

He frowned as he sat down opposite her. 'What's the worst thing he's done to you?'

'He's shouted in my face, slapped me, bitten me, punched me, kicked me, choked me, smashed my head into a mirror, raped me and pushed me down the stairs,' she listed. 'But I think the worst thing was making me miscarry. I think I would have made a good mum,' she said, her eyes filling with emotion.

'You still will one day.'

She wiped her eyes. 'Hopefully, if someone still wants me.'

'How could they not? You're beautiful.'

His statement made more tears fall from her eyes, which caused Bailey to nudge his nose under her hand in a bid to comfort her. She bent down and kissed him on his snout. 'I'm okay, boy.'

Cole nodded in the direction of the furry family member. 'He's just as worried about you as we are.'

She repeatedly ran her hand through Bailey's fur as she spoke. 'My cuts and bruises will heal. It's the mental stuff that might just take a little longer to repair.'

A reflective silence landed on the room as they each processed their brief conversation. It was only when the family pet walked over to the doors Kaidence had been gazing beyond, and lifted his paw, that Cole got up to let him outside. The fleeting exposure to the elements brought a momentary chill into the kitchen until the barrier was closed again. It caused her to shiver slightly. It wasn't that she was cold; it was because she was sleep deprived and in pain.

That's when her sister joined them with her son cradled in her arms. 'Morning,' she greeted them both as she walked over to her husband and kissed him.

'Do you want some breakfast?' he asked, heading to the fridge.

But she shook her head as she took a seat at the table beside her sister, who immediately cooed over her nephew. 'Just a cup of tea this morning please.'

'Is little man ready for his breakfast?'

She rocked him. 'No, he's not hungry yet. He'll let us know when he is.' She turned her attention to Kaidence. 'Did he wake you in the night?'

'I was so exhausted that a bomb could've gone off under me and I wouldn't have woken up,' she replied. 'Although it doesn't feel like I slept a wink.'

'That's because you went twelve rounds with an arsehole who tried to kill you last night.'

It may not have sounded like it to the untrained ear, but Kaidence heard the dig at her for not divulging the true extent of her relationship. She chose to ignore it, to not rise to her sister's sniping because she knew she was never going to get her to fully understand why she'd kept the abuse hidden. As she'd told her sister the night before, it was something no one could comprehend unless they'd had to suffer it themselves.

She decided to change the subject. 'Talking of last night, you'll never guess who I saw at the hospital while I was there.'

'Who?'

'Mattie Logan.'

Her brow furrowed. 'I thought he left town.'

'He did, but once he got his doctorate, he came home.'

'Why didn't he get in touch?'

'It's been years, he probably didn't know how. Besides, he's a doctor now – he probably barely has time for a social life, never mind looking up old friends.'

'We were more than old friends. We were practically family.'

'People grow up and lose touch all the time.'

'But you two were especially close, so much so that I expected you to end up together.'

'We never even dated.'

'That doesn't mean you didn't have feelings for one another.'

'Maybe once, before mum and dad died. But we don't know each other now,' she confessed. 'Still, it was nice to see him.'

'Did you give him your number?'

'No, but he gave me his.' She remembered searching her joggers for the scrap of paper he'd shoved into her hand.

'Are you going to call him?'

Cole placed his wife's mug in front of her. 'Easy darling, she's hardly going to be thinking about dating right now. She's barely out of her last relationship.'

'No, of course not, but she could do with as many friends as she can get.'

Kaidence sighed. 'I can't call anybody. I left my phone at the house so it's probably being analysed by the police for anything they consider evidence that they can use in the trial.'

'I'm going into town, so I can buy you a new phone until you get yours back,' her brother-in-law offered.

'That would be great.' She smiled at him. 'If you let me borrow your computer, I can transfer the money to your account.'

'Don't worry about that for now, we'll figure it out later.'

'God, I've got so much to sort out today,' she said, rubbing her forehead lightly. 'I need to contact work to let them know I need even more time off, at least until my face heals. I've got to shop for a new wardrobe without my bank card, which'll be interesting. Then I really should find a solicitor in case I'm charged.'

'What am I, chopped liver?' Cole asked. 'I'll represent you.'

But she shook her head. 'No, I can't let you do that.'

'You can and you will.'

'I don't want you to hear the details of everything that's happened.'

'I can handle it, K.'

'I'm not sure you can, CJ. Reading the words is one thing, seeing the photographs is another; especially when some of them are of your sister-in-law half-naked.'

Meredith did a double take. 'You took photographs?'

'Of every injury from every fight,' she replied with a nod.

'Do the police have them?'

'I told them where to find them.'

'Then you have enough evidence. How could you possibly face charges?'

'I stabbed him, Mimi. The police might deem that as an aggressive attack instead of self-defence.'

'Well look, if you won't let me defend you at least let me give you the number of my partner,' Cole pleaded with his bright blue eyes.

'Would she take my case?'

He shrugged. 'I can but ask.'

'I appreciate that.' She smiled before turning her attention to her sister. 'Have you still got the boxes I left behind when I moved out?'

Meredith nodded. 'They're in the attic. I'll get Cole to bring them down to your room.'

'Thanks Mimi. I promise I'll be out of your hair as soon as the police clear my place.'

Meredith reached for her hand. 'You're welcome here any time.'

She smiled and squeezed her hand in appreciation. 'Is it okay if I try to take a shower?'

'Given your current state, a bath might be preferable.'

She took her suggestion on board. 'I'm not sure how I'll get in and out of the tub though.'

'I can help you with that.'

Kaidence didn't want her sister to see the bruises or the scars Mitchell had inflicted but she knew the likelihood of her being able to do it alone were slim, so she admitted defeat. She wanted to prepare her for what she'd see. 'I've got battle scars.'

She could see Meredith swallow down her distaste as she nodded her understanding and got to her feet. 'Here, take your son,' she instructed the man she'd vowed to spend the rest of her life with. 'I'll go and run the bath,' she said, as an excuse to leave the room.

Meredith hated that she hadn't been able to protect her sister, especially when it had been the one thing she promised to do once their parents died. Tears of frustration fell from her eyes as she walked up the stairs to the first floor. By the time she got to the bathroom, she was a blubbering mess. She pushed the door to and turned on the taps before sitting on the side of the bath and letting her emotions run away with her, sobbing into the hand towel that had been hanging on a ring beside the sink. She couldn't comprehend how a man could hit a woman he was supposed to love, if Mitchell was even capable of such a sentiment. She should have known. She should have seen it. She should have insisted on answers the minute she started noticing the weight loss and demanded details when Kaidence stopped wearing make-up and styling her hair. She should have known, and she hated herself for not seeing it sooner.

They could hear Meredith sobbing from downstairs, and it affected them both in different ways. It made her husband angry, almost as much as the idea of someone laying their hands on his sister-in-law did, because there wasn't anything he could do to change it and he desperately wanted to. Still, he had to be strong for them, but it was difficult when he felt so helpless.

Silent tears rolled down Kaidence's face. She hadn't wanted to hurt her sister, but it was inevitable and now that Meredith knew, she couldn't take it back. How Meredith saw her was forever changed, because of Mitchell and because of her own inability to walk away without controlling how she left.

Cole looked over at the only sister he had. 'She's just processing what you told her,' he said, meaning it to comfort her.

She nodded and sniffed back her tears. 'I know. I just don't like it when she cries, let alone when it's my fault. But I had to prepare her for what she was going to see.'

'She knows. Just give her a minute.'

She took a deep breath as she forced her broken body to stand. 'I can't sit here and listen to her break her heart, I'm going up there,' she said, sluggishly moving towards the door.

He raised his eyebrows as she took her time disappearing out of the room. 'She'll probably be composed by the time you manage to get up the stairs,' he muttered under his breath.

Meredith was coming to the end of her breakdown when Kaidence reached her, and instead of wasting time with words, Kaidence perched next to her and wrapped her good arm around her sister's shoulders. They didn't need to speak, they just needed to grieve together.

CHAPTER TWENTY-TWO

The cold air bit against her skin as Kaidence sat outside in the garden taking in the sounds of the morning while Bailey ran around amusing himself. She'd replaced one home for another, but the prison sentence was the same. She hadn't left the safety of her sister's house in the five days she'd been there; the garden was as far as she'd gone. This was partially down to the state of her face, which had healed considerably, but she was hiding. She didn't know what Mitchell's status was, but she knew the minute he was able, he would come after her to finish the job. At least when she was in her own house she wasn't putting anyone else's life in danger.

She was still having nightmares about the night that had driven her here, and they were getting worse. They weren't always the same, but they all ended with her waking up in a cold sweat with her sister sitting on the bed ready to comfort her. Even after almost a week, she could still feel the knife in her hand. It had been the first time she'd ever attacked anyone, and although it had been to stay alive, it haunted her in a way she hadn't been prepared for.

She hadn't spoken to Jackson or Louisa since being interviewed at the station because the new phone her brother-in-law had procured for her didn't come with the numbers she had in the one she assumed was in the police's possession, and she didn't remember them despite the months of contact. She felt like a big chunk of her life was missing, despite only having them in it for a few months. But she'd come to rely on them, so having them keep their distance from her now was foreign to her.

She was going stir-crazy living under her sister's roof again, filling her time watching mind-numbing daytime television and assuming babysitting duty whenever her sister needed to pop out. She enjoyed being around her family for a change, after being kept away from them by Mitchell, but there was a reason siblings didn't share homes once they grew to be adults. It had been a long time since she'd had to escape to her bedroom whenever she wanted time on her own and her sister wouldn't let her cook any of the meals or help with any chores. It was as if she was being treated like a guest from out of town instead of family. It was wearing thin. But she needed to wait for the police to finish with her house before she could leave, because she knew Meredith would be offended if she checked into a hotel and she had enough making up to do without upsetting her any more.

She took a deep breath, inhaling as much of the fresh air as possible before making her way back inside. Meredith and Cole had yet to surface and she wanted to use that to her advantage. She headed to the fridge, removed the ingredients she needed to cook a fry-up breakfast and set herself to work.

Walking into the station to finish his shift, Jackson headed straight to his locker to change out of the uniform he spent most of his time in. His life had been remarkably emptier since keeping his distance from Kaidence. He enjoyed being around her. But he couldn't afford to have his relationship with her questioned, especially now that her separation from Mitchell hadn't gone as smoothly as they had hoped. It was killing him to stay away from her, particularly when she'd become as important to him as he hoped he was to her.

'Chase!' he heard bellowed from the doorway.

He peered around the wall of lockers. 'Yes?' he asked, seeing Detective Danny James.

'We're releasing Miss Hadaway's property today and my partner wants to know if you'll let her know seeing as you have an existing rapport with her.'

'Sure, I can do that,' he said, trying to appear nonchalant despite being thrilled to have an excuse to see her.

'You can claim salary because your tour is over,' Danny said, tossing him her house keys.

He caught the keys. 'No, her sister's place is on my way home, so it won't take me five minutes.'

'Okay,' Danny replied, leaving him to get changed.

It wasn't until Kaidence was halfway through cooking breakfast that her sister and brother-in-law emerged. But, although it was barely what most considered working hours on Saturday, they were dressed and ready for the day. All week Meredith had been dressed in attire she only deemed good enough to wear around the house, so to see they'd made an effort made her curious.

'Going somewhere?' she asked.

'Justin's got a paediatric appointment,' Meredith replied and crumpled her face in regret. 'We haven't got time for breakfast, sorry.'

'But I've cooked all of this.' Kaidence motioned to the spread she'd laid out on the table.

Cole walked over to the feast and picked up some bacon. 'Wrap it up, we'll have it when we get back,' he said, chomping on the meat.

'Some of it will keep I suppose, like the croissants, pancakes and fruit, but the rest of it will need to be thrown away.'

Meredith's brow creased. 'Did you make all of this?'

Her sister nodded. 'I got pretty good at distracting myself in the kitchen, so that I didn't have to spend any time with Mitchell.'

Cole grabbed a croissant and ripped off a piece before shoving it into his mouth. 'They're good. If you ever get bored of teaching, you could open a bakery.'

'We better get going if we're going to make our appointment,' his wife said to focus him. 'We'll be back in a couple of hours I expect.'

Kaidence frowned. 'How far away is the doctor's surgery?'

'She likes to get there half an hour before we're due to be seen and, although the surgery is only five minutes away, we leave quarter of an hour before in case there's traffic,' her husband clarified. 'It's forty-five minutes of my life I'll never get back.'

'Sometimes the wait is horrendous,' Meredith added.

Her little sister laughed. 'She does hate to be late.'

Cole raised his eyes in agreement. 'Come on then, let's get on the road.'

'See you later,' she called out after her hosts as they left her with her spread. She sighed.

She had wanted to do something nice for them and it had all been for nought. Although the food was fresh, she had to pack it away so that it stayed that way for when it would be eaten. It was as she contemplated what to do with it that there was a knock at the front door. She froze, unsure what her next move should be. In her own home, she was trained not to answer any knocking. Except this wasn't her house. *What if it's Mitchell?* The question echoed in her mind, but was quickly dismissed. If Mitchell wasn't in the hospital or locked up, she knew Jackson would have found a way to warn her.

She headed to the door and used the peephole to see who was calling. She breathed an internal sigh of relief and an involuntary smile met her lips as she unlocked the door and pulled it open.

'God, am I glad to see you,' she greeted him, reaching for his hand and easing him inside before closing the door behind him.

He was immediately struck by how much smaller Meredith's house was in comparison to Kaidence's. It was moderately bigger than an average home, but wasn't as grand as her sister's and despite the modern furniture and decoration, it felt homely.

'I think that's the happiest anyone has ever been to see me,' he said, as he was led through the hall and into the kitchen. His eyes landed on the breakfast she'd prepared. 'Jesus, are you feeding the forty thousand?'

'It was meant to be for my sister and her husband, but they had to go out. Are you hungry?'

'I've just finished a tour; I'm starving.'

She gestured towards the table. 'Well sit down and eat. If you don't it'll go in the bin.'

He rubbed his hands together as he headed to a chair. 'Don't mind if I do.'

'Cuppa?'

'Please.'

As she boiled the kettle and prepared his drink, she continued the conversation. 'So, what brings you here?'

'The detectives asked me to swing by and return your keys.'

'They're finished? I can move back in?' she asked, placing his drink in front of him.

He fished around in his pocket and pulled out the object he was there to return. 'I've got your keys right here,' he said, placing them on the table.

'Good, because I need to get back to my wardrobe,' she said, signalling to the clothes she was outfitted in.

She'd forgotten what kind of clothes she used to wear before she'd boxed them up to store at her sisters. They were more risqué than she'd been allowed to parade around in since dating Mitchell, and her occupation meant she dressed more conservatively anyway. She was uncomfortable in the skin-tight jeans and jumpers that were low enough at the bust to expose her cleavage, but they were the only clothes she had.

Her sentence gave him an invitation to look her up and down. Her attire was so different to what he was used to seeing her in; these clothes hugged and enhanced her figure, and apart from once when she was dressed for work in tailored trousers and a colourful blouse, he had only seen her in baggy clothes that disguised her figure.

He laughed. 'I think that's the most skin I've ever seen you show.'

'It's not by choice, believe me,' she said, pulling up the V-neck to try and cover her cleavage. 'I forgot how much skin I used to be comfortable showing.'

'You'll hear no complaints from me.'

The drive to her house was eerily quiet. Jackson knew instinctively that she was reliving the attack and there was nothing he could do to take away her apprehension, but he could prepare her for what she'd find.

'The house will be exactly the same as when you left it, minus some blood,' he told her as he drove towards their destination. 'But it'll look messier because of the fingerprint dust that's been used around the crime scene area.'

She nodded. 'As long as Mitchell's not there, I don't care what state it's in.'

'He's under police guard at the hospital,' he said, turning into her street.

'So he's not dead?'

Jackson frowned. 'No. It seems he's going to make a full recovery.'

'But I stabbed him.'

'And miraculously missed every vital organ,' he said, pulling up outside her house.

As he turned off the engine, Kaidence unclipped her seatbelt. 'Well, this is a new experience.' He questioned her with his expression. 'Walking into my house with a man who isn't Mitchell in broad daylight.'

'And let this be the first of many new experiences,' he said as they climbed out of the vehicle.

It was strange to walk back into the house she used to consider her home. All it felt like now was the place that had imprisoned her since Mitchell had moved in. When she bought it, a couple of years after getting her inheritance, she thought it would be the place she'd live forever; where she'd raise a family. But all the house reminded her of now was the worst time of her life since her parents' death. Deep down she knew it was inevitable that she'd put it on the market, although it wasn't evident until she stepped over the threshold how she truly felt. Now it was obvious that she wouldn't be able to move on until she sold the house and started over somewhere new, once the trial was finished.

She looked around at what remained of the battle she'd survived a week ago and it was hard to believe there had been one. There was barely anything out of place; if it wasn't for the dried outline of small pools of blood on the white tiles, there would be no evidence at all.

It felt like a lifetime since she'd been there, and she walked around as if the house was new territory she was trying to get familiar with. She entered the kitchen and exhaled.

'Why doesn't this feel like my house?'

'Probably because you've been away from it for a week,' he suggested. 'When was the last time you went on holiday?'

She raised her ungroomed eyebrows. 'I don't think I've had one of those for years.'

'Then it stands to reason that it'd feel strange after you've spent any time away.'

After a week of being closed up, the house felt stuffy, so Kaidence headed to the large windows behind the dining table and threw them open to allow some fresh air in. She exhaled. 'My God, it's going to be weird to be here alone, to be able to do whatever the hell I like whenever I want,' she thought out loud. 'He's been in my head for so long that being able to do as I please will take some getting used to.'

'You'll probably need a small adjustment period, but you'll get into the swing of things quickly.'

She searched the floor with her eyes. 'I don't see my phone anywhere so I'm assuming the detectives are keeping it.'

'They'll get it back to you as soon as they've transferred any data they need.'

'It's okay; I got a new one anyway. Besides, having a new number can't hurt. At least if they keep the phone, they'll know if Mitchell tries to contact me, which can only help to convict him,' she said, heading to the cupboard beneath the sink for the spray bottle of cleaning solution and a cloth.

Jackson laughed. 'You're itching to clean, aren't you?'

She half shook her head. 'I can wait until you go.'

'Or I could help?'

'You don't really want to help.'

'If it means I get to spend a bit of time with you, I'll help.'

She frowned. 'Haven't you just finished a shift at work?'

He shrugged. 'Seeing you must have given me a second wind.'

'Well, feel free to take a nap on the bed upstairs while I clean,' she said, spraying the floor tiles and wiping them over with the material in her other hand.

'I knew it! You can't fool me Miss Hadaway!'

'Hush, go and get some sleep while I'm busy.'

'Okay, but the furthest I'm going is the settee.' He smiled as he walked out of the room in the direction of the living room.

By the time Kaidence had got the house cleaned to the standard she'd been conditioned to keep it to, hours had passed and there was no sign of Jackson, but she could hear his gentle snores from the room across the hall. She was about to go in and nudge him awake when her mobile phone started to ring. She removed it from her pocket and when she saw that it was her sister, she looked at the clock to check the time.

'Hey Mimi.'

'Kaidence, thank God,' her sister sighed, relieved. 'When we got home, and you weren't here...'

Kaidence cut her off before she spiralled into all the horrible things she'd imagined. 'I'm fine. I got my house keys back, so I've been here cleaning.'

'You could have left a note.'

'Yeah, sorry. I didn't think to.'

'Well, do you want some help?'

Kaidence dismissed the suggestion, wanting to exploit her freedom a little longer. 'No, I'm almost finished. I'll come back in a bit and get my things so you can have your life back.'

'You don't have to leave yet if you're not ready.'

'I appreciate you taking me in, but I've got my own house, which is what I was waiting for, so it'll be better for me to get back to normality – or at least a semblance of it.'

'Okay, then I'll see you later,' Meredith said, ending the call.

Cole noticed his wife's demeanour as soon as she hung up the phone to her sister. 'Is everything okay?' he asked, concerned.

She nodded, but she was far from all right. 'Kaidence is moving back home.'

'Is that where she is?'

'She got the keys back, so she's cleaning it.'

He frowned. 'And she doesn't want help?'

She placed her mobile phone down on the coffee table as she lowered herself next to him on the settee. 'No, she's determined to internalise everything and keep me shut out,' she responded in frustration.

He tried to comfort her. 'That's just something she's been used to doing. It's got nothing to do with you.'

'But she's away from him now, she doesn't have to do it any more.'

'She's been accustomed to dealing with things alone for so long, she can't just shut it off. She's got to retrain her thinking, that's all.'

'Do you really think she's ready to go back to that house?'

He shrugged. 'She obviously feels like she is.'

'Yes, but do *you* think she's ready?'

'It's hard to tell with your sister.'

'Exactly. She's been quiet all week, like she's been reliving it repeatedly. She's not over it. So for her to think she can go back and live in the house where it happened...'

'Not to sound crass but she's been living there all this time with him and this obviously isn't the first time he's hit her. I think she can handle being back at home, especially now that Mitchell isn't there.'

'But how long before he gets out of hospital and comes after her? You're a solicitor; you know how long it takes for these kinds of cases to get to trial and he won't be locked up in the meantime. He'll be able to go after her and if she's at that house, he'll know where to find her.' She realised she was beginning to ramble and lapsed into silence.

'He'll be on remand, with conditions to prevent that happening.'

'Do you really think a piece of paper will stop him? It won't. He'll go after her on principle to stop her from testifying against him and this time, he will kill her.'

Kaidence sat at the breakfast bar with a mug of tea. She hadn't had the heart to wake Jackson as she had planned, so instead had been killing time replaying the events that had contributed to her nightmares. Her memory was hazy – the more time that passed, the more details she seemed to lose. This was unfamiliar, because she remembered every aspect of previous attacks as if she'd just lived through them, but this one was slipping away from her day by day.

She was blankly staring towards the hallway when a blurred figure appeared in front of her and spoke. 'You'll be dead before they get here, darling,' the figure said. Tears formed in her eyes. It was Mitchell. The shock of thinking he was stood in front of her made her focus as the tears spilled onto her cheeks. But he wasn't there. It was Jackson. He repeated his question. 'How long have you been finished cleaning?'

She reached up to dry her eyes as he approached. 'Not long,' she answered, still feeling the effects of fear in the pit of her stomach.

'I knew it was too soon for you to be back here,' Jackson said, walking over and wrapping his arms around her shoulders.

Rather than fight against his comfort, she leaned into it and almost immediately started to sob uncontrollably into his chest. She could feel the strength in his arms as he pulled her closer to his body. He'd always made her feel safe, and now was no different. He was the only one she'd allowed beyond the wall she'd built up to keep people out, the only one she felt she could reveal her vulnerability to safely.

He smelled exactly as she remembered – of deodorant with a hint of after-shave. She could tell he'd had a shower in the locker room after work because of the subtle scent of soap on his skin, though there was a modicum of sweat on his clothes from the nap he'd taken. It was slightly different to the last time she'd been so close to him, but he smelled good regardless.

Reaching the end of her emotional breakdown, Kaidence pulled away from him. 'I'm sorry. I don't know what's wrong with me.'

'In my experience, it's called relief,' he said.

She dried her eyes with the sleeve of the jumper from the past that she was still wearing. 'What's going to happen to him?'

'Do you care?'

'I do if it means he's going to be free.'

'He'll be cautioned and questioned. If there's enough evidence to charge him, he'll be released on remand until the trial.'

'He won't keep to any of the conditions of remand; the minute he's released he'll come after me.'

'Then he'll be locked up.'

'It won't matter if he finishes the job he started.'

'If he shows up here, call the police. You have enough locks on the door to hold him off until they get here.'

'Fat lot of good they'll do when he's got a key.'

'Then can I suggest you change the locks?'

'It's one of the first things on my to-do list.'

'A few hours ago, your priority was to get out of those clothes but you're still in them,' he said, waving a hand over her outfit with a smile, teasing her. 'I think you like them more than you let on.'

'I got so consumed with cleaning that I forgot to change and burn them.' She laughed, getting up from her seat. 'I'll go and get into more appropriate attire.'

'Appropriate for what?'

'I need to get my things from my sister's.'

'I can drop you off on my way home,' he proposed.

She hesitated. 'Do you have to go home?'

'I've just come off a twelve-hour shift. I could do with some sleep.'

'You could sleep here – there is a bed upstairs.'

'Do you think that's a good idea?'

'I think it's a brilliant idea, that's why I suggested it.' She laughed.

'I've got a few days off so it's not like I *have* to be anywhere.'

She smiled. 'Fantastic! You can sleep while I go to Meredith's and when you wake up, I'll cook for us.'

'You do like to feed me.'

'You're happiest when you're eating.'

He raised his eyebrows to agree with her. 'Most men are.'

The house was quiet as Kaidence walked inside. She didn't have a key to her sister's, but the front door was always unlocked in the day. She had one of those heavy-set PVC fire doors that you could pull the handle up on that gave it some resistance but didn't lock it until you used the key. She prepared herself for the guilt trip Meredith would certainly take her on as she walked into the living quarters to find either of the people who lived there. When she reached the kitchen she found Cole at the sink, cleaning the dishes that she'd left over from breakfast.

'I was going to do that,' she said, startling him.

'It's okay. I don't mind doing it, especially after you cooked,' he replied.

'But you didn't eat anything.'

'Oh yes I did.' He gestured to the half-empty plastic tubs.

She smiled. 'Where's Mimi?'

He took a deep breath. 'Upstairs. Cleaning.'

'Which means she's upset.' She sighed. 'Does she really expect me to stay here when I've got my house back?'

'I think she just wants to make sure you're okay before you leave,' he imparted, drying his hands. 'She's still beating herself up for not knowing what Mitchell was doing to you.'

'I can't do anything to change that. All I can do, the only way for me to be okay, is to move on. There's no point in dwelling on things. I've wasted enough of my life already; I just want to get on with living the rest of it.'

'I won't apologise for being concerned about my sister,' Meredith said, entering the room having overheard her.

Kaidence exhaled loudly. 'I didn't mean it like that, Mimi.'

'Of course, you did,' she spat back.

'My God, I'm twenty-eight. At some point you have to let me make my own decisions,' she countered with the same hostility.

'Don't fool yourself Kaidence, you've been making your own decisions for years.'

'And you've been disapproving of them for just as long.'

'Because you've always done as you please, damn the consequences.'

'Don't take it out on me because you got old before your time.'

'Do you think I had a choice?' the oldest sibling asked rhetorically. 'Jesus, you'd think you were the only one who lost her parents, well I lost them too. But I didn't have the luxury of falling apart because I had to take care of you.'

'No one asked you to!' Kaidence bellowed.

'You're my sister!' Meredith responded.

Kaidence threw her hands in the air. 'I can't do this,' she said, swallowing down a golf-ball-sized lump that had formed in her throat. When she spoke again, her voice was low. 'I haven't got the energy to fight with you just because you don't want me to go home. I know you're hurting, but I can't fix that. So I'm going to fetch my things and then leave,' she said, walking out of the room.

Cole had been standing by, allowing the sisters to clear the air but when they'd started shouting, he knew better than to get in the middle. He regretted that decision immediately when he heard the hateful things they were saying, but they'd been said, and no amount of wishing would take them back. He looked at his wife to see her looking back at him.

'Do you feel better?' he asked.

She shook her head as she lowered to a seat at the dining table. 'I didn't want to say any of that, but when I heard her talking about moving on, I got angry.'

'Then go and fix it before she leaves,' he advised.

'I'm not sure I know how to.'

He lowered himself into the chair beside hers and reached out to rest his hand atop hers. 'Just talk to her. She needs you, now more than ever, and you know you won't forgive yourself if you're not there for her.'

Kaidence moved sluggishly about the room that she'd been sleeping in, packing up the few items she'd acquired during her stay. None of it was important, just toiletries and clothing, which were easily replaced. But she'd wanted to come back to her sister's house, at least give her a proper goodbye. She regretted that decision now.

Fighting with Meredith had always come so naturally; it was something they'd done so much growing up. But after they lost their parents, they had become closer and the arguing had stopped. She hadn't wanted to spit out the hateful things she'd said, but she had to defend herself – and it was so easy to do when it involved family.

She was shoving clothes into an overnight bag when she felt the presence of someone else in the room. She spun to look in the direction of the doorway to find Meredith standing there.

Kaidence sighed. 'I don't want to fight.'

'Neither do I,' Meredith said, entering and perching on the bed. 'I didn't mean anything I said downstairs.'

'You did, and that's okay. It's probably about time someone said it. But I'm not that person any more, Mitchell saw to that,' she said. 'Just because I want to go home doesn't mean I don't need you. I do, more than ever, especially if I'm going to get through the trial. I just want my own space, surely you can understand that?'

'You've always been more comfortable with your own company than I have. I just worry that being alone will put you in danger once *he* gets out of hospital,' Meredith said, refusing to use his name.

'I'm changing the locks and having a security system installed by the end of the week. Plus, even the police had trouble breaking my door down, so I'll get to call triple nine before he gets to me.'

Her sister relaxed a little. 'Well as long as you've thought it through, I'm happy.'

Talk of their parents had brought them to the forefront of her mind, so on the drive back home Kaidence took a detour to their final resting place, somewhere she hadn't been for the entirety of her abuse. Although she knew it was irrational, she didn't want her parents to see her with bruises when she was at their graveside. She remembered the first time she was there as vividly as if it had happened yesterday. She'd been heartbroken then, and if she was honest, it hadn't really got to be any easier than it had been seven years ago when they'd passed.

She walked through the wrought iron entrance of the cemetery and immediately felt the warmth of the midday sun. No matter what the weather, whenever she passed through the gates, she felt the sun beaming down on her and, because she didn't believe the death of someone meant they were gone, she liked to think it had something to do with her parents watching over her. She took a leisurely stroll through the headstones, being careful not to walk over any bodies on her way, until she came to where they lay.

She took a deep breath as she searched for an opening – an excuse for her absence – but her mind drew a blank. 'I'm sorry I haven't been here for a while. It's been a tough eighteen months,' she started, being as honest with them as she would be had they been standing in front of her. Suddenly she started to cry. 'I miss you both so much. I wish you were here.' She allowed her emotions to show, not for the first time that day.

'Mitchell wasn't the man he let me think he was. You would've disapproved, not least because of what he did to me, but because he isolated me from Meredith. I thought he was the Prince Charming you told me to expect no less than, Mum, then he showed his true colours. But by then it was too late.' She paused. 'I put up with more than I should've and I'm now dealing with the consequences of that decision. I stabbed him last week and I'm so scared that I'm going to go to prison. But he was going to kill me, and I wanted to stay alive.' She continued to cry. 'I had to fight back; I couldn't put up with it any more. I just hope the evidence I collected helps to convict him and exonerate me, even though I stabbed him. I was angry, I wanted him dead, but I didn't want to be the one to kill him. I just wanted to get away...I guess I'll have to wait and see how things play out. At least I've got Jackson to help me get through it. If it wasn't for his help over the last couple of months, I'm not sure I'd have survived. He's the officer who knocked on my door the day after I'd taken a beating and he wouldn't walk away. I guess that's because he's had his share of trauma regarding abuse too. I'm so comfortable with him and, if he wasn't the officer who'd saved me, he'd be exactly the kind of man I'd date. I think you'd like him,' she said, as her tears dried up.

For reasons unbeknown to her, talking of dating sparked a vision of the childhood friend she'd been reunited with. 'Oh, while I was at the hospital, I ran into Matthew Logan. You remember he left town to study in London? Well, he's a fully fledged doctor now. I'm not thrilled he knows I was abused, but the upside is that he remembers me the way I was before; that I'll hopefully be again – one day. I just hope that he keeps in touch now that he's back home.'

The house was quiet. Justin was asleep, but it was a different quiet to any time before. Meredith hadn't uttered more than a few words since her sister had left, and Cole was concerned.

'Did you sort things out with Kaidence?' he asked to make conversation.

There was a heaviness that hung over them and had since she'd found out what Mitchell had been putting her sister through. They were both restless, dealing with their own demons for not seeing the signs.

She nodded. 'I can't help her, not the way I want to. She's got to deal with it in her own way, regardless of whether I like it or not. I don't know what it's like to live in fear of the person who's supposed to love you the way you love them, I've got no idea what it's like to be hurt by the hands of someone you're supposed to trust and I can't comprehend having to live with it all silently so that that person won't kill you,' she confessed. 'I'll never understand what kind of hell she's been through, so I won't presume to know how to help her. All I can do is be there, if she asks.'

CHAPTER TWENTY-THREE

It had been a week since she'd left her sisters' house. It had been a long week, alone. Jackson had been working and suggested they didn't spend much time together before the trial in case they were seen by anyone to do with the lawsuit against Mitchell. They'd spoken on the phone. But it was so lonely in that house without anyone for company. Meredith had been by to see her every day with her nephew, but the nights were hard, especially when she couldn't sleep. There was only so much cleaning and baking she could do before she got bored. Plus, they were both things that she used to do to save her from having to sit with Mitchell, and she didn't have to do that any more.

So much of her life was still dictated by the one she had with him. She still dressed so no one would pay any mind to her when she was out of the house. She still scraped her hair back and wore no make-up. She still stayed inside instead of venturing outside the confines of her grounds. She knew those things would change but she wasn't ready to alter her life that dramatically so soon after adding to the survival rate of domestic abuse. She would get there, eventually; it would probably only happen once she knew Mitchell was no longer a threat, though. She still feared him showing up on her doorstep, because he wasn't the kind of man to let her go without a fight – he'd so much as told her so.

There were nights that Kaidence sat and watched the cameras that she'd had installed for security in and around her property on the off-chance that no one had managed to get word to her that he'd left the hospital. She didn't expect the cameras to command her life so much, but she found herself running them on her laptop in any room she was in and she glanced over at them frequently.

Today she was going to take a huge step forward in forcing her recovery and step out of her house to go shopping with her sister, just as she usually would on a Saturday. It would be the first time she left the house all week, because it was the first time she felt ready. It was driven by Meredith, but she had refused every request every day she visited, much to Meredith's dismay. But this morning, she'd woken up wanting to get out.

She had consciously put on clothes she hadn't wore since meeting Mitchell because he disapproved of them in one way or another. The trousers she'd picked he wouldn't let her wear because they showed the curve of her backside and thighs, and the T-shirt was tight, emphasizing her perky thirty-four D sized breasts. She had put on a mid-thigh-length cardigan a dress size too big over the top, but the fact that she was wearing them was progress. She'd even slipped on three-inch-heeled boots that he didn't like because they made her almost the same height as him and he liked to tower over her.

The difference was evident to Meredith when she met up with her a few minutes later than arranged. 'You look nice,' she complimented her.

Kaidence forced a smile. 'Thanks. I feel nice.'

'Do you? Because you keep pulling that coat closed like you're uncomfortable that people can see what you're wearing,' Meredith countered.

'That's because I am.'

'You've just lost your confidence, that's all. They look great on you so stop fidgeting.'

Although her sister's words were harsh, Kaidence knew they were designed to diminish her discomfort. Meredith had always had a hard time delivering a compliment so that it sounded complimentary – everything sounded like a criticism – but it wasn't intentional, it was just the matter-of-fact way that she delivered them. Kaidence had got used to it over the years, but not everyone had the luxury of getting to know her sister well enough to learn that about her. Meredith had been friendly and trusting before the tragedy of losing their parents, now she was hard to befriend, and Kaidence knew her defences were designed to protect her from getting too close to people. She understood, because she had a similar guard, but hers was born of her relationship with Mitchell.

Kaidence glanced inside the carriage of Justin's modern pram to find him bundled up and asleep. 'How long have we got before he needs feeding?'

'Providing we keep him moving, it could be a few hours,' his mother replied.

'Then let's not waste time standing around,' Kaidence suggested, starting to walk towards the town.

It was as they walked, and her sister rambled on about nothing of importance, that she thought she saw him among the shoppers on the street. Her heart jumped in her throat, her legs began to wobble, and she trembled. Had he left the hospital without anyone notifying her? Or was she imagining him there? She stared at the spot where she thought she had seen him only for the crowd to part and reveal that no one stood there. She relaxed a little so she could continue to stay upright, but the possibility of having to see him again terrified her.

'Are you okay?' Meredith asked, noticing how pale her complexion had suddenly become.

She swallowed down her fear with a nod. 'Yes.'

'Are you sure, because you look like you've seen a ghost?'

She didn't want her day to be consumed by the man she'd managed to break free from, especially when it could so easily just be her paranoia. 'Just first-outing nerves.'

Kaidence sighed as she sat down at a table outside a coffee house inside the shopping centre. 'I forgot how painful it is to walk around in heels,' she said, removing her boots one at a time and rubbing her feet.

Meredith laughed. 'It's been a while since we shopped this much.'

'That's because Mitchell hated it. He only let me come and meet you because he knew it would make you suspicious if I didn't.'

She raised her eyebrows. 'Well, he seemed to know me well enough to know that about me.'

The younger woman shook her head. 'I told him that if you didn't see me regularly you'd call and if I didn't answer, you'd come to the house. He didn't want that, so he reluctantly let me meet you.'

Meredith frowned. 'Why would you warn him?'

'Because I would have paid for it if I hadn't.'

'Well that's all the talk of that man that I want to have today,' she said with a sigh. 'I'm going to go inside and get us a couple of drinks.'

As her sister stood up, Justin moving in his pram caught Kaidence's attention. 'It sounds like he's waking up. I'd get some hot water to warm up his bottle too while you're in there.'

It was as Kaidence sat pushing the pram backwards and forwards to hold off any hungry screaming from the baby that she saw Jackson walking towards her in his civilian clothes. She stared at him, not wanting to draw attention to herself but expecting him to notice her.

Jackson pretended not to see her as he stepped into her eyeline, but he had a sixth sense when it came to her and that meant that he would always notice her if she was close. He glanced in her direction, hoping not to be seen, to find her staring back. He couldn't help the internal smile that came from being so close to her. He considered walking by just to test whether she'd call out to him, but he didn't want to miss an opportunity to speak to her.

Getting closer, he nodded in her direction, acknowledging her. 'I see you've finally ventured out,' he said with a smile.

'Well, I couldn't stay hidden forever,' she countered playfully.

'Good, you should be living your life.'

That's when Meredith emerged from inside with a tray carrying the jug of hot water and two beverages, and Jackson rushed to hold the door open so she could walk through.

'Thank you,' she smiled gratefully.

Her sister introduced him as she placed her purchase on the table they had claimed. 'Mimi, this is Jackson, the officer I told you about.'

Meredith looked him up and down. 'Oh, hello. It's a pleasure to meet you.'

'And you,' he replied. 'But we've actually come across each other before.'

'Have we?'

He nodded. 'I barrelled into your sister at the supermarket once.'

She raised her eyebrows. 'That was you?'

'That was me,' he confirmed.

'Why don't you join us?' Meredith offered.

'I would but I've got to pop into the bank.'

'I've got to feed the little man, so we'll be here for a while. So why don't you go and do what you have to and come back to us?'

He looked at Kaidence for direction and she smiled. 'My sister doesn't really take no for an answer,' she said.

'Then I'll be back as soon as I can so that I don't hold you ladies up,' he said, taking his leave.

'He likes you,' Meredith said to her sister once Jackson was several feet away.

'We're friends,' she responded.

Meredith shook her head. 'It's more than that for him.'

'You're imagining things,' Kaidence replied with a laugh.

'I'm not. I'm sure if you made a pass at him, he'd reciprocate.'

Kaidence looked down at her cup, trying to avoid eye contact with her sister. But Meredith noticed her sister was attempting to evade her gaze.

'Did something already happen between you two?' Meredith asked.

'No! Of course not!'

Her sister shook her head emphatically. 'Oh, something happened, and I am going to need details.'

Kaidence smiled. 'It was one kiss and that was only because I was curious.'

Meredith laughed. 'I knew there was something between you two.'

'There isn't. His only interest in me is purely professional.'

'No, it isn't.'

'You met him for two minutes, so what, you think you know? You couldn't possibly know.'

'Seeing you two together, it's obvious.'

'No, it isn't.'

'You know you're acting like a teenager, don't you?'

'Am not,' she said, playing up the part.

———

Hours passed. Justin had eaten, been rocked back to sleep and was then returned to his carriage. They'd spent their time talking and laughing. It was refreshing for Kaidence to feel free enough to waste time in good company and it was just as invigorating for Jackson to witness her behaving so differently to how she'd been in the past. But it all came to an end when Meredith got to her feet.

'I better get back to get dinner started,' she declared.

'Then I better call for a taxi; I won't carry all of this on the bus,' her sister announced, looking at her loot.

'I can give you a lift home,' Jackson said. 'It's on my way anyway.'

Meredith frowned. 'Why didn't you drive?'

'Finding somewhere to park is more hassle than it's worth – I thought the bus was easier. I didn't plan to buy this much.'

'I found somewhere to park.'

'Because you have those mother and baby spaces. I don't have that luxury.'

'Well, Jackson parked.'

'Actually, I cheated and used a space at the station, then walked the few streets over,' he confessed.

'So, you offered me a lift and failed to tell me I have to walk, in heels, to fetch the car,' Kaidence teased.

He laughed. 'Since when are you high maintenance?'

'Since I spent all morning walking around the shopping centre in heels that I haven't worn for a very long time.'

'Well I could pull the car around for you, madam.'

'That sounds like a really good idea.' She smiled and raised her eyebrows playfully.

'Better still, I could carry you,' he mocked.

She laughed. 'You're funny.'

Her sister stopped the banter by approaching her and kissing her on the cheek as she embraced her with her free arm. 'It was great spending the day with you today. I'll see you Monday.'

'Actually, Monday I'm going back to work.'

'You are? Don't you think it's too soon?'

'It's been two weeks; my face is healed so there's no reason for me to sit at home going stir-crazy when I can be working.'

'Then call me when you're free. I love you.'

'Love you too,' Kaidence said, as Meredith walked away from them.

'Your sister is nice,' Jackson said, picking up her bags as they began the walk to his vehicle.

'No, she's not,' she countered. 'She's just polite in front of people who don't know her, so they think she's nice.'

He thumbed over his shoulder. 'That can't be an act.'

'It's not. It's just people who don't know her can't hear the condescension.'

'Have you thought that maybe you hear that because you're her sister?'

'Yes, because I know her.'

'No, you hear it because that's what you expect from a big sister, but it's not really there.'

'Oh, it's there. You'll see as, or if, you get to know her.'

He kept to her pace as they walked side by side in silence and it was a few minutes before she broke the peace.

'I thought I saw Mitchell on the street earlier,' Kaidence confessed.

'Well, I suppose that's to be expected. But he's still in the hospital, under the watch of PC West and Perez.'

'Will I be notified if he's released?'

'Yes, because I'll tell you.'

'He's been in hospital for two weeks. I wasn't in that long when I was in a coma.'

'I think it's just a precaution, because he's awake.'

'Has he been questioned yet?'

'No, they won't do that until he gets out of hospital because they'll want to record it and unless he's in an interview room, it can be compromised by background noise. They won't want to take any chances,' he said as they reached the car.

'Are you sure you don't mind dropping me at home? I thought we had to stay away from each other,' she said, watching him load her bags into the boot.

'We've just spent hours in the open drinking coffee, I hardly think taking you home is going to make much of a difference,' he replied, unlocking the doors so they could both climb inside.

'Are you sure you don't need me to lie on the back seat?'

'Just get in the front before I make you walk,' he joked, sliding into the driver's seat.

Doing as she was told, she slipped into the passenger's seat beside him. 'You know, you used to be more tolerant of my playful side.'

'That's because I rarely got to see it,' he said, putting on his seatbelt.

'Well buckle up, officer, because it's the only part of who I was that I know how to be,' she said, applying her harness.

'I suppose it's better than the alternative,' he commented, starting the engine.

He wondered if her change of attitude was due to any other alterations she'd made in her life, and he was curious whether it had something to do with the doctor who'd slipped his number in her hand two weeks ago.

'So, have you called that doctor friend of yours?' Jackson asked as he drove.

She frowned. 'No.'

'You haven't even called him to catch up?'

Not realising that jealousy underlay his words, Kaidence stared straight ahead. 'There'd be so much we'd have to catch up, I'm not sure I've got the energy for that right now, not while I'm going through all of this.'

'What kind of history do you have?' he asked.

She exhaled. 'Uh, our parents were friends from the time they were in high school, so we spent a lot of time together. I don't have a single childhood memory worth remembering that doesn't have him in it. We spent half terms visiting beaches and having picnics, and every holiday we had we took together.'

'But you lost touch?'

She raised her eyebrows. 'He wanted to be a doctor and his parents wanted him to study at the best university, so he went to London. He got on with his life and I got on with mine.'

'So, you're not going to call him?'

'I think the past is best left there.'

'Aren't you the slightest bit curious about his life?'

'A little, but if I ask questions, I'll have to answer questions too, and I'd rather he remembered me as full of life rather than what I've turned into.'

'You'll get that attitude back.'

She shook her head. 'I'll get my life back but being abused has a way of changing someone forever; I'll never be the same as I was.'

If he was honest with himself, he was relieved that she didn't plan to pursue any type of relationship with Matthew Logan. It was selfish and stemmed from his feelings for her that he couldn't admit to or act upon. He wasn't sure she would even return those affections, despite the kiss she had instigated. His hands were tied for the next six months until the trial anyway; at least by then he'd know how real her feelings were or if she'd only felt that way because of the freedom he represented.

***

Carla exhaled as she reached her desk with the freshly made coffee she had stepped away to make. The investigation into the domestic abuse case she'd been assigned two weeks ago was developing well, because of the evidence the victim had gathered herself. She had enough to charge him with a crime even if he denied there had been any abuse. But she didn't want to reveal the photos or the written accounts of each incident to Mitchell until she absolutely had to. For now, she'd use the pictures Officer Jessop had taken at the hospital on the night of the last attack.

She picked up the mobile phone she'd collected from the scene that belonged to Kaidence as she took her seat, and it started to ring in her hand. The identity of the caller was the accused, so she left it to ring and for voicemail to kick in because maybe he would get sloppy and leave a message. She waited patiently for the notification after the call cut out and then held her finger on number one of the keypad. It immediately dialled the computer-based system to access the message and she hit the on-screen speaker button so she could hear it out loud.

'You bitch! Do you think you can get away with stabbing me? You won't! I'll

catch up to you and when I do, I'll finish the job I started. You know how weak you are. You can't stop me. You got lucky this time. But I am stronger and smarter than you, so you won't see me coming. You better have military grade protection because when I get to you, you're dead. I'm even going to carve you into little pieces and scatter you all over the country so I can torture what's left of your family.'

The venom of his words chilled Carla to the bone. She had no doubt he meant every word, because men like him preyed on the vulnerable and depended on their fear. It was lucky that she'd intercepted this call so he hadn't been able to intimidate Kaidence. But Carla knew Mitchell wouldn't be able to stop at making threats over the phone; eventually when Kaidence didn't respond to them, he'd have the urge to pay her a visit and Carla had to make a case for him to be held in prison until the trial.

Kaidence's street was quiet as Jackson pulled up at the kerb outside her house and engaged the handbrake. He didn't want to presume he'd be invited inside and wasn't sure if he should accept if he was. He'd kept away from her as much as he could despite almost nightly phone conversations. But he didn't fear those being discovered because she had a new number, which was nothing to do with the investigation. However, he had no idea how to explain it if they were seen in each other's company.

'Are you coming in?' she turned and asked as she unclipped her seatbelt.

'I should get home,' he replied.

Kaidence shrugged. 'Eh, I had nothing special planned, I was just going to drink the bottle of chardonnay I brought and order takeaway anyway,' she said, opening the door, climbing out and heading to the back of the vehicle.

Jackson turned off the engine, removed his seatbelt and climbed out of the car after her. 'Let me carry those inside for you,' he said, popping the boot open.

'It's okay, I can manage,' she said, reaching inside to collect her shopping. 'If you're really not coming in.'

He laughed and relented. 'I suppose I could come in for something to eat.'

'Hey, don't do me any favours,' she countered, walking towards her front door.

He locked his car as he followed her into the house. But it wasn't until they got inside, and she shrugged off her long coat and oversized cardigan, that he first saw the outfit she was wearing. It was unlike anything he'd ever seen her in. It wasn't baggy to disguise her figure like her everyday clothing, it wasn't revealing like her clothes from the past had been, and it wasn't professional like the ensemble she wore to work. It emphasised her curves enough that it wasn't hard to imagine what was beneath them.

'Wow!' he exclaimed. 'You look nice.'

She looked down at her outfit to remind herself of what she'd put on that morning. 'I'm trying a new look – well, an old one,' she said, removing her boots and heading into the kitchen with her bags. 'I've got a perfectly good wardrobe upstairs that I can finally wear now Mitchell doesn't control every aspect of my life.'

Jackson followed her and immediately noticed the subtle addition to the room. 'You installed the security system then?'

She nodded as she started unpacking the bags containing food. 'Had the locks changed too,' she answered. 'The only thing I didn't expect was how much time I'd spend watching them. It's like my life is run by the cameras now. I'll be happy to go back to work to have something else to do.'

'You'll get out of that habit once he's behind bars.'

'If he's ever put there. I'm beginning to think he's playing on his injuries to make it look like I attacked him for no reason.'

'You had cuts and bruises all over your body and a dislocated shoulder – you didn't do that to yourself.'

'But the judge might think he was just defending himself.'

'You've got photos and journal logs.'

'Those are just pictures and words; I could've made them up.'

'You didn't.'

'We know that, but will a judge?'

'You've got scars,' he pointed out.

'All he has to do is create reasonable doubt and he won't be convicted,' she argued.

'Kaidence, where is this coming from?'

'Men have been getting away with hitting women for years, how is this any different?' she asked. 'All it takes is for the wrong judge to be sat in that courtroom and he'll be free to come after me.'

'That's not going to happen. He will serve time for what he did to you.'

'You don't know that.'

'And you don't know that he won't.'

'I've just got a feeling that my life is still in danger.'

'That's natural. But if you see this through, he will get a conviction.'

She exhaled. 'I didn't think the police were supposed to make promises they didn't know they could keep.'

He closed the distance between them and put his hands on her shoulders, forcing her to look him in the eye. 'Trust me, in the unlikely event that he's released, he won't come after you.'

She didn't quite grasp what he was implying. 'I wish I could believe that.'

'Believe it. I'll wipe him off the planet before he even has a chance.'

That's when she realised what he meant. 'Don't say that, Jackson. You're not going to risk everything just because I'm scared.'

'I let one abuser take someone I cared about once before; I'm not going to let it happen again.'

'You're a police officer and you're talking about killing a man.'

'It's not going to come to that. He's going to be put behind bars.' He was adamant.

'Still, I don't want to hear you talk like that.'

He smiled and saluted. 'Yes ma'am.'

It was only after they'd eaten and were a glass of wine down that Jackson could see that Kaidence had relaxed. Even though he had made a deal with himself to only stay as long as it took to eat, he was comfortable in her house and with her company, so he'd stayed longer. After their earlier conversation, he wanted to be there as moral support because he felt that she needed it.

During a momentary pause in the discussion they were having, Kaidence yawned.

'Tired?' he asked.

She nodded. 'I haven't been sleeping.'

'I thought you'd be sleeping better now.'

'I close my eyes and I am back there, stabbing him.'

'You were fighting back.'

'I know, but I relive it every night like I'm the aggressor.'

'You just need to change your perspective from attacker to victim because that's what you were – are.'

'That's hard to do when I could face charges.'

Somehow the conversation always came back to Mitchell, every time. It wasn't what either of them wanted, but maybe it was the only thing they had in common when they stripped everything back.

It was becoming obvious to Jackson that Kaidence's attitude towards him had changed in the fortnight she'd had her freedom. She didn't flirt playfully with him the way she used to and he wasn't sure if it was just because he'd put restrictions on their interactions, or whether it was due to her not needing him in the capacity she once had, but he felt the distance between them growing with every visit. He hated it. He had a feeling that he'd have to face the reality that he might have to live without her in his life at some point in the future.

CHAPTER TWENTY-FOUR

Although Kaidence was out of practice, getting up for work was easy. She was looking forward to going back to her own version of what was normal. She had been through the clothes she hadn't worn in a year and picked out an outfit she had always liked – a pair of black tailored trousers with a chocolate brown satin shirt tucked into the waistband. She didn't know how they looked on her; all she had to go on was what they had looked like the last time she'd wore them, when she had a full-length mirror.

She headed to her dresser, picked up her brush and ran it through her hair. She planned to keep it down today instead of scraping it back into a bobble as usual. It was another step towards breaking the restraints Mitchell had put on her. As she exited the bedroom, she picked up the black cardigan from the bed and headed downstairs to find something to eat.

It was once she reached the kitchen that her mobile phone started to ring. She checked the clock on the wall; it was barely seven, much too early for anyone to be calling. It wasn't until she saw her brother-in-law's business partner's ID on the screen that her interest was piqued.

'Morning Sarah,' she greeted her.

'Morning Kaidence. I'm ringing to give you an update on Mitchell.'

'What about him?'

'He was released from hospital yesterday and questioned.'

'Okay.' She waited for the next instalment of information.

'They held him in custody overnight and he's being arraigned this morning.'

She took a deep breath. 'All right. Do I need to be there?'

'No, this is just a preliminary hearing for him to enter his plea,' Sarah replied. 'Depending on his plea, I'm going to enter a motion for him to be remanded in custody until the trial but there's no guarantee the judge will agree, because the only criminal record he has is for drunk and disorderly.'

'So, what are you saying?' she asked, trying to read between the lines.

Sarah exhaled on the other end of the phone. 'He could be out on bail by the end of the day.'

Kaidence was stunned. She dropped to a chair at the dining table, searching her mind for her next move. She had fooled herself into believing she was safe while he was being guarded by the police. She hadn't been prepared for what would happen next. Knowing he wasn't going to let her go was different to being faced with it. There were endless thoughts that ran through her mind. Should she stay at home and risk him getting inside to attack her? No one would know because no one would be checking on her. Or should she go to work and put other people's lives at risk? At least there she would have witnesses if he did show up. She didn't know which option was best.

'I'm supposed to go back to work today,' she told her solicitor, almost in a whisper.

'Do that. I'll let you know how it goes in court and we can decide what we do next.'

'He'll come after me, Sarah. It'll be the first thing he does.'

'Let's not worry about that until we have to.'

Kaidence was distracted as she sat with her first cup of tea of the day after the phone call. She was preoccupied as she picked at the already cut-up fruit she'd prepared for work and had pulled out of the fridge for breakfast. She was still side tracked as she punched in the code for the alarm and left for work.

By the time she got to the school, she was running on autopilot. She knew she had to find time to sit down with Irene, the headmistress, to explain what was happening. She wasn't looking forward to that, but the head of personnel deserved to have fair warning in case Mitchell showed up on the premises and the police had to be called.

It turned out that she didn't have to instigate the conversation because as soon as she walked through the doors, Irene appeared from her office and called her inside. She immediately brought up the amount of time she'd had off, which prompted Kaidence to confess her reason for it. The instant the words were past her lips, she saw the sympathy on the sixty-year-old's face. She was surprised when her boss admitted that she'd been called into the office to be let go, but that her admission had made her rethink the decision. She was relieved, knowing that it was probably because of the older woman's affection for her that she'd stayed employed for as long as she had. But she found herself wondering whether it was best for everyone who worked there for her to walk away. The last thing she wanted was for any of her colleagues to get dragged into her drama if Mitchell came after her and she voiced those concerns to the woman she respected and admired.

Kaidence sighed. 'I want to be here. Teaching has been the only thing I've lived for this last year, but if Mitchell comes to the school to get to me and someone else gets hurt...'

Walking around her desk, Irene cut her off before she could finish. 'My darling, he's not brave enough to come here,' she said, sitting in the chair next to her and taking her hand. 'The whole reason he hit you behind closed doors is because he didn't want anyone to see what he was doing. Besides, he'd have to go through me first. You're safe in this building with people that love you.'

Kaidence didn't fight her on it. The truth was, she could use the distraction of being at work with her lively pupils.

She went to her classroom and did her best not to think of the one thing she couldn't help but think about. She even convinced herself she had seen Mitchell standing outside the school boundary watching her through the window. But she remembered Jackson saying that it was to be expected, and looked away before looking back again to find no one there. Her mind was obviously playing tricks on her because she hadn't heard from her solicitor yet.

By the time lunch came around Kaidence was completely consumed by her fear. She'd tried to push it to the back of her mind and not panic until she needed to, like Sarah had advised, but she couldn't concentrate. She hated to admit it, but she was about as much use to the kids she taught as she would've been if she'd stayed at home.

She was making her way to the staff room when her mobile phone started to ring. She turned on her heel and exited the school through the main entrance so she could take the call in private.

'Hi. Why are you calling? Aren't you at work today?' she asked right away.

She heard Jackson exhale and knew he was preparing himself to say something he wasn't looking forward to. 'Kaidence, he's out on bail.'

The wind was knocked out of her and she stumbled to lean against the nearest surface to stay upright. 'What does that mean?' she asked, unable to think straight.

'He pled not guilty and Sarah argued for him to be remanded in custody until the trial because of the severity of the abuse, but because the only criminal record he has relates to being intoxicated, the judge granted him conditions to stay one hundred feet away from you.'

'So why are you telling me this?'

'I was in court and I was going to call you anyway so I told Sarah that I'd tell you.'

'When did this happen?'

'About an hour ago.'

'So, he could be watching me right now.'

'He's got to stay away from you, or he could be held in prison until the court date.'

'Do you think he'll care about that?'

'If you see him, call nine-nine-nine. The court order means you'll get a quicker response.'

'That won't matter, Jackson, especially if he corners me on the street or if he's waiting by my car when I get out of work.' She started to panic.

'I'll meet you outside the school tonight and escort you home,' he said, thinking he was helping.

'Are you going to follow me around for the rest of my life? Because the minute I'm alone, the minute he thinks I'm vulnerable, that's when he'll attack.'

'I know but, bar from moving in with you, I can't be there all the time.'

'I'm not expecting you to be, that's why I had the cameras installed. But how much help are they going to be if he breaks into the house?'

'They'll prove he was there.'

'And help convict him after I'm dead,' she commented.

'Don't talk like that,' he scolded.

She took a deep breath. 'All right, at least I know what I'm dealing with. Thanks for letting me know.'

'I'll see you after work,' he said. But she barely heard him over the thoughts raging in her mind. 'Kaidy!' he called out to get her attention.

'What?'

'I'll be there when you leave, okay?'

'Yeah okay, see you then.'

She stood outside after she hung up. She was dazed. She couldn't focus on anything around her because all she could think about was the many ways Mitchell was going to hurt her. There was a time during one of the beatings she was taking that she prayed for death, but now that she was away from him, she wanted to live. She had to stop giving over her power to him and move past the fear he'd taught her to feel. But wanting that and making it happen were very different things.

By the time she'd finished work, Kaidence had worked herself up into a state. She'd barely been able to concentrate on lessons all day; all she could think about was Mitchell. Despite the restrictions given him by the courts, she knew he wouldn't keep to them and she was anticipating his next move, whether he had planned it or was acting on impulse. It was driving her insane. Since she'd spoken to Jackson, she'd had the feeling of being watched. She knew it could be just her paranoia at play, but it could just as easily be because she *was* being watched.

She didn't realise she was dragging her feet to leave until Jackson appeared in her classroom. In her anxiety, she'd forgotten he'd offered to escort her home.

'Are you ready?' he asked, walking towards her.

She took a deep breath. 'I suppose so.'

'You'll be more protected at home.'

She frowned. 'On my own?'

'You've got that hefty front door that even we had trouble getting through, you've got cameras and an alarm,' he responded. 'He doesn't know about the precautions you've taken, and he thinks he's got a key; that can only work in your favour because you'll have the chance to ring triple nine.'

'You're right,' she relented, picking up her handbag from her desk and leading him out of the door. 'I've been seeing his face everywhere today.'

'That doesn't mean he was there.'

'It doesn't mean he wasn't, either.'

He raised his eyebrows; she was right. 'Well that's why I'm here.'

Kaidence was on high alert as she drove back to the house, followed closely by Jackson in his car. She was sure she saw Mitchell on every corner at every traffic light she stopped at. She'd locked her doors so no one could get into the vehicle regardless of how much they wanted to, and she had Jackson on the phone through her in-car Bluetooth.

'You okay?' he asked when the lights changed to green and she didn't move.

She forced herself to refocus as she released the handbrake and continued home. 'I am ready for this nightmare to be over.'

'It won't be long until it is,' he said, trying to sound optimistic.

'Then why does it feel like these last two weeks have been the longest of my life?'

'Because the anticipation of a deed is sometimes worse than the deed itself.'

'Unless you've been living it over and over for a year,' she commented as she turned into her street. 'And the suspense is only going to get worse from now on.'

Her eyes darted from one possible place where Mitchell could hide to another as she pulled up on her drive. She felt her nerves keenly in the pit of her stomach and thought she was going to throw up as she engaged the hand-brake. She didn't turn off her engine, because she wasn't sure she was going to stay. She was tempted to drive until she ran out of fuel in whatever direction the flip of a coin told her to travel, with just the clothes on her back and the belongings in her handbag. But Jackson's voice broke through her dalliance with fleeing.

'Wait for me to get to your door before you unlock it,' he told her before she hung up.

The call cut out and, almost instantly, he was tapping on the driver's window. It took her a minute to react. Removing her seatbelt with her left hand, she turned the engine off with her right and grabbed her handbag from the passenger's seat as she unlocked her door and exited the vehicle. She locked her car, and Jackson guided her to the entrance of her home like a bodyguard would with his charge.

He stood behind her, acting as lookout, as she opened the door to give them access to the safety of her home and he heard her release a breath in relief once he closed the barrier behind them. She instantly punched the six-digit code into the panel for her alarm system, so it didn't notify everyone within earshot of unauthorised access and removed her coat.

'Now what am I supposed to do; sit and watch the cameras until he shows up? Because you know that's exactly what I'm going to do, don't you?' she asked, heading to the kitchen and putting her bag on the dining table.

Jackson noticed the room was slightly less orderly than it had been the first time he'd checked on her after his initial introduction – maybe she was rebelling against the clean streak she'd developed.

'It might not seem like it, but this is the best place for you to be,' he said.

'So, am I meant to stay inside this house for the rest of my life?' she asked, filling the kettle and putting it on to boil. 'Because it was one thing to be stuck in this house when it was more than my life was worth to step out of line, it's quite another to have to stay here when I'm on the verge of getting my life back.'

'I know that to be so close to living free only to have it snatched away is frustrating, but you just have to hold on for a little bit longer until the trial, and then you will be able to live anywhere and do anything.'

'If I make it to trial, because he'll never let me testify.'

'He's not going to have a choice, Kaidence.'

'Do you think he's above stabbing me outside the court?' she asked. 'He's not. So, if he doesn't get to me beforehand, he'll take a desperate last-minute pot shot, regardless of the consequences because, for him, to be convicted of murder is better than having me accuse him of something he will never admit to.'

'He just doesn't want people to know what kind of man he is.'

'Which is precisely why he will shut me up by any means necessary.'

'You've just not got to give him any opportunities.'

'So, I'm still being punished when the only thing *I* did wrong was pick the wrong man to let into my bed.'

'I know, it's not fair. But this is the hand we've been dealt.'

'We? I'm sorry but there is no *we* here. You get to leave and go back to your normal life. Meanwhile I've got to sit in solitary confinement until the court has time to convict him.'

'Six months is the standard wait for any case to be heard in court.'

'That's what Sarah said. But six months is a long time to put my life on hold, if I even have one by then,' she said, lowering herself onto one of the chairs at the table and leaning forward to rest her head in her hands.

He crouched on the floor in front of her. 'Listen to me, you are the bravest person I know. You survived a year of torture at the hands of this man – all you need to do is hold on for a little while longer.'

She lifted her head to look at him. 'I want to move on, to start healing. But I can't with this hanging over my head.'

'I know it's hard to see the light at the end of the tunnel but it's there, you just need to take a few steps,' he pleaded.

She sucked in a hard breath, pushed her chair back and got to her feet. 'Maybe I should just forget about pressing charges and take off; start over somewhere new.'

He shot up to his feet. 'That is absolutely your right. But if you don't make him accountable for what he's done to you in a court of his peers, you will be haunted by him for the rest of your life.'

'That's going to happen anyway. I'm not going to be able to just shake off the trauma he's put me through.'

'But once he's behind bars you'll be able to move on and leave this relationship in the past, like you're supposed to.'

'This is more than just a bad break-up, Jackson; it's going to take more than a shower and a bottle of wine to move on.'

'You know that I know that.'

She growled in frustration. 'I know, I'm sorry. I just don't want to be forced to live my life from this house. I need to be able to leave. Otherwise I might as well have stayed with Mitchell,' she said, reaching into the cupboard for two mugs and holding one in his direction. 'Coffee?'

He nodded. 'I've got time for a quick one before I've got to get back.'

She frowned. 'Are you still on duty?'

'I'm on my lunchbreak.'

'But isn't your shift almost over?'

'I'll have about two hours left when I get back.'

'Did you purposely take your break so you could fetch me from work?'

He shrugged like it wasn't a big deal. 'I knew you needed me.'

She sighed. 'You go out of your way for me and all I've done is act like a spoiled brat who can't have her own way,' she admitted. 'I'm sorry, Jackson.'

'Hey, you're scared and that's okay; it's normal.'

She finished making the hot beverages and placed his on the counter where he usually sat. 'I almost lost my job today,' she shared, leaning against the kitchen unit with her backside.

'For?'

'How much time I've had off work.' She paused. 'I had 100 per cent attendance before Mitchell started marking my face. But the first time he blacked my eye, a few staff members asked how I got it and I lied because I didn't want them to know what I'd allowed him to do. Then the second time, he split my lip. The same colleagues asked the same question and I lied again. They weren't convincing lies, so I was expecting one of them – any of them – to call me on it and insist I tell the truth. They never did and by the tenth time, they'd stopped asking altogether. So whenever I got any cuts or bruises on my face, I always took sick days. I was sure Irene, my boss, knew about the abuse because the teachers at that school gossip and there was no way the ones that asked me about my injuries didn't know exactly how I'd got them. But when I told her what Mitchell had been doing to me today, she was surprised, which is why she let me keep my job.'

'Sometimes people can't see what's right under their noses.'

'It's not her fault. I wasn't exactly forthcoming with a confession until I thought I was going to be fired. But if I take any more time off right now, I'm going to be unemployed for sure.'

'Surely she'd understand if you called her and explained the new development.'

'I don't want to though. I want to be at work.'

'I know, but the school isn't secure. He can walk inside at any time and cause injury to you, other staff members, or worse...those kids.'

She relented immediately at the thought of what he might do to the young students. 'You're right, of course you are. I'll give her a call later.'

He took a deep breath to motivate himself to leave. 'Right, I better get back to work or you won't be the only one on the unemployment line,' he said, moving towards the door.

Kaidence followed him in silence, feeling her isolation before she was even alone. She knew it was going to be a tough six months and, although she wanted to fight against it, she knew Jackson was right; staying safe had to be her priority.

He turned on his heel at the door to face her. 'I'm just the other end of the phone if you need me, no matter what time of day or night.'

She nodded, but didn't dare to make eye contact for fear of breaking down and begging him to stay. She didn't want him to go. She didn't want to be left alone.

'You are stronger than you think you are,' he said, sensing her vulnerability.

Again, she nodded but it was lacklustre in comparison to the previous one.

'This will work better if you at least pretend that you believe me.'

'For me or for you?' she asked, raising her chin to make eye contact.

'For me, of course,' he said, causing her to smile, which made him mirror her expression. 'That's better. Now I can leave with a clear conscience.'

'Go, before I hold on to your leg and refuse to release you, so you can't finish the rest of your shift.'

'I'll call to check on you later,' he said, rushing out of the house before he changed his mind about going.

Kaidence applied the deadlock, the chain and the two bolts at the top and bottom of the front door. She paused for a second before she turned to lean her back against the heavy wood and took in the silence that she had become accustomed to, but that somehow felt different now she knew Mitchell was free. She slowly slid down to the floor until she was sat with her knees pulled up to her chest. She was truly without anyone. His isolation had left her completely exposed and vulnerable. All the people who had vowed to be there for her were gone, busy living the lives they had before she'd interrupted them with her drama, and she sat alone; as lonely as she'd been in the relationship that had separated her from them in the first place.

She looked down the oversized hallway towards the back of the house and cursed her need to buy the bigger place when she could have settled for something smaller until the growth of her family warranted upsizing. She'd done it as a means of saving time, trying to find the perfect home to bring up children in once she found the man to do that with, because as soon as she stepped over the threshold, she knew she'd found it. Except now, the house that had been so ideal for her future was a prison.

Suddenly she shot up from the floor, as if a switch had been flicked to spur her into action. She headed to the kitchen and closed the curtains, being sure to leave no gaps for anyone on the outside to see inside. She did the same in the office and the lounge before heading upstairs to do the same in all the bedrooms. If she was going to be restricted to the confines of her house, she was going to make sure no one would be able to watch her once it was dark, and the blackout window dressings were a great asset for that. The only purpose they served was to make her feel safe moving about in her home, but that was better than walking around in the dark just to remain undetected.

While she was upstairs, she sat on her bed and took in the silence that she would have to get comfortable with if she was going to make it to the trial. It was horrible, she hated it. She knew she'd go out of her mind if she didn't channel her energy into something productive. But her options were limited. She didn't really have any hobbies. She only found out she had a forte for baking by accident, not because she was passionate about it. The only other thing she had discovered – by chance – during her time documenting her abuse was that she had a flair for writing, which was enough encouragement for her to decide to keep a diary to distract her from the four walls that surrounded her.

She was about to strip off her clothes to change into something more comfortable when she heard a sound from downstairs. Her breath caught in her throat and adrenaline made her heart pump a little harder in her chest as she listened for a repeat noise. There was nothing. But she was curious, despite her terror and she removed her shoes before slowly getting to her feet. She tiptoed towards the stairs and still heard nothing. She moved against the wall of the staircase, praying that none of the stair treads creaked underfoot as she stepped gingerly down to the ground level.

Reaching the cold tiles of the hallway, she listened for any signs of company as she breathed through her nose so she could hear clearly. Then in an instant she realised that if there had been an intruder, her alarm would have been triggered because only she knew the combination.

She relaxed in an instant and walked into the kitchen to retrieve her laptop from the table and returned upstairs. Once she was safely back on her bed, she opened the computer and loaded the cameras onto the screen. She flicked through each of them with the press of the right-pointing arrow key and studied each for any movement before moving on. Satisfied there was no one in or around the house, she removed the outfit she'd put on that morning and headed to the bathroom for a shower. She needed to wash the day off her.

As she stepped in and stood beneath the water, she let it wash away any desire she had to control the things she couldn't change. This was the turn her life had taken, and she had to let it ride out however it was going to, which would be hard. She'd found a newly developed strength from the couple of weeks that she had been living free, and trying to put the metaphorical cork back in the bottle was going to be tougher than she imagined it could be. She'd had a taste of life after Mitchell, when she knew he was being supervised, and she liked it. All the plans she'd once had for her life seemed possible again for the first time in a long time, and now they were being put back on hold.

Feeling clean and refreshed, Kaidence wrapped a towel around her wet hair before reaching for a larger one to wrap around her body. She didn't bother to dry herself off. Instead she headed back to her bedroom and sat on her bed in front of the laptop. Again, she flicked through each camera feed to be sure she was still safe. Happy there was nothing to cause alarm, she relaxed back on the mattress and stared up at the ceiling. It was getting dark outside and the only reason she knew was because it was hard to see in the room, especially with the addition of the blackout curtains.

After lying there for a while, she removed the towel from her body and put on her dressing gown to head down to the kitchen to find something to eat. It was when she reached the room she had previously spent the majority of her time in that there was a knock on the door. She froze as her heart jumped into her throat. The laptop was still upstairs, so she couldn't see who it was without looking through the peephole. As a precaution, she turned off the light she had flicked on upon entering the kitchen and headed towards the noise. She was a few steps away when the knock came again, frightening the life out of her. She sucked in the air in front of her as she covered her chest over her heart with her hand and stopped.

'Bitch! Open the door!' she heard shouted the other side.

She'd know that voice anywhere. It was Mitchell. She held her breath, convinced he'd hear her if she did breathe, and tried to think of her next move. She backed up, retracing her steps to get to her handbag on the dining table and allowed herself to breathe again. She fished around inside it for her mobile phone and immediately silenced it before sending a text to Jackson to tell him Mitchell had shown up. She patiently waited the lifetime it seemed to take for him to reply. *You're safe inside the house. Don't open the door and call 999.*

She exited the messages and did as instructed while she headed to the back of the kitchen, so that she wouldn't be heard, and as an extra precaution she lowered herself to the floor, pressing her back against the units and pulling her knees up to her chest while she waited for someone to pick up the other end. The call was answered after a few rings.

'Nine-nine-nine, which service please?' the operator asked as they were connected.

'Police please,' she replied, just loud enough to be heard.

There was a click as she was transferred and a different voice came down the line. 'Police emergency. How can I help?'

'Hi, my abusive ex-boyfriend had conditions from the court to stay a hundred feet away from me and he's banging on my door demanding to be let in,' she explained as best she could.

'What's your address?'

Kaidence relayed the information she asked for with her eyes trained on the doorway to the kitchen. She knew that if he managed to break through the front door – and that was a big if – her alarm would activate.

'All right, I've dispatched officers to your location. They're a few minutes out, so I'll stay on the line until they get there,' the operator said.

'Okay, thank you,' she replied gratefully. 'I've changed the locks, so he's probably just realised his key doesn't work.'

'How long have you been separated?'

'Fifteen days, since he tried to kill me.'

'You should be able to hear sirens now because they're around the corner.'

She got to her feet and walked to the window to peer beyond the curtains in time to see the flashing lights of a patrol car. 'Yes, they're here.'

'Then I'll leave you in the capable hands of the officers.'

'Okay, thanks,' she said, disconnecting the call.

Two seconds later, there was a knock on her door. 'Hello, it's the police,' they called out to her.

Feeling safe enough to answer, she pulled open the barrier to the world, but there was no sign of Mitchell, just two officers – one male and one female.

'Have you got him?' she asked with a frown.

'There was no one here when we arrived.'

'He was here,' she insisted.

'We'll do a full search of the grounds to make sure he didn't duck out of sight when he heard the sirens.'

'I've got a restraining order.'

The officer nodded as if she had already been informed. 'If he's not here we'll pay him a visit at the address on file to see if he can account for his whereabouts.'

The fog of Kaidence's fear evaporated, allowing her to think more clearly, and she remembered the security system. 'I've got cameras. He'll show up on those.'

'That'll be helpful.'

'I'll go and get the laptop,' she said, rushing upstairs to her bedroom.

After a few minutes she emerged, still in her dressing gown, with the computer in her hand. She rushed down to the officers and opened the lid to access the feed from the camera above the entrance. She rewound it until there was a figure on her doorstep and hit play, then paused the video almost immediately. There, as plain as day, was Mitchell banging on her door.

'That's great,' the male officer said, taking a phone from his pocket and taking a photo of the screen. 'That's all the evidence we need that he's breached his bail. We'll keep him detained until he can go back in front of the judge.'

'Thank you,' she said, feeling relieved.

'We'll let you know when we've picked him up,' the female officer said as they turned to leave. 'Be sure to lock up in case he comes back before we get to him.'

'I will,' she said, closing the door behind them and reapplying the locks.

She took a deep breath to steady the nerves in her stomach. She wouldn't truly feel safe until she got word that Mitchell wasn't coming back, but she was hungry, so she headed to the kitchen to make something quick and easy to eat. She loved cooking but cooking for one was effort she didn't have the energy for. She opened the fridge to check its contents and decided on a sandwich. She was chopping salad when notice came through to her that the officers had visited Mitchell's parents' house and had him in custody, so she completed her task and ate, feeling the most relaxed she'd been all day.

Once she was finished, Kaidence made her way back upstairs. She knew it was illogical, but she felt safer up there. She had a television and a DVD player in her bedroom that she used to use all the time before she shared her space, so she had plenty to distract her from the real reason she was stuck indoors. Now in her pyjamas, she put one of her favourite films in the player with the intention of lying in bed to watch it with the cameras running on the laptop, on what used to be his side.

She had only been alone in her house for a few hours, but she liked the freedom that knowing Mitchell was under lock and key afforded her. The thought of him triggered another, and she ran to the kitchen for the huge bag of popcorn she had in the cupboard. She was never allowed to eat in bed because he didn't like crumbs – so she was going to take full advantage of being able to now.

Meredith checked the clock. She had just put Justin down for the night and she was thinking about calling her sister because she hadn't spoken to her since spending time together two days ago. If Kaidence hadn't been returning to work today, she would have popped in to see her, but she didn't want to be accused of suffocating her.

'What's on your mind?' Cole asked, noticing she wasn't paying attention to the television.

'I'm wondering whether I should call Kiki.'

'I'm sure she would've called you if she'd heard any news.'

'I don't care about that; I care how she's doing.'

'You saw her on Saturday, how did she seem then?'

'Fine. But she's on her own and I said I'd be there for her.'

'And if she needs you, I'm sure she'll call.'

'So, you don't think I should contact her?'

'You could send her a text instead?'

'That's so impersonal. I prefer actually speaking to her.'

'If it'll put your mind at rest, call her.'

She sighed. 'No, I'll wait until tomorrow. She can't accuse me of being suffocating if I leave it three days.'

It was only nine o'clock by the time the film finished, but Kaidence was exhausted and ready for bed. She used the remote to turn off the television and closed the lid on her laptop before moving it to the bedside table so that she could access it in the night if she needed to, then she got comfortable beneath the duvet. Closing her eyes, she did her best not to think of the one person she instinctively thought about: Mitchell. She was settling into sleep when there was a knock at the front door. She reached to get the laptop and checked the camera feed over the entrance, only to see Mitchell standing there. Her heart leapt into her throat. He wasn't supposed to be free. She grabbed her mobile phone and dialled Jackson's number.

'Hello,' he answered chirpily after a few rings.

She didn't waste any time on a greeting. 'I thought Mitchell had been picked up.'

'He has. He's at the station.'

'Then why is he on my doorstep?'

'Hang on, I'll call custody and see what's going on.'

'Thank you,' she said gratefully, before hanging up and returning her attention to the laptop.

Mitchell was still stood there, banging on the obstacle in his way shouting all the profanities at her that he could think of. She watched with her stomach in knots as his anger escalated. She was anticipating his next move when Jackson's name lit up her phone screen. She answered without hesitation.

'He's still in the cells, Kaidence,' he said, getting straight to the point.

'Then he must have a clone, because he's at my door.'

'I don't know who's at your door, but Mitchell is being held tonight and will be put back before the judge in the morning for breach of bail.'

'Jackson, I'm looking at the camera feed and I am telling you: Mitchell is here.'

He exhaled audibly. 'All right, I'm coming over. But put a call in to nine-nine-nine so the officers who were there before can come back out because I won't be in uniform.'

'Okay, I'll do that now.'

⸻

The phone line went dead, and Jackson shoved it into his jeans pocket. He believed his colleagues when they said they still had Mitchell locked up in the cells, which meant Kaidence was paranoid, seeing his face on the cameras because of her fear of him. He was only going because he thought the news of her delusions would be better coming from a friendly face rather than two authority figures she'd only met that night.

By the time he pulled up at the kerb outside her house, the officers had the man who'd been causing the disturbance in the back of their squad car. As he climbed out of his vehicle, Jackson glanced into the back seat to see the familiar face of Mitchell, and a frown formed on his brow. He approached the officer standing at the bottom of the drive to find out what was going on, while his partner got Kaidence's statement and any footage she had.

'Jackson, what are you doing here?' Officer Ryan West asked.

'Miss Hadaway called me,' he responded. 'She trusts me, so I just wanted to come and check on her.' He motioned to the man in cuffs. 'I thought he was in custody.'

'Mitchell is,' West countered before pointing at the detainee. 'But that's not Mitchell.'

'Well who the hell is he?'

'His twin, Martin.'

'He's got a twin?'

'Apparently, and he's three sheets to the wind so we'll keep him in a cell until the morning.'

'Does she know yet?' he asked, gesturing in Kaidence's direction.

He nodded. 'Perez has told her – she didn't take it well.'

Jackson thumbed in the direction of the front door. 'I better get over there.'

'Okay.'

As Jackson made his way towards Kaidence, Officer Leticia Perez was walking away from her, and they crossed paths with just a nod of acknowledgement.

'So, Mitchell's got a twin,' he said as he reached where Kaidence stood.

Kaidence headed inside, silently inviting him to follow her. 'I thought I was going crazy.'

He closed the door behind him and followed her to the kitchen. 'You didn't know?'

'How could I? I never met any of his family.'

'Well the good news is that Martin's going to be detained in custody for the night so he can sober up, and he'll be released in the morning. The bad news is that Mitchell was telling the truth when he denied being here earlier, so he'll be released without charge.'

'I suppose that's only fair. He shouldn't be punished for something he hasn't done.'

He frowned. 'Are you the same woman I left a few hours ago?'

'I've accepted the things I cannot change.'

'In five hours?'

'All right, I'm trying to accept them,' she acknowledged. 'But Mitchell's been free since this morning and he hasn't come after me yet so I'm hoping I've got him wrong.'

'Unless he sent his twin as a distraction.'

'Why would he do that?'

'To see how you react.'

'I'm not sure he's that forward thinking.'

'You'd be surprised what plans a desperate man can come up with.'

'But as you said, I am the safest I ever will be right here.'

He nodded. 'I'm glad you've made your peace with that.'

'I wouldn't go that far; but at this point I'll do what I have to if it means I get to put him behind bars.'

The sun was almost up by the time Kaidence was ready to go to sleep. Jackson had left not long after the police had departed and then she returned to her bedroom with a brand-new leather-bound notebook. She had spent some time writing a diary entry in a bid to work through her feelings, hoping it would help her to balance her mixed emotions about hiding out to protect herself while Mitchell lived free. She felt a little better getting some of her bitterness down on paper; it seemed to take some of the weight off her shoulders. When she wrote, she was utterly honest about everything. They were, after all, just letters to herself. No one else would read them. It was like a form of therapy; something that she hoped would help with her nightmares. Of course, it would take a few more entries before she could work everything out of her system. But one entry was a start.

Bringing things to the forefront of her mind to put them into written form had meant she wasn't able to fall asleep when she tried just an hour after her usual bedtime, so instead she'd put another film she enjoyed into the player. She was still wide awake when it finished, so she flicked through the channels for something to occupy her until she was relaxed enough to try and sleep.

She was exhausted by the whole day's events, from constantly looking over her shoulder for Mitchell, to seeing his likeness in the twin that she'd known nothing about who had shown up on her doorstep. Still she had to fight to get comfortable and when she closed her eyes, Mitchell's image was waiting for her in the darkness. It wasn't until she started to drift off that she felt the knife in her hand, as if it was really there.

CHAPTER TWENTY-FIVE

It was Thursday by the time Kaidence felt that she needed fresh air. She only ventured downstairs for food or drinks and stayed there for no longer than she needed to. Being stuck inside was beginning to drive her stir-crazy. She'd spent the days filling her time with sitting on her bed going through night footage from her cameras and watching films she had forgotten she enjoyed. The chill that flowed in through the window she opened was a poor substitute for her garden, yet Jackson had given her strict instructions not to even risk going out there in case Mitchell was lurking in the shadows, waiting for an opportunity to strike.

It was almost ten in the morning. She was in the kitchen, standing against the corner of the cabinets at the back of the room drinking her first cup of tea and contemplating what to do with her day, when she heard a noise at the back of the house. Placing her drink on the work surface, she crept out to the hallway, being sure to stay sheltered by the staircase so she wouldn't be seen through the thin floor-to-ceiling windows at the side of the back door. There was a figure there, fiddling with the lock. The hoodie the individual was wearing obscured her view of their face, although her gut told her it was Mitchell. Her heart pounded in her chest as she weighed up her options: running upstairs for her mobile phone against making a dash to the office across the hallway for the landline on the desk, at the risk of him seeing her. She knew that if he saw her, he would be even more determined to get inside; he would resort to smashing the windows regardless of the consequences if it meant getting to her before she could call for help, so she opted for the logical option.

She rushed up the stairs, despite knowing it meant she'd be trapped if he got in, and retrieved her mobile from the bedside table before punching triple nine into her on-screen keypad. When she heard the click of connection, she barely had the patience to wait for the operator's question before she responded.

'I need the police,' she stated.

'Police emergency, how can I help?' the male voice at the other end asked.

She heard glass smash downstairs and she knew he was in. She panicked as the security system also alerted her to the invasion, loudly enough that it was going to make it difficult to communicate with the emergency services. She made her way to the en-suite bathroom and locked the door behind her.

'My abusive ex-boyfriend has broken into my house. I need officers here before he finds me and then kills me,' she demanded.

'Officers are on the way.' The operator tried to reassure her.

'They need to hurry,' she managed before the line went silent.

Removing the phone from her ear, she checked the screen only to find the call had disconnected and the keypad was visible. She tried dialling the number again, but her mobile was showing no signal, so instead she opened the browser to connect to the internet to contact the police, but that wasn't working either. She growled in frustration and rushed to squeeze herself between the toilet and the wall at exactly the time she heard pounding on the door above the noise of the alarm.

'I know you're in there!' he roared.

The familiar address came over the radio and Louisa looked over at her partner. Although she was behind the wheel, she knew that in his mind, they were already on their way and it was pure coincidence that they were only a few streets away. Jackson accepted the assignment as she turned on the sirens and spun the squad car around.

Without warning, the bathroom door came flying off its hinges in her direction, causing her to scream. But that didn't deter the man in the doorway. He smirked as they made eye contact.

'Hi Kaidence, miss me?' Mitchell taunted her, blocking her escape route.

'The police are on their way,' she countered.

He reached into his jacket pocket and pulled something out before holding it up for her to see. 'Nice try, but this little device blocks all phone signals, so I know you're lying.'

She didn't argue with him. It was better for him to think he'd bested her, because he wouldn't be in a hurry to escape and the police could catch him in the act of whatever he had planned to do to her. She just had to hold on for as long as it took for them to reach her. That's when she saw the glint of the blade in his other hand. He was going to exact his revenge with the same weapon she had used in the attack that had precipitated their break-up.

He shoved the signal blocker back into his pocket and barged past the barrier he'd knocked down to get to her. She knew her position was a huge advantage for him because there was nowhere for her to escape to and the room was so small; it was unlikely she'd be able to outmanoeuvre him and give herself a chance of freedom. Still, she wasn't going to lie there and make it easy for him. She got to her feet and stood with her back to the wall as he walked towards her.

As they got closer, the officers could hear the alarm ringing out and before Louisa had even fully ground the vehicle to a complete stop, Jackson was out of it with his taser drawn.

'I'll go around the back,' he shouted to her as she removed the keys from the engine and rushed after him.

She glanced at the front door; it looked to be secure, so it probably wasn't Mitchell's point of entry. Not to mention that it had been difficult for the police to break down with the Big Red Key, so it was unlikely he'd got through it. She followed Jackson at a run, and her instincts were proven right when they reached the back of the property to find the door wide open and the side window shattered into pieces on the floor.

'He's inside.' Jackson pointed out the obvious.

Louisa drew her taser and signalled with a nod that she was ready to enter.

Mitchell took one last step in her direction. 'I am going to enjoy this.'

She could tell from her year of experience that he was amused by his ability to get so close to her regardless of all the measures she'd taken to keep him out, and her safe. Despite being taller than her, he seemed smaller because of the confidence she had now and although she was scared, she puffed out her chest to make herself feel stronger.

She didn't dare speak, for fear of antagonising him. He was already angry, and she knew that it would be impossible to reason with him – if anything it would make him angrier. She just hoped her silence didn't have the same effect. She wanted to prolong his attack, because she wanted to survive. But she couldn't hear anything outside the room apart from the alarm, so she had to put faith in the police being close.

Without any warning, he thrust forward with the knife, sinking the blade low down into her abdomen, near her navel. It was an oddly specific place to stab her and it wasn't readily apparent why, but she knew he'd have a reason. He twisted the blade and she screamed out in pain as it ripped through the surrounding tissue.

Jackson had just reached the landing of the first floor and signalled to his partner to go right while he went left in the direction of the main bedroom when they heard a scream as clear as day above the noise of the alarm. Without hesitation, they both ran towards the pained cry. They didn't know what they'd find when they entered the bedroom. Jackson noticed the door for the en suite immediately and pointed it out to Louisa, who gained on the entrance to it, her taser held up with her finger on the trigger. Seeing Mitchell with his back to her, blocking her view of Kaidence, she shouted at him to drop to his knees and put his hands on his head. When he didn't react, Jackson stepped over the threshold to get inside the room.

'Mitchell, get on your knees and put your hands on your head,' he instructed.

As Mitchell moved, Kaidence screamed again and when he raised his hands, his right hand held a knife dripping in blood.

'Drop the knife,' Jackson ordered.

Lowering himself to his knees, Mitchell allowed the knife to fall from his fingers to the floor. The officers couldn't see his face because he was still looking at Kaidence, but she could see the smile on his lips, and she knew that meant he was proud of what he'd accomplished.

'I am going to cuff you. Do not move or you will be tasered. Do you understand?' Jackson stated in a commanding voice. He turned to look at his partner, who nodded to signal she knew what he wanted her to do without a word passing his lips. She walked inside the bathroom and stepped to the side of the doorway to be able to keep her taser trained on the offender in case he turned his attack on them. She glanced at Kaidence to find her holding her side as blood escaped through her fingers while she slowly slid down the wall to the tiles beneath her feet. Keeping one finger on the trigger of her weapon, Louisa used the radio on her vest to call for an ambulance as Jackson placed handcuffs on Mitchell, but no response came back.

'You do not have to say anything. But it may harm your defence if you do not mention when questioned something which you later rely on in court. Anything you do say may be given in evidence,' he cautioned the detainee.

Once he was secure, Louisa holstered her taser and checked on the welfare of the homeowner, who was bleeding out on the floor. Kaidence was struggling to stay conscious, so Louisa dropped to her knees to try and focus her into staying awake.

'What's the code for the alarm?' she asked, applying pressure to the wound.

'Jackson knows it,' Kaidence managed before passing out.

Louisa looked across at her partner as he searched Mitchell for any other weapons. 'This doesn't look good,' she told him.

Emptying Mitchell's pockets, Jackson found a small plastic box which had a switch and a green light on it. He was puzzled as to its purpose but risked flicking the switch the other way. That's when Louisa's radio crackled back to life.

Louisa realised what the device was. 'I think that's a signal blocker.'

'This is illegal,' Jackson informed the intruder.

'I don't care,' he countered smugly with a shrug of his shoulders.

Realising her request for an ambulance hadn't been heard, Louisa called it through again. 'We need to shut off this alarm,' she said to Jackson.

'I'll put him in the squad and shut it off. What did she say the code was?'

'She didn't; she just said you knew it.'

He nodded in her direction, automatically knowing what it was likely to be, as he helped Mitchell to his feet. He guided the prisoner, who had his hands handcuffed behind his back, out of the bedroom without speaking. As they got to the landing the man started to taunt him, assuming his interest in Kaidence was more than professional because of the way he'd confronted him on the hospital car park.

'It's going to be difficult for your girlfriend to give you any offspring now,' he said spitefully as the male officer held him by the bicep to influence the path they took.

That gave Jackson an indication of the type of injury Kaidence had sustained, and he was immediately angry. But he had to separate his emotions from the situation and act as he would at any other call. He kept his mouth shut, allowing Mitchell to incriminate himself on the body cam without any assistance at all.

'I thought about killing her, but this is so much better because now she'll have to live knowing she can't get pregnant,' he continued as he was guided down the stairs.

'Are you admitting to a purposeful attack?' the officer asked as they stepped out of the building and headed towards the police vehicle.

Mitchell didn't answer his question, but he did implicate himself further. 'I had to research exactly where to put that knife.'

His honesty was puzzling, especially when he'd been deceptive about the abuse up to this point. Maybe he'd been unbalanced by the police presence because he thought his signal blocker had prevented Kaidence from contacting them and being caught red-handed had forced his hand. Or maybe he just didn't care and simply wanted to ruin her life as a parting gift. Jackson had given up trying to figure out men like Mitchell; that was a job for detectives much more astute than him when they questioned him.

He unlocked the squad car and held on to the prisoner as he opened the door. He guided Mitchell's head to duck beneath the archway and secured him to the seat with the belt once he was inside. Slamming the back door of the squad car closed, Jackson went to the boot to get an evidence tube for the weapon that was still lying on the bathroom floor and then locked the vehicle as he headed inside.

He got to the panel for the alarm on the wall in the hallway and punched the only code Kaidence had divulged to him – her birthday backwards – into the keypad and hoped it was the right one. When he pressed the enter button the house fell silent and he breathed a sigh of relief.

When the alarm stopped sounding out around the house Louisa was relieved, but her ears continued to ring. It would be a while before they returned to normal after how long the alarm had been going, and that was evident when she didn't hear Jackson enter.

'I guessed the code.' He pointed out the obvious, approaching the knife and resting the tube on the floor while he put on the latex gloves he plucked from his pocket. He gestured to Kaidence. 'How is she?'

'Not good,' Louisa replied, still applying pressure to her wound. 'She's losing a lot of blood and she hasn't regained consciousness.'

He picked up the weapon before containing it to transport back to the station and then removed the gloves. 'I'll see if I can get an ETA on the ambo,' he said, leaving the room with the evidence.

Jackson had barely departed when Kaidence sputtered back to life, staining her bottom lip with blood. She gasped for breath; this pain was more than she could handle. She struggled to fill her lungs with air. But she didn't open her eyes, she couldn't. Taking one final gulp of oxygen, she passed out again.

When the ambulance arrived, her breathing was shallow, and her pulse was faint. The paramedics got straight to work doing their best to repair the damage so that she'd make it to the hospital for more extensive treatment, but they couldn't stop the bleeding or bring her round. They wasted no time getting her to the bus. Her condition was critical, and Jackson was worried enough that he had dialled the number he had for her sister before the ambulance put on their lights and sirens and left.

Meredith was at home feeding her son, like every weekday morning since she'd had him. She hadn't seen or heard from her sister since the weekend and figured that if she was needed, Kaidence would reach out. She hadn't. She'd respected her sibling's obvious need for space, as much as it went against her every instinct.

She removed the bottle from Justin's mouth and her mobile phone started to ring from its position on the dining table. The identity of the number meant nothing to her; still she answered it, leaving her son in his bouncer as she took his bottle to the sink.

'Is this Meredith Tate?' a voice at the other end asked.

She stopped moving. 'It is. Who's this?'

'It's Officer Chase, I'm ringing about your sister.'

Meredith's heart jumped into her mouth. 'Oh my God, is she okay?'

'She's on her way to the hospital.'

'Why? What happened?'

'Her ex-boyfriend broke into her house and attacked her.'

'My God, how serious is it?'

'I'm not going to lie to you; it looks bad. I advise you to get to Good Hope as quickly as possible.'

'Yes, okay. I'll get in the car now.' She started to panic. 'Thank you.'

Hanging up without waiting for a goodbye, Meredith immediately selected her husband's number and hit the loudspeaker button as she placed her phone on the dining table so she could get her son ready for a trip to the hospital.

Her worst fears had been realised. Although her sister had assured her of her safety with the extra measures she'd put in place, she had been subjected to more violence at the hands of her ex. The officer hadn't gone into the details of how serious her injuries were but given that she'd been prompted to get to the hospital as quickly as possible, she could only assume that they were life-threatening.

Jackson had headed inside the unsecured house while he was on the phone and immediately after hanging up, he took a deep breath. Seeing Kaidence's life in such danger had thrown him off balance, especially when he had been sure she was safest in the house she'd made more secure. Closing his eyes, he leaned against the interior wall at the bottom of the stairs. It killed him to act professionally, when all he wanted to do was exact his own kind of revenge on Mitchell, but his body cam footage meant he had to restrain himself. The minute he'd heard Kaidence scream, he had known he was too late to protect her from her ex, just as he had been the night she'd been forced to stab him. He was frustrated – since they'd met, he'd vowed to keep her safe and he was continually failing her.

Louisa walked inside the house to find her dejected colleague being held up by the wall and immediately knew how he felt; she shared a measure of his emotions too.

'Are you okay?' she asked, alerting him to her presence.

He opened his eyes and unstuck his back from the interior support. 'Yeah,' he responded with a sigh. 'I just hate getting here too late.'

'Me too, but it's the nature of the beast.'

'Well, I wish the beast would fuck off.'

The language he used surprised her. It was rare she heard him swear, so she knew he was truly upset.

'He's breached the conditions of his bail now, so he'll be kept locked up until the trial. Plus, he'll be charged with this offence too.'

'How much use is that if she's dead?'

'You can't think like that. You've got to put on your copper head now.'

'It's best if I don't focus on it,' he said. 'Let's just wait for the PCSOs to get here to babysit the property so we can transport him to custody.'

Kaidence lay in the hospital bed barely conscious. She was trapped in her mind. She could feel the pain in her abdomen. It was almost unbearable, but she had to endure it in silence. She couldn't communicate with anyone. She couldn't move her body and her mouth and eyes wouldn't open no matter how much she willed them to.

The pain was unlike anything she'd ever felt, and she'd had plenty of injuries to compare the agony against. Still, she'd never been stabbed before. She didn't know the nature of the damage he'd done; she just knew its placement was specific for a reason, even if that reason was only known to Mitchell.

She was in and out of consciousness, but even when she was conscious, she couldn't convey the anguish she was in. It frustrated her because she could hear the doctors standing by her bed; she just couldn't interact with them.

And just like that, she passed out again.

———

Meredith rushed into the emergency department, straight to the desk to ask about her sister. She'd managed to get a hold of her husband, who had met her at the hospital and taken over the care of their son before she went running inside. She had just one purpose in mind: to get to Kaidence. She still had no idea what her injuries were, and she didn't want to waste any time in case they were as serious as Jackson had intimated.

'I'm looking for my sister. The police told me she'd been brought in,' she said, speaking as speedily as she'd travelled to get there from the car.

'What's her name?' the receptionist enquired.

'Kaidence Hadaway.'

The desk nurse tapped at the keyboard on the computer and it seemed to take her forever to respond. 'She's been stabilised and taken straight into surgery.'

'What are her injuries? I've been given no information.'

She consulted the monitor. 'She was stabbed in the abdomen, which has caused some damage to her reproductive organs.'

Meredith frowned. 'What does that mean?'

'Unfortunately, all I can tell you is what the computer says, I don't know anything more than that.'

'I know, I'm sorry. But she's my sister and I don't know what's going on.'

Suddenly a voice came over her shoulder. 'Meredith?'

She spun on her heel to face the speaker and when she saw the man stood there in grey scrubs, it took her a while to recognise him. She frowned. 'Matthew?'

'Yes, hi,' he said, leaning forward to embrace her in a small momentary hug. 'Is everything okay?'

Her hand reached up to rub her forehead. 'The police rang and told me Kaidence had been attacked by her ex-boyfriend and it was serious. But all this woman can tell me is that she's in surgery because she was stabbed in the abdomen, which has caused damage to some organs,' she explained, flustered.

'I'm consulting in A&E at the minute, but I haven't seen her come through,' he said as he thought on his feet. 'Would you be okay to wait here? I'll rush up to the operating theatre to see if I can get some more information for you.'

Meredith nodded. 'Yes, thank you.'

The white tiles of the en suite were covered in Kaidence's blood; it resembled the scene of a murder. There were traces of splattered blood on the surrounding porcelain and some trickling down the wall where she'd been stood when she'd received the potentially deadly blow, but most of it was pooled at the foot of the toilet, where she'd been slumped fighting for her life.

As soon as he'd pulled himself together enough to focus on the end game, Jackson had rung for a repairman. Then he called to inform the detective dealing with her case of the new development, and she'd asked him to document the scene. There was no telling how long it would take the forensics team to get there, and she wanted to see the evidence of the attack that she'd be adding to the investigation against Mitchell as soon as possible.

Jackson had used his superiority to task Louisa with fulfilling Carla's request while he supervised the repairman, who had shown up in double quick time to secure the damage to the back of the property. He'd cancelled the request for the community support officers to attend the scene, simply because by the time they got there, the repairs would be finished.

'Are you done?' Jackson asked, appearing in the doorway of the bathroom.

She nodded. 'I've photographed every inch of this room,' she said from her crouched position by the lavatory. 'Her phone's here, shall I leave it?'

'Is it interfering with the crime scene?'

She shook her head. 'No, it's tucked behind the toilet. There's no blood evidence anywhere near it.'

He thought about it longer than he should have done. 'It's part of the crime scene, leave it where it is.'

Louisa pushed up with her legs and stood. 'She lost a lot of blood.'

He raised his eyebrows to agree with her. 'The forensics will come in and mark it out before photographing it themselves, so try not to disturb anything as you walk out.'

'It was hard enough getting in without doing that,' she countered, widening her stride to step in a clean space to exit.

'I'll just grab her keys from downstairs, then I'll reset the alarm and we'll transport Mitchell to custody.'

The waiting room was a lonely place when you were anticipating news of a loved one, no matter how many people were in the same position. The wait made time for imagining the worst, and Meredith couldn't help but do that. She felt completely alone as she waited for the return of the only staff member she knew. Cole had texted to let her know he'd returned home with their son because he felt the hospital was no place for a six-month-old baby to be, and she knew he was right. Plus, it meant she could focus her attention on the family member most in need.

She seemed to be sat there for hours before Matthew appeared in front of her again. But when she registered his face, she shot up to her feet. 'Anything?'

He took a deep breath. 'She had significant trauma to her reproductive system, and they couldn't stop the bleeding, which is why she required surgery. I don't know the extent of the damage, but they had to operate in order to save her life.'

'Could she die?' she asked, tearing up.

He reached out to place his hands on her upper arms. 'She has the best surgeons working to make sure that doesn't happen.'

All of sudden Meredith began to sob. 'I can't lose her too, Mattie. She's all I've got left.'

He pulled her into a hug to comfort her. 'I promise you; she is in excellent hands.'

Meredith stepped backwards, out of his arms. It was rare for her to show any emotions, so her breakdown made her feel vulnerable. But the shock of imagining her life without her sister in it had provoked a strong response that she hadn't been able to withhold.

'Do you need me to call someone to be here with you?' Matthew asked as she wiped the tears from her cheeks.

She shook her head. 'My husband took our son home. There is no one else.'

'Sorry, I didn't mean to...'

'It's okay.' She excused his apology. 'You know, since Mom and Dad have been gone, Kaidence and I have been closer than we ever were growing up. If I lose her...'

'Think positive, okay?' he encouraged, rubbing the top of her arm.

She sniffed back her tears. 'Do you know how long it's going to take?'

'There's no set time for this kind of thing. It'll take as long as it needs to take.'

'Then I better make myself comfortable.' She sighed.

'As soon as I hear anything I'll come and let you know. But I've got to get back to work.'

She nodded. 'Yes, of course, you go. We'll catch up later.'

―――――――――

By the time Mitchell had been booked into custody and Jackson had filled out his reports for the shift it was closer to lunchtime than their clocking-off time. They'd been due to finish work when the call had come through about the break-in at Kaidence's address, so it had prolonged the shift. Once he was showered and changed into his civilian clothing, he was ready to drop by the hospital, using the keys as an excuse to check in on the woman he'd been consumed with helping for the past three months.

He walked into the accident and emergency department hoping to get some information about the patient, but it was going to be difficult because he wasn't wearing his uniform. It was as he approached the nurse behind the closed-off desk that he heard a woman's voice call out his name across the waiting area. He turned around to find Meredith advancing towards him.

'How is she?'

She took a deep breath. 'She's in surgery, so I've been sat here, waiting.'

'Have you been given any indication what her injuries are?'

'Yes – Matthew saw me here so he went up to the operating theatre to find out what he could. She's got trauma to her reproductive system, but I don't know the extent.' She sighed and was suddenly hit with clarity. 'You were there, what happened?'

He took a deep breath. 'When we got to her, she'd already been stabbed.'

'Where?'

'It was low down in her abdomen.'

'Mattie said it caused damage to her reproductive system, so that would make sense.'

He dropped his head and rubbed at his forehead. 'That's what he meant.'

'He who?'

He looked up at her, not realising he had spoken out loud. 'Mitchell.'

'Did he say something?'

It was part of an investigation, so he was obligated not to divulge any information. But she was the only family Kaidence had and he wasn't there in an official capacity, so he gave himself permission to share details he shouldn't have. 'He implied that it would be hard for her to have children. He even said he'd researched where to stab her.'

'So, he intentionally tried to take away her ability to have a family? Why would he do that?'

He shrugged. 'He probably knows how important it is to her and it'll have everything to do with him maintaining some control over her even though she's finally away from him.'

'Oh my God,' she repeated over and over as she lowered herself onto a seat, putting her head in her hands. 'How am I going to help her through mourning for a life she can't have?'

'Hey, we don't know yet that he took that away from her,' he said, sitting beside her.

'Of course he has. They've been operating on her for ages now, there is no other explanation for that,' she said, looking him the eye. 'I don't know how she'll get over this.'

CHAPTER TWENTY-SIX

The two of them sat waiting in the area for an hour. Neither of them dared to leave for even a moment in case they missed a doctor looking for them. They hadn't spoken. They had nothing to say. Instead they sat in silence awaiting any news.

Meredith shifted in her seat with a sigh and checked the watch on her wrist. She had been running over the scenario of her sister being unable to have children in her head for as long as she'd been there, because she needed to. She had to prepare for how she would help Kaidence come to terms with the news Meredith was certain she would receive, especially after Jackson had confided in her what Mitchell had said when he'd been arrested.

All Kaidence ever wanted was to have a family, so she wasn't going to take it well. Meredith hoped she was wrong; that somehow the doctors could save her life and leave her with the ability to bear children. But she suspected that Mitchell had taken that from her as a parting gift. So she had to be the strength Kaidence would need.

Jackson watched Meredith shift in her chair and knew she felt as restless as he did. But they were both helpless to do anything other than wait. He bolted up to his feet, needing to do something other than sit, and walked over to the window to look out. There was nothing beyond it except the car park, but he couldn't stare at the floor any more. He stood there, watching any cars or people that went by for a minute before turning back to the room.

'What the hell is taking so long?' he asked rhetorically, vocalising his frustrations. He didn't shout because losing his temper wasn't going to help.

Meredith sighed. 'I guess it's really serious if it's taking this long.'

It was only a short time later when Matthew walked into the waiting area. Despite having been working, he'd kept updated on any developments with Kaidence. It was now hours since she'd been admitted to the hospital and he was finally able to give her sister some kind of update. He scanned the room for the woman he was looking for and, as he made his way over, he saw a man approach from the window.

'She's out of surgery,' the doctor told her as she stood to receive the news. 'She's not out of the woods yet, but I can take you to see her.'

Meredith turned to collect her coat and handbag from the floor to follow him, not really paying attention to whether Jackson was behind them.

'Is this your husband?' Matthew asked, not recognising the man with her.

'No, this is Jackson, one of the officers who's been helping Kaidence,' she replied.

'We've actually met,' the officer divulged. 'I was with Kaidence when she came in for treatment on her dislocated shoulder.'

'Sorry, I didn't recognise you out of your uniform,' Matthew said with a smile. However, he remembered the hostility he had been met with. It made him suspect that the officer's interest in his friend was more than professional. Still, he brushed it off.

Although he knew what to expect when he walked into her private hospital room, Matthew's breath caught in his throat when he actually saw her. He'd seen patients lying unconscious in their beds before, but it was completely different to see someone he knew, and had once been so close to, look so defenceless. It was a shock to his system, and it upset him. He'd never seen her so vulnerable, not even when he'd first learned of the abuse. But he forced down his distress for the sake of her sister. He knew Kaidence was in exactly the right place to receive the kind of care she needed.

Over his shoulder, he heard Meredith suck in a breath of shock as she lay her eyes on her sister. 'Oh my God,' she whispered in horror as her eyes welled up.

Matthew spun on the spot in an aim to be the comfort the older sibling needed but once he was facing her, he realised he was too late. Jackson already had his arm around her, supporting her as she threatened to collapse.

Feeling the strength of his support, Meredith turned to bury her face in his chest as she began to sob and Jackson instinctively wrapped his arms around her, to be the comfort she needed even though he was just as shaken by the image of Kaidence. Meredith was shaking, but tried her best to pull herself together; however, every time she felt strong enough to deal with the situation, the waterworks started again. It took a while for her to snap out of it, to finally be able to look at her sister without breaking down, although the tears still streamed down her face.

'She's still sleeping off the effects of the anaesthesia, so she won't be awake for a while. But you can sit with her,' Matthew said, once her emotions were under control.

Meredith slowly approached her sister's bedside. 'Umm, did they fix...' she started to ask, but she couldn't bring herself to finish the question as she placed a tentative hand on top of Kaidence's.

'I don't know, M,' he said with a shake of his head. 'I'm sure a doctor will brief you on the details when he does his rounds.'

Meredith lowered herself to the seat at the side of the bed, gripping her sister's hand. 'How long will she be like this?'

'There's no telling,' he answered regretfully.

'Okay, thanks Mattie,' she said, knowing he had to return to work.

'I'll pop back up after my shift to see if you've heard anything and if you're still waiting, I'll see what I can find out for you.'

She nodded as he left the room and Jackson approached the other side of the bed. 'She looks so fragile,' she said, trying to wipe away the tears that kept coming.

Jackson didn't respond. He was processing the image in front of him. He knew it wasn't helpful to her sister, but he couldn't pull himself out of it. Kaidence looked like she was asleep, but there were obvious signs of distress behind her closed eyes. He could see slight creases on her brow that Meredith couldn't from her position, and there was the odd occasion when he saw movement behind her eyelids.

He reached out to touch her hand, but before he achieved skin-to-skin contact, he slowly retracted his hand. She wasn't his girlfriend, he had to remember that. Despite his feelings for her, they were only friends. In fact, there was more distance between them now than there ever had been. He had noticed the detachment creeping in from the minute she'd got away from Mitchell and initially he'd put it down to the *no contact* clause he'd put on their relationship, but the phone calls were sparse too. The only times he'd seen her was in his professional capacity and the only real conversations they had were about Mitchell. So maybe now was the time he faced the reality that she was just a woman he'd helped reach her objective, which was his job, and she just didn't need him any longer.

'I think I'll get going,' he said, starting to walk towards the door.

'No, please...' Meredith implored, shooting to her feet. 'Don't leave me here on my own. I don't know what I'm going to say to her when she wakes up... *if* she wakes up.'

He couldn't refuse a damsel in distress. 'She's going to wake up,' he tried to assure her; the way Louisa had for him the last time Kaidence was lying unconscious in a hospital bed.

The hours of waiting had shifted to Kaidence's bedside. But being in the private room with her somehow made it easier for them to take mini breaks, whether it was to the bathroom or to get food and a drink. It was mainly Jackson who left, though; Meredith could only bring herself to do so when she was desperate for the toilet.

They'd been sat in silence for the most part, just waiting for the patient to wake up, which she showed no signs of doing. A nurse or two had popped in to check her vitals, and Meredith had tried to find out what the outcome was of the surgery, but they knew nothing, or they did and weren't sharing. She had simply been told to wait for the doctor. But waiting always felt like a lifetime when you wanted something.

Kaidence edged towards consciousness and the intensity of the pain came with it. A scream developed in her throat but didn't quite make it out of her mouth as she clenched her fist. She wanted to force her eyes to open but the agony radiating from her stomach was the only thing she could focus on. It was like the worst wake-up call she'd ever been privy to.

Meredith drew in a sharp breath, which in the silence of the room sounded loud. 'She squeezed my hand.'

Jackson got closer to the bed. 'Are you sure?'

'Yes, yes,' she responded, standing up. 'I think she's waking up.'

The effects of the trauma were immediately evident as Kaidence opened her eyes with an agonising moan, which made her sibling erupt into another breakdown. Watching her sister writhe on the mattress in distress was too much for Meredith to handle and she covered her face to disguise the upset she felt.

It was Jackson who was the first one to speak as he got close enough for Kaidence to hear his voice. He leaned over her head and stroked her hair in an aim to calm her down. 'Kaidence, you've had surgery, try not to move because you'll rip out your stitches.'

Her mouth opened and she let out another, quieter, moan. 'It... hurts,' she managed between struggling breaths.

'I'll get a nurse,' he said, rushing from the room.

'Jackson?' she mumbled.

Meredith wiped the tears from her eyes and cheeks. 'He's gone to get a nurse,' she said, announcing her presence.

Kaidence forced her eyes to focus. 'Mimi?'

Her sister forced a smile to her lips. 'Hey.'

'You're... here.'

'Where else would I be?' Meredith asked, reaching out to hold her sister's hand.

It was a few minutes later when Jackson returned to the room with a man in tow. The medical professional immediately approached his patient and checked her pulse by applying two fingers to her wrist.

'Hello Kaidence, can you tell me on a scale of one to ten what your pain level is?' the nurse asked in a slightly elevated decibel level.

'Ten,' she managed.

He reached out and pressed the small pump on the bed next to her, to administer a small dose of morphine to take the edge off her pain. He then lifted the button, so it was in her line of vision.

'This is a morphine pump; it will release controlled amounts of the drug to help with the pain. But there's a limit to how much you can have, so only use it if you absolutely have to,' he explained.

Kaidence nodded as best she could from her position. 'Okay.'

'You should start to feel better soon.'

'Thank you.'

As the nurse was about to make his way out of the room, Meredith stopped him. 'Will the doctor be in to see her now that she's awake?'

He nodded. 'He'll be in to see her when he does his rounds.'

'And when will that be?'

'In a couple of hours.'

Meredith smiled. 'Thank you.'

Kaidence lay in the hospital bed barely conscious. Her stomach hurt, even though her wound had been treated and dressed. Her body ached. It felt like there was someone inside trying to break out, making her sure her life was slipping away with each breath she took. Suddenly the pain increased and her breathing became shallow; she tried to move to make herself comfortable, but it was no use. She held in the scream on her lips. She just had to make it until the drugs got into her system. But every second felt like hours.

Lying there on the bed, her head and shoulders propped up by pillows, Kaidence replayed what had happened in her head. She could see Mitchell inches in front of her brandishing a knife and she remembered wondering whether he'd taken it from her kitchen or brought it with him. In an instant she had felt the steel sink into her body, and she had heard a scream. She hadn't realised right away that it was coming from her. But she had known it wasn't Mitchell, because he had had a smile on his face.

Her eyesight had blurred as the intensity of the pain took precedence over all of her senses. She vaguely remembered covering her wound with her hands to slow the bleeding and simultaneously feeling her legs giving way beneath her as she saw two blurry figures entering the room she was in. Subconsciously, she had known that help had arrived, so she had succumbed to the blackout that beckoned. When she'd momentarily come to, there were doctors standing over her. But she'd quickly lost her battle to the pain again.

Now she was trying to work out what damage had been done to her without having any information at all, except the location of the searing pain. The intensity was starting to get duller, which meant the drugs had begun to kick in, although its position was burned into her memory. It was low and close to her navel, so it wasn't designed to hit any of her vital organs, although she knew there was a reason for its specificity.

She wanted to stop her brain, to scream at it to be quiet, but it shouted thought after thought. She closed her eyes, willing herself to concentrate on something else, when she heard her sister's voice softly enquire whether she was okay. Her concentration on the pain had made her forget about her visitors.

Her eyes shot open and tears rolled down her face towards the bed. 'Mimi,' she sobbed.

Her sister grabbed her hand. 'I'm here.'

'What's going on? What did he do to me?' she asked, wanting to know the extent of her injury.

'We don't know yet. We're waiting for the doctor,' Meredith replied, disinclined to prepare her for the news she might get in case the doctors had performed a miracle.

'But it's serious, isn't it?'

Meredith couldn't bring herself to speak as her emotions created a lump in her throat. All she could muster was a nod of her head.

'Am I going to die?' Kaidence asked, starting to panic.

Seeing the older woman freeze once the question had passed her sister's lips, Jackson knew he had to field the answer she needed. He wanted to be honest with her, least of all because he always had been, but he didn't know how she was going to take it. He cleared his throat. 'Your friend Matthew said that you weren't out of the woods yet.'

The familiar slow trickle of tears leaked from her eyes. 'So I *could* die?'

Although he was shouldering the same worry, he feigned a smile as he leaned closer to her. 'I've already told you: you're made of tougher stuff than the average woman.'

'Then why am I so scared?' she asked as a sob escaped into the room.

'It's okay. Meredith and I are here and we're not going anywhere until you're ready to go home,' he said, projecting as much confidence as he could.

The pain took it out of her and, not long after she'd woken up, Kaidence gave in to the tiredness. She needed to recharge, to somehow process the danger her life was still in and shut off the torment rolling around in her head. Closing her eyes was the only way to do that and thankfully the morphine gave her enough relief to drift into a slumber.

Realising she was asleep, Jackson forced her unwilling sister to go to the hospital cafeteria for a break, while he sat on watch duty and waited for the doctor they had been anticipating all day. She'd made him promise to call her phone and hang up the minute the doctor stepped into the room so she could rush back to be there for Kaidence.

Kaidence looked so peaceful, which was such a contrast to the agony she'd been in when she'd first opened her eyes, and this helped to settle him. He sat down in the vacant seat by her bedside and watched the gentle rise and fall of her chest. He had been awake for over twenty-two hours and he was starting to feel it. The adrenaline he'd been running on since he'd heard the call over the radio had waned by the time he got to the hospital after his shift, so now he was running on empty. It was fatal for him to get comfortable; still he did it as he stifled a yawn.

Taking the chance afforded her, Meredith stepped outside the building and walked away from the crowd of smokers just beyond the doors so she could call Cole to give him an update. It was much quieter among the parked cars, which would afford her privacy when she inevitably broke down. She wasn't usually run by her emotions but the idea of losing her sister made her unable to be practical like she ordinarily would be, because they were all each other had left of the family they grew up in.

As soon as the call connected, Cole spoke. 'How is she?'

She felt the familiar sting of tears hit her eyes. 'In a lot of pain if the screams were anything to go by when she woke up. But the drugs must've kicked in because she's fallen asleep. There's still no sign of the doctor yet but Jackson's sitting with her while I take a break.'

'The copper? What's he doing there?'

'He was on call and came to the hospital after his shift to check on her.'

'He's really invested in her case, isn't he?'

His question made her laugh. 'I think it's her that he's invested in.'

'That's unethical.'

'Maybe, but it's human nature,' she countered. 'How's Justin?'

She missed him. Since he'd been born, she hadn't spent more than a few hours away from him but today had already been all of that time combined.

'He's a little cranky, but we're managing without you. So don't worry,' he answered.

It was quiet as Kaidence came to. She scanned the room as best she could for any signs of the visitors who'd been there when she'd fallen asleep and only found Jackson, grabbing forty winks in the chair by her bedside. There was no trace of her sister, which made her wonder if she'd imagined her being there. It wasn't until she saw the coat draped over the back of the seat the officer was on that she realised she hadn't.

There was just a dull ache where she'd been stabbed and she thought she would be able to move, but the pull of her skin when she tried made her stop. She blindly searched the mattress around her with her hand for the controls to the bed, hoping they were as easy to access as her medicine pump, and instead found the nurse call button. She pushed it, not wanting to wake the sleeping man for assistance. She knew the chances were that he hadn't slept since his shift, so she wanted to give him some time to recharge.

Kaidence smiled as she noticed a nurse enter. 'I can't find the bed controls and I'd like to sit up,' she explained. 'Can you help me?'

The man approached her position. 'Sure, I can let you up a little but any more than that could pull your stitches.'

'That's fine, I just want to be able to see more than the ceiling.'

'How's the pain now?' he asked, elevating the top of the bed slightly.

'Better,' she replied. 'Do you know what they did during my surgery?'

'I don't. But the doctor has just started his rounds, so he'll be in soon to tell you what happened.'

'Thank you.' She expressed her gratitude as a familiar face appeared in the doorway to her room.

Matthew smiled, happy to see his childhood friend awake and seemingly in no pain, 'Hey you. It's good to see you conscious. How are you feeling?'

'Like I've used up two of my nine lives,' she responded with a slight smile as the nurse slipped out of the door.

'Well, do me a favour: don't test to see if you've got any more,' her sister said as she returned to the room.

'I second that motion,' Jackson stated, waking to the new voices.

'Sorry Jackson. I didn't want to wake you,' Kaidence said regretfully.

He stood up. 'Ah, it's okay. I never needed more than half an hour to recharge,' he declared, stretching out the kinks threatening his neck.

'Has the doctor been around yet?' her childhood friend asked.

'The nurse said he's just starting his rounds, so he should be here soon,' Kaidence replied.

'We've been hearing that claim all day,' Jackson muttered.

It was a couple of minutes later when the doctor made his entrance, but when he did the two men excused themselves in order to give the women privacy. It made Meredith anxious. She didn't want to be the only visitor in the room to hear the reality of what they were dealing with, especially when she had an inkling of the news Kaidence was about to get; she had no idea how she was going to see her sister through it.

Kaidence had been a mother in her mind long before she'd been old enough to physically get pregnant. It was the only occupation she cared to have in her life. It's why she'd chosen to work with children and why she was so good with her nephew. So to have that lifelong dream taken from her by the man she'd finally had the strength to walk away from was going to make it more devastating than if it was because of any other reason.

The medical terminology the doctor used did nothing to ease Kaidence's fear. She didn't understand half of the words coming out of his mouth, but she knew it translated to bad news. The damage to her reproductive system had been severe, that's why they'd had to operate. It was when he declared that in order to save her life, they had to perform a hysterectomy that the implications really started to sink in. She knew what that meant and suddenly, the reason for Mitchell's knife placement made perfect sense.

She could see the doctor's lips moving as he continued to talk but she couldn't hear any sound; it was as if someone had turned down the volume so that she could process the news she'd been given. *Unable to have children.* Those were the only words she could concentrate on. They repeated in her head like a record on loop. What was her life worth if she wasn't able to have kids? She might as well be dead. It was the only thing she had ever wanted, since she'd been little. Distraught didn't even begin to cover her emotions.

She took erratic shallow breaths, unable to give her body the oxygen it needed as tears erupted from her eyes. She could feel her heart break as all her hopes for the future shattered into a million pieces and then suddenly, like a switch had been flicked, her breathing returned to normal.

Every woman took having kids for granted, except those who couldn't. Those women were the ones who were tormented every day by thoughts of something they could have done differently in order to get a different outcome. The chances were that nothing they could have done would have changed a thing...but she had been pregnant once. She'd known what it was like to feel the exhilaration of growing a person inside her, albeit briefly, and Mitchell had taken that away from her too.

If she'd have just left him sooner. If she had let him know that she wasn't going to tolerate his treatment of her. Or maybe she would have needed to go back to the beginning and never have given him a roof over his head.

All the wishing and hindsight was for nought now; the damage had been done, and it was going to affect her for the rest of her life.

Meredith's heart broke for her younger sibling, knowing what having children would have meant to her. She'd already had so many obstacles to endure and here was another one. She had expected Kaidence's reaction to be different; for her to scream and shout her protest against accepting it but, apart from the barrage of silent tears that flowed down her face, Kaidence was calm. It unsettled her.

As the doctor took his leave, Meredith reached out for her hand. 'Are you okay?' she asked, thinking how ridiculous a question it was after she'd uttered it.

Kaidence released the breath she'd been holding since hearing the update on her health and a sob came with it. 'Don't...I can't...' she said, keeping her eyes fixed on the hands in her lap.

***

Jackson stood alone outside the private hospital room looking in. He could tell by the energy beyond the door that the information they'd received wasn't good, which made him hesitant to enter. It seemed that her sister's worst fears had been realised, and they needed some time to process what they'd heard.

He didn't want to intrude. Besides, he had no idea what he was going to say to her. If Mitchell's statement was anything to go by, Kaidence was going to be distraught, just like Meredith had expected.

It wouldn't be so bad if he had back-up in the form of Matthew, but her childhood friend had followed after the doctor so he could find out the details of the surgery in case he had to explain anything they had questions about. So Jackson stood, just beyond the door, wishing he could muster the courage to comfort her. But what did you say to someone who'd had a future she pictured snatched from her by a man who didn't know her worth?

The room blurred around her as Kaidence struggled to control the thoughts in her head. She would never be hopeful that a missed period meant she'd fallen pregnant, or have morning sickness that sometimes lasted all day, and she wouldn't ever know the feel of the butterfly movement her sister once described when she was carrying Justin. Those were all things she didn't have a chance to experience before Mitchell had beaten her last pregnancy out of her. She was destined to be alone for the rest of her life, because no man was going to want her once he found out she was sterile.

She angrily wiped at her face to remove the evidence of her weakness from it. She had picked him and had stayed after he hit her for the first time. So what did she expect? It was all her fault. She deserved everything she had got for being weak and stupid.

'Kiki,' her sister said for no reason other than sensing the change in her demeanour. It wasn't until her younger sibling made eye contact that she saw the coldness her eyes emitted. 'Oh, Kiki,' she said, her face shrouded in sympathy.

'What are you doing here, Meredith?' Kaidence countered venomously, sniffing back her emotions.

She frowned. 'You're my family. Where else am I going to be?'

'You've got a son at home. Go. Be there for him. I don't need you.'

'You don't mean that,' Meredith said, choking back the tears that again threatened to spill from her eyes.

'Yes, I do. There's no point in you being here now. I don't need you any more, not that you were there when I did. So, go. Leave me alone.' She spat out the words, their volume slightly elevated. 'You're good at that.'

'Kaidence...' Meredith started, but her sister didn't let her protest the accusations.

'For fuck sake Meredith, GO!' she shouted, easily heard by Jackson, who paced the hall outside. 'It's too late to be my big sister now! Get the fuck out of my room! I. Don't. Want. You. Here!'

Meredith hadn't got the energy to stand her ground. She knew the hateful things her sister was sprouting were designed to push her away. She didn't mean them. She was externalising her pain and hitting out because she was grieving. But that didn't stop them hurting. She wanted to stand there, to let Kaidence take her frustrations out on her, and use her as a punching bag; she just didn't have the mental strength to take the punches.

Stung by her sister's words, and afraid of the feelings of guilt they threatened to raise in her, Meredith felt anger build. 'You want me gone?' she returned, at the same level she'd been spoken to. 'Because if I walk out of that door, I'm not coming back.'

Kaidence leaned towards her. 'Of course, because walking away is what you're good at.'

Meredith hesitated, seeing the agony in her sister's eyes, agony she could never fully comprehend. She wanted so desperately to be able to comfort her, but she was tired and not equipped to be abused without taking her words to heart. Silently, tears spilled onto her cheeks and slowly trickled down her face. She hated that she couldn't help her.

'Oh good, here come the waterworks!' her sister announced nastily to the surrounding private rooms. 'I don't know why *you're* crying, *I'm* the one in the hospital bed.'

Meredith spun to collect her bag and coat from the chair behind her. She hated that she had to walk away, but if she stayed, she would inevitably say something she couldn't come back from.

Jackson had heard enough. He knew what Kaidence was doing and why, but he couldn't stand by idly and do nothing. Stepping inside the room, he saw the tears running down Meredith's face as she barged past him on her way out.

He turned his attention to the patient. 'Do you feel better now?' he questioned harshly, giving her a taste of tough love.

She cut her eyes at him. 'I've got no idea why you're even here. Is it because we kissed once, when I was vulnerable? Newsflash, Jackson: I'm nothing to you, or are helpless damsels your thing?'

He took a few steps closer to her and gestured with his hand as if asking for more. 'Keep going, get it out of your system, because you can't hurt me the way you hurt your sister.'

'No? Is that because you're incapable of owning up to how you actually feel and hide behind that fucking badge instead?'

'It's my job on the line. You know that.'

'God forbid you put yourself out there, eh, Jacko?'

'Keep it coming, Kaidence, give it your best shot,' he said, his deep voice making him sound more like a police officer than he ever had before as he came closer still.

'You know, this is all your fault; if you hadn't made me believe I was worth more, I would've stayed with him so he wouldn't have come after me.'

'No, but you'd be dead by now.'

'Did you miss the fact that I've just been in fucking surgery for hours because I almost died?' she hissed. 'You've done a bang-up job keeping me safe, officer!'

'Have you got anything else you want to hit me with? Because I can stand here all night taking whatever you throw at me.'

'That's because you don't have a life outside of your uniform. You've hitched yourself to my wagon and I can't get fucking rid of you!'

'I'm here for you, just like your sister was.'

'Well, more fool you both,' she said, losing the urge to fight.

He stood by her side and placed an arm around her shoulders in an attempt to pull her into a hug. He knew she wanted to feel something other than anger and he had to force her to give in to it. She pushed against his chest as she finally broke down, but he was steadfast, circling her in his arms the best he could from his angle. Again, she averted his affection. With clenched fists, she hit him on the torso once or twice before they gained momentum. He allowed her a few blows, as she worked her frustration out of her system, while she cried. Eventually, she lost steam, enabling him to envelop her in an embrace which she didn't resist. Instead she collapsed against his frame, taking the comfort he provided.

Detective Carla Jensen slid the SD card that she'd found in the back of the journal she'd already read into the slot in her work laptop. She had been through all of the photos once, but she wanted to save a copy of them all for her files and view them again in case there was something she'd missed.

Opening the directory, she noticed a file format that was different to the others. It was a video. Reaching for the headphones she kept in the top drawer of her desk, she plugged them into the audio jack on the computer and put the ear buds in as she double-clicked the MPEG.

'My name is Kaidence Hadaway. The date is January seventeenth, two-thou-

sand and sixteen, and I'm documenting my injuries on film because I can't write an account of the abuse I suffered at the hands of my live-in boyfriend last night,' she said, waving a hand over her face to draw attention to the swelling of her eye and the purple bruising on her jawline. 'I made the mistake of putting lumpy gravy over his roast dinner and he drilled into me with his fists, again,' she continued as tears started to stream down her face. 'The reason I can't write is because when he kicked me in the jaw while I was down on the floor, I called out for him to stop and held up my hand to enforce it. So, he stamped on it.' She held up the battered body part to get it on camera too. 'They're getting worse and I don't know how to stop him before he puts me in hospital or the morgue. I want to tell someone, but, how can I? They can't help. I've got to try not to trigger him, except I don't know I have until he corrects me,' she said, breaking down. It was a few minutes later before she pulled herself together and reached out to stop recording.

Carla closed the window and removed the earpieces with a sigh as she threw herself against the back of her seat. She despised violent offenders, and Mitchell was the worst she'd seen for a while. It made her determined to see him locked up for the things he'd done. His most recent attack was just the evidence she needed to prove Kaidence hadn't been the instigator of the incident she'd been brought in to investigate.

Sitting in the canteen nursing a cup of coffee, decaffeinated because she was breast feeding, Meredith stared at the surface of the liquid. She hoped that the time it took her to drink it and eat the pre-made sandwich from the fridge was long enough for her sister to snap out of the terrible mood she was in. But she wasn't hungry; the fight with Kaidence had seen to that.

Although she knew the things Kaidence had said were designed to hurt her and get a reaction, there was a ring of truth to them. She had promised to support Kaidence through getting back to the woman she used to be once she left Mitchell, and she hadn't – despite showing up most days to visit. They had avoided the topic of the abuse and Meredith knew that was likely because her sister wanted to save her from the gory details. And if she was completely honest, she didn't want them. She was happy in her ignorance. It was enough to have seen the cuts and bruises Kaidence had when she showed up on her doorstep, without knowing the particulars of each time he had put his hands on her.

She hadn't been there for her, and she felt guilty about it now she had been called out on it. Yet, at the time, she had made excuses for her lack of participation by convincing herself that the two hours she spent with her sister every other day was enough; that her sister would ask if she needed her, when Meredith had known that she wouldn't. Not asking for help was a family trait. Even when they lost their parents, neither of them would admit to needing the other. Kaidence had turned to alcohol and Meredith had channelled her grief into an obsession with getting pregnant. They had come so far since losing them, but yet, so many things hadn't changed.

Meredith wished more than ever that their parents were alive because they'd know how to help Kaidence. Their mother had a knack of saying exactly what someone needed to hear to make them feel better, and their father would always be on hand to give them a strong shoulder to rely on. With them gone, the responsibility fell to her.

She pushed the chair out from under her as she got to her feet. Putting the strap of her handbag over her shoulder and draping her coat over her forearm, Meredith picked up the half-filled reinforced paper cup and the sandwich she hadn't opened and discarded them into the bin on her way back to the ward Kaidence was on. It was time to show her sister that she wasn't giving up on her.

CHAPTER TWENTY-SEVEN

The heavy rain hit the window of Kaidence's room, distracting her from the noise on the ward beyond her door as she lay ignoring the television in the corner. She'd been lying there for two weeks, feeling like the walls of her private room were closing in, preventing her from filling her lungs with air as she mourned the life she had imagined having.

She had been gradually weaned off the morphine and given tramadol instead, which she needed less and less with every day that passed. Now, she was only taking over-the-counter painkillers, something she could be doing at home. But the doctors had refused to discharge her unless she had someone to take care of her and, even though Meredith had offered, Kaidence didn't relish the idea of sharing a roof with her again so soon after the last time. So she begrudgingly stopped pushing to be released, despite her status changing to stable after a second surgery a week ago.

Every day Meredith would visit with Kaidence's nephew to try and keep her spirits up, but seeing the six-month-old she loved so much only served as a reminder of what she couldn't have, and she slipped a little further into her depression. She just wanted to be left alone, even though she was grateful her sister was still talking to her, considering her behaviour in the aftermath of her hysterectomy. They hadn't officially made up, because no one had apologised; they just didn't mention it and carried on as normal.

Jackson's visits on the other hand had been sporadic since her meltdown. He was only dropping in for a few minutes at a time before making his excuses to leave and, although he had assured her it wasn't because of the vile diatribe she had subjected him to post surgery, she was sure that was exactly the reason he'd put so much distance between them.

The person she saw the most of was Matthew. His job gave him the advantage of being able to pop in on his breaks and lunch hours. She even saw him on his days off, which had given him the chance to fill in the gaps since he left to further his career.

He talked about the life he had had once she wasn't in it any more, and about the relationships he'd started and failed at. He regaled her with stories about studying in London and the many cooking disasters he'd had while he was living alone, which made her laugh, even though laughing was the last thing she felt like doing in her sadness. She even managed a smile when he reminisced about the old days. But Kaidence was more guarded, and didn't do much talking. Even now that she *could* talk about the last year, she chose not to. Although she'd known Matthew all of her life, it had been a long time since they were close, so it was going to take a while to build the kind of trust they once had. She didn't want him to know the woman she had been moulded into for the sake of her own survival because she didn't plan on being that woman for long; she preferred to be remembered the way she had been before her life turned to shit. So instead, she told him about being a teacher because it was the only thing she had in her life, beside family. She just hoped she would be able to get back to it once she was out of hospital.

It was only seven o'clock, but the winter night meant it was already dark outside, which tempted Kaidence to turn off the television and get comfortable against the propped-up pillows to see if she could drift off to sleep. But as the thought crossed her mind, she had the urge to go to the toilet.

With more effort than it should have taken, she pushed the blankets from her body and swung her legs off the edge of the bed. The ten steps to the bathroom always took it out of her, because although she was virtually fixed on the outside, the inside was still repairing so it hurt when she moved.

Taking a minute to prepare for the pain she was about to be subjected to, she hoisted herself up off the mattress, so she was standing. She turned slowly on the spot to face the door and took a deep breath as she reached out to the overbed table for extra support and stepped forward. Carefully, she planted her foot down and steadied herself before taking the others unaided until she got to the door.

Leaning against the frame to catch her breath, Kaidence contemplated her next move. She had always taken the opportunity having visitors afforded her and asked them to help her get to the bathroom, but she hadn't had any today, so this was the first time she had to do it herself. She cursed her need to be independent when she knew she shouldn't, and thought about turning back so she could buzz for a nurse, but she had come this far and didn't have the energy to retrace her steps. As she braced for her next move, she heard Matthew's voice amid the voices of the ward.

'Hey, what are you doing out of bed?' he asked, rushing to her aid.

'I need the toilet,' she broadcasted to anyone in earshot.

'That's what the button on your bed is for,' he said, slipping an arm under hers to take her weight and guide her the rest of the way.

Kaidence, feeling the strength in his support, leaned against Matthew as they moved towards the bathroom only a few feet from her door.

The sound of the rain hitting the windscreen as Jackson drove the squad car towards base served as the perfect buffer to the silence they'd been riding around in all night. Although it wasn't an awkward silence, it was a rarity that only happened when he had something on his mind. Louisa only knew that it was Kaidence who was on his mind because he didn't go out of his way to talk about her like he used to, and would limit his response when she was brought up in conversation.

Louisa had been riding shotgun all shift, waiting for an opening to question him about Kaidence because although she hadn't had time to visit, she knew Jackson was still going to the hospital, albeit briefly.

'How's Kaidence?' she asked, biting the bullet, keeping her eyes peeled on their surroundings.

'I don't know,' he replied, concentrating on the road.

'Didn't you go to the hospital last night?'

'No.'

His one-word response made Louisa frown. 'Why not?'

'She doesn't need me there.'

'Has *she* said that or are *you* just making assumptions?'

'Meredith and that doctor are there for her.'

'So, you're just going to stop visiting? Because she's going to notice.'

'It'll make the next part easier,' he stated coldly.

She whipped her head around to look at him. 'What's the next part?'

'Me stepping back. It's time I started to act professionally.'

He had been thinking about it for a while and their distance had given him clarity. Essentially all she was to him was a case, and somewhere in the middle her kind nature had caused him to think there was more between them. He realised now that there wasn't. But her thirst for company, and the loneliness he refused to admit to, meant he'd mistaken it for something deeper. There was no doubting that he found her attractive and they got on well, but there was a difference between being friends and being in love.

'That hasn't bothered you before,' she countered, not really meaning it to come out so callously.

He was just as abrupt with his reply. 'She wasn't under investigation before.'

'It's not like you were sleeping with her.'

'But I've stayed overnight. It doesn't matter how innocent it was, that it was per her request, or even that I slept in a different room, it looks unethical and I can't afford for her to be called into question so close to getting Mitchell convicted.'

The fact was that a few days before, Jackson had stopped in to see Kaidence and when he got to her doorway, he had paused at the sight of her laughing with Matthew. It immediately made him question his place in her life now that he'd completed his objective. The chances were that he would just serve as a reminder of the violence she'd escaped, and he didn't want that. He realised in that moment that he had to step aside if she was going to get on with her life, so he backed out of the room before he was seen. The odds were that it would be a long time until she was over the trauma of the last year, but it was going to take even longer if he held onto her when he knew it was his own history with abuse that had been the reason that he'd fought so hard for her. Those were his own demons to deal with, and it was unfair to expect her to shoulder the responsibility for his happiness. He had to let her go.

Helping Kaidence back to bed, Matthew watched as she tried to get comfortable and he couldn't help but feel sorry for her, even though he knew that would be the last thing she'd want. He'd never seen her spirits so low and he felt powerless to help lift them. There wasn't going to be any way to make her feel better about having the rest of her life snatched away; he just had to be there with her.

Although they were the same age, she had always been the mature one when they were growing up. She was often the conscience he needed when his friends suggested anything that could get him into trouble, the voice of reason when he talked about giving up on his career choice, and she was even on hand to give him advice on girls whenever he wanted it. So now it was his turn to be there for her, to listen if she chose to offload her frustrations. But so far, he'd been the one who'd done most of the talking.

The room was silent, except for the television, as Matthew watched

Kaidence rest her weary battered body against the pillows. It was hard for him to separate who she was now from the girl he'd grown up loving, because he hadn't been around for the transition. But there was no mistaking that she was different.

'You look tired,' Kaidence said, tucking her hand under her cheek as she lay facing her visitor, who sat in the chair.

He smiled. 'I was on the early shift. But I managed a couple of hours sleep in the break room before I came up here.'

'You should have gone home to bed instead of coming to see me,' she said softly.

'Is my company really that bad?' he asked playfully.

But she didn't have the same humorous tone he was trying to draw out when she responded. 'No, but I'm not going anywhere, and you need your sleep.'

'It's only just past seven; if I'd have gone to bed, I would only have had my regular five hours and then been up all night. This way, I get to stay up past a toddler's bedtime and get up with the sun in the morning,' he responded with the same seriousness.

'Still, you've visited me every day, you deserve time off for good behaviour.'

'I don't want it; I like being here with you. But maybe you should do the talking tonight?' he said, stifling a yawn.

'What do you want me to talk about?' she questioned, hoping he didn't want full transparency about her relationship with Mitchell. The idea of describing all the horrible things she had gone through filled her with dread, and she didn't have the mental bravery to relive them, just for him to look at her differently.

He kept the eye contact they'd maintained at the top of the conversation. 'Just, tell me something real.'

Kaidence searched her mind for anything she could give him but all she could think about was the reason she was there and, out of nowhere, she became emotional. 'I'm going to be alone for the rest of my life,' she blurted out as tears broke the dam and spilled onto her cheeks.

He shifted to the edge of his seat and reached out for her hand. 'Hey, come on, you don't know that.'

'Of course I do, and if you're honest, you do too,' she said, wiping her feelings from her face with her free hand as she sat up. Despite her movement, she kept hold of his hand. 'I'm not exactly ready to start dating yet, but when I am, I know that no man is going to want to be with me once he finds out I can't have a baby.'

'If he loves you, that won't matter because there are so many other ways for you to be a family.'

'God Matt, I wish I could believe that. But you still remember the girl I was. Any guy I meet in the future will get this damaged version of her.'

'Her heart is just as big, and her life means just as much,' he said, squeezing her hand slightly to reinforce his statement.

'I've missed you so much,' she said, as more tears escaped her eyes.

He shifted to sit on her bed and pulled her to his chest for a hug. 'I'm sorry I haven't been around. I promise to be a better friend this time.'

But Matthew wanted to be much more than that now. Being away from her for so long, he had been convinced his feelings had gradually changed, but the moment he saw her in the emergency room, it was clear they had only been dormant. He wanted to confess how he felt about her and let her know he was an option for her future. But she wasn't ready, at least not yet, and the last thing he wanted was to put any undue pressure on her.

So, instead, he held her as she cried.

As Jackson walked in the back door of the station behind Louisa, Carla intercepted him on his way to the break room. Having read the diary entries in each of Kaidence's books, she knew he hadn't been completely honest the first time they'd spoken so she wanted to give him a chance to come clean; if he was caught off guard, he wouldn't have time to prepare a rehearsed response.

As they reached her desk, Carla silently gestured to the chair opposite hers for him to sit in. 'I'm going to ask you again about your relationship with Kaidence Hadaway,' she announced, taking her seat. 'And before you lie to me for a second time, you should know I've read every journal we found in the safe – including the one she had on you. So I suggest full transparency, no matter how damaging you think it might be.'

Jackson sighed; he had been afraid of this. 'We were friends.'

'Before the incident?'

He nodded. 'Before this incident, but not before the burglary that I was canvassing about.'

She checked her records. 'So you've been friends for three months?' He simply nodded in response. 'And is that all you were?'

'Absolutely,' he countered with a hitch in his voice.

Carla propped her elbows on her desk and leaned towards him. 'I need to know everything Chase, *everything*.'

'The lines blurred a little,' he surrendered.

'How much is a little?'

'We talked regularly on the phone, we spent time together socially and she met my family.'

'What aren't you telling me?' she asked, leaning back against her chair.

'We kissed, but it was only once and that's all it was – one kiss.'

Carla lightly rubbed at her brow in frustration. 'Fuck Jackson, that means you can't testify on her behalf in court.'

'It was nothing, and no one knows about it,' he insisted, knowing how important it was for him to give evidence.

'I still can't let you testify. If anyone found out, it could seriously compromise the case.' She was adamant. 'I'm sorry Jackson, but we're going to have to do this with your partner instead.'

'Are we interrupting?' a familiar voice asked from the doorway of the room where Matthew was still holding Kaidence.

She had stopped crying a while ago, but had continued to hold on to him, and he didn't have the heart to break the connection when it was obvious that she needed the release. He didn't know how long they'd been sat like that, but the sound of his mother's voice forced them apart.

'Mum?' Matthew quizzed as he stood up. 'What are you doing here?'

'Well, when you told us at dinner last night that our little candy was in hospital, we had to come and see her,' she answered as she and her husband approached them.

Seeing the faces of the two people who reminded her of her parents made Kaidence emotional again. She was sick of crying, but the response was involuntary. She had always considered them family and, with their only son in London, she had stepped into the role of substitute daughter without any effort at all. But shortly after she had lost her mum and dad, her weekly visits had stopped because they were a reminder of the two people she didn't have any more. It was too painful to be around them then, and although it had been six years since her loss, she had never got back in touch. She felt guilty now about not providing them with an explanation for cutting them out of her life, but at the time the heavy drinking she'd subjected herself to helped her to justify it.

Their time apart didn't seem to have dampened how they felt about her because as Barbara Logan reached her bedside, she embraced her in a way only a mother could.

Barbara was a petite woman, barely standing five-foot two in height, with kind hazel eyes and short blonde hair. She had always commanded the respect of everyone around her without demanding it, while still being warm and friendly. She wore her heart on her sleeve, giving her love unconditionally – a trait she shared with her son – and despite their previous distance, Kaidence felt her love for her.

'How are you doing, baby girl?' she asked, holding Kaidence for longer than she usually would, silently relaying how much she'd been missed.

'I am better for seeing you,' Kaidence responded, sniffing back her tears.

Pulling away, Barbara reached out to dry her eyes with her thumb. 'It's okay darling, we're here now. We'll see you right.'

'I really messed up this time, Mum. I think it's going to take more than a hug to set me right,' Kaidence said. Referring to her as Mum was something she'd always done, even when her own was still alive, and that was something she wasn't about to change.

'Ah honey, that waste of air was just a pit stop on the road to the man you're meant to end up with.'

'I wish I could believe that, but I don't think he exists.'

'Oh, he exists.'

'I don't suppose you happen to know who he is, do you?' Kaidence asked with a smile.

'I've known that since you were little, and he's been right by your side for just as long,' Barbara replied, before using her forefinger to point at Kaidence, then her son. 'There's a reason that you two have found each other again.'

A frown formed on Kaidence's brow. 'You think we'll end up together?'

Barbara nodded. 'Baby girl, anyone who saw you both growing up knows that.'

'Did you know that?' Kaidence asked Matthew with a laugh, expecting him to find the same delight in his mother's sentence as she did.

But his face showed no sign of amusement. This was his chance to be honest with her without piling on any pressure. After all, she had asked the question; he was just taking advantage of the opportunity it afforded him.

'I've known since I got to London,' he said with a wink. 'But I can wait for you for as long as it takes; I'm not going anywhere, Sprinkles.'

His confession threw her a little. Not because she hadn't considered him an option while they were growing up, but because neither of them had acknowledged the possibility to each other, even when the other kids would tease them about it. Hearing him admit it was something he wanted gave her a sliver of hope that she wouldn't end up alone.

'Please tell me you're not still using those horrible nicknames,' Derek Logan said, speaking for the first time since they'd arrived.

Matthew was more like his father in his appearance, sharing his strong jawline, eye colour and height, although the older man seemed to have lost a few centimetres in height with advancing age. Derek gave affection in a different way to his wife. Instead of showing it with a hug, he would give words of wisdom, and he wasn't shy about offering his opinion either, regardless of whether he was asked for it or not. So it wasn't a surprise to hear his feelings about their pet names; he had expressed it many times.

'Do you even remember where that nickname came from?' Kaidence asked her once best friend.

'Yes. You decided I needed a nickname after hearing Tommy Walker calling his girlfriend Muffin, and came up with Cupcake, for God knows what reason. Then after about a week, I tried to come up with one for you that was equally annoying. Except I couldn't come up with one, which led to you suggesting Sprinkles, because – in your words – there wasn't one without the other.'

'Ah, that's right. It was either Sprinkles or Icing and I did not want to go through life with that legacy.'

'God, if I'd have known that, you would've been going by the latter for sure,' he announced with a laugh.

Barbara smiled. 'It's like you two haven't spent a minute apart.'

'Well, my hospital sentence has given us the chance to get reacquainted,' the patient responded, resuming her sullen state. 'But I can't wait to get home.'

'Is there no word about when that'll be?'

She shook her head. 'If I'd just had the hysterectomy, the doctor would have released me last week. But because I had to have a second surgery and haven't got anyone at home, he's not comfortable letting me go.'

'Couldn't you stay with your sister?'

'She's offered, but she's got the baby now and I don't want to burden her. Besides, I stayed with her for a week about a month ago, and it ended with us fighting so I prefer not to go through that again.'

'I don't think it'll be much longer,' Matthew offered. 'She is improving by the day; she just needs to be able to make it ten steps to the toilet alone.'

'*She* made it seven steps to the door, which should count for something,' Kaidence said, showing obvious displeasure at being spoken about like she wasn't in the room.

'And how long did it take you to get there?'

'I took my time because I didn't want to overdo it. I *am* recovering from surgery.'

Although the humour of their conversation lingered, the air in the room felt heavy. Kaidence wanted to believe that their years apart hadn't had any effect on her relationship with his parents, but she knew it was implausible to expect they'd fall back into it as if no time had passed. Besides, the way she had just stopped her visits to them was less than they deserved, because they had always been there for her, especially when her own parents had died. She knew eventually she would have to give them an explanation, but now didn't seem like the right time.

It was Barbara who broke the silence that had fallen on the room. 'So, I've got to ask how on earth you wound up in this mess?'

'Mum!' Matthew objected to her question. 'I don't think she wants to talk about it.'

He was right; Kaidence didn't want to talk about it, even though it was always at the forefront of her mind. But not talking about it was exactly what had got her in this state, and she couldn't deny Barbara the particulars because she was the only mother she had left. She reached out to grab Matthew's hand, and silently relayed the message that it was okay.

'I had a lapse of judgement and let my boyfriend move in before I really knew him,' she said, boiling it down to a nutshell. 'It wasn't long after that that he showed his true colours.'

The older woman reached out to stroke her hair. 'Why didn't you leave before he put you in here?'

Kaidence took a deep breath. 'My self-worth has taken a severe hit since I lost mum and dad.'

'Where were your friends?'

'Those went along the way too. The only person I didn't alienate was Meredith, and I couldn't tell her.'

'But she's family.'

Kaidence nodded. 'I was too scared that she was going to confront said waste of air and get the same treatment I had. I couldn't do that to her. He was my mistake.'

'All that matters now is that you're away from him,' Derek said, putting an end to the conversation. 'It's time to start repairing – yourself and the relationships that suffered because of him.'

***

The hour that Matthew's parents were there seemed to fly by and before Kaidence was ready for it, they were saying goodbye with a promise not to leave it so long until they saw each other again.

It was just the two of them left, and Matthew showed no signs of going anywhere as he scooted the chair closer to her bed. He didn't want to leave her yet, because although he'd been there for an hour, he felt like they hadn't had any time together, and his employment at the hospital afforded him the luxury of staying past visiting hours.

'Shouldn't you be going too?' Kaidence asked, resting against the pillows, exhausted from entertaining.

'Are you tired?' he countered.

'No, I slept most of the day.' She told a half truth.

'Then why are you trying to get rid of me?' he asked with a smile.

'I'm not, but I know you haven't had a lot of sleep, and don't you have to work tomorrow?'

He shook his head. 'Actually, I've got a couple of weeks annual leave, which got me to thinking...' he said, scooting to the edge of his seat. 'Maybe I could spring you out of this place.'

She frowned. 'And how would you do that?'

'Well, I could stay with you while you recover.'

'At my house?'

Matthew nodded. 'If that's okay with you.'

His proposal was appealing; it was ten days before Christmas, and she didn't want to spend the holiday in hospital, despite being in no frame of mind to celebrate.

Kaidence pushed herself up from the bed. 'Do you think the doctors would go for that?' she asked, getting her hopes up.

'I can be here when the doctor does his rounds in the morning and we can ask. Anything to get you out of here, right?'

'I'm not one to look a gift horse in the mouth, but won't it drive you crazy living with me?'

'Are you kidding? We had so much fun the last time.'

She laughed, remembering the holiday. 'We were fifteen and with our parents, in another country.'

'True, but it would only be for a couple of weeks and the most important thing is that you'd be at home.'

'You'd really do that for me? Haven't you got plans for your time off?'

'I'm a doctor, I rarely have a life outside of this hospital, so spending that time with you is as much for me as it is for you.'

Kaidence's brow furrowed suspiciously. 'Have you purposely booked time off so that I could be released?'

He countered with a shrug. 'I've accumulated some holiday that I haven't been taking, and I thought this would be the best way to use it.'

'Well, if we're going to be living together temporarily, can I ask you about what you said earlier; when your parents were here?' Kaidence asked, bringing up the subject it had been hard to keep on the back-burner until they were alone.

Matthew had been holding his breath since his parents had left. She was always going to bring up the truth he'd confessed to; it was a part of who she was, and he was glad it hadn't changed, even if it meant he had to awkwardly stumble through an explanation.

'I know you're going through a lot right now, so I wasn't going to tell you, but then you asked, and I wanted to be honest.'

'Honest about what exactly?'

'I loved you once, and when you're ready, I'd like the chance to get to know you again and see where we end up.'

So far as he could tell from the time they'd already spent together, the foundation of who she had been growing up was still beneath the baggage she'd obtained since he'd left for London.

Her eyes softened as she realised what he was implying. 'I'd like that.'

CHAPTER TWENTY-EIGHT

The grey clouds in the sky threatened more of the rain that had been falling for most of the week. There was a freshness in the atmosphere even though the moisture lingered above them as Kaidence stepped outside the hospital for the first time since her arrival two weeks ago and filled her lungs with natural air. Matthew had managed to convince her doctor that she would do her best healing at home, with him taking care of her, but he had insisted she used a wheelchair to get to the car. Kaidence had been tempted to refuse, regardless of her laboured movement, however she didn't want the privilege of being discharged to be snatched from her so had agreed to be pushed to freedom. Her eagerness to get home was still apparent, though, when Matthew had barely stopped the chair beside his car and she tried to stand.

'Would you wait until I put on the damn brake?' he scolded her with playful amusement as he reached down to do exactly that.

'I can't help wanting to get out of here before they change their minds,' she said, clutching her bag of belongings on her lap.

'Relax, you're free, they can't change their minds,' he stated, taking her bag and putting it on the back seat.

'I've spent way too much of the last two months in this hospital, I just want to see the back of it.' She watched him close the rear door and open the one at the front.

'Well, injuring yourself launching out of the wheelchair isn't going to help with that,' he countered, lifting her to her feet. He gave her the support she needed to take the few steps from the back of the vehicle to the front passenger's side and once she was safely inside, Kaidence instinctively reached up for her seatbelt.

'I'm just going to take this back inside,' he said, taking hold of the wheel-chair. 'Don't leave without me.'

Knowing he was trying to be funny, she mocked a laugh as he closed the door and watched him make his way back inside. The jeans he wore hung off his hips slightly so that they clung to the shape of his curvaceous buttocks, the way all good denim should. *Damn he's got a great arse*, she thought, checking him out. There was no denying he was more aesthetically pleasing than he used to be, even though she'd always found him attractive. However, she'd forgotten just how much she enjoyed ogling his backside whenever he walked away from her, and this was a great refresher. It wasn't until he was on his way back that she realised that as sexy as he was in his scrubs, he was even sexier in his everyday clothes, and she imagined he looked better still out of them. She felt her cheeks flush as he climbed in behind the wheel and started the engine.

Looking across at her before disengaging the handbrake, Matthew noticed the colour on her face. 'It looks like the fresh air is already doing you some good.'

She giggled. 'Oh, it's not just the air.'

Her response made Matthew frown. 'Did I miss something while I was gone?'

'No, nothing.' She saved herself the explanation.

It had been a long time since she had looked at him that way and she knew it had been sparked by his confession the day before. Still, it had made her consider him as a suitor, sooner than she had expected to. She would be safe with him; she knew that, and perhaps that was the true draw of her attraction. But she wasn't about to rush into anything. She owed it to him, and herself, to be sure it was right before she potentially ruined years of friendship.

Meredith stood hugging herself on her sister's doorstep, waiting for her to get home. She had used her emergency key once she'd been told Kaidence was being released so that she could clean up after the police. She didn't want her sibling to walk into a scene still plastered in her blood because it was bound to trigger her to relive the horrific attack. Of course, Meredith knew that she'd be carrying around the trauma of what had happened anyway, but she wanted to minimise the damage.

She had dropped by the supermarket on her way to get some fresh shopping, and had discarded the out-of-date food in the fridge before cracking open a few windows to air the house. She had initially concentrated her cleaning on the bathroom, but once that was spotless, she changed the linens on Kaidence's bed and did some basic housework, so that it was one less thing for Kaidence to worry about as she recuperated.

She had closed up the windows as soon as she was finished preparing the house for its owner's return and had proceeded to make a stew for their dinner. But since receiving the text from Matthew saying they had left the hospital, Meredith had been looking out of the door for any signs of his car. She'd only made the move outside when she was sure they weren't far away. She just wished she'd had the foresight to stay inside, because even with her coat on, she was freezing.

Despite it being midday, the police station was eerily quiet as Carla made her way to the locker room to find Jackson. She had checked his rota and his tour had come to an end on the hour; she was hoping to catch up with him before he went home. She was still angry about the secrecy regarding his relationship with Kaidence, because it meant she had to find another way to introduce his testimony without him being called as a witness.

'Chase!' she called around the door to the men's locker room before waiting outside, pressed up against the wall.

Moments later he appeared in jeans and a plain black T-shirt. 'Detective,' he greeted her as he corrected his posture, standing with his shoulders back and overlapping his hands behind his back, much as he would have if he was being addressed by a superior in the army.

She encouraged him to relax with a downward wave of her hand. 'At ease soldier.' He loosened up and she got to the point of hunting him down. 'Did you know that Kaidence Hadaway was being released today?'

'No, I haven't seen or spoke to her for days.'

She seemed to accept his words despite his past deception. 'Ah, well, we'll give her a couple of days and then I want to arrange for her to be brought in so I can get a statement.'

He nodded to agree to her plan as she turned to walk away, and he headed back inside the locker room to continue his mission to get home.

His superior's question made him realise just how distant he was from the woman who just a few weeks ago he was spending all his available free time with. He knew it was his doing, but that didn't make it hurt any less. He missed her; it would be ridiculous for him not to, given how close they'd come to be in such a short space of time, but the bond he'd forged with her was a means to an end, and they'd reached that end.

As Matthew pulled into her street, Kaidence immediately spotted her sister and she sighed. Even despite the temperature of the winter afternoon, she was on the doorstep waiting, and Kaidence felt the joy of her homecoming evaporate. She should have been happy to see her; to be thankful Meredith had made the effort to offer her support, but she just wanted to be home. She didn't want to have to entertain, and that's what she felt she was doing lately: forcing herself to plaster a smile on her face when all she wanted to do was cry. She couldn't help feeling that her sister expected her to suck it up and get on with her life, putting her twenty-seven months with Mitchell behind her, but the scars were too deep, and she didn't think Meredith understood that.

She didn't mean her disappointment to show, though she didn't do very well to contain it when she vocalised her thoughts. 'What is she doing outside?'

'She's probably just looking forward to you coming home,' Matthew responded.

Kaidence sighed inwardly. She had forgotten how much her best friend used to defend her sister while they were growing up; it had been the subject of many arguments between them then, and she shouldn't have been surprised that it was an aspect of who he had been that hadn't changed.

'Well, she should have waited for me to get there before she showed up,' she spat out bitterly.

'You're really going to hold it against her that she didn't wait for you to get back before she came over?' he questioned. 'She probably just wanted to air out the place because it's been shut up for a fortnight.'

'You're right. I just wanted to get settled before I had visitors,' Kaidence acquiesced, as he pulled up on the double driveway beside her vehicle.

'She's not just anybody, Sprinkles; she's your sister,' he said, putting on the handbrake and turning off the engine.

Her eye roll went unseen as they simultaneously removed their seatbelts. His neutral stance was frustrating, especially when she just wanted an ear to bitch and moan into.

'Stay right there until I get to your side,' he insisted, hesitating before he moved.

Kaidence looked down at her attire. The grey tracksuit bottoms and oversized hoodie Matthew had purchased on his way to fetch her were loose fitting so they didn't interfere with her wound and offered more warmth than any clothes she had in her wardrobe, but she hated being seen out of her house in them because they were so different to anything she usually wore. She knew the neighbours who made it their business to report the comings and goings of everyone on the street would revel when they gossiped about her homecoming, and their disgust at her outfit would be top of the list, despite her just getting out of hospital. But she had no control over that; and at least she was home.

She was relieved to be out of hospital, even though she would be laid up doing exactly the same thing no matter where she was. There was something about being in your own space that helped the healing in a way the sterile environment of a hospital couldn't, and she was looking forward to being in her own bed.

Getting out of the passenger's side of the four by four was easier than the climb into it had been, because she had the advantage of being able to slide out of the seat. She wasn't very graceful in her landing, but Matthew was there to catch her and prevent her from collapsing in a heap at his feet. He moved quickly to her side to slip an arm around her, holding his other hand out in front of her hip to provide extra support for her to move. She slipped her hand into his, feeling the weakness caused by days laid up in bed more keenly in her legs than she had in her trips to the toilet, so was thankful for the assistance the man supplied, even if it meant she had to admit to needing it.

She was barely a step from the car when Meredith rushed to offer a hand, but Kaidence was less grateful for her help. 'I've got it,' she insisted, covering Matthew's hand on her hip with her own and gingerly stepping forward. She moved faster than her body was ready for, but it still took longer for her to get inside than she wanted.

'Where are we going?' Matthew asked as they stepped over the threshold.

'Upstairs, first door on the left,' Meredith responded, carrying the bag of her sister's belongings that she'd retrieved from the back seat.

Kaidence forced her eyes up from the floor towards the staircase and suddenly it was hard to breathe. She felt dizzy and sick. Her heart pounded in her chest loud enough that the world must have been able to hear it. She had wanted to be at home so badly that she wasn't prepared for the effect it would have on her. 'Just get me to the settee,' she managed through thick breaths.

'You should be in bed,' her sister insisted.

Matthew felt her weight increase and recognised her symptoms as a panic attack. 'Concentrate on regulating your breathing,' he advised. 'In through your nose, out through your mouth. It'll pass.'

She did her best to follow his instructions, but she wasn't strong enough to stay upright and stumbled into him. 'I need to get off my feet.'

Without wavering, he scooped her up in his arms. 'I've got you.'

'Let's get her upstairs,' Meredith urged him.

'No!' the younger woman bellowed, finding the strength in her voice that she didn't have in her legs. 'I can't lie in that bed staring at the bathroom where he attacked me, Mimi, I just can't. I thought I could, but being back in this house...' She stopped talking, unable to put her feelings into words.

'Then let's get you back to the car; you can come to stay with me,' the older sibling suggested.

'No offence Mimi, but I can't live with you again. I need my own space.'

'Then do you have another bedroom in this place?' Matthew asked, preventing an argument before it had a chance to start.

'Upstairs and round to the right.'

Meredith sighed and pointed to the door on their left. 'Take her to the settee. I need to change the sheets before she gets in it,' she said, making her way to the upper level.

Doing as he was told, the doctor effortlessly carried his friend into the room that had been pointed out to him and gently placed her on the three-seater opposite the television.

Kaidence grimaced, despite the care he'd taken to lower her gently; she felt a twang of pain from the surgery and adjusted her position to try to get comfortable.

Matthew hovered. 'What can I do to help?' he asked, feeling helpless as he watched her struggle.

'Can you get one of my pillows from my bed?'

He pointed towards the door. 'Up the stairs, first door on the left?'

She nodded. 'And while you're there, can you get me some pyjamas from the bottom drawer of my bedside table?'

'Pillow and pjs, got it,' he confirmed, swiftly leaving the room.

Now alone, Kaidence did her best to alter the way she sat so that the ache of her wound eased. She wanted to be able to spend her days on the settee and not confined to her bed, though she knew she probably should be in bed. She had been isolated enough over the past couple of weeks and if she had to lie in her bed, nothing would change. At least if she was sat in the main room of the house, she would have some company in the form of her new housemate.

'This house is beautiful,' Matthew said, returning to the room with the items she had requested and laying them down next to her.

'I know. It's a shame that I have to put it on the market,' she replied with a regretful sigh, placing the pillow behind her.

He frowned. 'Why do you have to do that?'

'Did you witness the panic attack I just had at the thought of going upstairs?' she asked rhetorically. 'I can't stay here.'

He exhaled. 'It's a pity. But it's understandable.'

She nodded her agreement. 'I loved this house when I bought it,' she said, looking around the room as though remembering back to the day that she'd moved in. 'The first time I walked in here, I saw kids running around being chased by the man I pledged to spend the rest of my life with and laughter bouncing off the walls constantly. But now all I see are the bad memories. So I can't stay here. I need to start over somewhere else; somewhere I can see my new future.'

'Well, we can sort that out while I'm here if you want to,' he offered.

'Sort what?' Meredith asked, returning to the room in time to hear the tail end of the conversation.

Kaidence sighed. 'Putting the house on the market.'

Meredith pointed to the floor. 'This house?' she asked, and frowned when her sibling nodded. 'But you love this house.'

'I do, but I have to leave it behind if I'm ever going to move on.'

'This isn't the first time he's hurt you and you've never talked about leaving before. What makes this time so different?'

Kaidence could see the look of horror on Matthew's face as the harshness of what her older sister had said sunk in. 'Because this was the first time that I truly felt like I was going to die,' she admitted, expecting the truth of her statement to resonate.

However, it didn't seem to. 'But he's being held on remand until the trial.'

Despite it being just a few weeks since she relayed how scared she had been at the thought of losing Kaidence, it was as though the minute Meredith knew the younger woman was going to be okay, she cast the incident – and all the circumstances of it – aside.

'That doesn't change the fact that it happened in this house, Mimi.'

'It means he won't be coming after you again.'

Shocked by the lack of compassion Meredith seemed to show for what had led to this point in her life, Kaidence looked over at Matthew for some indication as to which of them was being unreasonable, and the bewildered look he gave her sister was enough. 'Domestic violence isn't just physical though.'

'I'm not stupid; I know that.'

Matthew raised his eyebrows. 'Do you? Because it doesn't sound like it,' he said bluntly.

Meredith completely ignored him and continued, addressing her sister. 'I just don't understand why you want to sell your dream house when you know you're going to be safe here, especially with the security system you added.'

'A fat lot of good that security did me when Mitchell was sinking the blade into my gut.'

'He's caught now.'

'You're really not getting this are you?' the man between them observed.

'Let me try and explain this to you so that you get it; me staying in this house after that attack is like you keeping mum and dad's wrecked car in your back garden just so you can relive the pain of losing them. *Every. Single. Day.*' Kaidence added extra emphasis to the last three words. She didn't like to upset her sister by bringing up the painful memory of their parents passing, but she needed to make her understand.

But Meredith didn't counter with much of a reaction; just a simple shrug of her shoulders. 'Whatever you need to do,' she said, handing over the mobile phone she had found on the floor earlier that day. 'I only came in here to give you this. I put it on to charge not long after I got here.'

Taking it from her, Kaidence frowned, knowing the bathroom was the last place she had it. 'Did you clean?'

'I wasn't going to let you come home to a dirty house.'

As though the word sparked something in her, the patient looked hopefully at the doctor in the room. 'Can I take a bath?' she asked, getting excited by the thought.

He raised his eyebrows in her direction. 'Have you been able to have one yet?'

'No, but I couldn't get in the tub at the hospital and I really want to feel clean.' She growled up at the ceiling.

He approached and gestured for her to lift the oversized jumper to reveal the site of her wound so he could inspect it. He could tell by the colour of the surrounding tissue how tender it was; still, he gently ran his finger over her skin.

'These stitches don't dissolve. You have to keep them clean and dry until your doctor thinks it's time to remove them.'

Kaidence growled in frustration. 'You suck.'

'Can I give her a sponge bath?' Meredith suggested, knowing how important hygiene was to her sister.

'As long as you don't get that area wet,' he answered.

CHAPTER TWENTY-NINE

The decorated eight-foot-tall artificial Colorado spruce Christmas tree that took pride of place in the centre of the grand entrance hall made it easy for Kaidence to forget that she wouldn't be there at the start of the New Year – which was just twelve days away – and would be staying with Matthew temporarily. But she had been encouraged to dress the house for the festive period when she had contacted her estate agent to put it up for sale a few days ago. It was a marketing technique known as *staging*, which offered the buyer a glimpse of the property's potential and made for some great professional photographs for the website. It had worked, already generating a few offers despite how close it was to the holidays. So Kaidence wasted no time packing up whatever belongings weren't essential to everyday living and getting Matthew to take them to the family storage unit, to add to her parents' valuables that she and Meredith couldn't bring themselves to part with.

Kaidence's movement was still limited and her hysterectomy meant she wasn't allowed to lift anything, so Matthew had done the bulk of the work. But her refusal to be confined to her bed, sure that sitting upright on the settee was better for her recovery, had meant she had regained some strength in her legs during the five days since leaving the hospital. It made moving easier whenever it was required, although she was still a little unsteady when she used the stairs and needed Matthew's support.

Having his help was secondary to having his company, though, especially as they seemed to slot back into each other's lives with an ease they'd had since they were born. It was a welcomed change after being estranged for so many years, and having Matthew back in her life meant having his parents back too – even though it had been her fault that they'd lost touch in the first place.

'Are you going to be all right here on your own for a little while?' Matthew asked, appearing in the kitchen archway with a toolbox in his hand.

Kaidence, who had been sitting at the dining table for the better part of the day bubble-wrapping crockery and placing it into a box positioned on a chair by her side for convenience, frowned. 'Why? Where are you going?'

'Upstairs to fix the bathroom door,' he said, reminding her of the recommendations the estate agent had made so that she would be more likely to get the asking price.

Kaidence still hadn't been able to bring herself to go into the master bedroom, and she had tried. The morning after she was released, she attempted to get a clean set of clothes from her wardrobe but every time she got close to the door it would get hard to breathe, prompting another panic attack. Matthew had decided to move her belongings into the second ample-sized bedroom to save her the daily ordeal before taking the small box-room as his own.

'You didn't tell me you did DIY,' she said, taking the next plate from the pile and placing it atop the bubble wrap.

'You didn't ask.'

She smiled. 'I think I may have underestimated how handy you are to have around.'

'Well, wait until you've seen my handiwork before you jump to that conclusion,' he joked, as he disappeared from view.

Jackson knew she was home, though only because Carla had told him. He hadn't allowed himself to drive past before or after work, knowing he would make an excuse to knock on her door, and that would make it harder to keep his distance. But curiosity got the better of him when a week had almost passed, and he still hadn't heard from her – he had expected to hear from her, even if it was just a text. Now here he was, on his day off, giving himself permission to drive down her street.

The for-sale sign caught his eye immediately. He wasn't sure why he expected that she would stay in that house after all the horrible things that had happened there, but he hadn't considered the possibility of her leaving, especially now that Mitchell was being held on remand. He cruised to a stop at the kerb outside her property and, without giving it much thought, killed his engine. He couldn't just drive by. He had to speak to her.

The noise from the first floor was almost reason enough for Kaidence not to hear the knock on the front door. But when it came for a second time, loud and more determined, she knew she hadn't imagined it.

Gritting her teeth, she pushed the chair from under her as she got to her feet and took a second to steady herself before she shuffled her feet in the direction of the noise that came for a third time.

'I'm coming!' she shouted as loud as her lungs would allow.

She didn't give much thought to who she expected to see when she opened the door, but she would never have guessed it would be Jackson, because he had just stopped visiting with no explanation.

'You're selling up?' he asked, thumbing over his shoulder at the sign in the front garden, not bothering with a greeting first.

She turned on her heel, leaving it up to him to decide whether to follow her or not as she went back to what she was doing before he rudely interrupted. 'Hi Jackson, I'm fine. How are you?'

Taking the silent invitation she offered, the off-duty officer followed her to the kitchen, closing the front door behind him. 'You seem to be doing better,' he said, gesturing to her ease of movement.

She nodded as she sat back down, unsure why she was so angry that he was questioning her about leaving. 'I'm doing about as well as expected,' she continued, picking up a glass and wrapping it.

Even though it had only been a few weeks since they had spoken, the distance they had wanted to portray had developed without either of them realising it, and they had become strangers. But maybe that was because they weren't as close as they had convinced themselves they were.

The few boxes piled in the corners with the contents scrawled on the side in permanent marker confirmed her plans, but he needed to know how far she planned to go to escape the life she had when he'd happened upon her.

Jackson made his way to the bar stools in front of the breakfast bar, turned one to face her, and perched on the edge of the seat. It immediately drew her eyes to the taut straight-cut denim jeans that clung to the muscle of this thighs and she caught herself sneakily checking her own attire, which was a simple pair of leggings with a hoodie. She wasn't exactly dressed for visitors, opting instead for comfort.

'So, are you leaving?' he asked, breaking the awkward silence in the room by repeating his question.

'Yes Jackson, I'm leaving,' she confirmed abrasively. 'I can't stay in this house with these memories. Hell, I can't even sleep in my own room so the sooner I sell, the better.'

'Will you be staying around here?'

She shook her head. 'No, I need to start over somewhere new because the memories aren't just in this house; they're everywhere, and I'm not going to be able to heal until I get as far away from here as I can.'

Jackson knew her plan had always been to leave, but that was before Mitchell had put himself behind bars, so he had thought there was a chance she would stay. He searched for a way to keep the conversation going and the noise from above provided the perfect opportunity. 'Are you having some work done?'

'That's Matthew; he's fixing the bathroom door.'

'Oh. So, you kept in touch,' he said, recalling an earlier conversation they had had about Matthew.

'Yes well, he kept showing up in my hospital room and when he offered to spring me, I took him up on it. Otherwise I'd still be in there.'

He changed the subject, not wanting to engage in the verbal sparring match she was obviously spoiling for. 'Have you given your statement yet?'

'You'd know if you had bothered to text or visit during the last two weeks,' she spat out.

If her relationship with Mitchell had taught her anything it was not to pick a fight with anyone, because you never truly knew them. But she had always felt safe with Jackson – that she could say what she wanted, how she wanted, and he wouldn't hurt her.

He sighed. It looked like an argument was unavoidable. 'You know why I've been keeping my distance.'

He was right: she knew why they had originally made that decision. But she also knew that the circumstances behind that choice had changed, and the core of their relationship had always been honesty, so she didn't know when he'd become someone who would lie to her.

She nodded thoughtfully, taking a minute to consider leaving him blissfully unaware that she knew of the new information the investigating detectives had, but she was curious to see if he'd follow it up with another lie.

'That strategy made sense when Detective Jensen didn't know the truth about how much time we spent together, but she read all three of my journals; she told me when she returned them to me yesterday. It's the reason Louisa has to testify instead of you. So, do you want to give me the real reason I haven't seen you since my second surgery?'

He sighed, feeling a sinking feeling in his gut. He hated lying to her, but he had felt the need for it. 'I had to make a clean break.'

'Why?'

'Because holding on to whatever this was wasn't going to do either of us any good.'

'I thought that we were friends.'

'We are.'

'Friends don't just disappear out of each other's lives.'

He took a deep breath and rubbed at the tension starting to build on his brow. 'What do you want from me, Kaidence?'

'The truth.'

'The truth is that I would only serve as a reminder of all the horrible things you want to leave behind. So I thought I would make it easier.'

She sighed. 'You thought you would make it easier for you, without even thinking about how that decision would affect me.'

'You're right. But I got attached to you in a way that I shouldn't have allowed myself to.'

'You weren't the only one, Jackson.'

'Maybe not, but you were vulnerable; I knew better.'

Kaidence got to her feet and approached his position. 'You will *always* be the man who saved me,' she said, reaching out to grab his hand. 'And I know that somehow we translated that into something more than it was, but that's no reason for you to just walk out of my life. Your friendship helped to keep me alive and I'll be forever grateful to you for that.'

He affectionately rubbed his thumb along the back of her hand. 'I don't know how we stay friends after this.'

Kaidence released her hold on him and travelled the few steps back to her seat. 'It won't be that difficult. You won't even have to see me once I sell this place. But I would at least like to stay in touch.'

Jackson decided it was best to leave the possibility of contact lingering without fighting her on it, despite thinking it wasn't a good idea. 'Have you found somewhere to go yet?'

'I have been looking online and I've found a few possibilities. I think I've got a viewing in two days and if I like it, Matthew's going to put it in his name. That way nothing traces back to me.'

Mitchell didn't know about her connection to the doctor, so if he spent little to no time in prison, he – or anyone he knew – wouldn't be able to find her by searching for her name.

Recognising the voices downstairs as Kaidence and Jackson, Matthew made his way out of the bedroom. He eased the door into its frame, so as not to alert them to his movement, because the mention of his name piqued his interest and he intended to eavesdrop to see how the conversation progressed.

Matthew had soon realised how close his childhood friend had been to the officer from conversations they had about him. But he had taken a dislike to him, and he sensed the feeling was mutual. There was no real reason for it, beyond an unspoken competition for Kaidence's affection because of their shared interest in her.

His own fondness for her went back to their childhood, which had allowed him to know her prior to all the trauma in her life, but the fact he had left meant he had made way for Jackson, who knew her as the woman she was now, and that made him jealous because he had to get to know her again. He only wished he hadn't let their geographical distance come between them, because maybe his presence in her life would have been enough to deter Mitchell from treating her the way he had. Maybe. And that possibility would haunt him until he died.

The mention of the man she had known all her life made Jackson feel a twinge of jealousy. He could see the image of Matthew and Kaidence in her hospital room as clear as if he'd just witnessed it, and he couldn't help but feel bitter. He had been the one she confided in during the last three months. He'd given her the strength she didn't have to fight back and, when the time was right, he had helped her get away from Mitchell. But that hadn't stopped her replacing him.

'So, Matthew's been helping you out?' he asked, feigning interest.

She nodded. 'He's been a big help. We've practically packed up this whole house in the couple of days since I've been home.'

'So you'll be out of here before you know it then?' he asked with a twinge of sadness.

'Well, I'm not leaving until after the new year,' she informed him. 'We're having Christmas dinner here because I am determined to have at least one good memory in this house before I go.'

He couldn't help feeling insulted by her statement, because he had plenty of good memories attached to this house. But he chose not to pull her up on it. 'How are your nightmares?'

She sighed. 'I'm still having them, but now instead of stabbing him, I replay him stabbing me.'

'Have you thought any more about therapy?'

'I have, but I won't seek someone out until I get settled somewhere else, because I don't want to come back here for any appointments unless it's court related.'

Standing at the top of the stairs, Matthew waited for the opportune time to make his appearance and when she mentioned Christmas, he saw his chance to join them. It wasn't until he was halfway down the stairs that he heard Jackson mention her nightmares. He had been privy to those, having to enter her bedroom in the middle of the night when she screamed blue murder just so he could comfort her until she was calm enough to go back to sleep. They happened every night, and he was surprised to learn that the officer knew about them. But he reminded himself that Jackson was the only one she had been able to confide in up to now, so didn't take it to heart.

'Hi Jackson.' He greeted him as he entered the kitchen to find him perched on the stool.

'Matthew,' Jackson replied, dipping his head in acknowledgement, and almost immediately stood up. 'Anyway, you're busy, so I'm going to get out of your way.'

'I'll see you out,' Kaidence said, rising to her feet again.

Matthew knew it was his arrival that had encouraged the officer to leave, but it was hard to feel guilty about it. He knew his childhood friend gushed about how great he was and how helpful he had been in the short time they'd known each other, but he just didn't feel the same fondness for the man.

Kaidence stopped on the doorstep and pulled her front door to its frame. This wasn't how she wanted to say goodbye to him, but she knew that's what it was. He had played such an important part in getting her out of the abuse she hadn't let anyone else see that *thank you* didn't quite seem enough.

'Don't be a stranger, okay?' she said, reaching out to the lapels of his open jacket and pulling them together.

She didn't want to get emotional, but she felt her feelings creeping up on her all of a sudden. She tried to clear the lump that had formed in her throat by swallowing, but it seemed to get bigger as they stood awkwardly facing each other.

'Look after yourself,' he offered, searching his mind and failing to come up with anything better.

'I'll miss you,' she barely managed with strained vocals. She could swear she could see how upset he was at the prospect of not seeing her again, but it was fleeting, if it had been there at all.

'I'm going to miss you too,' he said, stepping forward and enveloping her in a hug.

She closed her eyes, feeling the safety of his arms as he held her. He smelled like he always did, of deodorant and aftershave, and it comforted her like it always had. It dawned on her that there was no smell in the world like it; it was unique to him. She wanted to bottle it; to take it with her so that she could take a sniff whenever she wanted to remember him. But she had to leave it, and him, behind.

He coughed as he released her and took a step back, trying to keep his own emotions in check. 'You're not the same person you were when we met, Kaidence.'

She shook her head. 'I'm not the person I was before I met Mitchell either. I'm someone else entirely, I just need to figure out who that is and where I fit in now.'

'I know I've said this before, but you're stronger than you give yourself credit for. Don't let that relationship define you. Live your life to the fullest. Don't let anything or anyone hold you back. Be great. That's how you win – by not letting him dictate the rest of your time on this earth.'

'I'll try not to.'

Jackson smiled a knowing smile. 'I remember you don't make promises, but do your best, for me.'

She nodded. 'I don't want this to be goodbye.'

'I'm sorry, but it has to be.'

'I don't know what I'm going to do without the pep talks,' she gulped.

'I'm sure I needed you a lot more than you needed me.'

'I find that hard to believe.'

He smiled. 'I'm going to go before I can't bring myself to walk away.'

She nodded her understanding. 'Thank you for everything, Jackson.'

'You're welcome,' he replied, leaning forward to kiss her on her forehead before following through and leaving her standing on the doorstep. He didn't dare to look back.

Kaidence watched him go, waiting for him to glance in her direction just one last time, but when he climbed behind the wheel of his vehicle, she realised he wasn't going to and went back inside. She had to wipe a tear from her cheek as she closed the front door and returned to the kitchen.

'Everything okay?' Matthew asked, sensing her sadness.

She gave him a small nod. 'We were just saying goodbye.'

Kaidence moved to the counter, where there was more crockery that needed packing, and started moving it to the dining room so as not to dwell on the end of her friendship with Jackson.

'Hey, let me get those, you're not supposed to be lifting yet,' Matthew said, taking the plates from her.

But he didn't quite manage to grab them all and Kaidence felt the plate slip out of her hand before she had a chance to stop it. She cursed as she dipped to pick up the scattered pieces, but when she felt a hand on her shoulder, she was back with Mitchell. Fear hit her in the chest like a freight train and she dropped to the tiled floor, landing on it with her rear and backing away from him with her hands raised – scared a lesson was coming.

Matthew could see the terror in her eyes and immediately regretted surprising her. 'Oh God Kaidence, I'm sorry,' he said, taking a step backwards, still holding the other plates. Being a doctor made it easy for him to be clinical about her physical injuries. But knowing about the abuse and seeing the aftermath were completely different things. It was a new experience for him to see her looking so terrified and he fought his natural instinct to approach her, opting instead to stand perfectly still, allowing her the time she needed to process the situation.

It was as though time froze as he watched her guard slowly start to come down. He didn't ever want her to be scared of him, and he could only reason that being in the house had contributed to her reaction.

Slowly she got to her feet and wiped away the tears that had fallen down her face. 'I'm sorry, that had nothing to do with you. It's just this was the room where most of the abuse was, and it's precisely why I'm selling.'

'Are you okay?'

'I will be.'

CHAPTER THIRTY

Time seemed to fly by and before she knew it, Kaidence was moving her belongings out of storage into her new house miles away from her home town and what little family she had left. She was lucky that her inheritance was substantial enough for her to be able to bid on a property before she had sold her own. She had still had to wait for the paperwork to be processed, but had been prepared to wait. She hadn't been prepared to move back in with her sister, even temporarily, so when Matthew had offered her his spare bedroom until she could move in to her new house, she had accepted without a second thought.

Getting to know him again after so long apart was just what Kaidence needed to take her mind off her past and to stop her focusing on what little future she was likely to have so far away from anyone she knew. And by the time she was settled in her new house, Kaidence was physically and mentally healthier. It had been easy for her to put on weight when she wasn't living in a stressful environment, and she had; enough that her curves were noticeable and her clothes fitted better. She had to retrain herself to care about her appearance, not necessarily going overboard with make-up or styling her hair but at least putting in a modicum of effort. She had even dusted off the clothes Mitchell had deemed too revealing for her to wear and was slowly regaining her confidence. It was Matthew's doing. He had picked up the mantle from Jackson, whispering a compliment in her ear when he saw her hiding behind her hair or covering up her blossoming figure to save from being noticed. He encouraged her to live as though no one was watching, and it worked to a certain extent. But she still checked over her shoulder whenever she left the house without him, which wasn't very often.

The plan had never been for him to move with her. But what had started with phone calls at all hours of the day and night when he wasn't on shift had gradually progressed to a pub lunch, which had extended to a full day together until eventually – after two months – Matthew had suggested relocating to be with her. They weren't a couple, because she wasn't ready to commit to him while she still felt the scars of her abuse so keenly, but each day was a day towards shaking it off.

She had even bought a mirror for her bathroom, which was a huge step forward. The item itself wasn't important, but the significance of it was. Since Mitchell had forced the back of her head into the last one she owned, she hadn't been able to bring herself to buy another. She had been lucky that she'd been facing him at the time, otherwise the scar would be on her face instead of in her hairline.

Not that she cared. She didn't rely on her looks the way she used to. She knew they had given her certain advantages, but if this nightmare had taught her anything, it was that people would always look past you if you gave them an excuse to, and it had been easy for her to go unnoticed once she changed her appearance. Abuse made people uncomfortable, pure and simple. There would have been outrage if she were a defenceless animal, but too many people thought it was easy to walk away from that kind of treatment if you were human. It was never that straightforward.

Now it was months since the stabbing and Kaidence sat in a small room waiting to testify. She was lucky she hadn't been required to show up to court and had been allowed to be questioned via video link because she wasn't sure she had the strength yet to face Mitchell. It had been seven long months while she waited for the trial, but she lived with the mental scars of his last attack as well as the physical, like a constant reminder of her relationship with him.

Her nightmares had stopped a few weeks after leaving her old home, and she was slowly shedding the shell of the frightened woman Mitchell had turned her into. In fact, most of the time, the memory of him drove the changes she made to her appearance, and she began to feel like the old Kaidence. Now, her hair had highlights and was usually only scraped back in a ponytail when she couldn't be bothered to style it, the clothes she wore showed off the shape of her body instead of disguising it, and she even wore a dusting of make-up on a daily basis.

But today, directed by counsel, she had no make-up on and the clothes she wore weren't unlike the ones Mitchell insisted she wore while they were together. This wasn't for his benefit, because she wanted him to know he had no power over her any more; it was for the judge and the jury to decide whether to convict. She wanted to be taken seriously, for them to have a visual of the way she'd lived with him and not have them make a judgement about her if she was too glammed up.

It was strange for her to hear the questions and answer them to an empty room, but it helped that she couldn't see anyone. She could be completely honest without feeling judged by the look on someone's face and when the emotions got too much, she could break down without having to see the smug look on Mitchell's.

The questions that came from her lawyer were delivered softly, but the ones asked by the defence were harsh and implied she was at fault. It made her angry and want to defend herself, but Sarah had warned her about doing that. So she kept her shoulders slouched and her voice the same as she responded, choosing her words carefully so they couldn't be twisted. Pretty soon, it was over.

As the court official turned off the camera and Kaidence relaxed, she realised she had balled up her fists so tightly that she had nail marks in the palm of her hands. She rubbed at them as she got to her feet and collected her belongings. It wasn't until she left the room that she stretched out her spine so that she stood straighter, and every step she took towards the exit fuelled her with an ounce more of the strength she had left on the street when she'd entered.

As she stepped out under the summer sky and felt the sun on her skin, Kaidence pulled the bobble out of her hair and shook her mane lose. She was a much different version of the woman she had been at any point of her life, but she had traits from each of them that she was proud of. She never classified herself as a victim; she was a survivor.

'Are you done?' Matthew asked, pushing himself off the wall he was propped against as she approached.

She smiled and nodded. 'Done.'

He turned and stuck out his arm for her to link onto. 'Then let's get out of here.'

She happily slipped her hand in the hole he provided and could feel the definition of his biceps. Although they weren't dating, the rekindling of their friendship has been exactly what she needed.

'Thanks for being here with me for this,' she said as they started to walk in the direction of the car.

'I didn't have anywhere else I needed to be.'

They walked in silence for what seemed like an eternity as Kaidence processed what she had just done and she got a sudden urge of bravery, not knowing where it came from.

'I think I want to go back for the verdict,' she announced out of nowhere.

Matthew's brow furrowed slightly. 'Are you sure?'

'I want to look that bastard in the eye when he's sentenced.'

'I get why, but what if he gets time served and walks out of the courtroom?'

She stopped walking and unhooked her arm from his. 'He has taken everything he can from me; he can't hurt me any more.' She couldn't explain the unexpected desire she felt to face Mitchell as his freedom was taken from him. But she suspected it had something to do with closure, and she wasn't entirely sure how she would react to being in a room with him again; she just knew she had to try.

Kaidence looked around. It was strange being back in her old neighbour-hood, although nothing seemed to have changed. She turned onto her old street in time to see a family of five exit the car on the drive of her previous dwelling. The father chased the littlest of three children on his way to the front door, scooping the youngster up into his arms, and she found herself smiling. That was exactly what had she expected to have in that house one day and although that wasn't what she got, she was glad someone was living it.

She still missed the life she had before Mitchell influenced it, and she had only gone back to her home town because she wanted to see the look on his face if he was sent to prison. The thought of him in a six-by-eight cell for any length of time was the only thing that had kept her going. She wanted him to atone for his sins, even though guilt was a concept he was unfamiliar with; having his freedom jeopardised was enough and he was facing three charges: one for rape and two for grievous bodily harm.

When she got to the courthouse steps, there were no familiar faces in sight, which she was thankful for. No one but Matthew knew she was coming back for this, and he'd been sworn to secrecy because she didn't want anyone to know, in case she changed her mind. She snuck inside the courtroom and sat at the back of the gallery, being sure to keep her head down so she wouldn't be recognised.

Reaching a vacant spot, Kaidence took the chance to look across to the dock as Mitchell was led in. He seemed so much smaller. She didn't know if it was because he didn't have the same power over her or simply because she had grown in confidence. But the sight of him didn't intimidate her like she expected it to.

Even now, Kaidence could see the arrogance of the man behind the plexi-glass. His belief that he would be vindicated and not vilified for his actions exuded across the room, despite his situation.

Kaidence had been told by her solicitor that Mitchell had entered a plea of not guilty for all charges, which was ridiculous, considering he'd been caught on Jackson and Louisa's bodycam with the knife in his hand. His defence representative tried to argue that he hadn't gone there with the inten-tion of hurting her, but Sarah said that she could tell it hadn't gone down well with the jury.

Kaidence kept her eyes locked on Mitchell as the judge spoke, asking the jury for their verdict on each charge. The foreperson stood and, somewhat proudly, announced a guilty verdict for each count against him.

She watched as he sank into his seat, his shoulders visibly hunching as the confidence he felt moments before dissipated. A feeling of empowerment washed over her and her posture grew with it. She held her head high as she listened intently to what the judge had to say, her gaze never wavering from Mitchell.

'Despite this being the first offence of this nature that you're facing charges for, I find your actions to be repugnant and depraved. Taking away this young woman's ability to have children and putting her life in danger, not for the first time I hasten to add, because she had the fortitude to leave after enduring a year of violence is inexcusable,' he started, giving the room a clear indication of his verdict.

Kaidence witnessed Mitchell's head drop so he was staring into his lap momentarily before he explored the room. Still she kept her eyes locked on his position. She wanted him to see her, so he'd know she was no longer afraid of him. She watched as his eyes seemed to skim past her only to return a second later and she forced herself not to look away. There was a flicker of self-satis-faction on his face, but it quickly changed to something she didn't recognise. Maybe seeing her resolute in staring back made him realise she was much different to the woman he'd forced her to become.

'My ruling is as follows. On count one, a sentence of five years in jail, on count two, a sentence of two years, and for the remaining count, a sentence of six years. Each sentence will be served consecutively to the other, which would lead to a total sentence of thirteen years,' the judge concluded.

Count one was rape, which carried a sentence from five years to ten. So Kaidence was happy with the minimum. Count two was for putting her in a coma – classified as actual bodily harm, which was anything from a fine to a maximum five years. So she was content with the term he'd serve. The remaining count, pertaining to the stabbing, was the one she had been most concerned about. That was the one that mattered. It carried a sentence of three years to life, so six years was satisfactory. It wasn't the best she could have hoped for, but thirteen years total was nothing to be sniffed at.

For the longest time, Kaidence had convinced herself that Mitchell's abuse was what she deserved because of the timing of her parents' deaths, but five months of therapy had helped her to see that she was worthy of more. She was a survivor, and what she deserved had no limitations.

The End

ACKNOWLEDGMENTS

Lynda, the jerk to my bitch; the Dean to my Sam, thanks for always being on hand to brainstorm and give me advice. Talking about my characters like they were real people is always strange, but it helps no end. I am lucky to call you my best friend and never underestimate having you in my life. I treasure the memories we've made along the way – too many to mention, and to think, it all started with a fan fiction I wrote about the Winchesters. Loves ya!

Sam, thanks for having the confidence in my ability to tell this story that I didn't always have. You made yourself available when a scene didn't sit right with me and give me your honest opinion on how to change it for the better. You're one of the best neighbours a girl can have because I get to call you my friend.

Tania, it started with you complimenting my nails when you were serving us drinks in the pub and blossomed into the most beautiful of friendships. I remember giving you a book of short stories that I'd handwritten for you to read, and you've been trying to get me to publish ever since. I love you more than I can express.

Mich, thanks for giving something I wrote the once over on more than one occasion and thanks for all the help and advice regarding self-publishing. You made the whole process less daunting and I appreciate it no end. Your words helped to inspire and drive me to get to the end of this book.

Judy, where to start? Your help has been immeasurable. This book would not be half as good if not for your input. I appreciate all you have done for me – it will not be forgotten.

ABOUT THE AUTHOR

Clare Bentley is a married mother of a son and a daughter, who are now adults. She was raised by a single mother and didn't care to know her abusive biological father, instead considering her stepfather to be her dad.

Playtime for her growing up was filled with creating scenarios to act out and making up dance routines to her favourite songs of the late 80s to early 90s.

She discovered a love of writing in secondary school English, which was the only lesson she cared to attend, and the only GCSE's she actually got a decent grade in.

She never really had a passion for anything other than being a mother until she was one, and that's when she decided to try her hand at writing.

It started with fan fiction, about Backstreet Boys, then *NSYNC and – more recently – the TV show, Supernatural. She loved it and met some incredible friends that encouraged her to use her skills to tell her own stories, with characters she created from scratch.

And that led her into the world of self-publishing.

Printed in Poland
by Amazon Fulfillment
Poland Sp. z o.o., Wrocław

55659681R00251